About the Author

Peter Tallon was a professional geologist who, after a period of prospecting in East Africa and Egypt, joined the construction materials industry rising to managing director of a multi-million-pound company. Married with two children and three grandchildren, he has lived in Suffolk for the last forty years where the beautiful coast and countryside form the background to his previous books. *Anno Domini — The Coming of the Messiah* is his fourth book and the first of a trilogy.

Anno Domini
The Coming of the Messiah

Peter Tallon

Anno Domini
The Coming of the Messiah

Olympia Publishers
London

www.olympiapublishers.com
OLYMPIA PAPERBACK EDITION

A CIP catalogue record for this title is
available from the British Library.

ISBN: 978-1-78830-820-5

This is a work of fiction.
Names, characters, places and incidents originate from the writer's
imagination. Any resemblance to actual persons, living or dead, is
purely coincidental.

First Published in 2020

Olympia Publishers
Tallis House
2 Tallis Street
London
EC4Y 0AB

Printed in Great Britain

Dedication

'For Lawrence, my eagle-eyed critic and proofreader.'

Acknowledgements

I would like to thank Neil Amos, my map maker, for turning my rough sketches into intelligible maps of the Roman and Judean world. Also, I thank Richard Maylam for his contribution in terms of ideas as well as corrections during the early phase of the production of this book. I really appreciate the patience of my wife, Jennifer, for accepting my semi-permanent presence in her orangery where her amazing display of flowers, shrubs and small trees seems to give me the inspiration for my most creative writing.

Finally, I thank Olympia Publishers for their patience and support during the production and publication of this book with them.

AUTHOR'S NOTE

Dates:

Whilst the Roman calendar is based on the solar year of 365 days, the Hebrew calendar is based on lunar years of twelve months which vary so that the Hebrew year can be 353, 354 or 355 days long. Because these are shorter than the solar year, there are seven leap years in every cycle of 19 years within the Hebrew calendar. Each leap year contains a 13th month of 30 days which brings the lunar calendar back into line with the solar year.

The long and the short of it is, it's difficult to make exact comparisons of historical dates between the two calendars which is why Hebrew dates in the text are compared only to the Roman month in which they take place. To make matters more complicated, Hebrew months do not coincide with Roman months. So a date early in the month of Sivan would be in May, but a date near the end of Sivan would be in June. Hebrew months are only used where the text relates to the Jewish part of the story.

Weights and Measures:

In order to save the reader, the constant need to recalibrate the weights and measures used two thousand years ago, which varied depending on where you lived, I have simply used modern equivalents so that the narrative flows more easily. Metric seemed too modern so I have used imperial units which at least seem a little more traditional.

Currency:

The imperial currency of the time was Roman, so denarii and sesterces have been used throughout though shekels are occasionally used as a unit of Jewish weight.

Personal names:

I have used the Greek form of names for Jewish people rather than original Hebrew/Aramaic forms. This makes it easier for the reader to identify with individuals who are recorded in the New Testament Gospels which, unlike the Old Testament, were originally written in Greek.

Historical Accuracy:

I have not altered any established historical events or characters, but some of the minor campaigns and two of the three main characters are fictional. The third, Judas, is of course non-fictional but he is depicted in a way more reminiscent of the recently discovered fragments of *The Gospel of Judas* rather than in the traditional Christian way. After all, it's the winners who get to write history so there is no harm in trying to even the score a little.

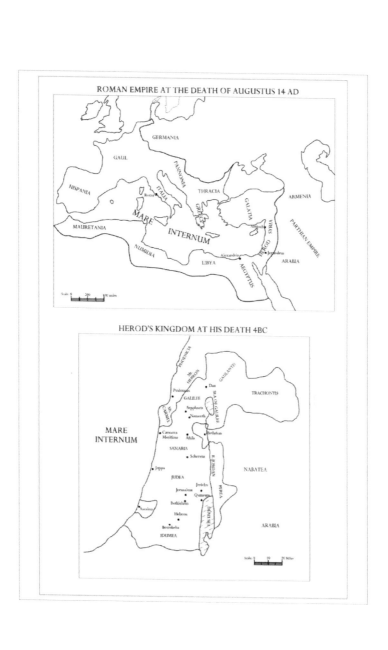

ROMAN EMPIRE AT THE DEATH OF AUGUSTUS 14 AD

HEROD'S KINGDOM AT HIS DEATH 4BC

PROLOGUE

The crowd was becoming restless. Nothing seemed to be happening. Above, the clouds were painted crimson by the late afternoon sun which was barely an hour from setting. At the top of a low hill called Golgotha, just outside Jerusalem, three crucifixes were silhouetted against the darkening sky. To each was bound a naked man.

A small clearing guarded by stern Roman legionaries kept the crowd a few paces distant from the suspended victims so that only close family and friends could gather and minister to their final needs undisturbed. The onlookers were a microcosm of Jewish society, peasants, artisans, tax gatherers and even a few rabbis and priests. Two in the crowd stood out as different, both bare headed, clean shaven with short cropped hair; unmistakably Romans. The taller one was young, about twenty-five years old, but from the quality of his raiment it was obvious he was from a good family. The other, shorter, stout and well into his fifties was me, Lucius Veranius.

My young companion, Marcus Longinus, turned to me, "Lucius, I am disappointed with this. Crucifixions are out of fashion in Rome and I can see why; this is utterly tedious."

"My apologies Marcus, but this has not been typical," I replied. "Normally, the dying shriek and cry out for mercy or death. Sometimes they swear and hurl profanities at their tormentors or babble with tears of self-pity."

"Well the two on either side have groaned a bit I suppose, but the one in the middle has been silent; inconsiderate to say the least. Why do they bend their knees then straighten them again so methodically?"

"To breathe. When they hang by their arms their lungs cannot inflate so they push upwards to gulp air then collapse with pain and exhaustion until the next gulp."

Marcus frowned, "Well we can't stay here forever. When will they die?"

"Very soon," said a nasal voice behind us. "Tomorrow is the Sabbath so they must be dead before then."

We both turned round and saw a tallish man by Jewish standards wearing shabby robes which, on closer inspection, had once been of good quality. He was a similar age to me and had clearly received some education for very few Jews ever troubled to learn our language.

"Judas Sicariot," I said. "Is it really you?"

"Lucius, I know it has been a good few years since we last met, but have I changed that much?"

"Unlike me, you have become thinner in the face but you seem to have worn well."

Judas addressed Marcus. "To whom do I have the honour of speaking?"

"I am Marcus Longinus, deputy to the Procurator Pontius Pilatus."

"And what brings such distinguished company to the execution of three ordinary Jews?"

The sarcasm in Judas' tone was unmistakable, but I chose to ignore it. "One of these men is anything but ordinary as well you know. Some Jews claimed he was a prophet, the Messiah and the true King of the Jews."

Judas shed his condescending attitude. "He never said any of those things though many of his followers did."

Marcus raised one of his elegant, well-manicured eyebrows. "So you knew him then?"

"Better than any man alive."

"Better than his own family?"

"Yes."

Marcus pointed to the middle crucifix. "Then why are you not ministering to him like the others?"

"Because I am not welcome; there have been too many lies and false witnesses."

Marcus was about to speak again, but I put my hand on his arm to stop him. Then turning to Judas, I said, "Jesus' death clearly pains you. I already know something of him and of you but, for the benefit of Marcus, would you like to tell us more about him?"

But before Judas could answer, the man called Jesus, also known by his cognomen the Christ, cried out for the first time since we had been watching. There were only a few words, all in Hebrew — the ancient language of the Jews — so I could not understand any of them, but despite the agony he was suffering, his voice was rich, melodic and pleasing to the ear. Its warmth seemed to draw your spirit towards him and made you want to hear it again.

"Judas, please tell us what he said?" I asked.

There were tears in his eyes as he replied, "How typical. He asked his father to forgive his tormentors because they do not know what they are doing."

"But I heard his father died some years ago."

Judas shook his head. "He is referring to his father in Heaven who sees all but is not of this world."

"How is that possible?" asked Marcus.

"Because his father is not the god of the Jews but the creator of everything and rules over all, including the god of the Jews."

"Even over Jupiter?"

Judas looked Marcus straight in the eyes. "None of your gods exist, they are merely inventions of the human mind."

I sensed Marcus bridle at that, so I quickly intervened. "Brave words Judas and dangerous too. Keep your voice down."

Judas pointed to the city where the great white walls of the Jewish temple stood out in the gathering gloom. "The Jewish god, Jehovah, does indeed exist but he is not the god of whom I speak. The god of Jesus is as far above Jehovah as a man is to a flea."

"But do not the Jews believe in just one god?"

"That is true Marcus, but the one true god is the god of Jesus who cannot be named. There are many lesser gods, angels, spirits, call them what you like. Jehovah is one of these. He rules this world alone and makes a poor job of it too. There are many other worlds with their own gods, all created by the god of Jesus."

By now Judas, who had ignored my request to speak quietly, was the object of a hostile frown from a man standing close by us. He must also have understood Latin and was dressed in the white robes of a temple priest. There was a sharp exchange between the two men in their own language, after which the priest disappeared in the direction of the temple.

For the first time Judas smiled, a surprisingly winning smile that seemed to warm his thin, angular face. His teeth were particularly white and contrasted with his olive skin and short, grey streaked, black beard.

"Are you in trouble?" I asked.

Judas' smile broadened still further, "I could not be in more trouble than I am already, and I certainly don't care what that priest thinks. My time in this world is strictly limited; all that remains unknown to me is my means of leaving it."

Marcus nudged me. "I've had enough of this. Shall we go?"

I was about to answer when there was a disturbance in the crowd to the right of us. Angry shouts accompanied a scuffle which seemed to be centred about two hundred paces from us further down the hill. For the moment, the victims suspended on the crucifixes were forgotten as all heads turned towards the disturbance which seemed to be drawing closer to us.

Marcus, whose young eyes were better than mine, whispered, "It's a Roman; I think he's alone. Should we help him?"

"Perhaps, but wait a moment; he seems to be managing perfectly well on his own." In fact, the crowd parted before him as waves before the prow of a fighting trireme. No doubt his appearance had something to do with it. He was unusually tall and wore the uniform of a senior centurion in full combat readiness. His helmet obscured his face and, instead of a shield, he carried a pilum, the standard legionary throwing spear. He soon reached the cordon of legionaries holding the spectators back and said a few words to the commanding officer who stood to one side to let him pass.

The centurion walked more slowly now until he stood about ten paces away from the middle crucifix. There were two women and two men attending Jesus the Christ. All backed away apart from one of the women as the centurion removed his helmet, revealing golden greying hair, which was rather long for a Roman soldier. He slowly placed his helmet on the stony soil beside his feet and adjusted the grip on his pilum. Then he drew back his arm and hurled the weapon with well-honed skill directly into the chest of Jesus. The victim groaned, exhaled the death rattle, and died almost immediately. The crowd jeered at this inconsiderate shortening of their entertainment, but made no move to break the cordon of legionaries.

Oblivious to the feelings of those behind him, the centurion paused for a moment in front of the limp corpse then bowed his head in what seemed a mark of respect, or perhaps a short prayer. Then picking up his helmet and placing it under his arm, he approached the woman who now stood alone at the feet of the dead man. I had not looked at her until now. Her face was finely sculpted, noble but lined with sadness. Although in late middle age, she was still slim and her hair, which was just visible beneath her long headdress, was still mostly black. She showed no fear of the centurion and the two conversed together for a while, but just as he was about to depart, she touched his arm in a manner that was revealing to anyone with experience of life.

After this extraordinary interlude, the centurion turned and walked back to the cordon of legionaries. For the first time I saw his face, but by now I already knew who he was.

"Lucius, what is it? What's the matter with you?" Marcus was tugging at my toga. "You look as if you've seen spirits from the underworld."

Without taking my eyes off the centurion, I said, "Well I might have seen one at least."

"What do you mean?"

"I know that centurion. His name is Caius Pantera. He saved my life in Germania. Please wait here Marcus, I must go to him."

I barged my way through the densely packed crowd, ignoring the curses of those I pushed aside. I had not seen Caius for too many years and now this opportunity to re-establish contact could not be missed. By the time I caught up with him, Caius was already half way down the hill. "Caius!" I shouted. "It's Lucius Veranius." He was only twenty paces away, but seemed not to hear.

"Centurion of the Third Gallica halt!" I bellowed.

Caius immediately stopped and slowly turned round as I pushed my way nearer to him. His eyes narrowed and his broad brow furrowed in an intimidating frown which would have unnerved anyone who did not know him. "Who calls!" he demanded in a low, menacing purr. By now, I was standing right in front of him. "Caius, do you not recognise me?" There was a short pause, then the tense face relaxed and the mouth widened into a broad, irresistible smile as I was grabbed by bear-like arms.

"By all the gods, old friend, I never thought to see you again. How goes it with you? Are you well? There is so much to say I do not know where to begin."

"I know why you did what you did a few moments ago. It was the right thing to do."

"Ah Lucius, you would understand." The frown returned. "So much has happened since we last met, not all good, and today marks another twist in my strange life. Hopefully, meeting you once more will make a change for the better."

"But first, we must make sure we do not lose contact again. Where do you dwell?"

"I have taken over my father's farm near Caesarea Maritima. There are vines, olives, goats and a view over the sea."

"It sounds idyllic, but it is two days' march from here." "I am renting a room above a tavern in Jerusalem."

"Then I would be honoured if you would stay with me instead." Caius seemed unsure. "Please, it would mean a great deal to me and my wife would wish to see you again too."

The broad smile returned to Caius' face. "Very well, let it be so."

I pointed back up the hill where I could just see Marcus waiting where I had left him. "Caius, I must explain my sudden departure to Pontius Pilatus' deputy procurator. Tell me where you are staying and I will come and collect you in half an hour."

When I reached Marcus, I was surprised to see Judas was still with him. The shadows were lengthening and the crowd was beginning to disperse. Either side of the dead Jesus, the other two victims were still clinging to life. One was whispering what seemed to be a prayer, the other retched and moaned in alternate spasms.

"I'm sorry I left you so suddenly, Marcus, but I could not let that centurion go without speaking to him."

"That's all right Lucius, but I think I see trouble approaching." Six grim looking temple guards were coming up the hill towards us accompanied by the priest who had argued with Judas.

"I think I'm about to be arrested," said Judas.

"I think not," replied Marcus. Like many old soldiers, I have often been critical about career civil servants but the next few moments altered my opinion entirely. Marcus waited for the priest and his guards to get within a few paces of us then halted them with a single word. It was in Aramaic, the language of the Jews and a tongue I understand reasonably well, but Marcus spoke it perfectly.

"Stop!" The priest halted immediately. "What do you want here!" demanded Marcus.

"We are going to take the blasphemer who stands beside you into custody," said the priest pointing at Judas.

"Judas is under my protection. I am here on behalf of the Procurator Pontius Pilatus."

"But the blasphemer has broken our laws."

"Then you must go through the proper channels before I release him to you. Your own Sanhedrin must request his release from Roman custody. Now go before I have you arrested for sedition instead." The priest muttered something under his breath and ordered his guards to return. He drew breath to say something, but then thought better of it and followed his men back down the hill.

Judas grinned from ear to ear. "Well done, Marcus. At least temple servants know authority when they see it."

"Maybe so, but I think it would be wise if we do not linger in this place. That priest will assuredly complain to my master who is residing in Jerusalem at present. They will receive an apology because I have exceeded my authority and no doubt the procurator will reprimand me in due course, but I can cope with that well enough."

I could see Judas had fallen on hard times and decided to help if I could. "Judas, I suggest you come with me and lie low until that priest has forgotten about you. If you will accept my hospitality, you can return the favour by telling me what has happened to you since we last met."

And that is how my story began. In my later years, I had intended as many old soldiers do, to write my memoirs which would have been read by no-one except my dear and dutiful wife. Instead, I have chosen to narrate accounts of two unusual men who led separate lives that nonetheless connected and overlapped from time to time. I have written the stories of Judas and Caius side by side because, in my view, they add to and complement each another. They are written almost exactly as they were recounted to me except where I myself feature in their lives.

I have now seen seventy-seven summers. It has taken many years to complete this work after that extraordinary day on the hill of Golgotha but, as I at last lay down my quill, I can comfort myself with the thought that I have created a work which will endure far longer than my memoirs would ever have done.

Lucius Veranius, written in the ninth year of the reign of Emperor Claudius.

CHAPTER ONE

Outside the cedar wood doors of the high priest's chamber stood a slim, anxious looking eighteen-year-old youth. It was late afternoon and the noise of hammering and sawing outside had just ended as the building work on the temple finished early that day. Tomorrow would be Hanukkah, one of the highlights of the Jewish calendar, and everyone wanted to be with his or her family before the festival began. The great doors swung open, pulled from the inside by temple servants, to reveal the high priest himself standing beside an unshuttered window observing the day's progress on the seemingly never-ending construction site on the temple mount in Jerusalem.

Simon bar Boethus cut a fine figure indeed. Adorned in his priestly blue robes and tall, blue and white head dress he looked every inch the embodiment of the most important man in Judea after King Herod himself. The afternoon sun seemed to shine on him alone as he stood deep in thought, oblivious to the youth who now waited at the threshold of his private quarters, unsure whether or not to enter the hallowed space. At last, Simon looked up and beckoned the youth to enter. He pointed to a lone chair, "Sit down Judas bar Menahem. Do not be afraid." The meanings of the words were clear enough, but the tone was cold and distant; there seemed to be little warmth in this man.

Judas sat as instructed but the high priest remained

standing, leaned on the wall and folded his arms, "So Judas, you know why you are here?"

"No Master."

"You are here because you have achieved the highest overall standard in your year. Your knowledge of the Torah is outstanding but also you have performed well in languages, finance, statecraft and the law. It is not often we have a student as gifted as you and less often still that the high priest interviews someone of such low rank as you. I trust you are honoured."

"Certainly, I am Master."

"Good. Your teachers tell me that you wish to continue working for the temple."

"That is true."

"Well you are not a Levite so you cannot be a priest but there is an opportunity in finance, temple income to be exact. It will require much travelling through Judea, Idumea, Galilee and even those parts of Samaria that have not deserted the true faith. How do you feel about that?"

"It sounds exciting, Master."

"Perhaps, but you will be seen by many as a tax gatherer; you will not be popular."

Judas shrugged, "I have not known popularity so I shall not miss it."

For the first time, the stern face of the high priest broke into a small smile, "Well said, young Judas; I may have chosen wisely. The popular ones often lack backbone. How soon can you start?"

"Immediately."

"But tomorrow Hanukkah begins. Surely you wish to be with your family?"

"Not really."

"Tut, tut, what is this! Your father, who has paid for your education, will wish to hear of your success. He will be proud of you and pleased to know that his investment in you has been worthwhile. Where is your home?"

"Jericho."

"But that is barely twenty miles away. You must leave at once, but you may return for duty as soon as Hanukkah is finished. Now you may go."

Judas stood up and walked towards the cedar doors, but as he reached them Simon called him back, "One moment Judas, I almost forgot." Then turning to the temple servants, he said, "Leave us and close the doors behind you."

When they were alone the atmosphere changed. From the cool formality of a few moments ago, Simon lowered his voice and became almost conspiratorial. "Judas, have you heard of the Zealots?"

"Yes, Master, but I know nothing about them."

"Your family is Pharisee is it not?"

"Yes."

"The Zealots stem from the Pharisee sect, but they have especially strong views about the independence of the Jewish people. I am told by your teachers that you also hold a strong opinion on this matter."

"Master, we are a great people, the race chosen by the True God himself. Yet, I do not understand why he permits us to be under the yoke of a pagan empire unless he is testing our faith."

"And what of Herod, our king?" The high priest saw the hesitation in Judas' eyes and added, "Judas, you may speak freely to me. This conversation is entirely confidential." The young Judas' head was spinning. To be spoken to like this by the high priest himself was as unnerving as it was exciting.

"Master, Herod is our king only because the Romans put him there, but he is more Greek than Jew. His father was an Idumean civil servant. There is not one drop of blood of the line of David in his veins. We await the Messiah, the one anointed to be the true King of the Jews who will bring us back to the glory our people once enjoyed."

"But Herod is rebuilding Solomon's temple."

"Yes, but with our money and for his own glory." Judas paused, "I am sorry if I have said too much."

Simon smiled again for he was pleased with the spirit in his new tax gatherer. "Judas, when you return after Hanukkah, I will introduce you to someone who shares your views. Abbas is the Zealot leader and is looking for young men like you to support his cause. You will not be obliged to do so; the Zealots only accept volunteers, but your new role travelling to temple properties throughout Jewish lands may be of use to him. Are you interested?"

"Certainly."

"Then remember that this conversation is not to be repeated. Herod has spies everywhere, even in the temple I dare say and the Zealots value secrecy. You will understand why in the course of time. Now, be off to your family and have a good Hanukkah."

***

II

Judas set off early next morning. This was a journey he did not wish to make. His mother, whom he adored, had died of a fever a year and a half before but, with indecent haste, his father had already taken a second wife who was about the same age as Judas himself. As a result, the comfortable cloth merchant's house in the middle of Jericho, where Judas had been born and bred, no longer felt like home. But, with the words of the high priest still ringing in his ears, he hoped he might somehow put the soured relationship with his father on a better footing.

The road from Jerusalem to Jericho was well trodden at this time of year. Although twenty miles long, it was mostly downhill from Jerusalem and easily covered in a single day by a fit eighteen-year-old. A smart, early morning rain had settled the dust to be followed by a weak but welcome winter sun which managed to create some heat through a high scud of cloud.

The small villages on the way were awash with hawkers of cheap wine, fruit, bread and stale figs which fetched exorbitant prices from the high-spirited travellers heading home to their families to celebrate Hanukkah. The hawkers were out to gain every shekel they could but would generally stop short of outright theft which was outside the hawkers' code. However, there were others lurking on this road with no such scruples; they would search for isolated pilgrims, usually after dark, who could be parted from their wealth with little risk.

During the afternoon, Judas crossed the low desert that surrounded Jericho and finally entered the city an hour before sunset. Although ancient and steeped in history, Jericho was only a small oasis settlement measuring less than two hundred and fifty paces at its widest extent, so it did not take long for Judas to reach the fine, bronze faced door that evoked memories of a delightful childhood dominated by a beautiful, loving mother. He looked ruefully at the wine he had brought for his father and the honey coated dates for his new... he could not bring himself to think the word 'mother'. This was a time when being an only child was painful. A brother or sister to share the burden would have been helpful now. On the other hand, that would have meant sharing his mother's affection; he would not have liked that. He drew breath and rang the great bronze bell at the side of the door.

After a few moments, the door was opened by a wizened, old house slave whose rheumy eyes took a while to recognise the visitor. Then, suddenly, the old man stood up straight and threw his arms round Judas gripping him with heartfelt affection.

"Master Judas! I never thought to see you so soon. What brings you here? Hanukkah, I suppose." The warmth from the old man relaxed the tension in Judas. He had half-forgotten the faithful, old Arethus, technically a slave but really a vital part of the family home. He gently unwound the sinewy arms clutching him and looked the old man in the eyes,

"It is truly good to see you, Arethus. It must be more than six months since I was last here."

"Eight and a half."

"As you say. How are the new, err, arrangements?"

Arethus answered in a strictly neutral tone, "Our master seems well content with his new wife." Then as an afterthought he quickly added, "As we all are of course."

"And Rachel?"

"She is young but confident. Although she has not run a household before, she is able to make decisions without the need to ask for advice."

"Enough!" said Judas. "The picture is clear. You had better take me to see my father."

6

Menahem had done well in life. Starting out as a cloth merchant's apprentice, he had combined hard work with a natural commercial instinct to advance and prosper. He now owned his own business and a fine house in the most desirable part of Jericho near the Well of Elijah. The central part of the house consisted of a small, square courtyard, which was open to the sky in summer, but could be covered with light, wicker panels attached to wooden beams in the winter. In the centre was a raised pool, which contained fish and water flowers, and around the walls of the courtyard were brackets which held oil lamps to provide light in the evenings. On this particular evening Menahem had just finished dining with Rachel as Arethus entered with Judas just behind him.

"Master, your son is here to celebrate Hanukkah with you."

Menahem put down his wine goblet and stood up with his arms outstretched, "My son, is it really you? This is unexpected and all the better for being so. Embrace your father." The two men held each other. Judas felt a pulse of affection for the father he still loved but who had become remote since the advent of Rachel.

"It is good to see you, Father; I have missed you."

"And now your new mother." Immediately, the warmth drained from Judas. Cold reality reasserted itself. He stepped towards Rachel who stood up with a slight wobble to await the embrace. Judas noticed her goblet was almost empty. There was no doubt she was a fine-looking woman, if a little short, but as she smiled her large, dark eyes showed no emotion, only the perfect blackness of a spider just before it strikes. The embrace was quick and superficial, but nonetheless long enough for the powerful perfume to send a surge of unwelcome sensuality through Judas' body. Her voice was a little lower in tone than he expected.

"Sit with us Judas and take some wine. Have you eaten today?"

"Yes, thank you," he lied.

"Yes, thank you, Mother," corrected Menahem. Judas managed to control the anger that welled up in him, but already he felt that this reunion would be short.

"Do not press him husband. These things sometimes take time." Rachel was clever; she was making certain that she would be free of blame, in her husband's eyes at least, when the inevitable rupture came.

For a while, the evening passed off well thanks in no small part to Arethus, who was permitted to remain, as Judas described his successful studies at the temple crowned with the offer of helping to manage the temple income from its properties outside Jerusalem.

"So," said Menahem. "The high priest himself offered you this career?"

"Yes, Father."

"Then I am truly proud of you. You have brought honour to our family, has he not Rachel?"

"Yes, husband, if you believe tax gathering is an honourable profession."

"It is not actually tax gathering, my dear. It is ensuring that the income from temple property and other assets is managed properly and does not find its way into the wrong purses."

"Of course, forgive me. I am only a woman and do not understand these matters." You are cunning as well as ruthless thought Judas.

"Very well," said his father. "I have a present for you which I have kept for an occasion such as this. Arethus, come with me, I may need some help with the lock."

For the first time since Rachel had entered the household a year ago, she was alone with Judas. She turned her dark, threatening eyes on him. "Do not think you can divide me from your father. If you try, I shall crush you like a cockroach."

"I will do what I think is right," replied Judas, uncomfortable at how pompous his response sounded.

"Fine words but empty. How do you know what is right! You are but an immature, selfish youth that believes what suits him is the same as what is right. Your mother is dead; accept it. Accept me and I might allow you part of your inheritance. If you do not then you shall get nothing."

Judas' self-restraint finally snapped. "How dare you speak of my inheritance! That is none of your concern, you painted Jezebel. My father would never cut out his only son." But instead of another fiery rebuke, Rachel's fearsome, yet beautiful countenance became more frightening still as the eyes half closed and a strange, triumphant smile revealed perfect white teeth.

"Look at me, you fool. I am young and healthy. I will give your father many children. I am carrying the first one now. It will be a boy, I know it."

Before more could be said, Menahem returned with Arethus who was carrying something under a small white cloth. The old slave placed it carefully beside the wine goblets and smiled as his master said, "Take off the cloth my son." Judas did as he was bid. His eyes widened as he looked at the magnificent silver dagger set in a jewelled scabbard that now lay between the goblets.

"Father, it's beautiful."

"Pick it up and remove the scabbard. It's a solid silver sicarius. Be careful, the blade is sharp."

Judas slowly drew the curved blade from its sheath, glimpsing his own face in the mirror-like metal. He carefully touched the blade, it was indeed sharp, and ran his fingers over the ivory handle which was inlaid with rounded stones of orange, green and black. The same type of jewels covered the silver scabbard which had been fashioned to fit the blade with perfect snugness.

"You like it then?" beamed Menahem.

"Of course, Father. It is both a weapon and a work of art fashioned by a fine craftsman, but I am not worthy of such a fine gift."

"Not now perhaps, but you soon will be. You will be able to wear it at important gatherings. When people see it, they will know that you are a man of substance. They will respect you. There are buckles on the back of the sheath which you can use to attach it to your belt.

Arethus, bring the box and key so that my son can keep his present in a secure place when he cannot wear it."

"I will wear it at all times," said Judas as he fixed the sicarius to his belt. "Except of course in the temple. I am truly grateful."

"It was your mother's wish that you should have it at Hanukkah."

Judas felt his eyes moisten as he thought of the person he loved above all others. "She would have been proud of this moment Father." A shadow passed across Menahem's face. Arethus shifted uncomfortably.

"My son, I did not make myself clear. I am speaking of

my wife Rachel."

Before Judas could respond, Rachel fanned the hot embers of discord into a flame of crisis, "Husband, I think I should leave your house. I did not realise I would cause such grief to your son." The fleeting moments of warmth between father and son suddenly ended.

"Never! You are my wife; you will remain at my side." Menahem moved menacingly towards his son and, for a few seconds, Judas thought he was about to be attacked.

Instinctively, his hand moved towards the hilt of his newly acquired dagger. But quick thinking Arethus stepped between them and the moment of danger passed, but not the anger.

"Judas, you cannot stay here," whispered Menahem hoarsely as he struggled to control his temper. "Else blood may flow. Arethus will see you to the door." Judas did not trust himself to respond, he would only have made matters worse, so silently he turned his back on his father and walked stiffly out of the courtyard towards the front door of the house.

"And do not trouble to return," shouted his father. "You are no longer welcome here!" Judas could only imagine the look of triumph on Rachel's face; pinpricks of heat ran down his back as he thought of it. Enough! He could not leave without saying his piece but, as he turned to go back and confront them, Arethus shuffled up to him and placed a leather bag in his hand.

"My boy, you must leave now. I will walk with you to the city gates. Come."

Half holding, half pushing, Arethus escorted Judas through Jericho's wide streets. The wise old slave felt that at any moment his charge might suddenly turn on his heels and rush back to confront his father. "Be patient, my boy. Time has

11

a way of seeing justice done if you let it."

"But my mother's memory is being desecrated. I cannot allow it."

"Your mother sees all you do. She will be pleased but she would not want you to risk everything for a memory."

"It's not the inheritance Arethus, it's the fact that my father owes his success mostly to my mother, for the dowry she brought and the advice she gave him. And now that harlot reaps the benefit."

"Judas, Rachel may not be perfect but she's not a harlot. Of that I am certain. Look, we have reached the city gates. Where will you go now?"

In truth, Judas had given that no thought yet. He had been too incensed to think beyond the immediate present. The gatekeeper heaved open the great west gate of Jericho, acknowledging Arethus as he walked a few paces beyond the gate to bid farewell to his surrogate son.

"I am only a slave, but would it be too much to ask you to embrace a tired old man who may not live to see you again?"

Tears welled up in Judas' eyes as he threw his arms round the small, rotund figure. "My dear Arethus, you have been a true father to me. I shall never forget you and, God willing, we shall see each other again."

***

III

The city gates shut with a thud and Judas stood alone outside Jericho's lofty walls. He looked up at the clear, starry sky and pulled his cloak more tightly around his shoulders. An almost full moon illuminated the arid, Judean landscape in silver light and, as he listened to the gatekeeper slide the bolts on the other side of the gates, he never felt more isolated. Jerusalem lay more than twenty miles to the west, he had no friends or family on the road back to the city and it was getting cold. There was no alternative but to start walking back the way he had come. If he felt tired, he could always find shelter under a thorn bush or in a vineyard and curl up in his cloak until dawn.

The first few miles were easy going, but then the road started to climb as he left the desert and entered the more fertile foothills west of Jericho. Now Judas began to feel the effects of his long walk earlier in the day; his limbs seemed to weigh heavy and his feet were sore. He was walking more slowly and realised he would soon have to find somewhere to sleep. He remembered an olive grove he had passed only a minute or two before, there would surely be plenty of cover there, so he turned round and began to retrace his steps.

He had only travelled a few paces when he saw something that stopped him dead in his tracks. Out of the shadow cast by the moonlight, two or perhaps three dark figures emerged from the very olive grove he was heading for. They were no more than a hundred paces away. Now he could see there were definitely three of them. The stealth with which they moved warned Judas they meant no good. Hide or flee; what was it to be? Fear devoured his weariness, he was young and fit so flight was his choice.

Judas broke into a fast trot, trusting to his youthful vigour to get him away. He looked back. The distance between him and the menacing shadows was growing. Maybe they were just travellers and not interested in him after all. That illusion was shattered when he looked back again a minute later and saw that the gap had not increased; if anything, it had reduced a little. Now there could be no doubt they were hunters and he their prey.

The next half hour was a period of growing terror for Judas. Highwaymen lived outside the law and did not regard themselves as bound by the standards of normal folk. They never robbed without murdering their victims; why risk survivors? Often, the pleasure of killing was as enticing as plunder to these evil outlaws. Lurid stories of their cruelty and skill in slow torture abounded, though in recent years their depredations had been curbed somewhat by Herod's flying columns of light infantry which kept the main roads safer than they used to be. But on this night, Judas' fate lay in his own hands; there was no prospect of help.

He glanced back again. To his horror, the gap had almost halved. Either his pursuers were extremely agile or, more likely, he was moving more slowly than he thought. The ache in his thigh and calf muscles was becoming unbearable; he had now travelled thirty miles or more in less than a day, the last two at a run. If he was caught, he would stand no chance against three hardened killers so he forced himself to speed up again; perhaps they would give up if he could keep them at bay just a little longer. He threw away his cloak and the bag of provisions Arethus had given him. Nothing could be allowed to slow him down.

Terror is a wonderful drug but, once cramp began to afflict his left calf muscle, Judas knew he could go no further. He staggered towards the top of a low hill which marked the entrance to Wadi Qilt; Jerusalem was still ten miles away. Now he could hear the footfall of his enemy, he would have to face them — his nemesis was upon him.

At the brow of the hill, about a hundred paces to the right of the road, a single, tall pine tree stood like a beacon marking the boundary between the Qilt and the valley of the Dead Sea. Judas remembered it from his outward journey earlier in the day. At least he could meet the highwaymen with his back protected by its trunk so, leaving the road, he headed towards it and turned to face his enemy with as much courage as he could muster. The wait could not have been long but in that short space of time he thought of his mother, Arethus and his lost home and how he would face death. He was even surprised at how calm he felt now that there were no longer any choices left for him to make. Above all, the resinous smell of pine made his senses reel; he would never be able to smell pine again without recalling this dreadful night.

At last, the three evil shadows appeared and paused at the top of the hill. They were barely twenty paces away; it could not be long now.

"There he is!" hissed a high pitched, snarling voice. "Thought he could escape the Lechem gang, did he? Now we'll see." Judas touched the hilt of his sicarius; these murderers probably assumed he was unarmed. The shadows moved menacingly towards him like three dark patches of malevolent fog slithering over the ground. The moon shone directly in Judas' eyes but he was ready.

The nearest shadow was but five paces away when it stopped. A hideous, low, rumbling laugh heralded the words every young man fears, "Well, well, seems we've found ourselves a pretty boy. Well worth the chase I'd say. Looks like we'll have fun this night."

When danger is close, the senses sharpen. Judas' straining eyes noticed that a small gap had formed between the shadow that spoke and the other two. They were overconfident. The last thing they expected was an attack. Judas took a deep breath and sprang towards the speaking shadow on his left drawing his sicarius as he did so. He thrust it deep into his enemy's stomach. For a terrifying, few seconds, there was no response. Had he misjudged his strike?

Then, a moment later, a foul, noisome stench made him retch as his erstwhile assassin coughed blood across his face and slowly toppled forward. Judas quickly withdrew the sicarius from cloying flesh and ran back to the pine tree; at least the odds were reduced to two to one, but the element of surprise had now been expended.

The two shadows on his right wavered. One of them whispered, "Yiztak, are you all right?" Before the wounded Yiztak could answer, the whole earth seemed to erupt with scores more shadows appearing from nowhere. A shout rang out "Seize them! Save the man by the tree!" The next few moments were utter confusion. The two threatening shadows were quickly overwhelmed; others surrounded Judas and the pine tree while yet more dragged the groaning Yiztak to his feet. Judas had no idea what was happening except that the newcomers, whoever they were, had saved him.

**

IV

The same voice that had ordered the capture of the highwaymen now issued more instructions. "Light braziers, take water to the man by the tree, bind the footpads and bring them to me." Soon many burning torches threw light on an encampment which spread outwards from the pine tree where Judas stood. A man dressed in a short white tunic with brown stripes on either side handed him a water bag.

"Drink, my friend, you deserve it."

"Thank you," croaked Judas. The water was cold and delicious. In his last moments of terror, he had not been aware of the tormenting thirst that assailed him. He drank all the contents of the water bag and, as he handed it back to his benefactor, asked, "Who are you?"

"All in good time. First, our leader will want to know who the man that faced three enemies alone with such fortitude was."

The commanding voice called out again, "Bring our brave friend to me. We must speak." Judas was led to an area about fifty paces square, which had been cleared of stones and vegetation, and was surrounded by many two-man campaign tents made of ox hide. Torches on long poles illuminated the enclosure casting wavering shadows across the faces of the men who were gathering along the edges to observe the events about to unfold. At the far end of the enclosure, sitting on a campaign stool, was a young man barely a year older than Judas himself. He was also dressed in the white tunic with brown stripes which seemed to be a kind of uniform, for all those gathered round were similarly attired. Burly men, presumably bodyguards, stood beside him, while to one side the three highwaymen were huddled in a pitiful group closely attended by more fearsome guards.

"Bring our friend a chair," said the seated man who, from the hurried reaction of his followers, was a leader held in great respect. With a generous, open hand gesture he bade Judas sit as soon as another campaign stool arrived. Then, with a wide, disarming smile, he began to question Judas.

"My friend, I know you must have much to ask which I shall answer shortly, but first I shall introduce myself and my band of brothers. I know you must be exhausted but are you ready for this?" Judas nodded. "Very well then. I am Elijah bar Abbas. In my father's absence, I have the honour to lead the Zealot brotherhood, the military arm of the Zealot sect." A thrill ran up Judas' spine; these were the very people he most admired. "The lone pine is one of our assembly points," continued bar Abbas. "And you were fortunate to choose it to make your last stand. My father is the leader of the Zealot sect, which is newly formed, and operates throughout Judea, Samaria and Galilee. Regrettably, he has been arrested by Herod and, consequently, I have called an assembly to debate what we should do."

Judas said, "Herod is not known for mercy or the rule of law unless it suits him. What makes you think your father still lives?"

"A good point, but even Herod would not murder the leader of an entire Jewish sect without some semblance of a trial. You seem to be well informed so perhaps you will declare yourself now."

At this point, Judas felt he should stand up, though he was not quite sure why; respect for Bar Abbas perhaps? Or maybe to make himself seem more important than he was? He swallowed nervously. Somehow, he knew that his next few sentences would affect the course of his life.

"First, may I thank you and your men for what you have done. You have assuredly saved the life of Judas bar Menahem, once resident of Jericho but now recently appointed financial assistant to the temple. My family is Pharisee."

Bar Abbas nodded and turned to speak quietly to one of his bodyguards. After a short conversation that was inaudible to Judas, the two men seemed to agree on something or other, and then the Zealot leader turned his attention back to Judas. "Joachim is from Jericho and he knows of your family. Your father is well respected in the community. Tell me about your temple appointment. Such positions are only allocated by the high priest."

"Indeed," replied Judas. "I was appointed by Simon to travel through Herod's kingdom assisting with the efficient collection of revenues owed to the temple."

"You are young for such a position."

"I studied hard and qualified top of my intake."

"But did you learn anything of practical value?"

"As well as religious studies and finance, I am fluent in Hebrew and Greek and speak passable Latin."

"Latin eh?" mused bar Abbas. "The tongue of our conquerors. That could be useful. When do you take up your duties?"

"After Hanukkah."

"You will be seen as a tax gatherer."

"I know I shall always be an unwelcome visitor, but at least I will be collecting for the temple, not Herod."

Then came the question Judas was desperate to hear. Bar Abbas leaned forward, "How would you like to serve the Zealot cause?"

"There is nothing I could wish for more than to be part of your brotherhood."

The Zealot leader frowned, "I am not offering that, at least not yet. You must prove yourself first, but from the way you confronted these vermin," he gestured to the three sorry looking villains who moments before would have cut Judas' life short. "You may soon be welcomed as a full brother." Bar Abbas was interrupted by a pitiful groan from the wounded highwayman. His broad, open face darkened, "Judas, these men would not only have robbed and humiliated you, they would have murdered you with unspeakable cruelty. The Lechem gang is notorious; its members are outside the law so we may do what we like with these three. Die they should, but you were their victim so if you feel merciful, they may be allowed to live at the cost of being blinded. What is your answer?"

Judas barely glanced at them. "I do not feel merciful."

"Good," said bar Abbas. He drew his thumb across his neck in the sign for execution. "Take them away." As the three were led whimpering to their deaths, he smiled grimly, "Judas you have passed your first test. Mercy is a luxury we cannot afford. It is a weakness which you do not have. So much the better. Now show me the weapon you used to defend yourself."

Judas unbuckled his belt and handed the sicarius to his liberator. Bar Abbas unsheathed the dagger and held the shining, blood stained, silver blade to the light of one of the torches. The golden flames seemed to dance in the reflection. A gasp of admiration went up from all those near enough to see.

"Solid silver," said Judas proudly.

Bar Abbas sheathed the blade again and handed the sicarius back then, raising his voice a little he announced, "Brothers, we have found a new friend this night. Let him be called Judas of the Sicarius, Judas Sicariot!"

CHAPTER TWO

In the twenty fifth year of the reign of Augustus Caesar, I received my commission as a centurion in the Third Legion Gallica. We were based in the great city of Antioch, one of the largest in the empire, and formed part of the garrison of our Syrian province which had the particular responsibility of keeping the Parthians firmly in place behind the east bank of the River Euphrates.

In the late winter of that year, the newly appointed provincial governor, Publius Quinctilius Varus, received a call for help from Herod, king of the old Jewish provinces of Judea, Samaria and Galilee, to quell a rebellion which had just broken out in Galilee. It was a plea Varus could not ignore because, as well as being an important client king in our empire, Herod was a personal friend of Augustus himself.

Within my century was a recruit who could speak Hebrew, a dying language, but one that had been spoken widely years ago. It was on the last day of February when, early in the morning, I received instructions to present this young legionary to the governor. My promotion was only recent; I was still a bit overwhelmed by my new status and had not yet learned to modify my behaviour to the quiet but firm attitude a good centurion should adopt.

My shadow preceded me as I strode across the parade square with the morning sun on my back. The morning wakening call had already been sounded and sleepy legionaries were spilling out into the square from the single storey barracks which lined all four sides of it. I entered the westernmost barrack and saw that one of the bunks was still occupied, so I whipped my centurion's cane across the feet of the supine form under the grey blanket that hid the rest of it from view.

"Get up, you, idle lump! The morning call was sounded ten minutes ago."

A tousled figure sat up and rubbed its eyes. "Have a heart centurion. I've been on guard duty all night. I'm excused first parade."

"Indeed, you are but you're not going on parade. The new governor wants to see you on a matter of great importance, though how that involves you I can't imagine. You've got twenty minutes, so get moving and be ready when I get back; full uniform mind you, nothing less for the governor."

Caius Pantera struggled unsteadily out of his bunk, stood up and stretched to his full height which was one inch over six feet. Although sun-bronzed from his six months' service in the legion, those areas of his body that never saw the sun revealed pale, northern skin. He glanced round the empty barrack room, put on his cloak, stepped into the blazing Syrian sunlight and trotted towards the camp baths. Within his allotted twenty minutes he had bathed, shaved and was waiting for me in full uniform looking the ideal image of a Roman legionary.

Together, we marched across the parade ground to the red brick praetorium, which housed the legate and his staff, where we were escorted into an office containing two men and a clerk.

The legate who commanded our legion, Marcus Tullius,

was standing to one side of his own desk while, sitting in the legate's chair, was the Governor of Syria himself. Varus kept us waiting in silence for a full minute before he put down the scroll he was reading and looked up at us from beneath heavy eyebrows that met in the middle.

"Caius Pantera?"

My companion touched his chest with the clenched fist salute. "Yes, Governor."

Varus was about forty years old, but his baggy eyes and receding hair made him look older. He was heavily built and his movements ponderous. "It says here that you speak Hebrew."

"Yes Governor."

"How so?"

"My mother was from Galilee. Hebrew is still common speech there."

"I thought Aramaic was the language of the Jews."

"Yes, but not everywhere. Galilee is backward and a long way from Jerusalem. Aramaic is not fully established there. Some Jews speak both languages."

"As does King Herod," pondered Varus. "You could be useful." He held out a flaccid arm whilst keeping his eyes fixed on Caius. The clerk hurriedly placed another scroll into his open hand. "These are orders for a cohort of the Third Gallica to be transferred to Jerusalem until further notice. I should like you Pantera to accompany it as I shall."

For the first time the legate, a scarred veteran of many wars, spoke, "I must protest Governor. To send legionary troops to Jerusalem gives the matter more importance than it deserves. We have five auxiliary cohorts at Caesarea. We could send two or three of those instead."

Varus sighed, "Marcus this is politics not warfare, at least not yet, and we want to keep it that way. Herod is in trouble with religious fanatics and his own bickering family again. By sending Roman legionaries we are showing our clear and absolute support for the king, not that he deserves it. If we leave him to his own devices there could be all out war." The legate did not reply, but he was clearly unconvinced. Varus returned his attention to Caius. "Your record shows your father came from Germania?"

"Yes, Governor. My father is from the Suebi tribe. He comes from a good family. He was a young warrior, just fifteen years old, when he was taken hostage by the great Caesar who, as you know, defeated the Suebi in battle. Later, he was permitted to join an auxiliary cohort in which he served Rome for twenty-five years. Upon his retirement, he was granted Roman citizenship and a parcel of land near Caesarea which is where I was born."

"So you were born a Roman citizen?"

"Yes, how else could I have joined the legion?"

Varus frowned. He was unaccustomed to such straight speech from a mere legionary, but he should have remembered that only citizens are allowed to join the legions. "And do you speak German as well as Hebrew?"

"German was the tongue of my childhood though I have not used it for many years."

"Are you German or Roman?"

At this, the legate interrupted, "Caius Pantera has taken the oath Governor. What reason have you to doubt him?"

"All right, Marcus, but I would like to hear it from him. Remember, the Germans are our blood enemies."

Caius drew himself up to his full height. He spoke with

pride. "I am Caius Tiberius Pantera, Roman citizen and legionary of the Third Gallica. I have loyalty to none but Rome."

Varus realised he had pushed too hard. There was almost a hint of apology in his voice. "Very good. You must understand that you are somewhat unusual for a plain legionary. I did not mean to doubt your loyalty. You may have value one day."

At that time, none of us could have appreciated the irony in those words.

Varus turned to the legate. "Marcus, we march tomorrow. We will take the coast road as far as Mount Carmel. There we will turn inland to Galilee and head first for Nazareth. Galilee is, so we are informed, the centre of the unrest..." While Varus debated with Marcus the pros and cons of marching through Galilee, I took the opportunity to observe his clerk. Brasidas was a gracile, well-educated Greek from Corinth who, I later discovered, had fallen into slavery through injudicious gambling. His movements were quick, like a stoat, and his brown, alert eyes darted from side to side missing nothing. It was obvious that Varus relied heavily on his administrative skills as he placed maps and documents under the governor's nose just seconds before he actually needed them, while at the same time making sure his master's goblet was kept topped up with lime juice. Brasidas soon saw I was watching him and, as our eyes met, a brief flash of humour revealed itself in an almost imperceptible rise in one of his eyebrows. At that moment, I realised he was intellectually superior to everyone else in that room.

***

II

On the morning of the first day of March, the Roman new year, the fifth cohort of the Third Gallica left Antioch bound for Jerusalem. As always, when soldiers were on the march, a crowd gathered to see us off. We numbered four hundred and fifty legionaries including officers, a troop of thirty cavalry and the headquarters staff; in all about five hundred men. My century was at the rear of the column as we marched out of Antioch's south gate on the road to Galilee. Everyone was in high spirits at the prospect of some action and the break from camp routine. The sky was cloudless and, though still early, the sun was already warming us through our red cloaks.

Caius, who was marching beside me, exclaimed, "What a day to be alive! Has anyone here been to Jerusalem?"

A voice from one of the files behind responded, "Yes. It's full of vagabonds and arrogant priests but the women! Wait till you see them. They're worth a visit any time!"

Someone else shouted, "All Jewish women are worth a look!"

"Yeah, but that's all you can do; look!" called out another voice. "You try and touch them and the family will cut your todger off!"

An old file leader, a commander of eight called Galerius, said "You kids should be satisfied with Syrian girls. They're just as pretty and a lot friendlier." He had hardly finished when a lithe, young girl of about sixteen years detached herself from the spectators on our left and ran towards us. Her long, black hair was uncovered, something no Jewish woman would allow in public. It seemed to float behind her in the gentle breeze until she stopped in front of Galerius, threw her arms round him and planted a long, lingering kiss on his lips before disappearing into the crowd again.

This was greeted by a chorus of bawdy comments but the old file leader, wiping his lips on his sleeve and smiling a toothless grin, called out to anyone who could hear, "There you are boys, that girl knows quality when she sees it! You're all plain jealous!" There may have been some truth in that, not the quality bit of course, but all jealous feelings were replaced by sheer joy when, a few hours into the march, the unfortunate Galerius discovered that his purse containing more than a month's pay had been deftly removed from his belt.

From Antioch to Mount Carmel is about three hundred miles, but the coast road was well maintained and the men were cheerful apart from Galerius, so we marched quickly and came within sight of the mountain in just sixteen days. Carmel is not especially high and has no peak, but it is still impressive because it rises sharply out of the sea at its north western end and trends south eastwards for fifteen miles or so, like a huge, pale loaf of bread. It dominates the land either side of it and when we first saw it there was still a little dusting of snow on its upper slopes, a remnant of the especially cold winter that had just passed.

That night, we camped at Ptolomais and the next morning we left the coast road and turned inland towards the Galilean border. Then everything changed. The first thing we noticed was a deterioration in the quality of the road. Instead of a dressed stone surface we now marched over dried mud, which is fine in spring and summer, but turns to a morass in winter rain. The rich farms of the coastal strip, which were neatly divided into a patchwork of fields by dry stone walls, soon gave way to poor quality grazing land suitable only for goats. Apart from the occasional olive grove and vineyard, the standard of land husbandry got worse as we moved further inland but, as far as I could see, this was more to do with the sparseness of the population than to the soil, for there were no towns worthy of the name, just well scattered villages and hamlets.

We crossed the Galilean border without knowing it because there were no markers, and by the time we ended the seventeenth day of marching since leaving Antioch, the atmosphere in our little column had altered from light hearted anticipation to a quiet, dark watchfulness.

Although we were still well within the boundaries of the empire, we sensed the enemy was close by, and the next morning we saw the first evidence of the presence of the fanatics who called themselves Zealots.

I was awakening from a restless sleep. The eastern sky was just beginning to lighten to a deep blue so, estimating there would be at least another fifteen minutes till the wakeup call, I wrapped my cloak more closely around me and turned over for a few more minutes dozing. I had only just resettled myself when a sharp cry from the front of the column woke us all up. Seconds later the alarm was sounded and we quickly stood to arms back to back along the road with shields facing outwards. It was a nervous moment and some of our young soldiers were ill at ease. I paced slowly between the two lines of my century peering into the darkness either side of us.

A young Gallic recruit with hair the colour of straw turned to me as I walked behind him, "What's happening Centurion? Are we under attack?"

"No lad," I replied. "At least not yet. Look to your front and report anything you see to your file commander."

"But I can't see anything."

"It will be light soon. Just stay alert, remember your training and all will be well."

We remained in position until sunrise then, as all seemed quiet, I went forward to the century in front of us to search out its commander Gnaeus Servilius, an old colleague of mine. I found him returning from the head of the column.

"Ah, Lucius," he said without his customary cheerful smile. "The enemy made contact during the night."

"How so?"

"We found a sentry with his throat cut. He was only eighteen. Must have been those bastard Zealots. The frightening thing is they came within a few paces of the governor undetected."

"This is their homeland Gnaeus. They know every ditch, every hiding place and they mean business by the looks of it."

"Well they certainly have no fear of us, that's for sure."

We resumed our march an hour later, many of us casting a wistful glance at the sad, little cairn of stones that marked the lonely grave of the young sentry. We marched in close order and full battle array as if in enemy territory even though we were in the domain of a friendly king. Apart from a few cavalrymen, my century was in the rear again. We were all on high alert scanning the terrain on either side of us for any sign of the enemy. I realised I had no idea what the Zealots looked like, so I made my way forward towards Caius, who had at least been born in Judea and might be able to enlighten me. Meanwhile a cold, steady rain had set in from the grey clouds clustering round Carmel's high plateau, drenching our cloaks and chilling our bones.

"Caius, who are these Zealots who come and go at will, undetected in the night?" I asked as I caught up with his file.

"I do not know any personally, at least not that I'm aware of, because they are a secret sect. They are not to be trifled with for they are fanatical about everything they do. They strongly believe that all the land comprising the old Israel of their King David should be beholden to no-one but their god, so they hate King Herod for being a Roman puppet. They follow an uncompromising version of the Jewish faith and despise all their own countrymen who do not agree with them. Above all, they use violence to get their way and are fearsome warriors who use clubs and long knives to bring down their opponents. Many are accomplished slingers; some are said to be able to hit a man four casts out of five at fifty paces, and, as we found out last night, they are masters of stealth."

Well, that was food for thought. I looked at Carmel's pale grey slopes on our right and wondered. There were numerous small ridges and hillocks that ran parallel with our line of march which could easily conceal a small army from sight. The land on our left was rising too. I felt my pores open as I thought of hundreds of malevolent eyes watching us as we walked into a trap.

Caius added somewhat unhelpfully, "It is said that the Zealots are strongest in Galilee, but their influence wanes as you go south to Judea." Nazareth was the main town in Galilee and that was precisely where we were headed.

As the morning progressed, we climbed higher up the road to Nazareth which was still a day's march away. The sense of being stalked became oppressive; we all felt it. At last, about noon, the storm broke. The rain had eased, blown to the east by a warming coastal breeze, and the men were anticipating their midday break when suddenly, we heard a cry of alarm from the head of the column followed by a rattling sound like hail on a sheet of metal. The horn sounded the 'stand to' so we halted and turned back to back in two long lines facing either side of the road. Within seconds we discovered what the rattling noise was as hundreds of sling stones struck our shields from the Carmel side of the road. The Zealots now revealed themselves from behind a low ridge some fifty paces away. They were scantily clad wearing nothing more than knee length white or grey tunics gathered at the waste by belts from which hung leather pouches containing the sling stones that were now smashing into our red, oblong shields.

The Zealots knew what they were about for they could see we had no archer auxiliaries with us and the ground separating them from us was too thorny and uneven to allow passage for our small cavalry escort. They were well out of range of our throwing pila so there was little we could do except cringe behind the relative safety of our wall of shields.

"Must be at least two hundred," said Caius as we awaited orders from cohort headquarters.

"Keep your head down and leave the counting to me," I ordered. "We don't want to give these bastards an easy target." Taking quick but cautious glimpses from behind my shield, I could see the slingers at least matched our numbers because the entire flank of the column was engaged. There was no need to discourage the men. I raised my voice so that as many as possible could hear, "Good estimate Caius, two hundred, perhaps a few less. Be patient, our time will come."

***

III

Our patience was sorely tried that day. We stood motionless for almost an hour under the heavy stone barrage. Though we were well protected by our large shields, it was inevitable that a few sling stones would eventually find targets. The young, straw haired recruit from Gaul let his curiosity get the better of him and lowered his shield slightly to take a quick look at the Zealots, only to be instantly struck between his eyes. The front of his skull was smashed; he was dead before he hit the ground. Howls of anger erupted from his comrades, some of whom began to throw back the sling stones out of frustration, but I ordered them to stop because their efforts were ineffective and they were needlessly exposing themselves to further danger.

Our lack of response only encouraged the Zealots who crept closer yelling insults and taunting us. The insults were of no consequence for none of us except Caius could understand them, but the slingers' accuracy improved as they got closer, some within twenty-five paces. We were well and truly pinned down, the rattle of stone on shield was deafening; to expose any part of your body now meant immediate injury or death. The men began to murmur; the humiliation of being bested by semi-naked savages was bad enough, but standing still waiting for death like lambs to the slaughter without striking back was intolerable.

I had just decided to launch an unauthorised charge, and to Hades with the disciplinary consequences, when at last, orders came from headquarters. They were brought by our cohort commander, Licinius Piso, a tribune of senatorial rank who ran behind the cover of the unengaged north facing files on the far side of the road, crouching as he darted past the small gaps between the centuries. Seeing my centurion's helmet, he part ran, part scuttled towards me, crawling the last few paces. He paused to gather his breath, eyes wide with fear; he was young for his rank. This was probably his first action but he managed to control the shakiness in his voice and remembered to ask the correct question first as he gasped, "Centurion, your casualties?"

"One dead, three wounded but none seriously."

"Very well. The cohort is heavily engaged; we have no choice but to attack." There was a groundswell of approval from all those who could hear him.

"Thank the gods," I answered. "When?"

"Now. You are the rear century and least heavily engaged. Deploy your men into skirmish formation and attack the enemy to your front. I shall support you with two more centuries while the remainder will stand fast on the road; there may be more of these beggars who've not shown themselves yet."

Although I did not appreciate the 'least heavily engaged' bit, these orders were just the tonic we needed. The prospect of hitting back was all we wanted. "Thank you, Tribune," I said. "We will move out immediately."

As Piso headed back up the column, I ran to the cover of a drainage ditch on the north side of the road and called my ten file leaders to join me.

"We're going to attack now, men."

"Bout time too," grumbled the toothless Galerius.

"Still fretting about your purse?" chided one of his peers.

"Enough of that!" I snapped. "This is going to be a tough

task so listen carefully. Leave your pila with the column; they will be useless for the work we must do now. We will advance at the trot in spearhead formation. Galerius, your file will take point position with two files slightly behind you on either side twenty paces apart. I will command the other seven files one hundred paces to the rear of you ready to support as the need arises. Stay close, do not get separated and hold your shields high especially while we're forming up. Any questions?" There was silence. "Very well, Galerius' file stand fast and the rest form up behind. The signal to advance will be three horn blasts."

Within five minutes, we were ready to attack. The Zealots could see what was happening and, even before we advanced, they began to retire covering their withdrawal with an ongoing swarm of sling stones. There could be no doubt they were disciplined and well led.

We moved forward at a trot which soon slowed to a walk once we left the road. The ground was uneven, full of tussocks of dried grass, sharp briars, brambles and low stone ridges built by the local farmers to retain the sparse topsoil which would otherwise wash away during the winter rains. It was impossible to maintain formation in such conditions. Although skirmishing formed part of every legionary's training, it was soon forgotten because this sort of work was usually left to the more fleet-footed auxiliaries. We had none with us which, I thought, was the fault of our commander, Varus.

We pushed on up Carmel's northern slopes. Our spearhead formation had now degenerated into a ragged line of twenty-four men with the other fifty or so clustered in an irregular group a bowshot behind. The sling stones still hammered on our shields as our enemies retired up the hill before us. We were not closing with them but at least we were taking no more casualties because their aim was faltering as they moved. I looked back at the column. We must have covered nearly a mile of bone jarring, sandal ripping ground but our young tribune was only now sending forward the two supporting centuries he had promised.

The file leader nearest to me, a tall, fine looking fellow from Pannonia called Ostorius Rufio said, "Centurion, look ahead. There are some buildings four hundred paces to our right front."

"They look like the huts of a shepherd's summer camp," I answered. "I think we'll halt there and wait for the other centuries to come up. I feel a bit isolated here."

"Don't worry Centurion," boomed Rufio. "These Zealot cowards won't dare come to close quarters with us."

I was not so sure, so I called in the leading files and together we occupied the cluster of dry-stone huts. There were five of them, each about four paces square and set in an irregular circle. All were roofless and seemed to have been used as rough shelters against the cool summer nights which affect Carmel's upper slopes when the breeze comes in off the sea. The interiors looked verminous so we rested outside the huts but within the protection of their curtilage while we waited for the two supporting centuries to join us.

Caius, who was beside me scanning Carmel's upper slopes, mumbled to no-one in particular, "Strange, those sling men seem to have disappeared into the ground. I can't see any of them."

"It's certainly gone very quiet," agreed Galerius. "Too quiet for my liking."

Rufio laughed, "Don't be an old woman, Galerius;

they've probably—" He was interrupted by a maniacal shriek from somewhere in the slopes above us then, suddenly, the earth seemed to belch out Zealots as swarms of them appeared out of a fold in the ground less than a hundred and fifty paces from us, which had concealed them until now. There were hundreds of them armed with clubs, spears and staves screeching like wild animals with the blood lust upon them. Despite the rough ground, they approached us rapidly.

"File leaders!" I bellowed. "Line the gaps between the huts. Galerius, Rufio to me! Your files will form a central reserve with me."

The files were already intermingled but quickly, instinctively, the men formed five solid lines of about twelve men each, linking all the huts in a ring of strong Roman shields and stone walls. We were like a fortified island facing the wild human tide about to engulf it. When the Zealot wave broke on us, we were ready, but only just. The two lines nearest the charge buckled but held. The clash of steel, shrieks of rage and fear and the hammering of clubs on shields created a mad cacophony of noise which made it hard to think. Soon the enemy, unable to break through, swirled all round our position like eddies of hate trying to find a way in. We were surrounded with no hope of escape but all our lines were holding for the present.

I looked back at the column. The two centuries sent to support us could see what was happening and increased their pace as best they could over the thorny terrain, but it was obvious we would have to fight alone for at least half an hour. The clouds had cleared and the day was warm. Despite the clamour around us, I looked skywards and saw two larks fluttering above our little enclave oblivious to the tumult less than fifty feet below. It is strange how small, isolated moments like that can stand out in your memory when they should be obliterated by events of far greater magnitude.

"Centurion, look to your left!" It was Galerius pointing out yet more Zealots approaching from the east to reinforce their comrades.

I barked out more orders. "Rufio, take your file to support the eastern line. Galerius, you stay here with me." I could sense Caius' frustration at being held back; he was part of Galerius' file. "Caius, do not worry," I said. "Your time will come soon enough."

Despite Rufio's help, the eastern line gave way within a few minutes and the wild-eyed warriors of Jehovah burst into our sanctuary.

"Galerius now!" I shouted, and together we led the century's last remaining file to try and plug the gap in our defences; there were just nine of us. The men of the Third Gallica were experienced soldiers who had learned not to panic in a tight spot. Seeing a determined group of their comrades running to their aid, they quickly reformed alongside us and suddenly thirty locked Roman shields slammed as one into the fearsome but unarmoured Zealots. A club hit my shield, I thrust my sword forward and felt the point sink into soft flesh. To my left, Caius used his shield like a battering ram forcing his opponents back by sheer physical strength. On my right, Galerius wielded his sword in short, stabbing thrusts, quietly swearing each time the blade struck home. Slowly and steadily, we gained ground a pace at a time. Just as I thought we had regained the perimeter, I stepped over what seemed to be a dead Zealot but, as I did so, he thrust up at my groin with one of their evil sicarius knives. Galerius had already seen him and parried the deadly blow with his sword then, with the experience of a veteran, he used the lower edge of his shield to break the Zealot's neck.

Before I could thank him, Galerius panted, "It's all right, Lucius; you would do the same for me."

The power of our counterattack seemed to discourage the Zealots. They began to give ground and the fighting broke up into isolated skirmishes. But this was dangerous for us because we lost the cohesion of a shield wall as the legionaries split up into small groups to pursue the scattering enemy. At this point, I failed as a battle commander because I should have recalled the men to await the arrival of the supporting centuries, but instead I thought the men deserved a reward for their courage and allowed a limited pursuit, not realising that the Zealots still had some fight left in them.

About twenty paces to our left, a group of Zealots suddenly turned on us and fought back; they certainly had guts and took us by surprise. Caius, Rufio and another legionary were momentarily isolated. I saw Caius fall. Rufio fought like a madman but, before I could reach them, the third legionary was cut down as yet more Zealots returned to the fight oblivious of the danger to themselves. The noise was deafening. The dust kicked up by the struggle made seeing and breathing difficult. Now we fought as individuals, not for the glory of Rome, but for ourselves and each other. The seconds passed like minutes; this was gutter fighting, blade, hilt, fist, shield edge, each man a gladiator fighting for his life. Blood stained the pale Carmel soil — Zealot blood for the most part — and at last our brave enemy finally gave way, beaten only by superior Roman weaponry and fighting skill, but not by any shortfall in raw courage.

We were exhausted. My sword was red up to the hilt; I was bleeding heavily from a thigh wound. Resting on my knees, I saw through sweaty eyes two legionaries being dragged away. I wiped the sweat away with a bloody wrist; Caius, barely conscious, was being hauled over the ground like a lump of meat while a weakened Rufio, still fighting as best he could, was surrounded by Zealots pulling him up Carmel's thorny slopes away from our vicious little battlefield. I looked at my own exhausted men stretched out on the ground wherever the fighting had ended, some gasping for breath, others examining their wounds; they were in no fit state to rescue their two comrades. Thirst was our enemy now.

We should have waited for the supporting centuries to arrive, but only the most disciplined commander could have followed correct post battle procedure by reforming his men into a defensive position to await a potential new attack. I did not have that much self-control and could not allow two of our comrades to be taken prisoner, tortured and murdered. I tied a rag round my thigh wound and staggered to my feet.

"Listen men!" I bellowed. "Those filth are dragging away two of our gallant friends to torture and death. Who will follow me to save them!" A ragged cheer stuttered from some of the dry throats nearest me, but there was no surge of support; the men had already given everything. It was unfair to ask more of them so, more in hope than expectation, I turned towards the retreating enemy and shouted, "Come on then!"

I heard some movement behind me, but did not look back in case my own courage failed, and set off in pursuit. After what seemed an age, I managed to close up to the Zealot rear guard, and stole a quick glance behind me. Only four men had followed but one of them was the ever-reliable Galerius; at least I was not alone.

It soon became obvious that the Zealots had also had their fill of fighting for they quickly gave ground before the unexpected pursuit. Exhausted but encouraged, I headed for the group that was being hampered by the weight of the legionaries they were hauling with them. I yelled our war cry, "Gallia Victrix!" and raised my sword to strike my first victim.

Then everything went black.

To the men in my century, it had been a desperate battle, but the laconic legionary record simply stated:

On the eighteenth day out of Antioch, the fifth cohort was engaged in a sharp skirmish with Jewish Zealots. Our casualties were four killed, nine wounded, two seriously, and three missing presumed dead. The enemy lost about sixty killed. All their wounded were finished where they lay.

CHAPTER THREE

The call to action came sooner than expected. Just three months after Hanukkah, Judas was summoned to Simon's quarters once more. This time, far from the calm, confident, magisterial being he remembered, the high priest seemed ill at ease, agitated almost. He had not been impressed by Judas' account of his encounter with the Zealots on the Jericho road, and now the young tax gatherer wondered if his recent appointment was about to be rescinded. He was not asked to sit.

Simon, who was seated at his bureau fingering through a heap of small scrolls, spoke without looking up, "So Judas bar Menahem, or should I say Judas Sicariot?"

"Well err..."

"It is of no consequence. There has been trouble in Galilee. One of our temple properties in Cana has been destroyed. Worse still, a detachment of Herod's personal guard was wiped out at the same time."

"Who by Master?"

"Zealots, who else!"

"I am sorry to hear about the property but should we not rejoice about Herod's guard?"

At last Simon abandoned his scrolls and looked Judas straight in the eyes. "No, we should not! Since Abbas' arrest the Zealots have lost their discipline. His son does not have the same respect for his betters and no appreciation that there may be more effective ways to achieve our aims other than mindless violence."

"Like what, Master?"

"Negotiation and persuasion. True, force will play a crucial role in due course and must always be there to support our bargaining position, but the time is not now. Herod has not long to live; his sons are weak and degenerate. Herod's death will be the time to strike."

"What will happen now?"

"Herod has requested help from Varus, the Roman governor in Antioch. Varus cannot refuse because of Herod's personal friendship with the emperor. That means we will soon have Roman soldiers here in Jerusalem which will hardly help our cause will it?"

"I suppose not, Master," agreed Judas.

"You suppose not, indeed! Herod's sons have never met Augustus Caesar. If bar Abbas had waited just a few months the Roman reaction might have been very different, but now we are guaranteed intervention."

Judas asked, "Why was our property in Cana attacked?"

"I am told it was a mistake. Some of Herod's guards were in the area and were ambushed by the Zealots. A few escaped and sought sanctuary in our house at Cana, but bar Abbas' men broke in and during the final struggle fire broke out destroying the building and all those inside including some of our servants."

"Master, why are you telling me this?"

Simon stood up, grabbing one of the small scrolls and pointing it angrily at Judas. "Because bar Abbas has had the gall to ask my permission for you to join his unruly mob!"

Suddenly, a light seemed to illuminate Judas' world. He was being asked to join the Zealots and a leader he greatly respected. The pleasure must have shown on his face for the high priest slowly put the scroll back on his desk and said quietly, "I assume you want to go?"

Judas tried to think of a form of words that would not offend his master too much, but even before he could open his mouth Simon shook his head and sighed, "No need to answer, it is written all over your face. I will not stop you for you are young and foolish. You had a great future serving the temple, but I suppose you must go. I cannot keep your position here open for you, others must have their chance, but once you have expended your youthful ardour, come back and I will see what can be done."

"Thank you, Master," replied Judas as humbly as he could. "I really do appreciate your patience with me."

"There is a servant of bar Abbas waiting outside to take you to him. He is staying in the lower city. Take care Judas, you are entering a dangerous world."

***

II

"Welcome, Judas Sicariot," beamed bar Abbas. "Come and sit with us." It was evening. Judas had been taken to the upper floor of a two-storey building, which was neither warm nor clean, in a poor quarter of Jerusalem. The street outside was narrow and crowded, though torches set high in the walls and maintained at public expense cast just enough light for a careful traveller to avoid stepping in something unpleasant.

Judas looked round the room which was no more than four paces square. In one corner were two crumpled sleeping mats that seemed as though they had seen rather too many years of service. To his right was an open window, too small to cast much light but large enough to release some of the smell of stale sweat. To his front, seated at a low table, were bar Abbas and another man whom he remembered from his encounter with the Zealots on the Jericho road. Judas sat down on a low stool opposite bar Abbas while the man who had escorted him from the temple was dismissed.

"Will you take some wine?" asked bar Abbas as he handed Judas a goblet.

"I would prefer water."

"As you wish," answered his host with an impish smile, hardly befitting the leader of a revolutionary army. He pointed to the man sitting on his right. "Judas, this is Joachim my second in command. He is more important to me than my right arm."

"I remember."

"Welcome, Judas Sicariot," said Joachim, who was a much older man. "We were all impressed by your courage at the lone pine."

Judas bowed his head a little. "Thank you." Joachim looked about the same age as Judas' father but there the resemblance ended. This man was gnarled and weather beaten, his skin dark and lined and his beard mostly grey; he might have been hewn from ancient oak. He gave the impression of immense physical strength controlled by experience and an iron will.

Bar Abbas took a sip from his goblet, "Judas, in a few weeks' time, my father goes on trial for treason. He will of course be found guilty and executed if we do nothing. We have also heard that the governor of Syria is sending Roman troops to help Herod deal with the unrest in Galilee."

"Fomented by you?"

"Of course. Anyway, Joachim has proposed a plan which might just save our leader, but for it to work we need you."

"Really?"

"Yes, because you speak Greek and Latin and we both feel we can trust you."

"I am honoured."

Bar Abbas frowned, "Well don't be until you've heard what will be required of you; it will involve some risk."

"I would not expect otherwise."

"Just as well then. Joachim, this is your idea so you can explain it to Judas."

The man of oak took a long draught from his goblet, wiped droplets of wine from his beard, and spoke in a deep, rumbling voice that sounded like distant thunder. "At first, I thought the coming of Roman troops was bad news but, upon reflection, this might well provide the opportunity we need to rescue Abbas. They will assuredly take the coast road from Antioch but our success in Galilee makes it likely they will turn inland either at Ptolomais or a days' march further south at Cape Carmel. In their place I would choose Carmel because that road goes through Nazareth, the centre of the resistance against Herod. A show of force there would be no bad thing from their point of view. Either way, we will be ready for them."

"Ready to do what?"

"Attack them of course, though not with the intention of driving them back, but to secure hostages of value."

This was indeed risky and not at all to Judas' liking. "How many of them?"

"Numbers do not matter for what we have in mind. Our attack will be sudden and well concealed."

"And we have almost a thousand men at our disposal, each one of which is just itching to measure his prowess against the Romans," added bar Abbas.

"Legionaries or auxiliaries?" asked Judas.

"Legionaries, I think," replied Joachim. "Which is to be preferred for two reasons. First, auxiliaries are lighter armed and more fleet of foot than plodding legionaries so we have less to fear from an active pursuit once we have completed our work. Second, only legionaries can provide the hostages of value we need to complete our plan."

Bar Abbas interrupted the older man as his enthusiasm for the plan got the better of him, "You see Judas, if we can capture a senior officer or perhaps two or three centurions, we will have something to bargain with. The Romans value their centurions highly, and while Herod doubtless cares nothing about them, the Roman commander certainly will. To him the return of his centurions in exchange for an obscure resistance leader will seem like a good deal."

"But Herod holds Abbas, not the Romans," said Judas.

"Indeed, and Joachim's plan depends on the Roman commander putting pressure on Herod to release him into Roman custody. Herod won't like it, but it will be difficult for him to refuse the man who has come to help him recover control of his realm."

"What if Herod still says no?"

Joachim responded before bar Abbas could answer. "Roman commanders are made of stern stuff. They do not abandon their men, only politicians do that, and I am sure that the much-vaunted friendship between Herod and the emperor would be severely strained if Augustus heard that the king had allowed his centurions to be killed when they could have been saved."

Judas remained silent as he considered all he had heard. To attack a column of legionaries without even knowing their number seemed hazardous, reckless even and yet…

The ever-enthusiastic bar Abbas could wait no longer. "Well, what do you think?"

"Give him time," reproved Joachim. "It is good to see one so young weigh the positives and negatives in such a mature manner."

"Unlike me, I suppose. Patience has never been my best attribute."

Joachim smiled, "It is also good to see such self-understanding in our leader." He turned to Judas. "I never had a son of my own. Abbas asked me to look after his in the event of something happening to him. I suppose my paternal instincts have devolved on to our unfortunate leader."

"Unfortunate! Never!" said bar Abbas; the bond between the two men was obviously strong.

Doing his best to respond to Joachim's compliment, Judas spoke in the most reflective manner he could muster, "The plan seems to me so outrageous it might just work. The Romans will never expect a direct attack on a legionary force. We will have the advantage of surprise and local knowledge. When do we leave?"

Bar Abbas laughed, "Now our young tax gatherer sounds as impatient as me! Do you not want to hear about your role in this?"

"Oh, err, of course," answered Judas, angry that his mature image of reflection had lasted only a few seconds.

"Your knowledge of Latin will enable you to speak directly to the Romans without intermediaries. Once we have secured our hostages, you will go to the Roman commander to bargain for the release of my father."

"Will the Romans respect a messenger carried by someone they regard as a rebel or just kill me?"

Bar Abbas shrugged, "I do not know and therein lies the risk I spoke of. You will need to use wit and intelligence just to reach the Roman commander. You do not lack either."

"I thought the risk lay in the battle to come?"

Bar Abbas looked horrified. "Of course not. You are too valuable to risk in a battle. A stray sling stone might finish you."

"The Romans do not use slingers," objected Judas. A deep throated noise came from Joachim which Judas interpreted as a chuckle. "You have not seen our slingers. Accuracy is not their strong point."

"All right then," acknowledged Judas. "I will happily take on this task, but I insist you allow me to attend the battle with the Romans."

"Bargaining already?" smiled bar Abbas. "This augurs well. Are you sure you won't have some wine?"

***

III

The Sabbath was over. The month was Nisan (March) and it was raining heavily. Judas looked to his right and left at long,

48

irregular lines of men crouching in the thorny undergrowth of Mount Carmel's north facing slopes. A breathless scout had just arrived at the Zealot headquarters, which was no more than a cluster of ox-hide tents hidden in a fold of the ground overlooking the road to Nazareth. He brought the news the Zealots had been waiting for.

Bar Abbas gathered his battle commanders around him and spoke quickly but without faltering. "My friends, our time has come. The Romans have turned inland and will be below us within the hour. Remember, our aim is only to engage them until we can extract prisoners of value. The slingers will attack first and draw the Romans up the hill towards us. The clubmen will stay with Joachim and me until we get the chance to isolate a group of the enemy. Then we will strike hard and fast. As soon as we have secured our prisoners, you will hear the call to withdraw. Obey it. We will then disengage and retire with all speed to our prearranged hideout. Any questions?" No-one answered. "Very well, you all know what to do. God be with you this day."

As the men moved off to their battlefield positions, bar Abbas spoke to Judas. "Stay beside me. On no account get involved in the fighting. Is that clear?" Judas nodded in acknowledgement.

The slingers, who accounted for three quarters of the Zealot force, moved forward down the hill to search out concealed positions near the road. The two hundred and fifty clubmen, specially chosen for their size and physique, stood silently in a group near their leaders. They looked formidable warriors. "I am glad they're on our side," smiled Joachim admiringly. "We must not waste them."

"Indeed, they would be difficult to replace," agreed bar

Abbas. "I hope they don't get carried away. That includes you Judas; you are here to watch and learn."

"That's twice you've said that," replied Judas, irritated that bar Abbas felt it necessary to repeat his order.

"I am sorry; it's just my natural concern. We cannot afford to lose you."

The rain passed and the sun had just made a welcome appearance when the head of the Roman column appeared as it rounded a bend in the road on the left of the Zealot force. Six or seven horsemen cantered forwards followed by the first of the legionary centuries. Soon, the whole valley seemed to be filled with armoured, red cloaked marching men; Judas began to fear their numbers would be too great, but at last the rear guard, which consisted of more horsemen, came into view and the entire column lay before the Zealots.

"How many would you say?" asked bar Abbas.

"About five hundred, a full cohort," answered Joachim.

"Very well, give the signal." Joachim stood up then raised and lowered his sword three times. Within seconds the slingers struck.

The head of the column was first to feel the assault. Judas had not known what to expect but the Roman reaction was remarkable. The column halted as one, as if it was a single animal reacting to an unwelcome intruder. Next, the armoured soldiers disappeared behind a blood red wall as long shields were turned and interlocked to face the attack. The shield wall was impregnable to sling stones and for almost an hour the slingers battered the Roman column with no apparent effect.

Bar Abbas was uneasy. "This is not working, Joachim. The Romans seem quite happy to sit on their backsides all day."

"And we will soon run out of stones," growled Joachim.

"All right then, pull the men back; we'll have to think of something else. Move the clubmen forward to the—" he was interrupted by Judas.

"Wait! Something's happening at the rear of the column. The shields are moving."

Joachim squinted and shaded his eyes, "Judas you're right; there's nothing wrong with your eyesight. Can it be...?"

"Yes, it is!" exclaimed bar Abbas. "They're forming up to attack. Excellent! Give the signal for the slingers to withdraw. Bring forward the clubmen, but keep them out of sight. I shall go down to meet the slinger commanders. Judas come with me."

By the time the two of them reached the irregular line of retiring slingers, it was clear that only one century was pursuing. The heavily armoured legionaries were struggling to keep pace with their lightly armed foe and their formation had been lost as they struggled up the uneven terrain.

Bar Abbas smiled, "This is perfect. Who'd have thought they would send only one century to chase us. The trap is closing."

"When will the clubmen attack?" asked Judas.

"Not yet; we need to draw the Romans a little further from their comrades until they're completely isolated."

"I don't think there'll be time. There's movement in the centre of the column." Bar Abbas peered appraisingly at the cohort and then called the slinger commanders to him. While he did so, the leading Romans halted amid a group of deserted shepherd huts to await support from the centuries that were now following behind them.

The young Zealot leader turned to Judas, "I need you to

take an urgent message to Joachim. Tell him to bring forward the clubmen as fast as possible, but using the ground to keep them concealed from the Romans. We must surprise these plodding legionaries if we can. I shall remain here with the slingers to make sure they keep out of the close quarter work; they have done their bit."

When Judas returned fifteen minutes later, closely followed by Joachim and the clubmen, the supporting Roman centuries were making good progress towards joining the advance century waiting amongst the shepherd huts. Just as before, bar Abbas gave his orders quickly but clearly, "We have half an hour to capture our prisoners and escape before the Roman reinforcements get here. Go for the officers, not the ordinary legionaries. There will be a centurion there — he would be a good prize. You will recognise him by the transverse crest on his helmet. The man who captures him will be rewarded. Eleazar, give the battle cry!"

Eleazar, a small man with a big voice, stood up and emitted the most blood curdling shriek Judas ever heard. Though the words were unintelligible, it had a dramatic effect on the clubmen. They roared an equally powerful response, a deep aggressive, animal growl and launched themselves at the Romans. Bar Abbas led them in person. Judas felt a tingle shoot up his spine and, despite his commander's explicit orders, found himself somehow swept up in the charge.

He was unarmed apart from his sicarius. He had no idea what he was going to do but, bellowing wordless shouts, he ran forward with the clubmen. For the first time in his life, he was experiencing the thrill, the terror and the madness of battle.

But the Romans were ready. They had turned the shepherd

52

huts into a little fortress, plugging the gaps between the buildings with lines of soldiers. The leading clubmen hurled themselves against the red shield wall which buckled but did not break. Very soon, a pile of Zealot dead lay at the feet of the legionaries. Other clubmen ran round to the far side of the defensive wall to try and find a way in, but they were blocked too. The attack seemed to be faltering. Then Judas, who was with the rearmost clubmen, saw bar Abbas gather a small reserve in the heat of battle and launch another attack. This time, the stubborn shield wall broke. The clubmen poured through. Judas knew he had just witnessed supreme battlefield leadership. Victory seemed imminent. He must play his part, and running forward he picked up a club from a fallen Zealot. But just as he reached the shepherd huts, he found the clubmen in full retreat.

They were dragging two wounded legionaries with them, but already the Romans were pursuing.

"Judas! I told you to keep out of this!" Bar Abbas could say no more because he was suddenly confronted by a small group of oncoming Romans; his disobedient tax gatherer would have to await his wrath. Before Judas could respond the Romans caught up with his commander and seemed likely to liberate their two comrades. One of the Romans was soon engaged by two large clubmen, but another bore down on bar Abbas with a bloodied sword ready to strike; he wore the transverse crest of a centurion.

Courage did not come into it. Judas saw the man he admired about to fall. Without a second thought, he ran up behind the centurion and clubbed him on the back of his helmet with all the strength he could muster. The helmet flew off the centurion's head, who crumpled at the knees and fell unconscious at bar Abbas' feet. Seeing this, the remaining Romans abandoned the pursuit and retired down the hill to join their exhausted comrades.

That was my first encounter with Judas Sicariot. The battle was over.

***

IV

The Zealots made good their escape and by nightfall had reassembled in a dry gulley on the south side of Carmel, safely out of range of their enemy. The atmosphere was jubilant. One of the three captives, the one Judas had struck, was a centurion and another was a section leader. To his acute embarrassment, Judas was being hailed by tough, hardened campaigners as a hero. Time and again, as he sat by one of the camp fires, he was asked to retell every detail of how he felled the centurion. It was difficult to make hitting someone on the back of the head sound interesting but his wide-eyed audience seemed not to mind.

"The centurion is a big man is he not?" enquired a young slinger. "Well not very big, but a good size," answered Judas.

"It is skill not size that counts," said a scar faced clubman. "And it is well known that the Roman army only promotes seasoned warriors to the rank of centurion."

"Surely, he was terrifying to behold?" insisted the slinger, but before Judas could dredge up yet another description, Joachim appeared out of the darkness. "Judas, bar Abbas wishes to speak with you. Come with me." A murmur of approval came from those nearby; Judas Sicariot was soon to be rewarded for his bravery. There seemed to be no envy within any of these extraordinary people.

Joachim took Judas to a camp fire a little separated from the rest. As they approached, bar Abbas glanced up at them and then looked back into the fire. Anger lined his young face. He remained silent while Joachim and Judas sat down in front of him; his knuckles were white as he gripped his battle club. Judas grew fearful and drew breath to speak but Joachim touched his shoulder and shook his head indicating he should say nothing. For a full minute, the Zealot leader stared silently into the flames and when he spoke at last, his voice was devoid of emotion. The usual enthusiasm was replaced by a cold monotone of controlled fury.

"Judas, you deliberately disobeyed my direct order."

"But I only—"

"Quiet! Do not interrupt me. Do you know the penalty for disobedience in battle?"

"I can guess," muttered Judas.

"Then can you give me a good reason not to have your throat cut?"

"No, I cannot."

Joachim intervened, "Eli, do not be too harsh; he is young and inexperienced. You were headstrong once."

"Did I ever disobey a battlefield order?"

"Never, but surely Judas' bravery should be taken into consideration?" Again, bar Abbas remained silent for a while. Judas now felt true fear, for this man's cold anger was terrifying.

"Discipline," said bar Abbas. "Especially battlefield discipline is vital if we are to beat the Romans. I should not have to say this to a man of your intelligence Judas. Fortunately for you, I always listen to Joachim, so you may leave now. I have no more use for you because I cannot trust you."

This was almost as bad as a death sentence. Judas could not face such abject failure. "Give me another chance," he pleaded. "I have learned my lesson. I will not fail you again."

Now, for the first time since they joined him by the camp fire, bar Abbas looked directly at Judas. The dark eyes seemed to mellow a little, "You must understand, Judas Sicariot, there will be no second chance. If you choose to remain, you will be subject to the same discipline as every one of us."

The light returned to Judas' world; he was not rejected after all. "Thank you, bar Abbas, you will not regret your decision."

Suddenly, the rock-hard countenance of the young leader vanished. The familiar, open face he had grown to respect and, yes, love as a brother, returned. "Well, in that case, you may call me Eli as my close brother Zealots do. Your bravery has earned you that right."

"Hurrah!" boomed Joachim. "We now have another full disciple. But Eli, what is the matter? You are still not happy."

"I am indeed happy that we have secured another brother, but unhappy that we lost sixty-two more in the battle today."

"But we captured our hostages including a centurion."

"But at a terrible price. Had I known the cost would be so high, I would never have fought the battle. It was supposed to be hit and run with minimal casualties. Instead, I lost almost one in twenty of my entire force."

"I understand," sighed Joachim. "The Romans fought well, but the men think it was a victory; best let them continue to think so."

Bar Abbas nodded, "As always Joachim your counsel is wise. I am tired now so let us meet in the morning to discuss our next move. Judas, remain with me a few more moments."

When they were alone bar Abbas said, "I am sorry if I frightened you, but I had to make you understand what is expected of a true Zealot."

"Am I now a true Zealot then?"

"Yes."

"Well, you did put the fear of God into me. Would you really have cut my throat?"

"Let us hope you never find out though you will soon experience fear again, not the hot, wild fear of battle, which you already know enough about, but the cold, chilling fear of being alone amongst enemies with no-one to advise or help you except your own resourcefulness. You will encounter greater danger than the rest of us, except my father perhaps, but if you survive, I see in you a possible replacement for me if I should fall. You are not ready yet, but in time you may be."

"I am honoured."

"And you have much to learn. This night, I shall content myself with explaining to you our ultimate strategy and the means by which this will be achieved. The only others who know this are my father, Joachim and two people in Nazareth."

***

V

The revelry in the Zealot camp was subsiding as exhaustion began to replace the post battle exhilaration of victory and survival. But Judas was far from tired as bar Abbas prepared to bring him into his confidence. The Zealot leader threw some more pine logs onto the fire and watched the sparks move upwards for a short while as he gathered his thoughts.

"Judas, despite what you may hear from my followers, we have no chance of winning our freedom through our own efforts alone. Herod's kingdom is divided. We have a king who has more in common with Greeks and Romans than his own people. Most of the Pharisees support him, the Sadducees remain aloof and are so few in number they don't really matter. The Essenes, who are most like us, are sworn to non-violence so the rest of our people are confused and accept subjugation because, in the absence of any alternative, it at least promises an easy life."

"Is our cause hopeless then?"

"No, not if we can find help outside the Roman empire."

"What help?"

"The Parthians will provide it if they are convinced we have a chance of winning. They will certainly need some convincing though. The last time they intervened in our land, more than thirty years ago, they achieved some early success but ended up being badly beaten by the Romans. We lost our last native Hasmonean king, Hyrcanus, and found ourselves with a low born Idumean puppet foisted upon us by the Romans instead."

"You mean Herod?"

"The very same. He has been our king ever since, but in order to unite Judea, Samaria and Galilee, the lands that were once Israel, we need a true king."

"I understand," acknowledged Judas. "But the Hasmonean leaders were not popular either and never controlled much more than Judea. The other provinces never really accepted them."

Bar Abbas now beamed his irresistible smile, "But I am not talking about the Hasmoneans. I am talking about a direct lineal descendant of King David himself! Not only that, if this descendant were to marry another of David's line, would not their progeny inspire all the Jews in the lands that were once David's domain?"

"Certainly, but could this happen?"

"It will happen; it is already planned! My mentor Joachim is married to Anna who is of the house of David. They have a beautiful though wilful daughter, Mary, who is betrothed to Joseph bar Jacob, who in turn is a direct descendant of King David. Their first son shall be the King of all Israel, the true Messiah."

It took Judas a few moments to digest such momentous information. It was difficult to believe. "The lineages, are they certain?" he asked hesitantly.

"Proven beyond all doubt and certified by the high priest himself."

"Is Simon one of us?"

"Yes, but covertly so at present. He has carried out the research in the temple records, some of which survived the Babylonian destruction. The proof is ready when we need to use it. Mary resides in Nazareth as does Joseph, who owns a construction business, but he was born in Bethlehem, the city of David."

"So the new King of Greater Israel will be the son of a businessman?"

"I know it doesn't sound very regal," laughed bar Abbas. "But we will ensure the new king is brought up properly and, with the kingdom of David re-united, the Parthians will surely come to our aid."

"But it will be many years before the new king will be old enough to lead his men."

"We do not have to wait that long. His mere existence will be enough. Others like us can pave the way until he is old enough to take command himself. But Judas, we must be vigilant for there'll be many Jews who will see the new king as a threat."

"I understand, so what happens next?"

"First, you must undertake the perilous visit to Jerusalem where, with God's blessing, you will negotiate with Herod and the Roman commander for the release of our leader. Then we must wait until Joseph and Mary deliver our Messiah. As you know, his coming has been foretold so, as soon as Mary's pregnancy is confirmed, we will get news to the Parthians to prepare for war."

"And what if Mary gives birth to a girl?"

"Then we will just have to wait longer, but her first born will be a boy; so says the prophecy. When he is born the Pharisees and Essenes will join us, Herod will be isolated and the Parthians will come."

Judas found himself borne up by the power of bar Abbas' inspirational faith. It would maintain them both in the years to come, but there was to be an unexpected and unwelcome complication, an intervention that neither of them could have foreseen. His name was John the Baptist.

CHAPTER FOUR

I woke up to a splitting headache. My eyes would not focus properly; it was so dark I could not tell whether or not my eyes were even open. Slowly I became aware of a point of light above me, and as my eyes slowly adjusted, I realised it was a small rectangular window. Next came the smell; stale sheep and sweat. I tried to sit up and groaned as my aching muscles fought against me.

"So you're awake at last," came a voice from somewhere behind me.

"Rufio, is that you? Are you all right?"

"A few cuts and bruises, but nothing serious unlike you two."

"How long have I been unconscious?"

"A day and a half."

"Where are we?"

"No idea."

"What of Caius?"

"He is on your left. He's badly wounded and has a fever. I fear for him."

I suddenly became aware of a voracious thirst. "Is there water?"

"Near the door in a large bowl on the floor of this stinking rat hole."

I dragged myself across the smelly, dried mud floor and

drank deeply; the water was tepid and stale but just then to me it tasted like spring water sent by the gods. Then, sitting up with my back propped against the door, I surveyed my surroundings in the dim light cast by two small windows. Our prison measured about ten paces by eight and was made with mud brick walls and a flat straw ceiling supported by wooden crossbeams. I was sitting at one of the shorter sides looking towards the far end where Rufio was sitting on a layer of straw which passed for a bed. To my right was Caius lying on more straw. He was still unconscious and shivering violently. I took another gulp of water and began to feel a little better.

"Rufio, the last thing I remember was chasing the Zealots. What has happened since?"

The big Pannonian came over to me and said, "All in good time. First, what of you, Lucius? You have a thigh wound. I washed it as best I could while you were unconscious, but we need to use our water sparingly. I have seen no-one since we got here and have no idea when or if our water will be replenished."

I examined the lateral cut across my left thigh. It looked bad, but it was not too deep and had scabbed up nicely though the edges were yellow with puss. Unlike Caius, I had no fever. "Thanks for your efforts, Rufio. I think I shall make a full recovery. You make a good nurse."

"Don't know about that," said the bluff legionary. "But it's got no worse during the last few hours."

"So what's happened since the fight with the Zealots?"

"Caius was already down and I was weakening when I saw you struck from behind by a clubman. The three of us were dragged away before the supporting centuries could reach us. We were allowed no rest. You two were dumped into a cart drawn by a mule and I was tied to the back and forced to walk throughout the night until we reached this horrible place. The Zealots never stopped and by the time we got here I could scarcely stand."

"Are we in a village or an isolated place?"

Rufio's brow creased with thought. "A small town I think."

"How many hours were we travelling?"

"All night and yesterday morning."

"What speed?"

"About half that of a legion."

"From which direction did the sun rise?"

"Directly ahead of us."

"That means we travelled about fifteen miles due east of the battle. I'm fairly sure we must be in Nazareth which is a well-known centre of Zealot activity."

Rufio asked, "Lucius, do you think the column will pass this way?"

"Sadly, my friend, it will already have done so and must now be heading south on the road to Jerusalem."

"So we're alone then." Before I could answer, the door supporting my back was thrown open. I tumbled backwards into blinding light and was hauled none too gently to my feet by two powerful clubmen and thrust back into the animal shed. Two more clubmen entered and stood to one side as a very different individual followed them in. He was slim, smartly dressed in clean, white linen and looked about thirty years old. With well-manicured hands, he beckoned us to sit and said, "Do any of you speak Greek?" Most legionaries based in the east picked up at least a smattering of this language, which was the most common tongue since the conquests of Alexander the

Great. It was widely spoken among the political and commercial classes, even in Herod's kingdom, and all educated Romans spoke it. That did not include us of course and Rufio always maintained Greek was an effeminate tongue and would have nothing to do with it. I knew enough to get by, though I do not suppose I spoke it well.

"I do," I answered.

"And who are you?" enquired the well-groomed newcomer.

"Who wants to know?"

"Fair enough. I suppose it does not matter if you know who I am. My name is Joseph bar Jacob. I am a man of influence in this area, one of the governing council."

"What area is that?"

"That I will not tell you. Now it is your turn. I see by your armband that you are a centurion."

"Centurion Lucius Veranius of the fifth cohort of the Third Gallica, which is on its way to Jerusalem to deal with your Zealot friends."

Joseph said quietly, "I am a Pharisee not a Zealot. I share some of their aims, but not their means to achieve them."

"Is that why we still live?"

Joseph smiled, "Actually no. You three are part of a larger plan. Herod has imprisoned a Zealot leader whose followers hope to use you as hostages in exchange for him."

"What if Herod refuses?"

"He assuredly would like to refuse but he will think twice before offending his Roman overlords will he not?"

It was I who thought twice. I was quite sure Varus cared nothing for us and would abandon us without a glimmer of conscience. However, our legate Marcus Tullius, would not allow three of his men to be so easily sacrificed. But he was far away in Antioch. I looked at Caius who was still shaking and said, "You may soon only have two hostages. The legionary who is still unconscious was injured in the fight with the Zealots. The wound on his right thigh is deep and full of poison; fever has set in."

Now the urbane, sophisticated Joseph was troubled. He walked over to Caius and lifted the field bandage that Rufio had placed over the wound. The smell was awful. Joseph turned his face away, revolted by the suppurating mess and said a few words to one of the clubmen who immediately left us. Then he turned to me again,

"Your comrade is seriously wounded and likely to die. My betrothed has medical knowledge; she may be able to help him, but I fear we are too late. She will do what she can." He seemed genuinely concerned, not about Caius as a hostage but as a man. There was humanity, almost gentleness in this pillar of local society.

I began to feel the first glimmer of hope that there might be a way out for us if the dice of fortune fell in our favour. But then all thoughts of the future were swept aside by what happened next. The clubman, who had moments before left us, returned accompanied by a woman I shall never forget. I was always a typical centurion, not especially imaginative or given to fine prose, but the woman who entered our dreadful abode would have defied the description of the finest poet. She was tall, her face was uncovered and she seemed to glide like an angel without quite touching the ground. It was as if there was an aura about her that lit up her surroundings in a warm light however horrible they were. I could not stop looking at her face which combined strong, noble features with a wide mouth that appealed to more base feelings. Everyone knows that Jewish women are attractive, I have seen many in my time, but none to match the betrothed of Joseph bar Jacob.

"Ye gods! What is this!" gasped Rufio."

"Hopefully, the person who will save Caius, and watch what you say. Our host may understand Latin," I answered.

The woman went straight over to Caius and pulled back the field bandage. Unlike Joseph, she was not disturbed by what she saw and examined the wound with clinical intensity. After a short while, she turned to her betrothed and spoke in Aramaic, the Jewish tongue we could not understand.

Then Joseph said, "Speak in Greek, Mary. Before you, sits Lucius Veranius, a centurion of the Gallica legion. He will understand you." For the first time, Mary looked at me. Her long, black hair fell in waves down to her shoulders. I should not have seen this but she had obviously come in haste and had no time to cover her face for non-family visitors. Joseph did not seem to mind.

When she spoke, in a voice rather lower in tone than I expected, I seemed to melt like snow in dazzling morning sunlight. "Lucius Veranius, I must tell you that your friend is dying. The poison has been in his wound for too long. It will almost certainly kill him."

"Is there no hope at all?"

"I will do my best but my medical knowledge is limited."

"Thank you."

"But I see you too are wounded."

"Only a scratch."

"It certainly is not," and without asking for Joseph's permission, Mary sat down beside me, examined my thigh wound and, with a feather light touch, pressed the edges of the infected area. As I watched, I could smell the scent of flowers that accompanied her which might have produced an embarrassing effect on me had I not felt too ill to react normally. Some puss emerged from one side of my injury which Mary wiped away then, taking a phial from a linen pouch that hung from her waist, she rubbed some white ointment into my leg until it was completely absorbed into the skin. The itching, which I had barely resisted scratching since I had awoken, immediately faded. With a slight nod of satisfaction, she stood up and, looking down on me, she almost smiled.

"The puss is good, Lucius Veranius. You will live, but I cannot allow your friend to stay here; he needs constant attention. What is his name?"

"Caius Pantera."

"Well, Caius will be moved to more comfortable quarters until his fate is clear."

I asked, "Why are you doing this? We are the enemy of your people. These clubmen would sooner kill us than see us cured."

The soft voice took on a hard edge and the warm brown eyes froze, "I share the hopes of these brave warriors. I do not do this for you, but because it is the wish of my betrothed."

I looked at Joseph, but his expression gave nothing away. Mary left us and was quickly followed by Joseph and the clubmen, who bore Caius' large frame with some difficulty. When we were alone again Rufio said, "What was all that about? Why don't they just kill us? I can't believe Zealots take prisoners."

"I'm sure they don't normally, but they want us alive for a good reason."

"A slow, painful death for public amusement; that's what I would do to them."

"I don't think so, not yet at any rate. Joseph said we are to be the subject of a hostage exchange; the three of us for a high-ranking Zealot leader. If the deal goes through, and I have real doubts that it will, we shall be freed. If not, then your prediction will happen. Either way we must try and find a way out of here once we know more about Caius' fate."

Rufio snorted, "Lucky devil; he'll be in no hurry to get better, not with that beauty mopping his brow."

"Maybe, but would you swap places with him?"

"Suppose not, but imagine waking up to her every morning. That Joseph's a lucky devil."

"They're not married yet, just betrothed. Amongst the Jews, it is quite common practice for a woman to live for a short while in the house of her future husband, though under close escort, until the time of the marriage."

"So Joseph's not plucked his flower yet?"

"You put it most elegantly Rufio."

"Well he'd better watch out or it might get plucked for him," laughed the big Pannonian. Prophetic words indeed.

***

II

While Rufio and I fretted in our prison, Caius was taken into Joseph's house where he could be treated properly. Much later, Caius gave me a full account of what passed and it is this that I shall retell now.

On the sixth day of our captivity, Caius' fever finally

broke. When at last he opened his eyes, he thought he must have died and gone to some new wonderful world instead of Hades, but he could not think what he had done to deserve such good fortune. Slowly, without sitting up, he looked at his surroundings as far as his aching neck would allow. He was in a large, clean room that was well lit by torches fixed into the walls. In the centre of the room was a brazier, which glowed cheerfully and gave out enough heat to keep the furthermost recesses warm.

Rich tapestries adorned the walls illustrating in bright colours scenes of hunting, harvesting and building; clearly this was the house of a person of substance.

In a large chair beside the brazier sat a woman in her late teens or early twenties, her head slumped forward in sleep. Somewhere incense was burning and, apart from a raging thirst, Caius felt a warm, comforting sense of wellbeing. Well, he thought, if this is the afterlife, I am happy to be here; but first I must do something about this thirst.

"Water," he croaked. "I need water." The woman in the chair immediately woke up, looked hard at him and hurried from the room. Caius was too weak to sit up unaided so he would have to wait for his drink. A minute or two later, the woman returned accompanied by a taller woman of a similar age, who sat on Caius' bed and touched his forehead with a cool, slender hand. She turned to her companion. "Ruth, the fever has broken. Bring a little wine with the water and some fruit." As Ruth left to do her mistress' bidding, the tall woman spoke in Greek. "Can you hear me Caius Pantera?"

"Yes."

"How do you feel?"

"Weak and thirsty. I did not know such feelings exist in

the afterlife."

"You are not in the afterlife."

"Are you not an angel then?"

At that, Mary could not help smiling, "Alas no, but I seem to be a good nurse though. You are very much in the real world."

Caius sighed, "Then, where am I?"

"All in good time. Here comes Ruth with your water. Do not drink too much at once."

With some effort, Ruth and Mary managed to heave Caius into a sitting position where he was able to quench his thirst at last, despite a sore throat caused by the fever. He completely ignored the instruction about not drinking too much and emptied the jug of its contents, but he did not feel like eating yet and his leg hurt.

"Where am I?" he asked again.

"I must not tell you that," answered Mary.

"How long have I been here?"

"Six days, though it is eight since you were wounded. Tell me how it is that you speak our ancient language. You called for your mother in Hebrew when you were delirious."

"It was my mother's tongue."

"So you are Jewish?"

"No, I am Roman, but my mother was born in Samaria."
"And your father?"

"He came from Germania."

"Your mother is Jewish, your father German, yet you call yourself Roman. How can that be?"

"All who join the legions must be Roman citizens, though most of us have never seen Rome."

"Your understanding of nationhood is very different to

mine. Jews are all descendants of Abraham and his wife Sarah. They lived more than two thousand years ago. Outsiders cannot simply become Jews as it suits them."

"Who was Abraham?"

"A great man selected by our God to create what we call God's Chosen Race. It seems to me that anyone can become a Roman if he chooses."

"Only if he qualifies. We accept only the best of the people we have conquered to be Roman citizens, which is why you are part of our empire and not we part of yours." Mary's brow furrowed and Caius quickly realised he had offended his beautiful benefactor. "Please forgive me. You have saved my life and now I have angered you. I do not even know your name."

"Your friends will tell you when you are returned to them, which will be soon by the looks of things. Ruth, stay with him until he sleeps again. I will come back in the morning." With that, Caius' angelic saviour swept from the room.

For the first time, Ruth spoke, "Do not worry, Mary has always been quick to anger but she is equally quick to forgive."

"Have you known her long?" asked Caius, still relishing the sweet scent Mary had left behind.

"Since we were children together. She has recently betrothed to the master of this house and, as her companion and personal servant, I have come with her to live here."

"I have never seen anyone so beautiful."

"Many say that. Joseph bar Jacob is indeed a fortunate man."

"Who is he?"

"An important man here. He is one of the town council elders and owns a construction business which is helping to build the new city called Sepphoris."

"Which is where?"

"Half a day's walk from here." Caius felt a twinge of guilt as he extracted information from this good-hearted woman, information he was sure his captors would wish to be withheld because Sepphoris was only a few miles from Nazareth, the hotbed of Zealot resistance to Herod. He now had no doubt where he was. At this time, he thought he was alone, probably a prisoner, but for some reason he was being kept alive by his ruthless enemy. Memories of the battle with the Zealots began to flood back; he needed time to think.

"Ruth, I feel tired now. What time of day is it?"

"It is the middle of the night. Rest easy now and try to sleep. I will be here if you need me."

When Caius awoke, he could hear voices, a man's and a woman's. The woman was Mary. He decided to feign sleep and listen. Fortunately, they spoke in Hebrew so he could understand every word.

"So you seem to have saved him then; well done. How soon can he re-join his comrades?" asked the man.

Mary answered, "It is difficult to say. The fever has gone and the wound in his leg is now healing but he may have broken a bone below the knee. The swelling suggests a possible fracture so he must keep his weight off it for a few weeks."

"A few weeks! That is most inconvenient. As well as this man I am obliged to accommodate five Zealot warriors to guard him, all of whom eat like starving wolves."

"Well, you can dismiss them then because there is nothing for them to guard. This Roman cannot walk, nor will he be able to for at least a month assuming his leg is not badly broken."

"Are you sure about that?"

"I cannot give you a precise timing, but as soon as he is able to hobble, I will tell you and you can recall the guards."

"As soon as he can hobble, we can lock him up with his friends again."

"You still want him to live, don't you?"

"Yes, for the present at least; just until we hear back from Jerusalem."

Caius heard footsteps leave the room, presumably the man's, because the next words were Mary's. "How did he pass the night?"

"He was restless," answered Ruth. "But he slept most of the time." There was a brief pause then Ruth added, "He is a fine-looking man is he not?"

"Fine looking or not, he is our enemy."

"Yes, but he seems too gentle to be an enemy."

"Perhaps," conceded Mary. "But do not allow yourself to like him. He will quite likely be killed before we can complete his cure."

"It seems a shame."

"Ruth, as long as men rule this world such things will happen. Now go and rest. I will watch over him. You have done well."

Now Caius' mind was spinning. His fate was to be determined by a message from Jerusalem; it was likely to be bad news. A fast rider could travel from Jerusalem to Nazareth in two days. He could not imagine what sort of message it could be that would decide whether he lived or died but, importantly, he had found out he had wounded comrades nearby. That gave room for hope however faint.

Once more, he became aware of the sweet scent of flowers

that always accompanied Mary; it was time to wake up. He turned over, sat up carefully to avoid putting any pressure on his leg and rubbed his eyes. Mary was sitting opposite and leaned forwards, "How are you this morning?"

"Much better I think."

"Ruth has made some broth. Will you take some?"

Now Caius realised he was ravenous. He had not eaten for nine days. Mary looked on as he devoured first one, then a second and finally a third bowl of lamb broth mixed with soft lentils and vegetables. He sat back on his pillows and said, "Please tell Ruth that was excellent. I never tasted anything so good."

"She will be pleased you liked it. Is there anything else you need?" Caius glanced down at his body. Apart from his chainmail armour, he was still clad in the clothes he wore in battle with the Zealots. Although his leg wound had been washed and bandaged, the rest of him was untouched. "You have already done more than any prisoner can expect from his enemy. I know not why, but..." He hesitated.

"You are my patient. Do not be afraid to ask."

"I would really appreciate a bath. Cold water would be fine. Is it possible?"

Mary said, "The Roman addiction to cleanliness is your one undeniable virtue. I will arrange it. The water will be warm and we have olive oil for you to use to cleanse your skin. We do not have a strygil but a sharp scraping knife should suffice instead."

"You are well informed of our ways."

"Not all Jews live their lives in one set of clothing."

"I suppose I must stink."

Mary smiled, "I have smelt worse, but not much worse."

"Then the sooner I bathe, the better for all of us!"

It took about an hour for Ruth to fill a copper tub with warm water. She and Mary supported Caius as he hopped unsteadily on his good left leg to the small room where the inviting tub awaited him.

Ruth said, "If you rest your weight on the tub, you should be able to undress yourself. Will you be able to get in and out unaided?"

"I shall have no trouble lifting my own weight, which is much less than it was nine days ago," replied Caius.

"Then we will leave until you call. There is a robe for you to use after you have finished. I will clean your uniform later."

"And make sure you are fully clad before you call us," added Mary. Caius suppressed the remark that entered his mind; he did not want to antagonise her again.

As soon as the women left, he undressed and lowered himself into the blissful, warm water. He lay there, relishing his good fortune, until the water began to go cool then, using the olive oil and scraping knife which had been left within easy reach, he did his best to remove the grime that had accumulated on his skin since the battle with the Zealots.

When the scraping was done, he heaved himself out of the tub, dried his body on some woollen towels and put on the white robe that had been left for him. Then taking a last look at his little enclave of contentment, he called out to the women that he was ready. They could not have been far away for they reappeared in seconds.

Mary asked, "Do you feel better now?"

"Much better thank you. A warm bath puts life back into the most weary limbs and I am the cleanest I have been since leaving Antioch."

Ruth giggled, "Dressed in that white robe, you look more like a temple priest than a Roman soldier."

"It is all that's available and I am most grateful for it."

"Actually, you are far too tall to be a priest and your straw-coloured hair—"

"That's quite enough, Ruth," interrupted Mary sternly. "We must get him back to his bed. Are you ready to return?" Caius nodded, so Ruth and Mary each took hold of one of his large arms and supported him as he slowly limped back to his quarters.

Whether it was the feeling of well-being or simple lack of concentration Caius could not recall, but when he was but a few paces from his bed, he stumbled and briefly stood on his injured right leg. A violent, sharp pain shot up into his waist. He began to topple over; the women suddenly had to bear his full weight. Ruth crumpled but, somehow, Mary held him up on her own and part carried, part dragged him to his bed.

For a few seconds as he lay there, Caius could not respond to the women, both of whom were urging him to tell them what they could do to help; the pain was just too great for speech but slowly, as the intensity subsided a little, he was able to mutter, "I felt something crack just below the knee. I'm not sure what happened. Maybe the bone has broken."

Mary quickly examined the leg. "Ruth, there is a phial in my room near the mirror; you know the one. Bring it please. Hurry!" Ruth ran from the room. "Caius, we have something to ease your pain. You will feel better soon. I think your leg may already have been broken; you put your weight on the fracture when you stumbled."

"And it would have been much worse if you, and you alone, had not prevented me from falling. I do not know whether it is your strength or beauty that I admire most. You already know my name; may I know yours?" Caius thought it prudent not to reveal that Ruth had already told him.

"My name is Mary."

"Then whatever the future may hold and whatever our differences may be, I thank you from my heart Mary."

"You are a strange one Caius, so different from what I was led to expect."

"I hope that is a surprise and not a shock."

"It is." Further conversation was ended by Ruth's speedy return.

Mary held the phial to Caius' lips. "Sip, do not drink. A few drops should be enough." Caius followed Mary's instructions and soon a pleasant, warm sensation flowed through his body as the liquid from the phial took effect. The pain in his leg grew numb and was replaced by a dull but eminently bearable ache.

"By the gods, that is powerful medicine!"

"It is also poison if taken in large quantities," replied Mary.

"Nature extracts a price for everything so please do not leave that phial within my reach," said Caius.

"You have delayed your recovery; you may need it again. If so, I will bring it back."

***

III

For Caius, the following days were long stretches of boredom alleviated by the anticipation of Mary's visits. To begin with,

Ruth was always present but after a week or so Mary would allow her a break from her work which would leave the two of them alone. Joseph would visit from time to time to check on Caius' progress, but he seemed preoccupied with business matters in Sepphoris and seldom stayed long.

Caius' first objective was to find out the names of the comrades who were sharing his captivity, albeit in humbler circumstances, but Mary steadfastly refused to give him this information saying only Joseph could provide it. Joseph, however, would say nothing except that Caius would see them both soon enough. So there were two of them. After two weeks Caius plucked up enough courage to try and discover more about the young woman who was so ably nursing him back to health. He chose one of those welcome occasions when Ruth was absent.

"Mary, I spent my childhood in Caesarea Maritima so I know something of the ways of the Jews. My mother was a Jew as you already know. I must say I am surprised, pleasantly surprised, that your husband permits you to tend me. I thought Jewish men kept their women hidden away."

"Most do but not all. My father, Joachim, educated me like a man because he has no sons. My mother, Anna, approved of this for she comes from a family of forward-thinking people who some might say are tainted with Greek ideas. Those who believe that the law should be imposed in exactly the same way as in the days of Moses think modernisers like us are heretics. Be that as it may, I am thankful for my father's broadmindedness which extended to ensuring I am betrothed to a man of similar views to himself."

"Betrothed? You are not married?"

"No, but soon to be. Ruth is my guardian and companion

in this house until the marriage takes place."

"When will that be?"

"Yom Kippur, in six months' time."

"That is a long time to be living in the same house as your future husband, but not yet his wife."

"You may think so Roman," sniffed Mary. "But Joseph is an honourable man. He would never betray my father's trust."

"Of course not," agreed Caius quickly as he saw Mary's expression darken. "And by the looks of this house, he will take good care of you. It looks more Roman than Jewish."

"Indeed, I am happy for that. Joseph has learned advanced building techniques thanks to his contracts in Sepphoris, which is being built mainly for wealthy Greek and Roman residents. We even have a hypocaust which heats our floors in winter."

"How very Roman!" And for the first time, they both laughed together.

A month after Caius' fall, he could walk short distances with the aid of a stick but, despite broad hints from Joseph, Mary showed no inclination to send him back to his fellow prisoners. Although cleansed and well-scrubbed, Caius began to fret about his appearance; his beard was growing thick, but all Romans prefer to be clean shaven. The opportunity came when Mary and Ruth were changing the dressing on his leg.

Ruth, always more forward than Mary, said, "Your beard is a different colour to your hair; it's almost red."

"Yellow hair and a red beard is a common combination in men from Germania, but as a true Roman, I would dearly like to shave my beard off. In my kitbag is all I need to shave if you would be kind enough to bring it with a bowl of warm water."

Mary said, "Ruth, I will fetch it while you finish off dressing Caius' leg. I will also bring a mirror."

Soon all was ready and Caius found himself looking into silvered glass, but was appalled at how thin his face had become. He opened the small, leather bag that legionaries carried at all times to store their personal effects and took out his sharp, iron razor and some herbs which he put in the water and rubbed to create a lather. The women watched in fascination for Jewish men never shaved.

"What herb is that?" asked Mary.

"We call it soapwort. This is the last I have."

Ruth examined it and pronounced, "I recognise this. It is sold in the market."

"Then go and buy some and bring back a whetstone to keep Caius' razor sharp," said Mary.

Caius rubbed the foam over his beard and began to shave. As he looked in the mirror, he saw Mary watching him intently. Without turning round, he said, "I suppose this must seem strange to you. I believe Jewish men do not shave."

"That is true. The beard is part of their manhood."

"Do we shaven Romans appear unmanly to you?"

"I might have thought so once, but not now."

When the shaving was done, Caius rinsed his face and turned round. "Thank you, Mary, that feels so much better."

"Good. I know you Romans like your hair cut short. Yours is now long and uneven. Would you like me to cut it for you?"

"Mary, just at this moment, I cannot think of anything I would like more."

"Very well, but I have not done this before. Sit down while I fetch some scissors."

Caius sat as ordered then Mary combed his hair through and set to work. She had never stood so close to him before. Her scent combined roses and jasmine, sweet but not sickly. The gentle touch on his hair sometimes lingered a little longer than he expected. He had never felt like this before. He closed his eyes, quietly indulged his senses and drifted heavenwards.

Suddenly, a sharp nip below his right ear brought him back to earth. "Caius, I am so sorry. I have cut you. I did not mean—"

"Mary, it's nothing — especially after what I've been through. Anyway, you did warn me you have not cut hair before."

She stopped the bleeding, which was hardly anything, with some damp linen, stood back and said, "All finished." Caius stood up and faced Mary. Their eyes met and held each other for a few long seconds. He hesitated, then stepped towards her. She did not back away.

"I'm back! There was plenty of soapwort in the market," announced Ruth as she entered the room. The precious moment was shattered. Caius picked up the linen cloth, which now had red blood stains on it, and wiped his newly shaven face as nonchalantly as he could.

Mary turned to Ruth, "You were quick."

"The market was but half full." Sensing the atmosphere, Ruth asked, "Have I interrupted something?"

"Of course not. I have just cut Caius' neck while I was cutting his hair. Nothing more."

"Nothing serious, Ruth; I think I'll live," joked Caius trying to relieve the tension.

But the moment had passed. Neither Caius nor Mary knew if it would ever come again.

As the days passed, always at the back of Caius' mind was the brief conversation between Mary and Joseph he had overhead when he had first regained consciousness about news from Jerusalem which would determine his fate. That news could not be long in coming and so, on another of those welcome occasions when he was alone with Mary, he decided to risk asking her a question he knew she should not answer.

"Mary, you and Ruth have done wonders nursing me back to health, yet I do not understand why my enemy is keeping me alive when I would have expected to have had my throat slit weeks ago. Romans and Zealots do not take each other prisoner."

Momentarily, he thought he saw Mary's eyes dampen as she answered, "I am truly sorry that you think of me as your enemy."

"Of course I don't; quite the opposite. In fact, my feelings for you are entirely inappropriate for a man to have for a woman already betrothed." Caius wondered if he had said too much but the smile Mary gave him melted any lingering doubts he had gone too far. The ice was broken.

"Dear Caius, God made us as we are. We cannot control how we feel but we can control how we behave. I am betrothed, but I will also do whatever I can to save you." Caius held out his hand and Mary clasped it; a simple action but one which sent a wave of emotion through his body. It was enough; they both knew they could speak openly now. In fact, neither spoke for a while; the simple sensation of holding hands tightly, their first physical contact outside nursing, was enough to satisfy the feelings that had developed between them, for now at least.

"He is staying tonight in Shunam and should be here by noon tomorrow."

"I will make sure Joseph is here to greet him. You have done well, Reuben." Turning to Ruth, Mary ordered, "Take this man to our visitor quarters and see he is made comfortable for the night. Then come back here with the phial; you know the one."

Ruth escorted Reuben away and quickly returned with Mary's phial, the one that had eased Caius' pain when he stumbled on his broken leg. By then Mary had gathered her thoughts and gave Ruth her instructions like a clear minded general. "Have the guards had their wine yet?"

"No, but it is due about now," answered Ruth.

"Pour six drops from this phial into each of their ration."

"Six!"

"We must be sure they are asleep. They will have sore heads in the morning; nothing more."

"I understand."

"Meanwhile, prepare food for three hungry men which should last for at least two days then, when you are sure the guards are asleep, come back to me for your final instructions."

When Ruth returned, Mary had transformed herself. Her face was made up as if for her wedding day; she wore linen of green and white. Her hair was uncovered and her scent heady and sweet. "The guards are asleep?" she asked.

"All the devils in Hell could not waken them," answered Ruth.

"Is Caius' uniform ready?"

"Yes."

"Very well, give this written message to Ephraim, it is the

message that Reuben brought, and tell him to deliver it to Joseph in Sepphoris without delay."

"But Ephraim is unfit and overweight."

"Exactly, which gives us more time, but you know how pompous he is. He will be honoured to deliver such an important message even if it does arrive rather late."

"And he is Joseph's head steward, so it is his responsibility to ensure the message arrives safely," said Ruth, entering into the spirit of conspiracy.

Mary thought for a moment, "Which is our largest donkey?"

"Gebel, but he is too spirited for Ephraim."

"I was not thinking of Ephraim. Prepare Gebel for a journey," said Mary embracing Ruth warmly. "And, finally, you are my dearest and most trusted friend. Please make sure Caius and I are left alone and undisturbed for one full hour. When the hour has passed, we will be ready. Is that clear?"

Ruth smiled broadly, "Completely clear."

"When you return, I would like you to help us release Caius' comrades, but that is not an order; you do not have to."

"Of course, I will."

"We will try to arrange things so that when the guards finally wake up, they will think the prisoners' escape was their fault. Then we must trust in God to see that justice is done."

And, thought Ruth, that there are no consequences from what is about to happen.

CHAPTER FIVE

It was just six days since the battle with the Roman cohort. Judas stood outside the Jerusalem temple wondering what the next few hours would bring. He had arrived in Jerusalem accompanied by two Zealot clubmen, Reuben and Daniel, whom bar Abbas had assigned to him as his bodyguards. They spoke little but obeyed Judas as if he were bar Abbas himself; yet, they had great difficulty obeying Judas' last order, which was to wait for him in the safe house where he had met bar Abbas and Joachim in Jerusalem only a few weeks ago, while he went on alone to the temple. Judas had abandoned any idea of attempting to meet Herod and the Roman commander under a flag of truce. Instead, he had concocted a story which he would first try out on Simon. If the wily high priest believed it then there was a good chance Herod would too.

He shivered a little as the cool, spring morning breeze strengthened and strode purposefully up the steps on the south side of the temple, through the Hulda Gates and the imposing Royal Portico where the Sanhedrin court customarily met, and entered the temple's outer courtyard known as the Court of Gentiles. As usual, this area was packed with vendors of all sorts of goods but there was no time to stop and look around. He continued onwards, through the Court of Israelites until he reached the main temple building which housed the administrative centre and, above all, the Holy of Holies.

The temple guards recognised Judas and allowed him passage to the high priest's antechamber. He found himself looking forward to meeting Simon again but felt a twinge of conscience that he was about to deceive this venerable man. He need not have worried. The door to the antechamber was opened by a palace servant but instead of Simon, a young man no older than Judas himself greeted him.

"Welcome back Judas bar Menahem. I heard you had left temple service." It was the arrogant Caiaphas who had been one of his fellow students. Although not especially gifted in an academic sense, Caiaphas had a bearing of confidence which was supported by a low animal cunning. He was certainly a fine looking individual of above average height, with widely set, dark, unfathomable eyes and, when he chose, he could charm the birds from the trees. He was also hugely ambitious and had set his sights on nothing less than the high priesthood. Judas hated him.

"Where is Simon!" he demanded.

"In Hebron," replied Caiaphas smugly.

"Why is the high priest in Hebron?"

"He is not in Hebron."

"What do you mean?"

"Simon is no longer the high priest," gloated Caiaphas. This hit Judas like a sling stone and he was momentarily lost for words. "King Herod has appointed Simon's half-brother, Joazar, as high priest," continued Caiaphas. "He was dissatisfied with Simon's tolerance of the Zealots."

"But Joazar is fat and lazy!"

"True, and unlike Simon, he ignores Herod's sexual excesses which suits the king perfectly. Joazar has already delegated all decisions except those directly affecting the king personally, to his chief secretary, Ananas bar Seth." This was even worse. Ananas came from a long line of distinguished priests and believed all senior roles in the temple hierarchy should be reserved for a select few families. Needless to say, Judas' family was not one of them, but then neither was Caiaphas' which was some consolation.

Having regained his composure, Judas said, "I have come with an important message for King Herod and the Roman commander in Jerusalem, but in view of what you have just said, I think Ananas should hear it."

Caiaphas cocked a supercilious eyebrow, "Do you indeed? Well, you can tell me and I shall be the judge of who may or may not hear it."

It was with the utmost difficulty that Judas stopped himself from planting a fist on Caiaphas' aristocratic nose but he restricted himself to a single sentence, "My message is for Ananas, not his lackey."

Now it was Caiaphas' turn to restrain himself. "The chief secretary only conducts interviews by appointments made through me. He is not in the temple today."

"Very well, I will see him tomorrow then. Tell him the message comes from Elijah bar Abbas."

"The son of the Zealot leader?"

"The very same."

"But how do you know him?"

"That is none of your business."

Caiaphas did not respond immediately. He realised that confrontation was getting him nowhere, yet he needed to know more if only to impress Ananas. Perhaps subterfuge might work. He sighed wearily and forced a smile to match his attempt at a conciliatory tone, "Judas, please sit down."

"I prefer to stand."

"As you wish, but I will sit. I have been on my feet since dawn." Judas kept his thoughts to himself as Caiaphas continued, "I ask you to forgive me for the bad start we made today. It was my fault and I regret it." Judas was expected to respond but he remained silent. "You must believe me when I tell you that Ananas will see no-one without making an appointment through me. I will of course make the necessary arrangements but I assure you it would help if I could give him a brief summary of your needs. He likes to prepare for his meetings which is why he never sees anyone without an appointment first."

This made sound sense to Judas. As a student he had never ceased to be surprised at how well informed Ananas always seemed to be. Perhaps a conciliatory response to Caiaphas' request would be wise. "Very well," he said. "The essence of my mission is to propose a compromise between the Zealots and the Roman commander here in Jerusalem. A few weeks ago, I was sent north to Cana by Simon to discover more about the destruction of the temple property there. When I arrived, I was ambushed by some of bar Abbas' followers, blindfolded and taken to a filthy, flea ridden village just outside the town."

"Can you be more precise about the location?"

"No. As I say, I was blindfolded. Apparently, there had been a battle in which the Zealots captured three Roman legionaries, one of them a centurion. The Zealots wish to negotiate an exchange of these three Romans for bar Abbas' father. I am the unwilling intermediary."

Caiaphas nodded, picked up a scroll of parchment and wrote a few words on it. Then he put down his quill and said, "It seems you have stumbled upon a matter of state."

Good thought, Judas, my story is accepted.

"Judas, would you mind if I offered you some advice?"

"Go ahead."

"I think it a bad idea if you inform Ananas of your intentions. He is no lover of Zealots. He believes they undermine the established order, of which he is part. It is likely that he will oppose your hostage swap. Is that what you want?"

"I don't really care," lied Judas. "I just want to complete this task and be finished with the Zealots."

"The Zealots do not forgive failure. The only way you can be rid of them is to succeed in your mission."

"Then do you support the Zealot cause?" Caiaphas shook his head. "No, but if you succeed and gain the credibility of the Zealots, you may be of use to the temple one day."

Judas was by now completely confused. Perhaps he had misjudged Caiaphas. "Then what do you suggest?"

Caiaphas picked up his quill again and spoke as he wrote. "The Roman military commander in Jerusalem is a tribune called Licinius Piso. He is camped with his men in the lower city just inside the city walls. He will probably favour your plan because to the Romans, one rebel leader is much the same as any other and of little value compared to three legionaries. But there is a complication. Although Piso commands the troops, he will not make the decision."

"Herod?"

"Not really. The Governor of Syria, Quinctilius Varus, accompanied Piso to Jerusalem so he is in overall command."

"How does that affect my mission?" asked Judas.

"Probably a great deal. Varus comes from an ancient Roman family. Rumour has it that he is very ambitious with eyes set on nothing less than a senior consulship. To him being

Governor of Syria is just a stepping stone towards high office in Rome. He will be well aware of the friendship between Herod and Augustus Caesar, so he is unlikely to take any action that will upset Herod who, as far as the Romans are concerned, has kept us unruly Jews in good order for the last thirty years while at the same time never failing to pay the taxes due to Rome in full. In short, he is a perfect puppet king."

"Then it seems my mission is doomed."

"Not necessarily. Go to Piso first. Persuade him to make a strong case in favour of the prisoner exchange. It will certainly make Varus and Piso look like heroes in the eyes of their soldiers but, ultimately, it will depend on how much Varus values the opinion of his men."

For the moment Judas was convinced by Caiaphas' logic. "Caiaphas, your reasoning is indisputable. I will follow your advice."

"Good. Then take this note I have just written with you to the Roman camp. It's written in Greek, but every educated Roman understands Greek. It should at least gain you an audience with Piso."

"Thank you. I shall go immediately and I apologise for my part in our earlier dispute."

Caiaphas handed the scroll to Judas. "I suggest you leave it till tomorrow morning. It is past noon now. The Romans tend to carry out their business in the mornings and amuse themselves for the rest of the day. Why not return to your lodgings and prepare what you will say so that you will be all the more effective tomorrow?"

"I shall," answered Judas.

***

II

Judas' mind was a whirl of confusion as he strode across the temple's outer courtyard. He was not fooled. Caiaphas hated him just as much as he hated Caiaphas, yet the young priest's advice seemed so sensible as to make him wonder if he really did want to see Abbas freed. Maybe he had his own agenda or perhaps he fostered a covert sympathy with the Zealot cause. Still, Judas decided he would not accede to Caiaphas' suggestion of waiting till tomorrow to see Piso. Instead he would try and secure an audience at once. It was a decision that probably saved his life.

Caiaphas' note certainly had an effect, and within a few minutes of his arrival at the Roman camp Judas was ushered into the tribune's palatial tent. Licinius Piso sat behind a light campaign table, upon which were some bowls of fruit left over from his midday meal. To his right was a pile of scrolls awaiting his attention, which had just been brought in by the governor's clerk who stood behind him. Apart from two guards, no-one else was present.

Judas assessed Piso to be in his early twenties, which was young for a tribune. His brown hair was close cropped in typical Roman fashion, but his blue grey eyes suggested antecedents from further north. He was a fine-looking man and no doubt at least one female heart would have been saddened when he left Antioch. He pushed a bowl towards Judas and said in almost accentless Greek, "Would you like some fruit?"

Judas was too nervous to feel hungry but took an apple to be polite. Piso quickly read through the scroll Judas had brought. "It seems you have news of three of our comrades?"

"Indeed."

"Are they well?"

"Two, including the centurion, suffered minor injuries in the battle but the third has a serious leg wound."

"Will he live?"

"I do not know, but he is in good hands."

The clerk standing behind Piso interrupted, "The centurion is Lucius Veranius, sir. The other two are Ostorius Rufio and Caius Pantera."

"Thank you, Brasidas. I gave the order to attack to Lucius myself. I am relieved to hear he still lives, and also the others of course." The tribune turned back to Judas and pointed to the scroll. "It says here you are Judas bar Menahem, a temple servant. Were you present at the Carmel skirmish?"

A skirmish! That was not how the Jews saw it thought Judas. "No," he answered, but found lying to the open faced, young Piso surprisingly difficult. He then explained how he had come to be the bearer of the hostage exchange proposal and how he hoped to get back to a normal life as soon as possible.

Piso raised his eyebrows, he did not seem convinced, then beckoning Brasidas forward and speaking in Latin he said, "Do you believe this, Brasidas?"

"I am not sure, sir, but I think he is hiding something."

"Well, we will accept him for what he says unless we find reason to do otherwise. After all, the lives of three fine legionaries hang in the balance."

Brasidas glanced at Judas. "I agree, sir; we have no real choice." Judas, who could understand every word they said, now saw the clerk in a new light; he was an adviser as well as a servant.

"Very well, Judas bar Menahem," said the tribune. "I will support your hostage proposal, but Governor Varus and King Herod will decide. I am glad you came to see me first because I think they might need quite some persuading, especially Herod."

"Thank you, Tribune," replied Judas. "And may God give you help in your task."

Judas left the Roman camp in good spirits. He was confident that Piso could persuade Varus at least, though Herod would be another matter. He headed towards the safe house, which lay just beyond the market area, excited at the thought of bringing the good news to Reuben and Daniel, but when he was less than a hundred paces from his refuge he felt a sharp blow to the back of his neck which rendered him momentarily unconscious. He sank to his knees in the middle of a narrow street, but just as he was coming to his senses, he was grabbed by the shoulders and hauled roughly to his feet. Then, staggering and stumbling as he went, he was dragged up the road to the citadel unable to wriggle free from the iron grip that held him fast. He remembered being pushed through the palace gate and shoved down some stairs into a smelly, dark passage and, just as he was thrown into a filthy chamber; he was able to see that his captors were two of Herod's Galatian guardsmen.

Then everything went blank.

***

III

Judas awoke to a severe neck ache which made it almost impossible to turn his head. He could feel warm sticky blood around his knees and elbows but could see nothing. Around him was absolute blackness. He was lying on a cold, damp, stone floor and the smell of death and ordure was overwhelming. He slowly raised himself into a sitting position and peered into the darkness but there was no sign of light in any direction. Utter silence blanketed his ears. He began to wonder if this was Hell and he had died, but the smell and discomfort were all too lifelike. Having decided he was still alive, Judas set his logical mind to work considering his situation.

Clearly, he had been attacked and imprisoned shortly after seeing Licinius Piso. The tribune seemed honourable but perhaps he was just clever or devious. But if he was responsible, he would have had to act within seconds of Judas' departure from the Roman camp, yet it had been Herod's Galatian guardsmen who attacked him, not Roman soldiers. Judas decided his original judgement of Piso was correct.

Then who else knew of his plan? Who else would know where to look for him? Caiaphas! Of course, it must be him. He had even suggested that Judas should visit Piso and he would certainly have had enough time to have him followed. The fact that it was Herod's men who took him proved beyond doubt that Caiaphas, and probably Ananas too, were the king's creatures. Simon bar Boethus was clearly not malleable enough for Herod's liking, which was the real reason he had been replaced as high priest. It all made sense now.

"So," whispered Judas quietly. "It all falls into place."

"Awake at last!"

Judas leaped to his feet, half stunning himself on a low, wooden crossbeam. "Who's that!" he shouted in panic.

"Welcome to King Herod's hospitality, and you have no need to fear me." The gentle reply came in a voice that seemed oddly familiar. "I have flint and tinder here somewhere, which I will light and then we can see each other."

After some rustling and scratching sounds, a small, red glow appeared. Soon, the glow moved upwards then a second, stronger glow appeared as a small wall torch was lit. The darkness fled to the recesses of the stone chamber and Judas was obliged to shield his eyes to allow them to accustom themselves to the brightness, which though not great, seemed like blinding sunlight after the pitch black of seconds before. In front of him stood an old man dressed in rags. His long grey hair and beard were matted with dirt and he bore the red weal marks of torture on his skin, yet he stood tall and straight and had the bearing of one accustomed to command.

He held out a grimy, wooden goblet, "Would you like some water? It is all I have to offer, I'm afraid." Despite the long, filthy fingernails, which appalled the fastidious Judas, raging thirst overcame his scruples and he gulped down the water. "Thank you. Who are you?"

The old man smiled, revealing that most of his teeth were gone, probably knocked out by his captors. "As the incumbent in this dwelling, I believe it is my privilege to ask you that question first."

"Of course. I am Judas bar Menahem, born in Jericho but now a temple servant."

"And I am Abbas bar Joel, a resident of Jerusalem."

"Eli's father?"

Abbas stepped back, suspicion written across his face. "You said you are a temple servant. Why should I trust you?"

"Well I used to be, but now I am one of Elijah bar Abbas' brotherhood and you are the man I seek—"

Abbas held up a hand to stop Judas. "Judas bar Menahem, you give your trust too easily. I may not be who I say I am. I could be one of Herod's spies planted here to find out as much as possible from you." Judas shamefacedly looked at his feet, angered at how careless he had been. "I do not mean to chastise you," said the old man. "You are young and speak from the heart which is no bad thing. Just be careful, that is all."

"Thank you, Abbas, I know I have much to learn; I will not make that mistake again. Your son is well and sends his greetings along with a message of hope." Judas then recounted the purpose of his visit to the city and how Abbas' freedom was to be negotiated, at the end of which the old man shook his head sadly. There was deep wistfulness in his voice.

"Judas, the plan sounds eminently plausible but it will not work. Eli is assuming Herod can be reasoned with. He cannot. He will never release me whatever his Roman masters may want. He is more cunning than a fox, more vicious than a cornered rat, more voracious than a starving spider and more vengeful than the dark angel himself. When he sees you, as he must now that the Romans know you are here, be very careful because he will try to trick information out of you. Above all, he wants my son's head for he has correctly surmised that the Zealot cause revolves around him. So beware of any proposal that puts Eli at risk because if my son thinks he can save me, he will indeed take risks he should not."

"But then what will happen to you?"

"I will never leave here alive. Any agreement Herod

makes will be broken. He wants Eli more than me but best of all, he wants us both."

That was clear enough. Judas did not doubt that Abbas was a wiser man than his son, yet the father was making it plain that the son was the man who would lead the Zealots to freedom. He decided to risk another confidence. "And what about the King of the Jews?"

"Herod or the Messiah?"

"The Messiah, of course."

"What has Eli told you?"

"The Messiah will be born in Bethlehem," replied Judas. "Of parents now living in Nazareth who are both direct descendants of David himself. The betrothal has already taken place."

"Then Judas, you are indeed within Eli's inner circle. That information is restricted to a select few."

"When your son told me he didn't even mention that you knew."

Abbas chuckled, "He must have forgotten that it was my idea in the first place. It was I who researched the lost genealogical archives and selected the Messiah's parents. None were more surprised than they when they were informed."

"It is a wonderful idea, but why now? Rome is stronger than ever."

"Rome is the cause. Our people have gone through bad times before, but we have always regained our freedom. We were prisoners in Egypt and later in Babylon, but we survived through God's will and the determination he gave us. But Rome is the greatest power in history. Unlike other empires, it builds it strength steadily, incrementally and digests its conquests before embarking on new ventures. Now it is at peace and likely to remain so for a long time yet because it has conquered everyone except for a few wild tribesmen who aren't worth conquering, the longer we leave it, the stronger Rome will become; the prospect of throwing off its yoke recedes each day. We need help, and soon."

"The Parthians?"

"They would help, but what we really need is the Messiah." The old man's eyes seemed to glow as he warmed to his cause. Despite his filthy, ragged clothes and unwashed hair, the likeness to his son was now remarkable. He seemed to grow in stature as he spoke. "Since the Romans came, foreigners have swarmed into our sacred land. They build great cities full of wealthy people who must be fed by the country dwellers. They buy land at inflated prices turning our sturdy peasant folk into labourers struggling to rent the land they once owned. Worst of all, these foreigners bring with them false gods that appeal to the baser nature of humankind and spread corruption. It has even reached the temple. Now our people are restive; they have had enough, especially in Galilee. They will fight when the Messiah comes to lead them."

"How will they know the Messiah?"

"You ask a good question Judas for there will be many charlatans and imposters who will seek to benefit from the anger of the Jews. Never has the time been more ripe, for rebellion and false messiahs."

"Then how do you know that your messiah will be the true one?"

Abbas thought for a moment then, gripping Judas by the hand said, "You must have faith. The road we must follow has been shown to me by God himself."

"But how?"

"Through revelation. Some of us are chosen to receive God's messages directly. Usually, this happens just once or twice in a lifetime, but a select few receive his words many times. We call them the prophets. The rest of us are just ordinary men but after revelation we are never the same again."

"What form does revelation take?"

"I do not know if it is the same for all, but for me it was like a waking dream. I still am not sure if I was awake or asleep when it happened. That was over twenty years ago, before Eli was born, but what I saw in my revelation remains crystal clear as if it was imprinted on my memory like a branding iron. That is how I know it was not just a vivid, yet ordinary dream."

"Will you tell me what you saw?" pleaded Judas.

"Some, but not all; there are parts for me alone, parts that empower me to have no fear of death."

"Then just speak of what you can."

"You already know that the Messiah will be of David's seed and born in Bethlehem, but he will not be what the Jews expect. He will not arrive in majesty and glory, but as a humble man preaching the power of love. This will cause some to doubt him but he will lead his people using the power of his will; he will not need the superficial trappings of royalty which are so precious to Herod. The most difficult thing for us Jews to accept will be that his message will be for all men, not Jews alone."

"Even Romans?"

"Especially Romans."

"But will he deliver us from them?"

Abbas' response left Judas none the wiser. "He will be King of the Jews, but he will also become King of all men. The course of his campaign is not for me to know, but my revelation showed that you, Judas bar Menahem, also called Sicariot will have a vital role to play in it."

"How did you know my other name?"

"It came to me in my revelation. Revelations do not lie. I can also tell you that though your life will be fulfilled, regrettably, you will not find happiness."

"I would prefer fulfilment over happiness if that must be the choice. The former is long lasting; the latter can be ephemeral."

Abbas smiled, "You are wise beyond your years Judas, which is just as well. You will be reviled because your actions will be misunderstood by all except the Messiah himself. Your reward will come in the next world."

"Then I shall be content."

**

IV

Judas' imprisonment lasted nearly a full month during which he learned much from Abbas. Whereas bar Abbas was the warrior and master tactician, his father was the thoughtful strategist who encapsulated into a single cause the plethora of hopes and ideas in many Jewish minds to rid the land that once formed the old Kingdom of Israel of all foreign influences, especially those of Greece and Rome. The people who dedicated their lives to this cause became the Zealots. Abbas seemed to Judas more like a respected teacher than a war leader though he showed no fear of the fate that awaited him when he ceased to be useful to Herod.

According to Abbas' meticulously kept calendar, Judas' release came on the twenty fifth day of Nisan (early April). It was presaged by the sound of metal lined boots approaching their cell at a fast march instead of the shuffle of the lice ridden gaoler, who provided the meagre rations that were just enough to keep them both alive. The heavy cell door swung open and four huge Galatians entered. The commander spoke in execrable Greek, "Which of you is Judas bar Menahem?" To his horror, Judas suddenly realised that his appearance must have deteriorated so much during the last month as to make him indistinguishable from Abbas.

"I am," he answered.

One of the other Galatians threw some clean clothes at him.

"Put those on and come with us," rasped the commander.

While Judas was dressing, Abbas mused aloud, "Four large guardsmen to escort little Judas. You are honoured."

"Perhaps, but I expect I'll soon be back here."

"I think not. Remember, the king will try to trick you so act like a simpleton, pretend to believe him and say as little as possible. Hopefully he will under-rate you. That way you might leave here alive."

Sadly, those were Abbas' last words in this world. In fact, only two of the Galatians escorted Judas out of the prison. Ominously, the other two remained behind.

Judas was not taken to the audience hall in the palace, but to a chamber in Herod's private quarters. The reason quickly became obvious as Judas, who was now thin and weak, was hauled into the king's presence. His immediate sensation was a revolting smell which made even the stench of the prison more bearable. Heavy wafts of incense failed to mask the unmistakable odour of putrefying flesh which had a nauseous effect on Judas' half-starved stomach. To his left, the source of the smell sat in a large, green armchair; it was King Herod himself. Although he was almost covered in a loose fitting, voluminous, purple cloak, which hid his decaying body except for the head, forearms and lower left leg, he presented a grotesque figure. One leg was propped up on a padded stool and heavily wrapped in bandages that were once white, but now were stained with vile ooze from the suppurating sores in the king's flesh. Behind his grey beard was a blotchy, puffed up face in which two small, dark, beady eyes observed him like a predatory bird. Immediately to Judas' front sat Piso and to his left the Governor of Syria. Varus was more or less what Judas expected, if a bit fleshy.

Unlike Piso, who was too polite to notice the stench in the room, Varus held a pomander to his nose. Standing behind them both was Brasidas, whom Judas remembered from his interview with Piso a month earlier. No translator was needed as all understood Greek.

Piso spoke first. "Judas bar Menahem, I have explained your proposal to exchange the bandit leader for three Roman legionaries to King Herod and Governor Varus, but they wish to hear it in your own words."

"That may be so, but first you may explain to me why I was arrested and thrown into a stinking prison for a month just after I met you," responded Judas defiantly. He hoped a show of spirit might add to the credence of his cover story.

Piso, red with embarrassment, began searching for an answer but before he could say more Varus, who suddenly abandoned his demeanour of affected boredom, intervened. "It seems this Jew could do with another month's confinement to teach him some respect for his betters. Jew, you will speak as instructed now or you will be thrown back into the stink hole where you belong."

Deciding further defiance was pointless Judas, speaking more respectfully, repeated the offer he had already made to Piso. After he finished, there was a short silence then, for the first time, Herod spoke. Ulcers in his throat had turned his voice into a hoarse whisper; normal speech was painful. "You are a vile Zealot."

"I assure you I am not, Your Majesty." Lying to Herod was easy.

"I say you are. You should have your head cut off for insolence." Judas judged it best to remain silent. He glanced at Brasidas who seemed to be stifling a smile.

"How do you know our men are still alive?" asked Varus.

"They were alive when I left them. I would not be here otherwise."

"And what if we refuse?"

"The Zealots will kill your men."

Piso interrupted his commander's interrogation, "Governor, the lives of three Romans for one Jew; that must be a good bargain."

"But that is not what is on offer Piso. It is three common soldiers for a general."

Herod agreed, "Well said Governor. We must hold what we have."

Now the young tribune began to show his mettle, "The men won't see it that way."

"They will obey their orders Piso," answered Varus.

"You would not say that if the legate was here."

Now it was Varus' turn to redden, not with embarrassment but with anger. "Marcus Tullius commands the Third Legion Gallica. I am the Governor of Syria and, as such, I command him. Do you understand Tribune?"

"Well, well," interjected Herod. "I am sure Augustus Caesar would not wish to hear his officers bickering in front of a Jewish king and a bandit Zealot. Perhaps we might consider some sort of arrangement." Herod was relishing his self-appointed role as peacemaker between the two squabbling Romans but not as much as Brasidas, whose eyes were positively twinkling with mirth.

"If we are to discuss this seriously," continued the king, "I think the Zealot should leave this chamber until we have made a decision."

For an account of what happened during Judas' absence we have Brasidas to thank, who related the story at a later date in a different country far to the north.

No sooner had Judas been escorted out of the chamber than Piso launched another verbal assault on Varus. "Governor, you do not seem to understand the effect on morale if you abandon your men when it is within your power to save them. I know all three of them. I sent them forward to attack. We owe them our support."

"I understand how you feel," said Varus, trying his best to be patient. "But I do not need a lecture from you on morale. I myself commanded the Nineteenth Legion in some tough fighting when we subdued the wild Celtic tribes south of the Danube ten years ago. I know all about loyalty. King Herod clearly has a plan in mind. Let us listen to him before making hasty decisions."

Both men looked towards the king and waited. At last,

after a suitable pause for effect, Herod spoke, "You will not be surprised to learn that I have given this considerable thought since we captured that wretched bandit waiting outside. He pretends he is an innocent bystander but I do not believe him for a moment, yet if we use cool judgement we may yet secure the release of your legionaries, retain Abbas in our custody and capture his son, who is now the real driving force behind the Zealot rebels." Only Herod knew that at that moment Abbas was already dead.

"If all three objectives can be achieved, we shall indeed be in your debt," replied Varus unctuously.

Herod smiled, exposing rotting tooth stumps; no part of him seemed free from corruption. "Firstly, Abbas will remain where he is; we will not risk losing him. Instead, we will find someone who looks sufficiently like him from a distance. The meeting place for the hostage exchange will be a small village called Mukhmas, which is close to Wadi Qilt on the road from Jerusalem to Jericho. We will get there early, well before the appointed meeting date, and prepare an ambush. I suggest we tell our young Zealot emissary that each side should be limited to thirty men, but bar Abbas himself must be present to give us the comfort of knowing we are not walking into an trap. If all goes well, you will recover your men and we will kill or capture Elijah bar Abbas and thus cut off the head of the Zealot cause."

"Who will command the mission?" asked Piso.

"Attalus, my guard commander. We will send two hundred Galatians who will wait hidden in the foothills around Qilt. You may, if you wish, provide the thirty men who will be the escort to the false Abbas, but this must be a Jewish operation, not a Roman one."

Piso, who was not convinced that the Galatians would turn up when needed, said, "So we Romans are the bait, but we must rely on you to provide support when the fighting starts?"

"The Galatians are fierce warriors and love to fight. You need have no concerns regarding their reliability; they have proven themselves often enough. At this moment, it is far more important we convince our Zealot scum prisoner that we really mean to exchange Abbas for your men."

Piso demurred. "Well I am not happy with this plan. Not only could we lose our three legionaries, we could lose another thirty Romans if your Galatians are less reliable than you think."

"Now, now Tribune," reprimanded Varus, who was eager to retain the favour of the influential king. "It seems to me that King Herod has come up with an eminently workable strategy which has a good chance of success."

"Very well Governor, then I urgently request I take command of the thirty Romans who will be put at risk by this operation."

"Accepted, Piso," replied Varus, who had no concern whatsoever about the wellbeing of his recalcitrant tribune.

Herod, satisfied with the outcome of the spirited debate, recalled Judas and the two guards. "Judas bar Menahem, we have decided to show mercy even though your insolence does not justify it. We agree to the prisoner exchange but only on the terms I shall now recite. The place of exchange will be the village of Mukhmas at the Wadi Qilt, a day's march out of Jerusalem."

"I know it," acknowledged Judas.

"The time will be noon seven days from today. Each side will bring thirty men for protection, no more no less, and the exchange will take place in the open ground outside the village."

"Thirty men seems a lot for a simple prisoner swap."

"That's because the hills are full of bandits like you."

Judas did not bother to argue; he did not want to anger the king again now that his own release was imminent. "I will take your terms to the Zealots. You will know within two days if they have been accepted."

Herod leaned forward, wincing with pain as he did so. "Now go before I change my mind. If you ever see me again, you will know your miserable life is about to end."

Judas turned to leave but the king had not quite finished. "One more thing. Bar Abbas himself must deliver the Romans to us; no-one else will do. Is that clear, Judas the Bandit!"

"Very clear, Your Majesty."

***

V

The palace gates slammed shut behind him. Judas looked up at the dazzling, blue sky, which he had not seen for so long, and breathed in fresh air and freedom. He might look like a ragged, starving beggar but just then he felt like a king. He knew he must head for the safe house but experience had taught him caution; he was sure to be followed. Without looking behind, he walked down from the citadel towards the market place, which was usually crowded, and where it should not be difficult to lose anyone shadowing him.

Judging from the position of the sun, it was about an hour before noon; the market would be at its busiest. Judas walked slowly towards the centre of the city with the temple on his right-hand side as if he was in no hurry but simply relishing his freedom. When he reached the market, he strolled along the stalls of the wine vendors and stopped to examine some wines for sale, only to be chased away as a vagrant. The smell of fried fish from the nearby eating area clawed at his empty stomach. As he wandered slowly past the olive oil stalls, the aroma of freshly baked bread reached him, but alas he had no money and could only dream of tasting these delights.

For the first time since leaving the palace, Judas took a quick look behind him. Amongst the bustle, all seemed as it should be apart from one ordinary looking man who stopped for no apparent reason then backtracked to a vegetable stall and began looking at some of the produce there. Judas walked a few paces further then took a left turn into another part of the market where the cloth makers and weavers displayed their wares. He stopped at a stall and glanced back, this time more stealthily. Sure enough, the same man was there observing him at a distance of twenty paces or so. Judas walked on until he had almost reached the northern edge of the market where it abutted a residential area honeycombed with narrow streets and alleys. He stopped, checked he was still being followed, then suddenly ran out of the market and disappeared into the warren of small streets outside. Herod's hound had lost its scent.

Back at the safe house, Reuben and Daniel had been fretting. A month had passed since Judas had disappeared and there had been no word. Reuben, the senior in rank of the two, decided they must get word to bar Abbas for instructions, so Daniel left the safe house while Reuben remained behind in case Judas came back. This was just as well for the day after Daniel left, at about noon, there was a loud banging on the door which startled the small dog in the downstairs apartment into prolonged yapping. The tenants were not at home so Reuben cautiously went down the stairs and opened the door. Before him stood a thin, bedraggled figure that he did not at first recognise.

"Reuben, by all the devils in Hell, let me in!"

"Judas?"

"Who else!"

Reuben ushered the half-starved Judas upstairs where Herod's erstwhile prisoner collapsed onto a chair and gasped, "Something to drink, something to eat, but first of all a bath and some clean clothes!"

"Yes, but this is not an inn. The water will be cold and you will have to bathe in the yard at the back. I will fetch food and clean garments while you wash yourself."

"Thank you, Reuben, and then I will answer your questions but hurry, we must leave this afternoon."

"Why?"

"I must see bar Abbas as soon as possible. I have spent the last month with his father."

Two days later, Reuben and a revived Judas reached bar Abbas' spring camp which was located in the hills twenty-five miles north of Jerusalem. Only bar Abbas' personal bodyguards, some fifty men, were present because the remainder had been sent back to their homes to tend their flocks, plant crops and spend time with their families. Hit and run warfare was not a full-time occupation; the Zealot treasury could not afford many professional warriors.

There was a cool wind blowing from the northeast, and although the morning sun was shining from an azure blue, cloudless sky, the air was still cold. The three men who sat talking together on the stony ground a little apart from the rest were sheltered from the wind by a small thorn bush. They were huddled in blankets to keep out the cold.

"So you are certain my father will die come what may. Will he not even get a trial?" asked bar Abbas.

Judas answered, "He is probably already dead. Herod was lying through his rotting teeth, though the Romans obviously believed him. It was all too simple, too easy. At the end of the meeting, when Herod insisted that you personally should be present at the point of the hostage exchange, I knew there was no hope, for this was exactly what your father predicted. Herod is desperate to capture you too. If we go to Mukhmas we will be walking into a trap. Eli, I am sorry."

"Then our plan has failed. All those brave men who died in the battle at Carmel; their lives have been wasted."

"Not necessarily," growled Joachim. "We may yet salvage something from this."

"How so old friend? We have heard from Judas that my father is almost certainly dead even as we speak."

Joachim put a gnarled hand on his young leader's shoulder to steady the emotion welling up inside him. "Alas, there is nothing we can do for your father now. His contribution to our cause was huge, but his work is finished on this earth. Now he can rest and enjoy his reward with God. But it is Herod's duplicity that gives us an opportunity. From what Judas told us, Herod believes we will take his bait. Well, let him think so because he is not the only one who can prepare an ambush. We could get to Mukhmas two days before the appointed time and hide in the hills. When his men arrive, we will have a surprise waiting for them."

Bar Abbas looked his old adviser directly in the eyes. He even managed a small smile. "That is smart thinking Joachim."

"Age sometimes brings wisdom, Eli."

"Indeed, but we must make sure we have enough strength to succeed. How many men will Herod send?"

"Who knows? He thinks we will bring thirty, so we must assume at least two or three hundred."

"And we only have a few days to get word to Herod saying we agree to his terms, gather our forces and get into position around Mukhmas. But our men have been dispersed to their homes. How many can we gather within the time available?"

Joachim rubbed his chin thoughtfully, "I estimate about five hundred, plus your bodyguard."

"Good, that should be enough. Send out the word. Anyone who cannot meet the deadline must keep away; we don't want latecomers drifting in and unwittingly revealing our positions. Mukhmas must appear to be the sleepy village it has always been. Unfortunately, no-one may leave the village after we arrive so apologise to the elders for me. If this works, my father will not have died in vain."

"May I come?" asked Judas.

"No, and that is a clear order which this time you will obey for you have not completed your existing task," answered bar Abbas. "You must go to Nazareth and execute the Roman hostages. Reuben and Daniel will accompany you. When that is done, I have another, more difficult task for you. You may refuse it if you wish because it will be dangerous."

"You know I will not refuse."

"Yes, Judas, I know, but it will require utmost skill and diplomacy."

"Then why choose me? I have just failed your father."

"Judas, you are the best man for the job. As far as my father is concerned, I now realise I sent you on an impossible mission. It was my strategy that failed; there is no reflection on you."

"Thank you. Then tell me what I must do."

Bar Abbas shivered with cold and pulled his blanket more tightly around him as the chill wind strengthened. "In northern Galilee there is a problem looming. You know our land is awash with rumours that the coming of the Messiah is imminent. Well this has led to a crop of false messiahs claiming the throne of Israel. All but one has been discredited. The exception is a namesake of yours known as Judas the Galilean. The fact that he was born in Bethlehem has given him credibility to some at least, and consequently he has been able to assemble enough misguided followers to enable him to become a nuisance. I need hardly tell you that false messiahs are the last thing we need if we are to persuade the Parthians to come, so we must encourage this man to join us or desist."

"Do we know where to find him?" asked Judas.
"Somewhere in northern Galilee. If you go to the city of Dan and ask, he will find you. His power base is there."

"Dan! But that's almost in Phoenicia!"

"Bar Abbas smiled, "Yes, it is a long way but not the end of the world. Nazareth is almost half way there, so when you have dealt with the Roman hostages, send Reuben back to me to report and continue on to Dan with Daniel."

"I will leave immediately."

"Not immediately; there is someone here I wish you to meet." Bar Abbas signalled to the group of men nearest to him and a short, thick set man got up and approached them. He was well into his fifties with hair and beard almost completely grey. His portly frame and delicate pale hands suggested indoor living and no manual labour. He beamed an affable smile and addressed bar Abbas, "How long are you going to keep me in this frozen wasteland? The warmth of Jerusalem beckons."

"Hardly the attitude of a true Zealot," laughed bar Abbas. "But you will be pleased to know that you will be on your way this day."

"Thank Heaven for that, and as for being a true Zealot, my contribution is intellectual rather than physical."

"Of course it is Caspar. Now here is the man we have been waiting for so please introduce yourself to Judas Sicariot."

Caspar turned to Judas and, to the acute embarrassment of the young Zealot, bowed and said, "I am honoured to meet you Judas Sicariot. I understand you are held in high esteem here. I am Caspar bar Hillel, resident of Babylon but now on assignment to Eli bar Abbas. I have been selected by the Jewish community in Babylon to assist the Zealot cause."

"How will you do that Caspar?" asked Judas, still uncomfortable with the huge respect afforded to him by the older man.

"By bringing the Parthians to help us throw out the Romans from our ancestral homeland. I have been given charge of the Babylonian Jewish bureau in the temple and will remain there until the Messiah is born. When I have seen him with my own eyes, I will send word to our friends in Babylon who have the ear of the new Parthian king, Phraates. With his help we will regain our freedom."

"The Parthians have always been our friends," added bar Abbas, "and they will come when the time is right. We have decided that you, Judas, will have the honour of being

115

appointed the mentor and guardian of the Messiah during his childhood. This will start as soon as his mother is known to be with child. You will watch over and protect the Messiah's family and give him all the learning you have acquired during your studies in the temple. We already have a house prepared for you in Nazareth which you may start using after you have completed your mission in Dan. We can also afford a small allowance for the expenses you will incur carrying out your duties." The enormity of this responsibility left Judas speechless.

"You are lost for words young man," laughed Caspar. "That is how it should be. I hope we will meet again and soon. You will find me at the temple." Then speaking to bar Abbas again he said, "May I go now?"

As they watched the round figure depart, bar Abbas mused aloud to no-one in particular, "I hope we can trust him. He is not what I expected. You have not said much Joachim, what do you think?"

The man of oak answered, "I have met men like Caspar before. They affect an image of softness, weakness even, but under that gentle exterior there is an iron will. Did you not notice the outline of a sicarius beneath his cloak?" Both bar Abbas and Judas were obliged to admit they had not. "Caspar is as dedicated to our cause as any of us. You can most certainly trust him."

"Thank you, Joachim, that is good to know," acknowledged bar Abbas. Then turning to Judas, he said, "Well my friend, now it is time for you to leave us. When you reach Judas the Galilean's camp keep your wits about you. Try to estimate the number of men he has, how well they are armed, how warrior-like they seem, anything that might be helpful to us."

"I understand."

"And, finally, you should know that the Galilean is said to be volatile, unstable and capable of wanton cruelty, so choose your words carefully."

Judas set out with Reuben and Daniel later that morning but three days later, when they reached Nazareth, the three Romans were gone; the mission had begun badly. As he headed north towards Dan, Judas felt a deep sense of foreboding.

CHAPTER SIX

Night had just fallen; Rufio and I settled down to another tedious night. Rufio, who never had any difficulty getting to sleep, was already snoring, but I lay awake as usual wondering what the next day would bring; probably boredom and nothing else, but at least that meant there was still life and a little hope. Suddenly I heard a faint scratching sound on the other side of our locked door. It was too deliberate to be rats. Was this the moment of fate?

"Rufio," I whispered. "Wake up." The snoring continued so I got up and shook him, "What in Hades!"

I put my hand across his mouth. "Quiet and listen." We stayed still, our senses now on full alert, as the door creaked and slowly opened. A small shadow entered carrying a candle followed by another much larger shadow.

Now there was no need to whisper. "Come on, Rufio, let's sell our lives dearly!"

The larger shadow spoke in Latin, "There'll be no need for that, well not tonight at least."

"Caius!" We both shouted together.

"Quiet, we must not wake the guards."

As our eyes adjusted to the flickering candlelight, I recognised the other shadow as Ruth, Mary's personal servant, who used to bring us food from time to time. She placed three wicker baskets in front of us and addressed me in Greek.

"These are provisions that should last you for two or three days. There is also a bag of food for the donkey that will carry Caius. Caius will tell you what has happened but you must leave now; your enemy is coming and will be here soon."

Clearly, the hostage exchange with Herod had failed. We sat for a moment bewildered by this sudden change in our fortunes. Ruth spoke with greater urgency. "Hurry, your executioners are near. They are in Shunam only six miles from here. Do not travel in daylight; if you see them, they will see you and then it will be too late."

I said, "Thank you Ruth, and Mary too of course. Perhaps we may meet again in happier times."

"Perhaps, but go now. The pursuit will be determined."
Rufio and I quickly gathered our meagre possessions and the provisions Ruth had brought. We quietly left our prison and entered a courtyard where five Zealot clubmen lay in a deep sleep. I looked up at the clear, starlit sky, a beautiful sight I had not seen for over a month. The moon was near half full and bright enough to light up the courtyard in a blend of stardust and shadow, but my brief moment of bliss was shattered by a cry from Ruth. Rufio had picked up a club and was about to dash out the brains of the nearest, sleeping Zealot. Before I could speak, Caius grabbed his arm and snarled,

"Rufio, by the Furies stop!"

"What's the matter? Better to finish them off now than fight them later."

"There'll be no killing here tonight."

"But they're our enemy," objected Rufio. Caius gently, but firmly took the club from Rufio. "We are being given our freedom to prevent killing here. We must respect our benefactors' wishes."

Rufio shrugged, "All right then, it was only a thought."
From my perspective, this was an illuminating exchange.
Rufio was a file leader, senior to Caius, but the younger man's
authority was unquestionable; he would certainly shape up
into an excellent centurion in due course. It was time I
intervened. "Quiet both of you! We're unarmed so take a club
each; we may need them."

Ruth opened the courtyard gate. We shuddered as it
squealed on rusted hinges but the guards slept on. Outside a
large, grey donkey was tethered to a post. Ruth said, "His name
is Gebel, it means mountain. Caius cannot walk properly yet;
Gebel is the only donkey we have who is large enough to carry
him. He is a good beast, but he is young and can be
temperamental. Treat him kindly and find him a good home
when you reach Jerusalem."

"We will," I replied. "I wish we had the means to pay
you."

"It does not matter."

"But what of you and Mary? Will you not face the wrath
of the Zealots for releasing us?"

"They will not know it was us. It has been arranged that
the guards will be blamed." Then placing a bundle in my arms,
she added, "Here are three cloaks of Judean style. Wear them
to make you look less like Romans."

"That won't be easy."

"Well unlike Caius, at least you still have your beards. He
will need to keep his face hidden as best he can. And remember
to go round Shunam, not through it. Your enemy is there."

There was enough light from the moon and her flickering
candle to enable me to see Ruth clearly for the first time,
because although she wore a hood to hide her hair, her face

was uncovered. I think this was an error caused by the tense circumstances she was in. Like most Jewish women, she was remarkably attractive and without the overshadowing presence of her mistress, she was a star in her own right.

We thanked Ruth and manhandled Caius onto Gebel. Then, taking the southerly road to Jerusalem, we left Nazareth with the moon and stars lighting our way.

***

II

The road from Nazareth to Jerusalem lies through Shekhem. It was the obvious route for our pursuers to take but Caius' local knowledge probably saved us. He proposed a more westerly route through Samaria, which would add at least a day to our journey, but would throw the Zealots off our scent. It also meant the Zealots would overtake us, so when the two roads met again further south at Nasbe, they would be between us and Jerusalem. But we could not travel fast because of Caius; they would catch up with us anyway quite soon, so taking the diversion through Samaria would at least give us more time and be unexpected.

Our journey began well. Gebel carried Caius without difficulty while Rufio and I exulted in our new found freedom. Simply being able to walk again, something one normally takes for granted, was a sheer delight. As we slowly picked our way round the perimeter of Shunam, I thought about the Zealots. By the time they reached Nazareth and found their birds had flown, we would have about half a day's advantage over them, but that would quickly diminish. I began to worry that they might catch us even before we reached the junction where the Samaria road left the main road to Jerusalem. "I estimate we have six hours before dawn, so that means we will cover about fifteen miles before we must stop," I said to Caius.

He thought for a short while as he always did when responding to a question that required computation. "Then we'll have to hide up for the day because we will still be on the main road to Jerusalem. The road junction to Samaria is at least twenty miles away."

"We could push on for the extra few miles in daylight," suggested Rufio. "The Zealots won't have caught up with us by then."

"Can you manage a non-stop twenty-mile march Caius?" I asked.

"Certainly, if Gebel can." I looked at the large, grey donkey. He stared straight back at me. Somehow, I felt that he would play an important part in our survival before too long.

It was a hard march. There had been no rain and the road was dusty. While the evenings were still pleasantly cool, the cloudless days were starting to become hot. We pushed on throughout the night but by dawn we were beginning to flag. Rufio and I now realised how unfit we had become thanks to our enforced captivity, but Gebel continued to carry Caius with ease. Around mid-morning, we passed through a small town, whose name I forget. Our appearance obviously created suspicion amongst the townsfolk, who stood silently watching us from outside their crude, mudbrick dwellings. Any or all of them could have been Zealots for all we knew. Even their small, tan dogs growled and snarled at us as if we were creatures from another world which, in a way, we were. We felt a great sense of relief when we left that hostile atmosphere behind, but all three of us sensed the enemy was near.

About an hour's march beyond the town, we reached a fork in the road. Caius directed us to take the smaller, right hand road which was the less direct route to Jerusalem and would hopefully send our pursuers the wrong way. All this time Caius was unusually quiet. Rufio and I were waiting to hear all about the pampering he had received while we were stuck in our stinking animal shed, but he answered our questions with as few words as possible.

Finally, Rufio could stand it no longer. "Caius, look at us. Lucius and I look like ragged vagrants, unshaven and shaggy haired. We smell like a rat-infested dung heap. Yet you are properly groomed, your uniform is washed and you smell like a whore's parlour. Are you not going to enlighten us?"

Caius answered, "I'm sorry, Rufio. You are indeed entitled to an explanation. Let us make camp and I will give you a full account of what happened."

About two hundred paces from the road, we found a sheltered spot shaded from the sun by overhanging rocks, which was hidden by a spur of white rock from the view of any itinerant travellers. A small, clear stream ran nearby where we could wash and Gebel could take a long, well deserved drink. We cleared stones from an area of ground so that we could lay out our cloaks on a smooth surface and sat down to eat the rations Ruth had given us. What a treat after the basic fare Rufio and I had received in Nazareth! By the time we had unpacked the baskets, a feast of fresh bread, cheese, dates and shelled nuts awaited our attention. Ruth had even thought to include small pitchers of wine in each basket.

I suppose we ate half our food and drank all the wine, but

that was to be expected from two of us though Caius, who had obviously been fed well during our captivity, ate more modestly. We carefully repacked our food, which I estimated would last two more days, then I fed Gebel with some turnip-like vegetables Ruth had prepared for him. While the donkey's soft muzzle snuffled in my hand, I looked round at our little enclave and enjoyed the smell of wild garlic, which the warm afternoon sun drew out of the small, white flowered plants that grew all around. That was one of those moments I still remember well; I felt at peace with the world.

"We have about four hours till nightfall," I said. "We should try to get some sleep before tonight's march. How fares your leg Caius?"

"Healing well, provided I don't try to use it too much."

"Then before we settle down, perhaps you would answer Rufio's question as to why we are so ragged and you so well groomed."

Caius gave us a seemingly detailed account of all that had happened since he regained consciousness; how Mary and Ruth had nursed him back from the edge of death, how important compassion was to the two women and how that had driven them to save us from Zealot vengeance. The story satisfied Rufio, who went off to relieve himself before sleep, but I knew Caius better than that, and during Rufio's absence I said, "Caius, you are not telling us everything."

"That is true."

"Why not?"

"I cannot speak freely in front of Rufio. He would not understand how certain things happen."

"Then speak now while you can."

Caius winced as he felt a twinge from his injured leg, then

he managed to summon up enough courage to be open with me. "Lucius, it is love; Mary and I. I am young and inexperienced but despite that I know she is the woman fate has sent me."

"She is betrothed to another man."

"I know but that did not stop..." Caius' voice trailed away.

"Have you plucked Joseph's flower before he has himself?"

"Lucius, please understand. She saved not just me but all of us. She is remarkable, there is no-one like her." Before more could be said, Rufio returned. Our conversation was ended, for now at least, but I hoped Caius would wish to speak of Mary again before too long.

After we left our little camp, the road began to climb as it skirted the foothills of Mount Gerizim, the mountain sacred to the Samaritans, a Jewish people who do not recognise the authority of the temple in Jerusalem. The Samaritans are despised by other Jews as being unfaithful to the laws of Moses, but the land in which they live is bountiful because of the generous rainfall it receives compared to the low-lying coastal areas. The night became cold as we climbed, but walking kept Rufio and me warm enough. Caius occasionally dismounted and walked for a while to exercise his leg, but nobody spoke much; we were immersed in our own thoughts.

Two more, night marches, brought us to the junction where our road was reunited with the main road to Jerusalem. The great city was now just ten miles away. We found a disused quarry where stone had been extracted to maintain the road and decided to spend the remaining night hours there. Our food was finished and we were tired apart from Gebel who seemed to have limitless energy. He had decided that I was his new master, no doubt because I shared my bread ration with him. I never knew a donkey who liked bread so much; Gebel could not get enough of it. Wherever I slept, he insisted on sleeping beside me. On the march, he was never more than two or three paces from me. He behaved more like a loyal dog than a donkey, and with the intelligence to match.

There were perhaps two hours till dawn. Another full day doing nothing followed by a night march with no food lay ahead; yet Jerusalem was so near. Suddenly Rufio broke the silence and voiced the thoughts we were all having. "Do you realise that Jerusalem is only four hours away? If we keep going, we could be at cohort headquarters by mid-morning surrounded by friends and good Roman food."

"But two of those hours would be in daylight," said Caius.

"So what? The Zealots have probably given up the chase by now. We've seen neither hide nor hair of them since we left Nazareth."

"True," agreed Caius. "But they will have travelled fast and realised we must have taken another route. Between this road junction and Jerusalem is just where they would wait for us. Lucius, you are in command. What do you say?"

My sympathies lay with Rufio. Safety was so near, we had endured so much; surely it would only be a small risk to push on. "Let's go now." Even as I said the words, I started to regret my decision, but Caius did not object and Rufio whooped for joy so, putting my doubts to the back of my mind, we stepped out briskly towards Jerusalem and safety.

The Nazareth to Jerusalem road was a main highway in Herod's kingdom, well-trodden and maintained. We managed five miles before dawn broke. Soon we came across other travellers heading in the opposite direction to us. An hour later, we breasted a small crest in the road and there, directly in front of us barely a mile away, was the great city itself overlooking the Kidron valley. The morning sun seemed to turn the white walls into shimmering gold. Overtopping the city was the Temple Mount where Herod's magnificent temple seemed to proclaim itself a small part of Heaven descended to earth. Our spirits soared.

Caius dismounted from Gebel, "I think I shall walk the rest of the way; the exercise will be good for me." We began to chatter about all the things we would do when we reached the city; having a hot bath, a big meal and how pleased our tribune, Piso, would be when he saw us, but as we approached a village of about twenty dwellings, I noticed a man watching us intently. He was leaning against a mudbrick wall and wore a plain, dirty white tunic reaching only to mid-calf, which was shorter than normal.

I quietened my chattering companions, "Look straight ahead and listen. I think that man to our front left staring at us might be one of the clubmen who held us captive."

He certainly looks like a Zealot," agreed Rufio. "Shall I club him just in case?"

"No, there are bound to be others. He already suspects us so just keep walking and try to look relaxed. I may be mistaken, but be ready for trouble."

We walked steadily onwards doing our best to appear casual, and when we were within ten paces of the would-be Zealot, I thought Rufio's suggestion of clubbing him might be a good idea after all, but before I could say anything, the Zealot suddenly became agitated and ran inside the door of the building behind him, almost tripping over a stall of onions that half blocked his way.

There was no need for caution now. "Run!" I shouted. "And don't look back, they know we're here!" We broke into a fast trot. Caius was hobbling but seemed to be managing and Gebel entered into the excitement by cantering, which is something a donkey seldom does. We left the village behind and I started to hope that maybe I had misjudged our suspected Zealot, but then Rufio, who ignored my order about looking back, panted, "There are five of them." I looked round and, sure enough, five clubmen were in hot pursuit and closing the gap rapidly.

Caius said, "Five Zealots against three Romans. What do you think?"

Rufio replied, "Reasonable odds; what do you say, Lucius?" We were untrained in the art of club handling, but it was worth a try. We could not outrun the Zealots so, although Jerusalem was less than a mile away, it might just as well have been on the far side of the Middle Sea as far as we were concerned. We would have to fight to save our skins.

"Halt!" I ordered. "About face! Enemy to the front!" Legionary training does wonders in tight corners, and within seconds, we had turned to face our enemy with clubs drawn and the fire of battle upon us. The Zealots also halted about thirty paces away, but made no move to come to close quarters. We looked at each other, puzzled by this apparent reprieve, but soon understood the reason. The Zealots sheathed their clubs and took slings from their belts. Then they drew stones from pouches hanging from their waists and soon we were under fire from lethal sling stones against which we had no defence; our oblong shields were far away lying somewhere on the thorny slopes of Mount Carmel. Slingers are not especially accurate, unlike archers, but we had no protection so it was only a matter of time before one of us was hit. I was angry with myself for not foreseeing this.

We waited for a while with stones whistling past our ears. I had just decided we would have to attack when Rufio received a glancing blow to his forehead. He slumped forwards like a felled ox ready for sacrifice. The Zealots let out whoops of triumph while Caius and I heaved Rufio's limp body over Gebel's back. There was no point in standing simply to be picked off one by one, so we turned and ran. Immediately, our enemy followed but this time they closed with us because at two to five the odds had swung in their favour. Two of them, slightly ahead of the rest, caught up with Gebel and began trying to haul Rufio off his back. Everyone knows you should not approach a male donkey from behind, especially in a stressful situation, but in their excitement these two seemed to have forgotten that basic rule. As they were struggling to move Rufio's large frame from Gebel, the donkey, bless him, let out a loud bray and lashed out with his hind legs in three violent kicks. The effect was decisive.

Both Zealots tumbled to the stony road clutching various parts of their nether regions and howling as if the world was about to end.

Caius slowed down and looked at me, "Three Zealots against two Romans?"

"Good enough," I panted.

We halted and faced about again, clubs at the ready, but wisely the remaining three Zealots decided to break off the attack and ran back up the road, picking up their injured comrades as they went, and headed northwards as quickly as they could. A friendly nudge in my back reminded me who the true hero of the day was and, feeding him the last few morsels of my bread I said, "Well, we can thank Gebel for our deliverance. Because of him we'll be with our comrades in less than an hour."

"I'll drink to Gebel," laughed Caius, and in truth that donkey had won both our hearts. But the day of our deliverance was slightly marred by the fact that when we reached our cohort camp, Piso was away on another campaign.

**

III

The Galatians are an unusual people. They are Celtic in blood and language, much the same as the people in northern Italy, but their origin was in the wild lands north of the River Danube. There is an aggressive streak in their nature and two or three hundred years ago, war and famine forced them to leave their homeland. They wandered for years, slowly plundering their way through Macedonia and Thrace until they reached the Dardanelles. They remained there for a while but eventually found enough ships to enable them to cross the narrow straights to Asia, where they continued terrorising any people whose lands were unfortunate enough to lie cross their erratic route. Eventually, they settled in a fertile region now known as Galatia which lies between our provinces of Asia and Cappadocia. However, they brought their predatory ways with them and, after decades of upsetting their neighbours, they found a place in life as mercenaries serving the highest bidder. This may seem to be a harsh judgement, but on the other hand the Galatians gained a reputation for loyalty as well as for their warlike qualities, which spread well beyond the confines of Asia and Cappadocia.

Thirty years ago, Herod, newly transplanted to his throne by Rome, was regarded as a foreigner by many of his subjects because he came from Idumea — a land bordering the south of Judea, but not part of the traditional lands of the Jews. But his army was primarily composed of Jews, so he could not be certain of its loyalty which was why he decided to employ three thousand Galatian mercenaries to be his bodyguard to protect him against his own people as well as his external enemies. Rome was perfectly at ease with this arrangement because it was about to absorb Galatia as a province into its own empire. It might sound strange to talk of mercenaries and loyalty in the same sentence, but the Galatians had a fierce pride in their professionalism and now, at the end of Herod's reign, they were thought by many to be the most reliable troops in the east, apart from us Romans of course!

The morning of the fourth of May dawned chill and clear. It was still too early in the year for the sun to have much warmth before breakfast time, but the conditions were perfect for marching. Piso sat astride his horse outside Jerusalem's northern gate watching the heavily armoured Galatians march out of the city. Behind him was our cohort's cavalry troop drawn up in three files of ten troopers each. At full strength a troop consisted of thirty troopers commanded by a senior file leader called a decurion, plus the standard bearer or signifer. Our troop had sustained no casualties during the skirmish at Mount Carmel so, apart from one trooper who was sick, Piso's troop was complete.

Beside Piso stood the Galatian commander Attalus who, like most of his people, did not trust horses. He was an old, seasoned campaigner and one of the few remaining Galatians who had come to Judea at the beginning of Herod's reign. He looked up at Piso, his bright blue eyes shining like lapis lazuli from his sun bronzed face. "It's infantry that wins battles," he growled in atrocious Greek.

"Indeed," agreed Piso. "Any legionary would say the same, but against lightly armed bandits, cavalry might be useful."

"How many battles have you fought in?"

Piso reddened, "Well, just one and even that was not really a battle, just a skirmish."

Attalus admired the young man's honesty. "You can get killed just as easily in a skirmish as in a battle. Are you talking about the fight at Mount Carmel a couple of months ago?"

"Yes."

"Then from what I heard, you Romans fought well that day. Did you command?"

"The Governor of Syria was the senior officer present. I was his deputy."

"Varus!" snorted Attalus. "Then it must have been you who controlled the battle. Glad to have you with us."

"Glad to be here. I know I have much to learn," answered Piso, delighted to be complimented by an experienced veteran like Attalus. He began to wonder if he had misjudged the quality of the Galatians.

Once on the road to Mukhmas, the designated meeting point for the hostage exchange with the Zealots, Piso's horsemen trotted to the front of the column where they could scout ahead. After they turned right, off the main road and on to the track which led to Mukhmas, a messenger from the centre of the column arrived and asked Piso if he would join Attalus to discuss tactics. This was another honour for the young tribune so, leaving his decurion in command, he trotted back down the column to meet the Galatian commander.

"Walk with me," said Attalus. Piso dismounted, leading his horse himself, and fell into step with the Galatian.

"How is our false Abbas?"

Piso answered, "All is ready. One of our file leaders is covered in Jewish clothes from head to foot. No-one will notice the difference from a distance."

"Good. How does he feel about it?"

"Not happy. He keeps moaning that his false beard is too prickly."

"That's no surprise," smiled Attalus.

"His comrades are highly amused, which doesn't help, but at least it's only for a day or two."

Attalus pointed to the hills either side of them which were getting higher as they marched eastwards. "You could hide an army up there."

"But we're a day early for the meeting."

"I know, but my old antennae are twitching. We are but two hundred and thirty all told."

"It was agreed both sides should bring only thirty men."

"What we are doing, so can the Zealots."

"I suppose so," acknowledged Piso.

"I would feel reassured if you take your cavalry ahead of the column and reconnoitre the land around Mukhmas. It's about four miles away. If all is clear, send a messenger back and select good ground for an ambush while you are waiting for us to catch up."

"Very well," said Piso. However, as he remounted his horse, Attalus added, "Be cautious, Tribune. If you encounter the enemy do not engage them. Just count their numbers as best you can and come back here at full speed. No heroics, you have nothing to prove."

"Of course not!" laughed Piso as he galloped off. Needn't have wasted my breath, thought Attalus as he watched Piso disappear into the dust cloud kicked up by his horse's hooves; he's too much like I was at his age.

Piso led his men up into the Judean hills at a steady canter, free at last of the plodding Galatian infantrymen. Excitement infused the horsemen for this was the first action they had seen since Carmel, where they had merely been spectators playing the role of bodyguard to Varus. Soon they reached the lip of the Wadi Qilt valley where they paused to rest their horses before descending a steep, perilous looking goat track which led down to the dry river bed.

The decurion called out to Piso, "Single file here, sir; the track is narrow and unstable." Piso realised he had forgotten to give that order but, still flushed with excitement answered, "Give the order Decurion, and you may lead."

They reached the bottom of the valley without mishap and crossed the waterless river bed; apart from a few light showers, there had been no rain for many weeks. The track on the far side was in better condition and in less than twenty minutes they had reached the eastern lip of the wadi, where Piso ordered another brief halt to rest the horses again. Mukhmas was now less than a mile away.

He estimated ten minutes had passed and was about to give the order to mount when the decurion approached him, "Tribune, look back to the west; there is a dust cloud."

Piso was irritated by the delay, "Your name, Decurion."

"Quintus Paterculus, sir."

Piso could see a low, pale brown cloud rising above the hills through which they had just cantered. "What of it Decurion, that must be the column coming up behind us."

"Begging your pardon, sir, but that cloud is too large to be from a marching column alone." Just as he spoke, a distant metallic noise reached them, wafted in their direction by the gentle westerly breeze. It was barely audible, but both men immediately recognised the sound of battle.

"Thank you, Decurion," said Piso. "I am sorry if I was short with you. Order the men to mount up. We will return to the column at full speed."

By the time they approached the column, it was about two hours after noon. Piso halted the troop just before a ridge which separated them from the sound of a ferocious conflict taking place on the other side. The men were eager to engage but Piso, remembering his training, dismounted along with his decurion to walk the last few paces to the top of the ridge. Before them opened a spectacular view of a desperate struggle in which the Galatians were being assailed on all sides by a much larger Zealot force. Attalus had formed his men into a rough square in a wide, flat bottomed valley with craggy hills on either side. All round the square were clouds of slingers discharging their lethal stones at close range and encouraging the heavily armoured Galatians to break their formation and chase them. The Galatians dared not do so because interspersed amongst the slingers were knots of clubmen waiting for a gap to form in the square. If the square crumbled, Attalus and his men were lost.

Even as he watched, Piso saw a group of about fifty

clubmen charge where the wall of the square was thinnest. The Galatians buckled, the wall bent inwards but held — just. Inside the square were the dead and wounded; it looked like Attalus had lost almost half his men already.

Piso turned to his decurion, "Quintus, there is no time to lose. I am not a cavalryman as you know. What orders must I give?"

"Sir, deploy the first two files into a single extended line; we need width not depth to deal with the Zealots. I will lead with the signifier. Two hundred paces behind us you will lead the third file also in extended line. We charge at the canter, not the gallop, to retain order."

"Must I lead the second line?"

"Essential sir and standard cavalry practice for, as commander, you will decide where you are needed most. Retaining a reserve is vital for a successful charge."

"Then let's get on with it."

"One more thing sir. You will need a spatha, the long cavalry sword. Your short infantry gladius will be useless for fighting on horseback. You have no shield?"

"I wasn't expecting a battle."

"There are spare swords and shields with the pack horses. I'll have some sent to you while we are forming up."

Years of field exercises now showed their worth; in less than five minutes, the lines were formed and the horn sounded the advance. The two lines trotted forward with Piso at the head of the second, now armed with his long sword and oval shield. For the first and only time in his life, he was about to take part in a formal cavalry charge.

Just as the first line breasted the ridge, the horn sounded the charge. The horses recognised the sound as well as the troopers; Piso felt his arm almost pulled out of its socket as his mount surged forward with no encouragement from him. The first line disappeared over the ridge and moments later the second, with Piso in front and waving his spatha in mad circles above his head, reached the summit. Seeing the enemy, his men let out a roar; the horn was still sounding the charge — nine notes rising in threes to a final extended tenth. Piso felt a tingle run up his spine, he almost lost control; he found himself roaring too — no words, just a mad, animal yell; by all the gods, this was ecstasy!

By now, the Zealots realised their victory was far from secured. Quintus led the front line to the left of the Galatian square, where most of the enemy seemed to be, but they did not wait for the cavalry and began to run before the troopers reached them. A fleeing enemy is a horseman's perfect target and soon the long cavalry swords were plying their bloody trade amongst the defenceless, terrified Zealots. Piso could see that the left of the square was no longer threatened so he directed his men to the right, where the Zealots were still in some semblance of order. Despite cavalry procedure, he and his men abandoned the restrained canter and charged at the full gallop. The next few moments were vague in Piso's memory; order was gone, blood lust was upon him, and all he could remember were screams, blood and sword thrusts. For a short time, he lost the last vestiges of discipline. Fortunately, the Zealots ran and gradually sanity returned. He began to calm down; the enemy had fled and his men were waiting for their next orders.

"Tribune. Are you all right?" It was his decurion.

"I think so."

Quintus rode up beside Piso, "Well done, sir; well done,

indeed."

"We've won then?"

"Certainly. It's remarkable what an effect a well-timed cavalry charge can have even with only a few men."

"Our losses?"

"One man wounded, sir; knocked off his horse by a lucky sling stone, but he'll recover."

"Good, and well done to you Quintus."

"Thank you, sir."

Piso paused, struggling to find the right words, then blurted out, "By holy Jupiter, that was beautiful. I never experienced anything like it before. No wonder you joined the cavalry."

Quintus, who was at least ten years older than the young tribune, smiled, "Cavalry work is mostly patrols, scouting and guard duty. I have been in the legion for twelve years, but that is only the second charge I have made."

"Really, but you led the charge like a veteran."

"Tribune, may I have your permission to speak openly?"
"Of course, you have earned that right."

"Well, the image the cohort has of you is that you are rather too genteel to be a real soldier, but when the men hear how you performed today, they will change their minds."

"How so?"

"You fought like a Nubian berserker! You cut down more Zealots than any of us!"

Piso glowed warmly inside, delighted he had won the respect of his men. "I know I lost control."

"But only after you directed your line correctly."

"I don't remember actually killing anyone; it's all rather a blur."

"Then look at your sword, sir."

Piso looked down; his sword was bloody to the hilt, so was his forearm. He was more shocked than surprised, "I didn't know I had it in me," he said more to himself than Quintus. "The spatha is a fearsome weapon. I would like to keep it to remind me of this wonderful day."

"It's yours, sir, and it's only as fearsome as the man who wields it."

One of the Galatians was signalling to them; it looked like Attalus. The after-battle chat was over.

Piso ordered, "Take over here, Decurion; I must go to the Galatians." Then he rode over to Attalus and dismounted beside him. The Galatians had had a bad time of it. Dead and wounded littered the ground; blood stained the pale-yellow ground dark red. The grizzled, old warrior grabbed Piso's hand in his huge paw and wiped away blood from a head wound with the other one. "Are we glad to see you! You got here just in time."

"Glad we could help. We came as soon as we could but we never got to Mukhmas though."

"No matter, we walked straight into a trap. There never was going to be a prisoner exchange. I should have heeded my instincts, but your men did well Tribune and I take back what I said about cavalry never winning battles."

"Thank you."

"And I shall see that Varus and Herod hear of your contribution to our survival. But now we have much to do; collect the dead and tend the wounded and, in my case, write a report. We'll camp here for the night and double the guard. I think the Zealots have had enough, but they might try and surprise us again."

The Galatians do not bury their dead; their custom is cremation and, as the sun set, a pyre of thirty-eight bodies burned and sparked into the darkening sky. In such arid surroundings, it had taken all afternoon to find enough brushwood for the pyre, but the Galatians knew their business and gathered enough without having to sacrifice the baggage carts, which were needed to carry the forty-four who were too badly wounded walk. The Zealot wounded were dispatched where they had fallen alongside their dead. The corpses were left to the scavengers of the night.

Attalus and Piso sat together staring into the flames. "I knew all those men and their families," said the Galatian sadly. "This has been a tragedy for us."

"But at least we won the battle."

"True, but at what cost? Piso, I fear for the future. Herod is a tyrant but at least he is strong. When he dies, and it will be soon, all Judea, Samaria and Galilee will explode into rebellion. The Zealots will run wild and, quite frankly, they frighten me. Today they fought us to a standstill yet they are but half naked, poorly armed savages. They have no thought for their own preservation; I don't know if it is raw courage, lunacy, or their faith but if they ever acquire proper weapons, equipment and basic military discipline, there will be no holding them."

"They fought like that at Carmel too," agreed Piso. "But surely their reserves of manpower cannot sustain the losses they take?"

"Who knows? I suppose we will find out eventually."

The depleted Galatian column arrived back at Jerusalem in the afternoon of the next day. Attalus led his battered men to their quarters in the citadel, and Herod's wrath, while Piso and his cavalry continued round the city walls to the Roman camp where good news awaited him. Only a few hours earlier his three lost sheep, who were supposed to have been exchanged at Mukhmas, had already returned to the fold.

"Where are they?" he asked Brasidas, who was the bearer of the welcome tidings.

"They have bathed, been fed and issued with new uniforms, and are now telling their story to their comrades in Veranius' century. I should imagine it makes interesting listening."

"Leave it an hour to give me time to bathe and wash away the gore of battle, then bring them to my office."

By the time we met Piso, we had already heard of his exploits with the cavalry. He was overjoyed to see us. Brasidas stayed with us, smiling but saying nothing, as we swapped stories with our tribune till late into the night; he would not have got a word in edgeways even if he had tried.

***

IV

Three months passed. Piso had sent Caius home to his father's farm in Caesarea Maritima to recuperate from his leg wound while Rufio and I relaxed in the welcome monotony of camp life. Shortly after the battle at Mukhmas, Varus returned to Antioch taking Brasidas and our brave cavalry with him as his escort — which cheered Piso greatly — for although he was sorry to see the horsemen go, he was now Officer Commanding all Roman forces in Jerusalem — namely, his own cohort.

It was clear that our stay was not going to be short, so we constructed a more comfortable camp by substituting wooden barrack huts for campaign tents just outside the city walls. This was just as well because it was now high summer and the huts were cooler and airier than tents. Each hut was designed to contain a century of eighty men and, as a centurion, I had my own private room — which doubled as an office and sleeping quarters — at one end of the hut.

During the day, I would usually keep Gebel tethered outside my quarters shaded from the sun by an awning taken from one of the redundant campaign tents. At night, camp regulations required him to be returned to the animal park at the north end of the camp; we were now firm friends.

It was the seventh day of July; I remember the date clearly because I was sitting in my office signing and dating the guard duty roster for the night shift. The evening meal was about an hour away and I was beginning to feel hungry. There was a knock at my door and a smiling Rufio entered. "You have a visitor, Lucius."

"Show him in."

"It's a her."

"Then show her in." I recognised the perfume before she entered, but allowed Rufio to do the formal introduction. "Sir, may I present Ruth, our beautiful benefactor."

"Please sit," I said, and moved a chair opposite my desk. Rufio showed no inclination to leave so I added, "You may go Rufio," he hesitated. "Now!"

Ruth sat down and threw back her hood. Although her hair

was covered, her face was unmasked. She was as lovely as I remembered but looked tired. She did not speak and then I realised she was troubled so I began the conversation.

"Ruth, you saved our lives; we are indebted to you. Speak and I will do whatever I can."

"I have walked from Nazareth to Jerusalem. I am thirsty. May I drink?"

"Of course, I will send for some water."

"Wine would be better," she said with a mischievous smile.

"Then wine it shall be; I have some here." I poured out two goblets and handed one to her. She drank it in a few gulps and placed the empty goblet in front of me, so I refilled it. This time she took a sip and said, "I need to speak to Caius."

"I am sorry to tell you Caius is not here. He has been sent to his father's home in Caesarea Maritima to recover from his wound."

"How far away is that?"

"About two day's walk."

Suddenly, the proud bearing of this fine woman seemed to collapse; she was not just tired, she was exhausted.

"Ruth, you may speak to me. I will pass on your message to Caius, or if it is urgent, I will send a runner. You took a risk coming here alone; thieves and murderers patrol the roads at night."

"I came with a caravan."

"There are no caravans between Jerusalem and Caesarea. Whatever you say to me will be passed to no-one but Caius. I give you my word on that."

Ruth was undecided. She took another sip from her goblet. "It's a long story and I have not eaten today."

"Then we shall dine together here in my quarters while you speak." What I write now is the story exactly as Ruth told me.

The Zealot execution party reached Nazareth on the morning after we three Romans left. Joseph returned from Sepphoris just before them and was horrified to find the hostages had escaped. The Zealot leader, a certain Judas Sicariot, questioned the guards who were at a complete loss to explain what happened. One suggested their wine had been tampered with but he was ridiculed. It was obvious to Judas that they had all been drunk and failed to secure the hostages' door properly. He ordered them to set off immediately and recapture us or face bar Abbas' wrath; the Romans could not have got far because one of them had a serious leg wound. Then he departed on another mission further north.

For the next two months, Ruth thought that was the end of it, though Joseph was unusually silent. Both Ruth and Mary expected him to question them as to how the hostages escaped while in their custody, but he said nothing. Life resumed as usual until one morning, when Ruth was brushing Mary's hair before breakfast. Normally, at this time, Mary liked to chat about the day ahead but this day she was silent and tense. On the infrequent occasions her mistress was like this, Ruth knew it was best to keep quiet too.

Suddenly, Mary said, "I am with child."

Ruth dropped the brush and fumbled to pick it up again as she tried to compose herself. "Are you sure?"

"Of course I am. I have missed the last two months."

"Was it Caius?"

"Yes, you know it was."

"What are we going to do?"

"I must tell Joseph before it shows, then he will decide."

"He won't be pleased."

"He'll be livid. Ruth, please stop speaking the obvious. I have thought about this a great deal and the only course open now is honesty."

"What of Caius?"

"He must be told, but only after Joseph has made his decision. Joseph is a kind, and good-hearted man, if a little dull. It is his right to decide what to do with me. Only then can I determine the nature of my message to Caius."

"He could have you stoned."

"We are not actually married so the law would not allow that; nor would my father. Anyway, that will not be Joseph's choice; of that I am sure."

"When will you tell him?"

"This morning at breakfast. I would like you to be there too." A little later, Joseph got up from the breakfast table and said, "I shall be leaving for Sepphoris this morning. Is there anything I can get for you Mary?"

"No thank you, Joseph and please sit down; I have something to say." He was taken aback by the firmness in her voice and did as he was bid while Mary briefly left the room and returned with Ruth. Then she sat down opposite him and spoke calmly but remorsefully too.

"Joseph, I have let you down. I am with child. I am truly sorry."

The colour drained from his face. He looked down and gripped the edge of the table hard until his knuckles turned white. He remained silent for a while, staring at the ground but seeing nothing. When at last he looked up again, he seemed ten years older. His voice was hoarse, "It was the Roman?"

"Yes."

"He forced you?"

"No."

He paused again then said, "I never believed the guards let the Romans escape. Did you think I would not notice the missing donkey? I thought you released them out of misplaced mercy. I never thought… Do you love this man?"

"Yes."

"Does he love you?"

"I believe so, but marriage is not permitted in the legions."

"I see. So what do you want to do?"

"The choice is yours. I will abide by whatever you decide."

Joseph nodded, "You are right, I must decide what will happen. I will not go to Sepphoris today. I need time to think; I will call you at sunset, both of you."

It was a day of anxiety for both women made worse when Joseph told them at sunset that he was still not ready, but would see them first thing in the morning. After a sleepless night, Mary and Ruth finally met Joseph in the reception room; the same room where Caius had been tended and Mary's child conceived.

Joseph looked haggard; he had not slept either. "Well Mary, it seems there is indeed a choice. Either I send you back to your father's house with all the disgrace that will entail to both families, or I accept the child as my own and we bring the marriage forward so that it can take place before your pregnancy becomes obvious. I give you the choice, so which is it to be?"

"To remain with you," said Mary without pause or

hesitation.

"But you and this Roman love each other."

"In this life, one cannot always have what one desires."

Joseph's stern tone softened, "Mary, I love you too. I will not insult you by suggesting your love for the Roman is merely youthful desire; regrettably, I am sure it is not. I blame myself for not giving you the attention you deserve and being too preoccupied with my work in Sepphoris. I will do better from now on and will prove my love for you. Any man could love you and, in time, I hope you will be able to love me. But if you are to stay, I have three conditions which you must accept. First, you must never see the Roman again. Is that agreed?"

"Yes," answered Mary. "But he must know of the child's existence. Judea is volatile, anything could happen; the child may need protection."

"Mary," Joseph tried to hold her hand but she pulled away. There was silence. The tension in the room was almost tangible. For a short while Ruth thought all was lost and Joseph would send them away, but he wanted Mary too much. "Very well, I agree," he said and held out his hand again. This time, Mary responded. She had taken him to the brink and he had conceded; the critical balance had shifted. Mary, if not in control, was certainly in the ascendant, but she was intelligent enough to realise that Joseph must be allowed to retain his self-respect.

"Joseph, I will keep my promise not to see Caius again. Ruth will go to Jerusalem and speak to him." For the first time that morning, Joseph looked straight at Ruth. His eyes were cold, baleful almost. Her blood ran cold; there was trouble ahead, but as yet he did not address her directly.

"My second condition is utmost secrecy. Only the three of

147

us and the Roman can know of this because great events depend on it. People must believe that I am the father and so I must bear the shame of the act committed outside marriage. If the child is a boy, he will be the Anointed One, the Messiah, and the true King of the Jews. We cannot let slip the Messiah is half Roman."

"Only a quarter," said Mary helpfully. "Caius' mother was a Jew."

"As you say," agreed Joseph blandly. "But my final condition is the one that may be the most difficult for you, and before you answer I must tell you I will not compromise on it."

"Go ahead then."

Suddenly, Joseph's voice hardened in a way that neither of the women had heard before. He looked again at Ruth and hissed, "This woman must go! I accept I should have been here more often, but she was here all the time. She could have stopped this; she is a bad influence on you." Mary tried to speak, but he would not allow it. "Ruth, what is your purpose here?"

By now, Ruth was shaking with fear; she had never seen Joseph so angry, so full of hate. She answered hesitantly, "To be Mary's friend and companion, to look after her and see she comes to no harm."

"Good, and have you been successful?"

"I suppose not."

"Did you encourage Mary to be with the Roman?"

"No, but I did not discourage her."

"So, by your own admission you failed."

Mary could bear this no longer, "Stop! Stop! This is cruel and unjust. You are blaming her for my failings. Ruth only followed my instructions."

For the first time, Joseph uncharacteristically raised his voice. "Maybe, maybe not, but I will no longer have her under my roof!"

"But at least allow her to stay until I have given birth. I want no-one else near me."

Joseph bit his lip in frustration. He wanted Ruth gone, but he dared not risk losing his betrothed. "Very well, but just until the birth. After that, she goes."

Ruth realised it was hopeless to fight; to do so would risk the security of her mistress, something she could not allow. "Mary," she said. "I am two years older than you. It is true I could have done more to prevent what happened. I will go now or after the birth, whichever is decided."

Joseph, ashamed of his brief loss of self-control, resumed his usual calm manner, "Ruth, I have no intention of throwing you out onto the street. One of my under-managers in Nazareth is looking for a wife. Ehud is a good man; he may find you acceptable."

It was an unfortunate choice of words and turned Ruth's fear into anger. Fire pulsed through her veins; now she would stand up for herself come what may. "Sir, I may be of humble birth but I am not a prize heifer to be sold in the market. Nor do I care if this man finds me acceptable or not. I will not marry a man I do not know or like."

While Joseph struggled before Mary's strength and beauty, he could easily cope and even understand Ruth's outburst. "Ruth, say no more now and talk with Mary. No-one expects you to marry against your will. I can arrange a meeting with Ehud for you. At least talk with him awhile."

Ruth ended her story just as our evening meal arrived.

"And did you meet this Ehud?" I asked.

"Not yet, but I suppose I will when I return."

"You do not sound enthusiastic about it."

"Jewish men are so serious. I would rather marry someone from another people, a Roman perhaps. Rufio is a fine-looking man."

I felt a bit disappointed when she said that. "Rufio is indeed a strapping fellow, but I doubt he would be the sort of husband who would make you happy. Also, he has twelve more years to serve with the legions before he can marry. And you would not be able to communicate; he only speaks Latin and Pannonian." In truth, Ruth did not seem too downcast by my response. I added, "And you have only really met one Roman, Caius, and he is exceptional not typical. Now, would you like to hear about our adventures after we left you?"

My story took us to the end of our evening meal. Ruth particularly enjoyed hearing about Gebel's contribution to our escape, and when I had finished, she said, "I saw him tethered outside your quarters when I arrived. He looks in good condition."

"He is. He loves a little bread after his meal, only a little mind you; too much affects his digestion."

"Would you mind if I take him home with me? He will certainly ease my journey."

That came as a shock. I had allowed myself to become too fond of the young donkey. Putting a brave face on it, I answered, "Of course you may; he is part of your household anyway. I shall miss him though."

Ruth gently put her hand on mine, "Thank you, Lucius, and thank you for listening. I must leave before it gets dark."

"Have you somewhere to sleep?"

"I have accommodation in the city. A caravan leaves for Nazareth tomorrow."

"Then I will escort you and Gebel to your quarters."

We walked slowly into the lower city. The lamps on the main streets were being lit and the shops were shutting up for the night. Ruth stopped in front of one of the better inns in the city. "Well this is where we say goodbye."

"At least Joseph does not expect his servants to travel on a small allowance."

"Whatever you may think after what I have told you, Joseph is a kind and gentle man. His patience was pushed beyond endurance by Mary and me."

I gave Gebel a hug and stroked his long ears. He seemed happy enough. "Ruth, I will make contact with Caius as soon as possible."

"And I will send word when the child is born if I can. It will be in Bethlehem in case it's a boy. There are many conflicting prophecies about the Messiah, but they all agree on one thing; he will be born in the City of David, Bethlehem. Remember, after you have spoken to Caius, only five people in the world, including you, will know of the Messiah's true parentage."

"I understand." I turned to go but Ruth stopped me. "And one more thing." She kissed me gently on the cheek, "You are a good man Lucius Veranius. Caius is not the only exceptional Roman."

CHAPTER SEVEN

By the time Judas and Daniel reached Dan, the battle at Mukhmas was about to be fought. Reuben would have reported back to bar Abbas by now with news of the escape of the hostages. Upon reflection, Judas was not too saddened by this. The hostages had turned out to have no value anyway; no blame for their escape could be attached to him, and he had been spared witnessing their executions.

It was late in the afternoon. About three hours of daylight were left as the two weary travellers entered the city by the south gate. City was hardly the right word. Named after the tribe that settled in the most northern part of the land that later became Israel, everything about Dan was backward. You could smell the city almost before you could see it because the drains were not properly maintained, the streets were shabby, narrow and unwashed and, apart from the market place, there were no open spaces.

"Not like Hebron," moaned Daniel as he was bumped into a wall by a large, hairy man carrying a side of raw meat over his shoulders.

"Nor Jericho," agreed Judas. "I hate to think what their inns will be like. We'll try the market place first."

There was no shortage of inns fronting the market place, some bearing exotic names like 'The Traveller's Dream' or 'Stay Once Stay Forever', but all looked unsavoury and unwelcoming. Judas selected the one calling itself 'The Inn of the Faithful' in the hopes that its customers might be more religious and therefore perhaps cleaner than most, but as they entered the premises he gagged at the smell of stewing, fatty mutton; he would not be eating there that night. They had to call four times before someone came to attend to them. A scruffy, overweight woman with matted, unwashed, greying hair shuffled into the reception area from a door at the back of the inn and glared at them. "Well?"

Judas answered politely. "Madam, we would like accommodation for the night."

"Sharing a room?"

"Preferably not."

"That's double the price then."

"We expected no less."

"Two silver shekels."

"Madam that is equivalent to two weeks' work for a skilled man."

"Take it or leave it."

Judas fumbled in his pouch for the exorbitant fee. "Business must be good if you can afford to charge such outrageous rates."

The woman's eyes narrowed, "You're not from these parts with your high and mighty ways."

Judas sighed, "Alas no, we are from Jerusalem."

"You Judeans think a lot of yourselves. What is your business in Dan?"

Judas handed over his shekels and thought this might be a good time to mention his mission. "We seek Judas the Galilean."

"Herod's spies, are you?"

"Hardly that. We bring a message from the leader of the Zealot sect, Elijah bar Abbas."

The woman stepped back as if she had been struck, but pocketing the shekels at the same time. "I don't know anything about the Judas you seek. You will have to speak to my husband."

"And when can we do that?"

"He'll be back this evening." Then pointing to a worm-eaten door hanging on a single hinge she said, "That's your room and the one next to it is your friend's. My husband will speak to you as soon as he returns."

They had no idea when or if this woman's husband would turn up so, removing the insect infested blankets and mattresses that covered their bunks, both men lay down on the bare boards to rest. Within seconds, they were asleep.

It seemed to Judas that he had only just closed his eyes when he was woken by rough shaking. It was dark, he was confused; for a moment he thought he was being robbed and began feeling for his sicarius, but a man's voice said, "Hurry, the Messiah does not like to be kept waiting. We have a two-hour march ahead of us."

Soon, Judas and Daniel, both still half asleep, stumbled out of the inn accompanied by four of Judas the Galilean's men. There was a slight greying in the eastern sky suggesting dawn was less than an hour away; they must have slept all night. The air was cool rather than cold; the coming day would be hot so they walked at a good pace in order to finish their journey by breakfast time. After crossing a small stream, one of the headwaters of the River Jordan, they followed a winding goat track up into the foothills of Mount Hermon which lies to the northeast of Dan. There were no stops for rest, just two hours of hard, uphill walking, but Judas and Daniel were young and fit and kept up with their escort without difficulty.

It was already getting warm when they arrived at the Galilean's camp, which was not large consisting of just fifty or so black and brown hide tents. At four men to a tent, this meant that the entire band of the so-called Messiah numbered no more than two hundred; not enough to threaten bar Abbas but enough to be a nuisance.

There was one white tent, bigger than the rest, which was where the escort halted. One of them went inside. A minute later he reappeared and said to Judas and Daniel, "The Messiah wishes you to rest. You will be brought food and water. For now, he just wants to know your names. He will come to you when you have cleaned yourselves and eaten. There is a stream behind his tent where you may wash."

After Judas and Daniel had rinsed away the dust and dirt of five days' continuous travel since leaving bar Abbas, they enjoyed a breakfast of bread, cheese and goat's milk; they had not eaten since the morning before. Just as Judas finished his bread, he became aware of being watched. Standing silently outside the white tent was a small, slender figure dressed in a voluminous white, riding robe, the garb of desert nomads except they generally preferred black. It was far too large for him. His black hair was full and long, easily reaching his shoulders, and his face was delicate beneath his thin beard, child-like almost, but although he was smiling his eyes remained cold.

The voice was thin and high pitched and could easily have been a woman's. "Welcome to my humble abode."

Judas and Daniel stood up. Judas said apologetically, "We did not see you, sir." The thin voice took on a hard edge.

"Address me as Lord."

"Yes, Lord," responded both men together. Well he's not modest then, thought Judas, but he looks dangerous.

"Why have you come here?"

"We have a message from Elijah bar Abbas, leader of the Zealot sect, for Judas the Galilean," answered Judas.

"Then let us hear it." The Galilean made a simple hand gesture. About twenty of his men reacted immediately and gathered in a group behind Judas and Daniel; the atmosphere suddenly became threatening.

Judas did his best to sound confident, but his voice wavered slightly. "Lord, the Romans are our common enemy together with Herod, their puppet king, yet we fight separately. If we were to co-operate, we could have an effect out of all proportion to our numbers."

"Does bar Abbas wish to join me then?"

"Well, it would be the other way round. He has many more men than you."

"How do you know how many men I have?"

"I have counted your tents."

"There are only a few of my followers here. I have thousands and their numbers grow every day."

Judas continued, "If we join forces, bar Abbas would naturally be in overall command, but you would still have direct command over your own forces operating within an agreed strategic framework."

"And what is the aim of this agreed strategic framework?" The last three words were heavily laced with sarcasm. The Galilean's voice remained calm and steady, but something in his eyes warned Judas to be wary.

"Lord, together we would help to fulfil the prophecy; the

coming of the true Messiah." It was too late to retract the words. Judas immediately knew he had made a mistake. The Galilean's calm countenance now gave way to involuntary twitching on one side of his face; his eyes started to flicker this way and that; when he spoke, he began to foam at the mouth,

"Has no-one told you who I am?"

"Lord, you are the great leader called Judas the Galilean."

"Fool, I am the Messiah, the anointed King of the Jews. Everyone knows it. Get on your knees and worship me!"

It was too late to change course now. Judas tried to be as reasonable as he could, but there was no reasoning with this man. "Lord you cannot be; the Messiah is yet to be born."

"On your knees, both of you, or you will feel my anger!" But Judas and Daniel stood their ground. The Galilean made another hand signal and one of his clubmen stepped forward. Then he pointed to Daniel, "Him!"

Before Judas could react, the clubman struck Daniel with a mighty blow to the side of his head. It killed him instantly. He fell headlong landing at the Galilean's feet, blood and brains spattering his white robe.

Judas surged forward seething with rage and shock, "You little bastard! I'll kill you for this." Before he could grasp the effeminate throat, he was firmly pulled back by the Galilean's men. But at least he had seen terror in the false messiah's eyes when it seemed he might reach him.

The sight of blood and the exercise of his power seemed to settle the Galilean; when he spoke, he resumed his aura of calmness. "You will return to bar Abbas and tell him what you have seen. You will also say that I will allow him to join his forces to mine if he wishes, but all will be under my command. Finally, tell him to wait no longer for the Messiah, for I am here. Now go."

Judas was escorted down the winding goat track by three grim faced, burly clubmen. Although still shocked by Daniel's murder, he had the presence of mind to try and engage them in conversation to find out more about the bloodthirsty maniac dressed in white, but none would speak until they reached the stream just outside Dan. There, his escort left him but one of them, their leader, hung back just long enough to whisper when his comrades were out of earshot,

"He terrifies us; you saw what he did to your friend, but he does far worse to those who disobey him."

"But he is only one small man."

"He has spies living among us. We do not know who they are. I must go now."

* * *

II

The five day walk back to the Zealot spring camp was the most depressing Judas ever made. Shocked and alone, he avoided Dan and took the south road to Nazareth and Jerusalem. He even toyed with the idea of using the more easterly road, which followed the Jordan valley and would bring him to bar Abbas via Jericho, for just now he craved company and would have liked to see his father, but Rachel made that impossible. So, he trudged back the way he came, disconsolate and apprehensive about the reaction his report of the missing hostages and Daniel's murder would generate when he met bar Abbas.

Bar Abbas and Joachim listened quietly as Judas recounted the details of his journey to Nazareth and Judas the

Galilean's camp. They sat inside a campaign tent for protection against the hot afternoon sun, and when Judas had finished, neither said anything for a while. Eventually it was Joachim who spoke first.

"We must settle the score with that Galilean monster."

"He is a problem we must resolve," agreed bar Abbas. "But it will be a distraction. Why can't we Jews ever unite? Herod is dying, an opportunity to rid ourselves of Rome is coming, yet all we do is fight amongst ourselves."

"I do not know why God made his Chosen Race so quarrelsome," sighed Joachim.

"The Messiah will unite us," said Judas.

"Which one?" replied bar Abbas bitterly.

Joachim placed his hand on his young leader's shoulder, "Eli, we have had setbacks before but we always win through. The Galilean will pay for his crimes, but right now our most urgent problem is weaponry."

"How so?" asked Judas.

Bar Abbas replied, "Judas, you were not present at the battle we have just fought at Mukhmas. Our men fought like lions. We surprised Herod's Galatians and sent many of them to their gods, but thanks to their heavy armour and large shields, we were unable to break them before help came. No matter how brave our men are, slings and clubs are no match for body armour and finely tempered swords."

"Can't we make them?"

"Not in the quantity we need."

"And not soon enough," added Joachim. "Word from the palace is that Herod has only a few months to live. When he dies, our chance will come."

"Then we must buy weapons," suggested Judas.

Bar Abbas nodded in agreement. "Joachim and I were coming round to that idea too, but they will not be cheap. When the time comes, we will be able to put two thousand men into the field. Half will be clubmen; it is they who will exchange their clubs for proper swords and armour. The slingers will remain mobile and unarmoured. The cost of a thousand swords, shields and armour will be huge."

"We do not have enough in our treasury," said Joachim. "We will need to call upon our wealthier supporters who have already been generous."

"Nor can we buy from within the Roman empire because anyone who supplies us will be executed for treason. We will have to go to one of Rome's enemies," explained bar Abbas.

Judas frowned, "But there are hardly any left; Rome has beaten them all into submission except Parthia."

"The Parthians again," sighed Joachim. "I sometimes think we hope for too much from them. Although they hate the Romans almost as much as we do, they will still charge a high price for what we want. They are hard businessmen as well as tough warriors."

"But all that will take months," said Judas. "Herod won't delay dying just to help us."

Bar Abbas shrugged, "Well, enough of that. It is a problem that Joachim and I must resolve. Meanwhile, Judas, it is time for you to take up residence in your new home in Nazareth and get to know Joseph. Your relationship with him needs to be handled carefully for your role as guide and teacher to the Messiah, his son, must not conflict with his duties as a father."

"I understand."

"Furthermore, Joseph is one of those wealthy supporters of our cause that Joachim mentioned earlier. Unfortunately, these people, who come mainly from the commercial class, are dwindling in number because the Romans, for all their faults, have brought peace and stability through Herod's harsh rule. As you know, business flourishes in a peaceful environment; it may be the peace of fear but it is still peace. The result is that there is a growing body of well-off people who are not only enjoying the benefits of a humiliating peace but are also prepared to trade off our independence to generate greater wealth still. To them, we have become the enemy, not the Romans. Even the temple priests seem to be getting rather too comfortable with things as they are, so we must always be aware of the threat of enemies within our own people. But men like Joseph have not allowed their commercial success to cloud their judgement about what is right for God's Chosen Race. While we have men like him behind us, there will always be hope."

Judas left the Zealot camp with bar Abbas' words still ringing in his ears.

***

III

The property in Nazareth was simple but delightful. The house was rectangular in shape with a reception room at the front and a cooking and wash room at the back. Both rooms were flanked by a large courtyard from which steps went up the side of the house to an upper floor consisting of a bedroom and a small garden where Judas could sleep in the open on warm, summer nights. The dwelling was located near the noisy market in the crowded lower town with its outer walls shared with adjacent properties, but for Judas the sheer joy of being master in his own house for the first time in his life made any apparent shortcomings inconsequential. He had been given an allowance which, though small, was more than adequate for his simple needs. For the first time since his mother died, he was happy.

Joseph's large house was in the upper town where the wealthy people lived. Although Judas had visited it less than three weeks ago on his journey to Dan, he felt anxious about his reception as he walked up the stony street towards it. He had allowed himself two days to settle in, but this meeting could be put off no longer.

It was Ruth who opened the door. "Yes, Judas, we have been expecting you. The master is in his office. I will take you to him." She led him up the stairs, which were within the house not outside, a sure sign of wealth, and left him at the door to Joseph's office. The door was open and Judas could see a man bent over his desk scratching away at a scroll with a goose quill.

Joseph looked up, "Judas Sicariot, do come and sit with me. I am just finishing off my business accounts or trying to." Judas sat down in a padded easy chair opposite Joseph and looked around. The room was light and airy with open windows in three of the four walls. The upper town was quiet compared to the lower and here, on the upper floor of Joseph's large house, was the ideal working environment. But despite these benign circumstances, Joseph was clearly struggling with his accounts.

At last, Judas said, "May I help sir? Business accounting was part of my training at the temple."

Joseph put down his quill and sighed, "I can build a wall brick by brick to the finest tolerance, I can carve wood to make cabinets and furniture which are unequalled in Galilee, but accounts I cannot master. Your help will be most welcome." He handed over the scroll.

The sight that met Judas' eyes was appalling. A jumble of words and numbers was liberally interspersed with blotches and scratchings out. Some attempt was being made at recording cash in and out, but there was no evidence of the concept of profit and loss. Judas cleared his throat and asked, "How are you taxed?"

"By the amount of work I do."

"So you're taxed on revenue without knowing how much profit you make?"

"Well, I suppose so."

"That's the worst form of tax because the tax gatherer takes his cut whether or not you make a profit."

"Yes, but I must be making a profit otherwise I would not still be in business."

"True, but if we get your accounts in order you can be taxed on profit which is how it should be. You are most certainly paying too much tax now."

"Clearly, I need help then," acknowledged Joseph.

"First, we need to keep two sets of scrolls, each with a vertical line drawn in the centre. The first will be your daily cash book recording cash received on the left and cash spent on the right. The second will be your monthly profit and loss account with the value of work done shown on the left and the cost of materials and man hours carrying out that work on the right. How do you bid for work?"

Now Joseph showed more enthusiasm as this was a task he understood well. "I do a detailed estimate of all materials needed for a contract and how many man hours will be needed to complete it. Then I add a figure for profit and bid accordingly."

"Well, that's a start I suppose; we can talk about marketing later. At least you have all you need to prepare your monthly profit and loss account."

Joseph's enthusiasm waned again. "The trouble is finding the time to keep my records up to date. I am needed on contract sites most days and when I am finished, I'm usually too tired to start writing up accounts."

"Would you like me to get you started at least?"

"I should be forever in your debt."

"Then I will start at once."

Joseph and Judas never did get round to discussing the main purpose of Judas' visit that day, both knew what it was anyway, and over the next few weeks Judas was able to get Joseph's accounts into good order. All seemed to be going well until Joseph returned from one of his frequent visits to Sepphoris late one afternoon. Judas was just about to finish work for the day, having completed the cash book, when Joseph strode into the office with a face like thunder. "Government agents! I really dislike them!" Joseph never swore, but for once it seemed he might.

"What's the matter sir?"

"Yet again, I've been tricked. My men are working on a government contract which I have not told you about because it's confidential. I agreed a price with Herod's agent and the contract was signed. Midway through the contract, he asked me to put in security doors which are expensive and require extra building work. That part of the contract is now complete but when payment became due, he claimed the extra work was part of the overall bid price."

"But surely you agreed a contract variation?"

"Yes, but only verbally. He seemed so reasonable at the time and I was too busy to go back to my lawyer and sort out the necessary paperwork. Variations often happen in contract work but I now realise verbal arrangements are too easily broken." Joseph gradually calmed down as he was speaking and asked, "Judas, are you about to go home?"

"Yes sir."

"Please wait a few moments, I need to talk to you."

"Of course." Judas sat down in the padded chair opposite Joseph and waited.

"Judas, I need a business manager, someone to look after the accounts, prepare and manage contract administration, take care of the finances and all the other essential parts of running the business that I do so inadequately. If I had someone like that, I would be free to concentrate on the things I am good at, estimating, cost negotiation and managing the construction work. That way the business would grow because we could take on more contracts simultaneously if I knew the administration was being managed properly. We work well together, you and I, do we not?"

"Certainly."

"Then would you accept the business manager position? I would pay you well and we will not allow it to interfere with your prime mission of guiding the Messiah when he is born."

"I would be honoured sir."

"Excellent, then you must stop calling me 'sir'. Use my name as all my friends do."

"Yes, err, Joseph."

"Tomorrow, I must return to Sepphoris; I would like you

to come too so that you can meet my lawyer who is also a rabbi. He will draw up the papers for your employment; you will be seeing a lot of each other from now on. You can also visit the contract I was speaking about. We are building a high security compound for storing military equipment."

Judas' eyes widened as he recalled the conversation with bar Abbas and Joachim only a few days ago bemoaning the lack of weapons for the Zealot forces. "In that case, Joseph, there may be a way for you to recover your losses from Herod's agent and much more besides."

Judas threw himself into his new role as business manager with enthusiasm. In later years he often looked back on this period of his life with great satisfaction. The workload was vast and occupied most of the day, but he had never been troubled by hard work and, for the first time since leaving the temple, his intelligent, agile mind was being truly stimulated by the cut and thrust of the commercial world. He quickly learned the basic principles of construction work and soon earned the respect of Joseph's workers. Above all, he felt valued and appreciated.

His business relationship with Joseph gradually developed into a friendship, partly because they were so different, Joseph being a good practical leader with a winning personality, while Judas was the ascetic, intellectual, incisive thinker; the perfect second in command. But they shared two traits which bonded them even more tightly, a hunger for success and dedication to the Zealot cause.

About two months after his arrival in Nazareth, Judas received an unexpected visitor to his little house. It was the Sabbath and, as there was no work to be done, he was enjoying a leisurely breakfast in his courtyard. The visitor was Joseph. This was the first time his master had come to Judas' dwelling; it was obvious something important had happened.

Judas unlocked the courtyard door, which opened directly onto the street. "Come in, Joseph, have you breakfasted yet?"

"No, I'm not hungry," answered Joseph as he sat down on a bench in the courtyard.

"You look troubled," said Judas.

Joseph was ten years older than Judas but today he looked old enough to be his father. "I am bringing forward the date of my marriage to next month."

"Well that will be short notice for your wedding guests but it is no cause for worry. Would you like me to help organise—"

"I haven't finished yet," interrupted Joseph.

"Sorry."

The older man took a deep breath, "The reason I am bringing the date forward is because Mary is with child."

That news hit Judas like a thunderbolt. Joseph, the epitome of good manners and proper behaviour had sampled his fruit before the harvest. He tried to reassure his friend, "These things happen," he said blandly. "Mary is beautiful; any red-blooded man would understand."

"I doubt her father will."

"Perhaps not, but does Joachim need to know before the wedding? Will it show?"

"That is why I am bringing the date forward, but Eli and Joachim must be told. If it is a boy this will not be just any child, it will be the Messiah."

"I understand. And how is Mary?"

"Remarkably calm and in good health."

167

"Am I allowed to congratulate you both?"

Joseph looked directly at Judas with eyes that seemed distant, lifeless almost, not the look of a first-time father. "Certainly, you may, but I have a favour to ask you."

"Anything."

"Would you personally take this news to Eli and Joachim? I know I should, but I feel I can't face them, especially Joachim."

"Of course I will, but please try to cheer up. After all, it is a wedding and a birth we are talking about, not a funeral."

Judas set out the same morning and reached bar Abbas' summer camp at the lone pine three days later. The news of the coming of the Messiah spread quickly amongst the Zealots and everyone began to celebrate, except Joachim of course. Judas thought it useless to point out the child might be a girl; it would have seemed churlish. Against a background of singing and laughter, he stood in the shadow of the lone pine with bar Abbas and Joachim, for it was three hours after noon and the day was hot. "What progress have you made with your search for weapons?" he asked.

"None as yet," answered Joachim. "We have decided to ask Caspar for help. He will be able to strike a better deal with the Parthians than we can."

"You may not need to," said Judas, relishing the moment. "Joseph has won a secret contract to build a weapons store for Herod in Sepphoris. The contract is about half way to completion. Allowing time for the store to be filled, you should be able to take what you want quite soon."

"Will it not be fortified and guarded?" asked bar Abbas

"Certainly, but Joseph will copy a set of keys to the

security gates, so a stealthy, night time burglary might be arranged."

"But this is wonderful news!" exclaimed bar Abbas. "When can we do this?"

"The contract should be finished next Adar (February) so, allowing say two months for the weapons to arrive, we could aim for Ayar (April) or Sivan (May)."

"And the Messiah will be born in Sheva (January). The timing is perfect!" Then realising what he had just said, bar Abbas quickly added, "I'm sorry Joachim, I did not mean..." he did not know what to say next.

"That's all right Eli. What's done is done. I will say my piece in private to Joseph when I see him."

"But we must still get word to Caspar about the Messiah's birth. And Judas, when you return to Nazareth please congratulate Joseph; about the weapons store I mean."

"And about the forthcoming birth," added Joachim generously. "Reuben will accompany you for extra security."

Judas smiled, "His muscle will be welcome."

***

IV

The wedding took place on the third day of Thishri (September). Understandably it was a muted affair, the guests being restricted to family and a few close friends; Judas was included in this group. Also included was Joseph's cousin, Joab, who lived with his family in Bethlehem. Joab had offered to provide his home for Joseph and Mary when the time of the birth approached; thus, the requirement of the messianic prophecy would be met because the Messiah would be born in the City of David. All agreed that Mary looked particularly beautiful in her wedding dress, which was well designed to cover the fact that she was already five months pregnant. Above all, Joachim reduced the underlying tension by embracing Joseph on his arrival in a genuine act of forgiveness.

Autumn seemed to pass quickly as the excitement began to build, but Judas noticed that the only person who seemed unmoved as the great event drew near was Joseph himself. A month before the anticipated date of the birth, Joseph called his entire household together after the evening meal. Judas was also present because he had been working late that day. When everyone was assembled in the big reception room, Joseph stood up and spoke. "The time has come to tell you all what will happen over the next few weeks. Six of us will travel to Bethlehem. We will join the next caravan to Jerusalem and then continue on to Bethlehem which, as most of you know, is less than a day's journey from Jerusalem. Mary and I will be accompanied by Judas, his friend Reuben, Ruth and Deborah-"

Joseph was interrupted by a gasp of astonishment from the back of the room. "Well what's the matter Deborah?" he demanded impatiently.

A middle aged, portly woman answered, "Sir, Jerusalem is many days away, more than a hundred miles I dare say. You can't expect me to walk all that way."

Someone sniggered, "Jerusalem! She can barely walk to the toilet!"

"Enough of that!" reprimanded Joseph, trying not to smile. "Deborah, you have born many children and assisted at many more births yourself. I would not want anyone except you to attend Mary when her time comes. You will not need to walk because we will take five donkeys, one for each of the women and two to carry the baggage. You will ride Gebel; he is the largest."

"And the only one large enough to carry her," quipped the same joker as before to general laughter. Deborah drew herself up to her full height, what there was of it, and flattered by Joseph's compliments, announced grandly, "In that case sir, it will be my pleasure to accompany you on such an important journey. Ruth will assist me?"

"I would be honoured," answered Ruth without waiting for Joseph's approval.

"Well that's settled then," said Joseph, "and in my absence Ephraim my steward will be master of this household."

Ephraim, who was much the same shape as Deborah, smiled as his sense of self-importance was nurtured. He announced grandly, "Your household will be in safe hands, sir."

"I know. Tomorrow, when you oversee the packing, allow for a journey of about two months."

"It shall be so, sir."

Although the journey to Bethlehem was planned to be done in short, easy stages, it was mid-winter and the going would be hard. The caravan set out from Nazareth in a cold, unrelenting drizzle driven on the back of a stiff, northerly breeze. Joseph's party travelled with Reuben walking in front and himself and Judas at the back. They were all wrapped in heavy cloaks which kept them warm while they were moving and doubled as blankets at night. Towards the end of the third day, the wind freshened and it began to rain so heavily that the caravan master called an early halt amongst the half-ruined remains of Shekhem, which had once been a thriving town but was now largely deserted. As they prepared their evening meal in the shelter of a roofless building, Deborah approached Joseph.

"I don't like the look of your wife, sir; she is pale and shaking with cold. This journey is taking its toll. She should not be travelling in my opinion."

"Thank you, Deborah, but we must go on; there is a prophecy to be fulfilled."

"Mary is tough, but you are asking too much of her. If she is tired, so is the child inside her."

"I know, but we must stay with the caravan; it's not safe to travel alone in Samaria. I will ask the caravan master to slow the pace a little."

Deborah was not convinced. "I have had six children by three husbands and none of them understood what women go through to bear their children. You think your precious prophecy is more important than your wife's life. You're all the same!" And with that she waddled off to help Ruth prepare the evening meal.

Mary had overheard the conversation and came to put her arm round her husband. "Deborah means well, but I am strong and we are already half way to Bethlehem."

He kissed her on the cheek, "Thank you, Mary. I would not see any harm come to you. If you want anything you have only to ask."

The caravan reached Jerusalem three days later. Mary's condition had worsened so Joseph decided they would rest in the comfort of a city inn for two days before setting out on the final leg of the journey to Bethlehem. The rest seemed to improve Mary's condition considerably and everyone was in good spirits when they started out again. The journey was short and they expected to be at Joab's house well before nightfall. The road between Bethlehem and Jerusalem was always busy, so it was safe to travel without the protection of a caravan, but during the afternoon Mary started to feel nauseous. Suddenly, she fainted and began to slide off her donkey but Joseph, who was walking beside her, managed to catch her before she fell to the ground. He removed his cloak and laid her gently on it by the side of the road while the rest of the group gathered round.

Mary soon regained consciousness and whispered hoarsely, "I think it's coming."

Having given Joseph a look that could kill, Deborah said, "She's going into labour, sir. We must find shelter immediately."

"But she's not due for another month!"

"Nature will have her way, sir, especially if her patience is tested."

"But we can see the lights of Bethlehem less than a mile away. We can be in Joab's house in an hour or so."

Before Deborah could answer, Mary shouted, "For God's sake man! Do you want your baby born on the roadside! Do something! Now!" The blasphemy stunned Joseph into silence.

Deborah smiled grimly, "That confirms it. She's definitely in labour now. Don't be shocked sir. It is well known that even the most cultured women sometimes curse and swear at this time. It's nature's way of helping them cope."

And now, the quaint, portly woman took command. She was in her element. "Reuben, find shelter and firewood. It's freezing cold. Mary must be kept warm. Joseph, go with him and help; you're no use here. Judas, Ruth, help Mary back onto the donkey and be prepared to unpack enough blankets to make her a proper bed to lie on. Also unpack all our water and the cauldron; I'll need plenty of hot water and towels. Ruth, you will assist me at the birth."

Fortunately, a hamlet too small to have a name, lay only a short way ahead. The houses, eight in number, were all small but Joseph went to the largest and knocked on the door. It was opened by a short man made shorter still by being bent with age.

"Pardon our intrusion, sir," said Joseph. "We are travelling to Bethlehem but my wife, who was due to give birth there, has gone into labour early. We need shelter for the night."

The old man looked fearsome, but the tone in his voice suggested compassion. "Hardly surprising in this weather. Where is she?"

"About two hundred paces behind us."

"On her own?"

"No, there are six in our party and five donkeys."

The old man pondered for a moment. "My house only has two rooms, but I have a storehouse in the courtyard which could be made comfortable."

"In this weather, anything will do that has four walls and a roof. How much will you charge for it?"

"I will not take anything. Come." He led Joseph and Reuben to a building as large as his house which was half full of spare parts for ploughs, wagons and other agricultural implements, but at least it was weatherproof.

Joseph said, "You have been very kind already, but may I

trouble you for the hire of a spare bed, if you have one, for my wife to lie on?"

"I do have a spare bed which became available recently. You may use it for as long as you need."

"Thank you. May I ask your name?"

"Ezra."

"Very well, Ezra; now I will go back and bring up the others while Reuben here can start preparing your storehouse for us. He will also carry the bed to it."

"There is firewood at the back and you may stable your donkeys in the courtyard," said Ezra. "But don't let them eat the plants. You can take water from the village well which is just outside the front of my house."

In less than an hour, the travellers' prospects had changed from a freezing night at the roadside exposed to the elements, to a warm, dry shelter which easily accommodated all six of them. The storehouse measured about ten paces by five. There were no window apertures but, because it had been a stable at one time, it was possible to leave the upper half of the door partly open to release the smoke from the fire, which now burned in a brazier provided by their unlikely benefactor. Deborah and Ruth had divided the building into two roughly equal halves by erecting a screen of cloaks and blankets tied to a rope down the middle of the storehouse; one half for the men and the spare agricultural parts that Reuben had neatly stacked, the other for the women.

By now, Mary was well into labour. She was strong but Deborah predicted there would be many more hours yet before the baby was born because this was a first birth. The men made sure there was a plentiful supply of hot water and food, but there were long periods when they could do nothing except listen to the hushed voices of Deborah and Ruth interspersed with Mary's increasingly blasphemous cries. The night wore on, Mary's ordeal was getting worse; the men felt more and more useless.

Suddenly, Deborah shouted, "Push!" Mary screamed. Deborah shouted again, "Push! I can see the head. Push again!" A final piercing scream; then there was silence. Joseph was shaking. He got to his feet and called out, "Is she all right?" There was no response from the other side of the screen. "Please someone answer me," he pleaded.

"Quiet!" It was Ruth's voice. Then, like a shaft of sunlight suddenly appearing from black thunder clouds, the sound of a baby crying lit up their hearts.

"Mother and baby are fine," said Deborah. "Wait a few moments while we get them ready, then we'll come for you. Oh, and by the way Joseph, you have a son."

"Thank God," whispered Joseph.

"And the Messiah is with us," said Judas and, for no understandable reason the men shook hands with each other as if the triumph had been theirs.

A minute later, the screen was pulled back. Mary was sitting up in her bed with folded blankets supporting her back and holding a bawling bundle. Her hair had been combed and she was smiling a smile that would melt any man's heart. Deborah and Ruth, also beaming, stood either side of her like protective angels. It was a picture of complete happiness that engraved itself on Judas' memory forever.

"Joseph, come and hold your son," said the new mother.

As Joseph peeled back the soft, woollen wrap, Deborah commented, "He has brown hair. There must be northern blood somewhere in your ancestry."

"Hittite women were popular in King David's time," responded Judas knowledgably. "The Hittites provided mercenaries for David and Solomon. Most were blue eyed and some had fair hair; you can still detect their influence amongst our people, especially in the north." No-one noticed the brief glance of relief between Mary and Ruth.

There was a knock at the half open stable door. It was Ezra. He was wearing a crumpled nightgown and leaning on a stick. "Is everything all right? I heard a scream."

"Come in," said Joseph. "Mother and baby are well."

"And what you heard is quite normal in child birth," added Deborah.

Ezra smiled wistfully, "My wife and I were never blessed with children, so I have little knowledge of these things. Is it a boy or a girl?"

"A boy," answered Mary. "His name is Jesus."

"A good name," said the old man approvingly then, seeing Reuben on his knees he asked, "Why is this man kneeling?"

There was an awkward silence which was eventually broken by Joseph. "Well, Ezra, you might as well know that you have provided shelter for the birth of the true Messiah. Both Mary and I are of the line of David and this child is the true King of the Jews, the anointed one."

"Then I must kneel also," and slowly, stiffly and using his stick, Ezra lowered himself to his knees. In respectful silence, Joseph, Ruth, Judas and Deborah all followed suit.

The solemn moment did not last long. "Would someone help me up?" asked Ezra. "I seem to be stuck down here." Getting down was hard enough for his creaking joints, but getting up again was quite beyond him. Judas and Reuben raised him carefully to his feet and, when at last he was safely balanced again, he turned to Joseph. "There is of course already a King of the Jews, vile and cruel though he is. You will all be in danger when he finds out."

"We have protection enough from the Zealots, at least for the moment," replied Joseph. "But now the Messiah is here the Parthians will surely come to our aid and get rid of Herod and the Romans too."

Ezra was not convinced, "I wouldn't count on it. I remember the last time the Parthians came to save us; the Romans made short work of them and chased them away without much of a fight. And if they are coming, they had better come quickly. This sort of news will spread rapidly and soon reach unfriendly ears."

***

V

Ezra's words made sound sense. Shortly after dawn, Reuben was dispatched to Jerusalem to take the great tidings to Caspar. Just as he was leaving, Ruth surreptitiously thrust a small roll of parchment into his hands. "When you reach Jerusalem, go first to the Roman camp. Ask for Centurion Lucius Veranius and give him this message in person; no intermediaries." Reuben was not the questioning sort and accepted this addition to his mission without demur. But nor was he stupid and, as he left, he noticed a fresh grave just outside the village. He could read just enough to make out it was a woman's grave and he recalled Ezra's comment that the bed Mary was using 'had recently become available'.

Reuben was young and fit, and he reached the temple

before noon having already delivered Ruth's message to the Roman camp as instructed. Walking up the imposing outer stairway, he entered the temple through the Hulda Gates and stopped briefly to admire the beautiful columned portico which lined the outer wall of the Court of the Gentiles. This, the outermost court, was where most of the day to day business in the temple took place; here he would find Caspar. As the name suggests, the Court of the Gentiles was open to Jews and non-Jews alike. It was a hive of noise and activity, more like a market than a temple. Traders' stalls were everywhere but, unlike the main Jerusalem market, they were in no particular grouping or order. Reuben passed by sellers of food cooked ready to eat or uncooked to take home, cloth merchants stroking their goods as if they were all precious silks from lands far to the east, trinket stalls of metal objects mainly of copper or bronze but sometimes gilded with silver, and money lenders flanked by large, silent bodyguards. But by far the greatest number were the sellers of live animals for sacrifice. Depending on how much money you had, you could buy anything from a fine bullock or sheep down to a humble pigeon as long as the creature was unblemished. The temple took a cut from each sale and charged again for the sacrifice itself, which took place in one of the inner courts and could only be witnessed by Jews. Blood sacrifice to the Jewish God was the main purpose of the temple and one of its primary sources of income; the smell of burning flesh and ordure pervaded the entire temple complex, and though unnoticed by those working there on a daily basis, it was all too obvious to visitors.

At last, Reuben recognised Caspar sitting at a stall near the west wall between a money lender on his right and a booth on his left where one of the temple priests was accepting animals for sacrifice and payment for the prayers that would accompany them. Reuben waited while Caspar finished talking to a customer and watched him hand over a small scroll. When the customer departed Reuben introduced himself.

"I am Reuben, one of bar Abbas' men. I bring the news you are waiting for."

"I remember you," replied Caspar.

"The Messiah was born in the early hours of this morning just outside Bethlehem."

Caspar beamed, "At last, but keep your voice down. There are many here who will feel threatened by him. Did all go well?"

"Yes, though the Messiah was in a hurry to get here and arrived early. Thanks to a man named Ezra we were given shelter last night in a village a mile from Bethlehem where the child was born."

"Well I suppose that is near enough for the prophecy to have been met," mused Caspar. Neither man noticed that the priest in the next booth had stopped preparing a goat for sacrifice and was listening intently.

"Well," said Caspar. "I think the bureau for Babylonian affairs will shut early today. Help me pack up then come to my lodgings where we can eat and celebrate these momentous tidings. I have a few matters to finish off in the city so I will come to Bethlehem the day after tomorrow. Then, if all is well, I shall leave directly for Babylon."

"Pardon my interruption, but did you say the Messiah is born?" It was the priest from the adjacent booth. Reuben was flummoxed and said nothing but Caspar sensed danger.

"Why do you ask?"

"Because the Messiah is the rightful King of the Jews. He must be protected from the monster that calls itself Herod."

Reuben relaxed believing the priest was with them and, before Caspar could intervene, blurted out, "The prophecy is fulfilled; he is with us."

"Then let us thank God," said the priest. "Where exactly did you say he was born?"

"Enough!" snapped Caspar. "Who are you? Declare yourself!"

The priest looked at Caspar and smiled, "I am but a humble temple priest who would like to pay his respects to the Messiah. My name is Joseph Caiaphas."

Reuben set out for Bethlehem in the afternoon. Meanwhile, back at Ezra's storehouse Joseph was thinking about the return journey to Nazareth. Judas was out collecting firewood, so the planning was done with the women.

"How soon will you be ready to travel?" he asked Mary.

"I'm not sure. I feel comfortable but still very tired."

"Not for a week at least," interjected Deborah. "There are wounds that must heal before she rides a donkey. If we go too early, we could cause infection to set in."

"I understand," acknowledged Joseph. "I had better advise Ezra that we'll be here a bit longer."

Ruth said, "He won't mind, he's enjoying the company."

Mary added, "Despite his forbidding appearance, he is a gentle man."

"And recently widowed if I'm not mistaken," observed Deborah thoughtfully.

"How can you tell?" asked Joseph.

"There is a sadness about him. I have seen it before. Also, he frequently says 'we' in conversation, then checks himself and changes it to 'I'. It is typical of bereavement."

"We are indeed fortunate we found him," agreed Joseph. "If he has lost his wife, he must be devastated. Every man needs a woman if he is to live life to the full."

Ruth, who had been preparing the evening meal with Deborah and was acutely aware that her time with Mary was soon to end, could not keep the bitterness out of her voice. "Is that so? Then what are you doing about Judas? He is part of your household now and old enough to marry, yet he is still alone."

"He is learning the business but I do realise he will need a wife soon."

"Not so fast," said Deborah. "I think Judas may not be comfortable with women."

Joseph was shocked at the implication. "Are you suggesting he would prefer a man?"

"Women, especially older women like me, can sense these things."

"But it is against God's law."

"Man's law, I think you'll find. Where is it forbidden in the ten commandments?"

"But it is clearly stated in scripture."

"Written by men. Why would God create someone who cannot obey his own law?"

"Deborah, you are becoming blasphemous."

"Really? A typical male response when you have no answer."

Mary decided it was time to intervene, "Sometimes it is better to end a conversation before a discussion turns into an argument."

Ruth, who was still dwelling on the unwelcome change in

her life that would take place once they returned to Nazareth, was not ready to be silent. "As far as I can see, it is men's laws that govern our lives every bit as much as God's. Men decide when we come and where we go, what we wear, what we eat and when. Above all, men decide who we will marry."

"You are not obliged to marry Ehud," said Joseph, knowing full well what was troubling Ruth.

"What choice do I have?" But realising she could say no more in front of Deborah without raising awkward questions in the older woman's shrewd mind, she stifled her bitterness and sighed, "Perhaps choice is not always a good thing."

"Perhaps," agreed Joseph. "But Ehud will look after you. He has a good future in the business."

"And a temper if he's thwarted," sniffed Deborah.

Just as Mary was about to intervene again, Reuben returned with news that Caspar would soon be visiting. The flurry of plain speaking was ended but not forgotten.

About noon the next day, Ezra paid one of his increasingly frequent visits to his guests. "I was thinking of your journey back to Nazareth. It is a great distance for a mother and her new born baby, so I thought you might like to take my wagon. It is sturdy and has a cover so you will have shelter as you travel if needed."

"But Ezra, that is most kind," replied Joseph. "Are you sure you don't need it?"

"Certain. Take it as my gift to the Messiah. You will need two of your donkeys to pull it." Just as Ezra finished speaking, loud braying erupted from the courtyard outside.

"That's Gebel," said Ruth. "I wonder what's bothering him." Seconds later, two Roman soldiers burst into the store house. Reuben picked up his club and Judas felt for his sicarius.

"We come in peace," said the first, who wore the helmet of a centurion. "But you must leave now. Herod's soldiers are just a few minutes behind us!"

CHAPTER EIGHT

The summer and autumn of year twenty-five of Augustus Caesar's rule passed quietly in Jerusalem, but it was the calm before the storm. The city was alive with rumours about the imminent coming of the Messiah which, to us Romans, was a matter of supreme unimportance. Our indifference was, however, misplaced for Herod was sinking rapidly and no-one could predict what might happen when such a strong king finally met his maker, even though he had planned the succession carefully. On the morning of the winter solstice, the first inkling of trouble came from Piso, who had befriended Caius, Rufio and me as far as rank would permit since our escape from Nazareth.

It was now cold and we spent most of our time within the warmth of our wooden barracks. Word reached us that something was happening in the citadel because the Galatians were parading in full armour, so Piso left our camp and went to see Attalus to find out what was afoot. Since the Battle of Mukhmas, he had become a respected and popular figure amongst the Galatians and was able to enter Attalus' opulent quarters unchallenged.

"It seems like your men are preparing for a winter campaign," he said as he sat down opposite the Galatian commander, who was now a firm friend.

"Regrettably, that is true Licinius; we are being winkled

out of our warm nest to undertake a most unpleasant errand."

"Must you travel far?"

"Only as far as Bethlehem, but our orders are to kill all male babies in the city and the surrounding villages."

"But why?" gasped Piso.

"Word has reached Herod that, at last, the true Messiah has been born in Bethlehem. He has a better claim than Herod to the Jewish throne because he is a direct descendant of King David, the great Jewish hero."

"So why doesn't Herod just kill the Messiah?"

"Because he doesn't know exactly where to find him so, typically, he'll take no chances. All the male babies in Bethlehem must die."

"Why doesn't he get his own army to carry out this horrible deed?"

"He knows Jewish soldiers would never obey an order like that; he has never had much control over them at the best of times, which is why he employs us as his bodyguard. He has no authority over Roman troops so it comes down to us. There will be a terrible reaction when news of this leaks out."

"Why can't someone just get rid of him? He's half dead anyway."

"More than half I'd say," agreed Attalus. "But no-one has the nerve. If a plot like that failed, Herod's vengeance would be unimaginable."

"How do your men feel about it?"

"They are professional soldiers just like you Romans. They are sworn to Herod by a personal oath of loyalty; they will do their duty."

"When do you leave?"

"In about an hour. We should get to Bethlehem this afternoon and complete our task by nightfall. It would be unwise to stay there after what we're going to do, so we'll undertake a night march and get back here in the early hours."

Piso walked slowly back to our camp pondering on what he had just heard. He needed to talk to someone, so he went to the centurions' mess where we were planning guard duties for the day.

"What's the news from the citadel, sir?" asked Severus Pollio, our senior centurion. As Piso recounted his meeting with Attalus, I soon realised that Caius' baby was the target of all this activity because we had just received Ruth's secret letter the previous morning telling us about the birth. How Herod found out so quickly was baffling. I could only conclude at the time that his spies were everywhere, so as soon as Piso finished I asked, "Sir, when do the Galatians depart?"

"They are leaving as we speak."

"Then may I have permission to talk to you alone?"

"Of course. I was about to inspect the sentry posts anyway so walk with me."

A depressing drizzle had set in so we wrapped ourselves in our red cloaks and began to walk. I had to choose my words carefully to maintain the secrecy about the Messiah's true parentage. "Sir, I must ask you for indefinite leave and for Caius also. I estimate we will be away for only a few days."

"Go on Lucius, you are clearly troubled."

"Caius has a new born son by a woman in Bethlehem. The child will get caught up in this messiah business; we must rescue him."

"Certainly, you must and his mother too. There will be a bloodbath in Bethlehem today because the parents of the male children will not meekly hand over their sons to be killed."

"May we take two horses so we can overtake the Galatians?"

"Yes. Has Caius fully recovered from his leg injury? I heard he returned to the cohort only a little while ago."

"He is recovered as far as he will ever be. He will always have a slight limp but it is barely noticeable and does not impair him as a legionary."

"Very well, but Lucius, when you get to Bethlehem have you considered what you will do?"

"Not yet, sir."

"Well you cannot return this way without walking straight into the Galatians so you will have to head south." Piso paused in thought for a moment. "I have an idea. There is a cohort of auxiliary cavalry stationed at Hebron, about two days' march south of here. They are Germans, excellent soldiers. I will write a note to their commanding officer requiring him to give you shelter and protection."

"Thank you sir, you have been most helpful."

"It is my duty to be so, Lucius. And do not hurry to return to Jerusalem for there is likely to be a violent reaction to the massacre in Bethlehem. Make sure the woman and child are safe before you come back; we can manage without you both if necessary."

"Yes sir."

"Finally, Lucius, my only order to you is to avoid conflict with the Galatians. They are our only friends here, so if things do not go well in Bethlehem you must walk away. Is that clear?"

"Yes sir," but we both knew that if pressed, it was an order I could not obey.

As we trotted our horses past the grim-faced Galatians, Caius asked, "Lucius, do you know where we are going?"

"Bethlehem."

"Yes, but where in Bethlehem?"

"I don't know. When we get there, we'll ask. Ruth's letter did not mention the exact location."

"How big is Bethlehem?"

"Don't know that either; never been there."

"Well thank the gods we have Piso as our tribune. He's a gentleman, but he's a soldier's soldier too."

"And a true friend to us both," I added, as we at last reached the head of the Galatian column. Now we could travel at a steady canter and reach Bethlehem an hour before Attalus' men. It was not much of a breathing space and hardly enough time to track down Mary and her new son and then get them clear of the impending slaughter.

Just after midday, we saw of the City of David about a mile and a half ahead of us. The drizzle had lifted to be replaced by a chilly breeze, but at least the sun had reappeared as the lowering clouds began to break up.

"Bethlehem looks rather a big place," said Caius as we slowed our horses to a walk to pick our way through a small village.

"Certainly, bigger than I expected," I replied mournfully. "When we get there, we'd best split up; you start at this end while I'll ride to the far end and work back towards you. We'll meet somewhere in the middle. The trouble is that neither of us speaks Aramaic, but at least—" I was interrupted by the loudest donkey braying I ever heard.

Caius looked round, "What in Apollo's name is that!"

"If I'm not mistaken, it's Gebel."

We quickly dismounted and entered a small courtyard where Gebel was tethered with a few other donkeys. Although time was short, I felt obliged to give him his regulation ear stroke greeting as we passed before entering the large outhouse at the far end of the courtyard. The scene that met us was not what I expected. Instead of a mother, father and servant, there were four men and three women. The two younger men immediately grabbed their weapons, which was understandable; even Joseph did not recognise us at first for we were wearing helmets. I quickly expressed our peaceful intentions and we took off our helmets as a gesture of friendship and to be recognised. Mary and Ruth already knew who we were, but when Joseph saw Caius he frowned. "Why have you come here?"

"There was no choice," answered Caius. "Herod has found out about the Messiah. He is sending men to kill all the male babies in Bethlehem."

"Surely even he would not do such a thing?"

I answered, "He would and he is. There is no time for debate. His Galatians are only minutes behind us. You cannot take the Jerusalem road, but there is refuge in the south at Hebron."

The oldest man present walked to the door. "I will prepare the wagon while you all get ready for the journey. It will be ready when you are."

Packing up, removing evidence of the child birth and loading the wagon as the old man called it — to me it looked like a simple cart — seemed to take an age. Caius and I mounted our horses while the family and companions said their goodbyes to the old man.

Caius pointed back up the Jerusalem road. "Hurry, the

Galatians are almost here." The drizzle had dampened the road so there was no dust cloud to give early warning of their approach. I turned to Joseph, "You must go now or all will be lost. The Galatians will not spare you because we are here."

The wagon rattled out of the courtyard carrying Mary, the baby and a round matronly woman called Deborah; Joseph was driving. Ruth rode Gebel and the two younger men trotted behind her. Caius rode with me at the rear but just as I was leaving, the old man grabbed my bridle and stopped me. He seemed to see into my soul, "Why are you doing this?"

I could not lie to him, "For the child and his mother."

"Is that all?"

"It is enough," and pulling my bridle out of his grip I galloped after Caius.

The old man called after me, "I will offer the Galatians refreshment. That will delay them a few minutes. God go with you!"

For a while, no-one spoke as we hurried along the Bethlehem road. Despite Joseph's urging, the donkeys moved at little more than a walking pace. Caius and I were still in the rear; we kept nervously looking back but, by the time we reached a bend in the road and lost sight of the village, the Galatians had not appeared; the old man's ruse must have worked.

We trotted up beside Joseph, "It looks as though the old man has saved us. What's his name?" I asked.

"Ezra."

"Then may his god reward him for what he has done. When we reach Bethlehem, do not stop for anything and pray for the souls of your people who are soon to die. There is nothing we can do to prevent what is about to happen." I turned my horse to return to the rear. Caius did the same but not without a fleeting touch of Mary's hand. The touch was reciprocated but Joseph did not see it. So despite everything, passion had not waned between them.

As we left Bethlehem behind, I thought I could hear the first screams of the massacre drift towards us on the chill breeze. It had been a near thing.

***

II

In the afternoon of the second day of our journey, we approached Hebron. It had been an odd two days. The two young Jewish men spoke only Aramaic which neither Caius nor I could understand. I would have liked to talk to Ruth but Joseph guarded his womenfolk like a mother hen, which under the circumstances was hardly surprising, so the opportunity did not arise. While grateful for our intervention, he made it clear that the sooner he was rid of us the better.

Hebron is an ancient city and is supposedly where Abraham, the ancestor of all the Jews, is buried together with his family. It is colder than Bethlehem because of its greater altitude, and by the time we reached it, the cloudy wet weather of Bethlehem had been replaced by a cold, blue, winter sky. But it was good to see the sun again, which raised our spirits a little, for we were all downhearted by the slaughter of the innocents that had bloodied the city of David. I think we carried a feeling of guilt for doing nothing to help Bethlehem's unfortunate citizens.

The German camp lay on the south side of Hebron. We could smell it before we could see it because just as Rufio believed Greek was an effeminate language and refused to speak it, so Germans believed that bathing was only for soft city dwellers and wore the same clothes on their unwashed bodies until they fell off. Their camp consisted of a cluster of tents on both sides of the road to Beersheba, but most space was taken up by a large fenced paddock on the east side of the road where their big, well-groomed horses were penned.

Caius, who knew more about horses than I, purred with admiration, "They are beautiful, look how their coats glisten in the sun."

I looked at two soldiers leaning on the paddock fence. "It's a pity the Germans don't take as much care of themselves as they do their horses."

"They are a scruffy lot," laughed Caius. "But I'm glad they're on our side."

There was a tent, larger than the rest, in the centre of the group on the west side of the road so we headed for it, threading our way through scores of tents pitched in no particular order or pattern; Severus Pollio, who was our camp commander as well as senior centurion, would have turned red with fury if he could have seen such a shambles. The Germans seemed uninterested in us and got on with their camp chores without even challenging us though, to be fair to them, Caius and I were obviously Romans and allies. They were tall, fine looking men, mostly clean shaven though some sported long moustaches, but the most obvious difference to us, apart from their woollen trousers, was the remarkable range in the colour of their hair which they wore long almost to the shoulder. Some had hair like Caius, the colour of ripe wheat, others pitch black like a typical Roman, but there were also all shades between including red, brown and ginger. Some tied their hair in a knot at the side of the head, which was released when they wore their lightweight version of the legionary helmet. Those on guard duty wore only a light mail vest; in fact, their protective body armour seemed hardly adequate but, on the other hand, their huge broadswords suggested that attack rather than defence was their primary interest.

We halted outside the large tent and Caius and I dismounted. Joseph parked the wagon behind us and we waited. No-one came out so, after a few minutes, I walked over to the half open tent flap and called, "Is there anyone there?"

Inside, the silence was broken by a mixture of shufflings, grumblings and what I took to be German curses. At last, a man emerged rubbing his eyes like a mole caught in sunlight. He was extraordinary. Of middle age and medium height, he had the reddest hair and whiskers I ever saw. Beneath the whiskers, a scar was just visible which crossed his lips in a diagonal line; clearly an old war wound. His build was, to be charitable, portly but his hands were huge; both of mine would easily have disappeared into one of his great bear paws. When his eyes eventually focused, for he had been drinking, he beamed a wide smile made even more remarkable because, apart from one useless upper front incisor, his mouth was toothless.

"Ah, Roman, velcome! I Friedrich von Vechten, commander der Batavian cohort. At your service. Und sie?"

"Lucius Veranius, centurion of the Third Gallica legion stationed in Jerusalem."

"Ah gut, gut. Beg pardon, but ve sleeping after midday meal mit plenty vine." It would have been churlish to point out that midday had passed over four hours ago, so I handed him Piso's letter addressed to the cohort commander. "It is from the supreme commander of the Roman forces in Jerusalem." Piso would have laughed at my inflated description of his rank, but technically a cohort commander of auxiliary troops and a legionary cohort commander were of equal status and I did not want this German disputing Piso's seniority. Friedrich slowly opened the scroll and looked at the writing. It might just as well have been written in ancient Babylonian because it was obvious, he did not understand a word of it.

"Vat do dis zay?" I began to explain slowly but the German was clearly struggling to follow me. Eventually, he put one of his huge hands on my shoulder and smiled his toothless but charming smile again, "Halt! I have man here who vill speak und hear for me." Then turning back to the tent flap, he bawled in a voice any centurion would be proud of, "Hermann! Kommen sie hier bitter!"

A moment later, another even more remarkable man appeared. Man was perhaps not the right word for though immensely tall, even Caius had to look up to him, he could not have been more than sixteen or seventeen years old. He was the antithesis of his commander, elegant, clean shaven and, unlike every other German we had seen, he was dressed in Roman fashion. He looked like a fish out of water except for his golden hair which hung down to his shoulders in the same style as his comrades. It would not have been difficult to believe he was a god come down from Mount Olympus.

"Dis Hermann vill speak," said Friedrich.

And now came another surprise for this god-like creature spoke in classic, unaccented, Ciceronian Latin. "Good afternoon, my Latin name is Arminius. Give me a moment while I read this letter to my commander." It seemed strange to hear him speak in his own guttural language as he translated Piso's letter to Friedrich. Whether it was his upbringing or just his good looks that were the cause I cannot say, but he was extremely confident for one so young, too confident, for when he had finished speaking to Friedrich he did not wait for a response but addressed me again without bothering to ask my name. "Have you read this letter?"

"No, it was sealed when I handed it to your commander," I answered.

"Your cohort commander requires us to provide protection for your companions, which we will do, even though he does not have the rank to give my commander orders. He says there is trouble in Bethlehem."

By now, I had decided this handsome youth was also an arrogant prig but, with difficulty, I remained polite. "Herod is having one of his periodic massacres, but this time he has gone too far. He has chosen all the male babies in the city as his victims."

Arminius' sky-blue eyes flickered onto the bundle that Mary was carrying. "You should know that we have orders direct from Antioch to move to Egypt; Alexandria to be exact. The Greeks and Jews are at each other's throats again but our Egyptian based legions are far to the south patrolling the Nubian frontier. We are the nearest so now we must be the ones to stamp out the rioting in the city, which we will." I did not doubt that. I also observed he was completely unmoved by the plight of the babies in Bethlehem. "Your friends will have to accompany us; we will be leaving tomorrow."

I said, "I must consult with my companions."

"Very well. Call me when you have finished your consulting." With that he disappeared into the tent.

I looked at Friedrich who was shaking his head, "Ah die jungen dese days; very proud."

I asked, "What is his rank?"

"Err… adj, adjten…"

"Adjutant?"

"Jah, adjutant but I not choose. Ve all from Batavian tribe; good people, but he Cheruscan." Then, with the international gesture of contempt, he spat on the ground. "Hermann coming to Rome as child hostage ven General Drusus defeat Cheruscan tribe eight years ago. Now he more Roman dan German, but ve Batavians are friends to Romans here," he pointed to his heart. "But Cheruscans I nicht verstehen. Maybe friends to Romans here," he pointed to his head. "But nicht here I tink," he pointed to his heart again.

"Well that seems clear enough," murmured Caius, who was standing behind me.

"Ve eat and drink again in two hours. You join us jah?"

"It will be an honour, Friedrich," I replied with some foreboding; a headache next morning beckoned.

We found a small area of unoccupied ground near the large tent and settled down to camp for the night. One of the Germans, without being asked, came over and prepared a fire for us while we put up the cover on Ezra's wagon to shelter the women. When all was ready, we sat round the fire while I recounted my conversation with the Germans, at the end of which Joseph said, "I am not happy about going to Egypt. I have arranged things in Nazareth so that we can be away for two months, no more."

"I understand," I replied. "But you cannot go back yet. While Herod lives, nowhere in his kingdom will be safe for you. It will not be long because he is very near death."

"People have been saying that for years yet he is still here."

"True, but you must go with the Germans or risk everything. Look how quickly he found out about your child."

"Of course you are right," agreed Joseph. "I will plan for an extended absence from Nazareth." He then spoke in Aramaic to the two young men who I had no doubt were Zealots. A heated discussion followed between Joseph and the one called Judas, but at last agreement seemed to be reached. While all this was happening, Caius and Mary kept gazing at each other so much that I had to give him a surreptitious kick to bring him back to his senses.

Eventually, the Aramaic conversation came to an end and Joseph announced in Greek, the language most of us could understand, "Our course is decided. Reuben and Ruth will accompany Mary, Jesus and myself to Alexandria. Judas will escort Deborah back to Nazareth where he will take full charge of my business affairs until we return. I will send a letter to Ephraim with them advising him of the change of plan. As for you two Romans, you must do as you please."

I felt a bit hurt at the way we had been summarily dismissed, but I did not let it show. "Caius and I will accompany you to the Egyptian border. Once we are sure you are safe, we will return to our quarters in Jerusalem. Meanwhile, please tell your Zealot companions that, as far as we are concerned, there is a truce between us until you enter Egypt. After that they will be our enemy again, but we will not raise our hand against them before then."

***

III

Even though I had been careful not to drink too much with Friedrich, I could not get to sleep that night. Partly, it was the fault of the Germans in the tent nearest to Caius and me. There seemed to be a contest going on whereby whoever could break wind the loudest would be the winner. Actually, it was not the increasingly loud anal explosions that kept me awake, but the hoots of guttural laughter that greeted each one. Even so I reflected, as I tried to sleep through the noise, and mercifully I was not sharing their tent; there was an engaging simplicity about these people which was difficult to resist. I had already seen what an educated German could be like in the form of Arminius, but much preferred the unspoilt, if crude, version in the next-door tent.

It must have been about midnight when I gave up trying to sleep. Something was troubling me deep in my soul as if I should have said or done something, but I could not work out what it was. Caius was in a deep sleep, so I decided to leave our little campaign tent and have a walk around the camp. There was no moon, but the night sky was awash with stars that shimmered in the chill night air. As I pulled my cloak tightly around me, I noticed a figure wrapped in a blanket hunched next to our fire.

"Joseph, is that you?"

The figure looked up, "Can't you sleep either, Centurion?"

"For heaven's sake, call me Lucius. I am not your enemy."

"Then Lucius, come and warm yourself by the fire." Joseph prodded the fire with a stick and a few reluctant sparks soared upwards and disappeared into the night sky. "Are you alone?"

"Yes," I answered.

"Good, I have been meaning to speak with you before we go our separate ways."

I sat down beside him; my walk would have to wait. For a while, Joseph was silent, as if he was thinking about how best to explain what was on his mind. Eventually, he gave the fire another firm poke, took a deep breath and said, "I owe you an apology."

"How so?"

"You and Caius have undoubtedly saved the lives of my family and friends at no small risk to yourselves, yet I have barely thanked you."

"That is understandable given what happened in Nazareth."

"That was not your fault, Lucius; yet I have blamed you in my heart as much as Caius. As far as Caius is concerned, I am trying my best to hate him, but he is a difficult man to hate."

"Everybody likes Caius; he just has that effect on people."

"I know only too well," agreed Joseph bitterly. "Now I must live the lie about the Messiah because of my love for Mary." I wished I had chosen my words better. "There were three hostages in Nazareth," he continued. "Does the third know the secret? Why did he not come to Bethlehem with you?"

"I could not bring Rufio for two reasons. Firstly, he knows nothing about Mary's baby so to bring him would have raised questions in his mind. Secondly, when the crisis came, he was indulging himself in the flesh pots of Jerusalem so I couldn't have found him anyway. Have your companions been asking questions about us?"

"One of them has?"

"The one named Judas?"

"Yes."

"And your answer?"

"I simply said the Romans were paying off a debt of

honour, which is true to a certain extent, and refused any further questions from him."

"That was a good answer, Joseph. I shall make sure Caius and I say the same if the occasion arises. Does Judas know that we were two of the three hostages?"

"No, and he never will. As long as he has no reason to link you to that, our secret will remain safe. You will understand that the last few months have been hard for me. I have to pretend to be happy yet I know my wife still loves Caius. I am not blind. I see the way they look at each other though they try to conceal it. I can and do accept the baby but it's the ongoing love that's so difficult to stomach."

"The only comfort I can give is that after we reach Egypt you will never see either of us again. It is said that time is a great healer. I am too young to know, but I am certain Mary will come to love you. You will have your own children together which will forge a strong bond between you. Remember also, your children will not be burdened by being the Messiah."

"That is an astute observation Lucius and something I have already thought much about. I cannot help wondering what will happen to Jesus; he will certainly be at the centre of world changing events which he won't be able to control."

"And neither can you so there's no point in fretting about it. I suppose the first thing you must consider, after his personal safety, will be his education, but how do you educate a Messiah?"

For the first time since we left Bethlehem, I saw Joseph smile. "Lucius, you have a way of getting straight to the point. There is no precedent for teaching a Messiah but we have done our best. There is a highly intelligent, well trained temple servant who has been allocated to guide Jesus through his early years."

"Judas again?"

"Yes. He has been through the rigorous training of a temple priest though he could not actually become a priest because he is not of the Levite tribe. He has knowledge of philosophy, law and the Torah and is fluent in many languages."

"Including Greek?"

"Yes."

"So he understood all my conversations with you without my knowledge?"

"And your conversations with Caius too because he also speaks Latin. I am embarrassed by that now, but we had no idea how things would work out so I thought it best not to reveal Judas' skills."

"It was risky because Caius and I might have said things you would not want Judas to hear."

"About Mary and Jesus, you mean? Yes, it was a risk, but only a small one. I am sorry."

"There is no need to be. I cannot be angry because Caius and I have just done the same thing."

"In what way?"

"You heard our discussion with Friedrich which required young Arminius to translate into Latin?"

"Yes, but I could not understand what was said."

"The point is that Caius is a fluent German speaker; his father is German and, just like Arminius, he came to Rome as a boy hostage. But there the similarity ends for he became a Roman citizen and joined the legions; I cannot see Arminius doing that."

"Then why did he not assist Friedrich when he was struggling to speak with you?"

"He would have done if Arminius had not been present but, just like you, we were cautious."

"Well Lucius, it seems we are not so different."

"When we spoke earlier about you going to Egypt, you seemed to have an argument with Judas?"

"He wanted to come too because of his commitment to Jesus, but in the end, he understood his true value would be in running my construction business while I'm away. Accountancy is another one of his skills and there is not much you can teach a tiny baby yet, even a Messiah."

"It seems you are most fortunate in having this Judas with you."

"Yes, though," Joseph hesitated. "Well, there is something about him I cannot quite understand. He is deep. I could not have a relaxed conversation with him like we are now having. I feel that all my words are not only being heard but evaluated, so I find myself being careful about what I say. Affection is not easy for him to cope with so we remain the best of acquaintances without being true friends. Yet despite that I trust him utterly."

"A complicated man indeed."

"And dedicated to the Zealot cause. He led the execution party that arrived at my home only hours after your escape. I am grateful now that you avoided the fate the Zealots had planned for you even if it did require help from within my household."

That last comment was really a question. I chose to ignore it. "So Judas is ruthless too?"

"You have to be if you wish to be a Zealot. That is why I

am not one though I agree with their aims and support their cause."

"How will you manage in Alexandria?"

"We Jews are heavily inter-related. I have an uncle who owns a flourishing cloth business in the city. I just hope he has not got caught up in the rioting that Arminius spoke about. He will give us shelter until it is safe to return to Nazareth."

"And what will happen to Ruth when you return?"

Joseph looked at me quizzically, "You are interested in her?"

I suddenly understood why I had not been able to sleep that night. I was indeed interested in her but had not done anything about it. "Well, yes," I answered. "But I have not said so."

"That is just as well because she is betrothed to one of my managers. He has a bright future in the business and will be able to look after her well."

So, I thought, she must have accepted Ehud after all. Trying to hide my disappointment, I said, "Well I hope he can cope with her; she is highly spirited."

"Wild is how I would describe her. She has not been a good influence on Mary and could have prevented what happened with Caius. I cannot forgive her for that."

"But then there would have been no Messiah."

"Certainly, there would in due course, and a Messiah with the correct parentage, not half Roman."

"Quarter Roman. Caius' mother was a Jew."

"Do not split hairs with me Lucius Veranius, it is unbecoming in a centurion." The reprimand was not too serious for, despite being on opposing sides, we were in danger of becoming friends. "And it is only because of Mary's insistence, that Ruth is accompanying us to Egypt, otherwise I would have taken Deborah instead."

My night time conversation with Joseph had cleared my mind and the noisy Germans had fallen asleep. I decided to abandon my walk and return to my tent. "I feel ready for sleep now so I'll bid you goodnight. I suggest you do the same; there is a long journey ahead tomorrow."

"I will shortly," replied Joseph. "But I think I'll stay here a few moments longer." He poked the fire again and more orange sparks flew up into the night sky. He still had plenty to think about.

***

IV

We reached the Egyptian frontier and the limit of Herod's kingdom three days later. Judas, Deborah and Gebel had already begun their return journey from Hebron, so it was just Caius and I who bade farewell to Joseph's party and the Germans at the border city of Gaza. At last we could give our horses their heads and cantered along the well-maintained coast road with the wind in our hair. It was good to leave the slow-moving cart behind and by the time we reached Jerusalem the following evening I had, in the true tradition of a legionary, forgotten about Ruth; or so I thought.

For more than two months, Herod clung to life desperately, perhaps he feared what the Fates had in store for him, but the old scorpion still had a sting in his tail. Nor had the anger caused by the slaughter in Bethlehem diminished; a heavy sense of foreboding was in the air.

It was the fifteenth day of March, the Ides, a date made notorious in our history by the assassination of the greatest citizen Rome ever produced, Julius Caesar. Just after breakfast, Piso summoned all the centurions to his office. "Gentlemen, we have been asked to witness an execution up in the citadel, so I have volunteered you to accompany me." To the groans this received, he responded, "I am told that the victim is a person of high rank which is why independent witnesses are required. Cheer up, it will be a break from the routine of camp duty."

I trudged up to the citadel alongside Severus Pollio, our senior centurion. He was a skilled and intelligent soldier as well as a rigid disciplinarian. "This is strange Lucius," he said. "Herod is on his deathbed."

"What, again!"

Severus smiled, "This time it really is true. Word is he'll be dead by tomorrow or the day after at the latest, yet he still finds time to order an execution. He must hate the condemned man. I wonder who he is."

"Ah well, we'll find out soon enough."

We entered the citadel through the heavily fortified gates, which was the only access through its lofty walls. The courtyard was lined with stern Galatians who, since the killing of the babies in Bethlehem, dared not venture outside the citadel in groups of less than twenty. We Romans were given seats on a raised platform outside Herod's palace, which was on the opposite side of the courtyard to the gates. Apparently, everyone had been waiting for us because as soon as we sat down proceedings commenced.

The main door to the palace opened and out walked two

parallel lines of white robed priests, six in each line, followed by the current high priest Joazar, dressed in his rich blue, ceremonial robes and tall, cylindrical, turban style hat. They walked slowly to the centre of the courtyard where an executioner's block had been placed. The high priest stood beside the block where he read out the charges against the accused from a scroll. His voice was rich and mellow. The language he used was Aramaic so none of us could understand except Severus, who was of Syrian parentage and knew enough to translate the essentials for me.

"Apollo's balls!" he whispered. "Herod's going to kill his son and heir, Antipater."

"Why?"

"It seems he's been plotting treason. Probably some truth in it, though; Herod's hung on far too long."

"Why are we needed as witnesses?"

"It's not so much for the execution, more for us to hear the declaration of Herod's new successor, another one of his many sons, Archelaus."

When Joazar had finished, he looked up to a small balcony on the top floor of the palace for approval. Although we could not see beyond the balustrade, there was no doubt that was from where the dying king was supervising the whole morbid event. Then, at a signal from the high priest, the palace doors opened again and a tall man of about thirty-five appeared. I had never seen Herod but from what I had heard, this man did not look at all like his father.

Bareheaded and dressed in a short brown robe gathered at the waist by a belt, he strode purposefully towards Joazar with dignity and apparent contempt for what was about to happen. He spoke quietly to the priest for a few seconds and received some kind of blessing. Then, turning to face the balcony, he made an exaggerated bow, which I am sure was sarcastic, knelt beside the block and placed his head on it ready for the executioner to strike.

Unlike our priests, Jewish priests are skilled with weapons because they carry out so many blood sacrifices. One of the priests stepped forward and unsheathed a broadsword which he had been carrying concealed in his robes. With no formality or ceremony, he struck off Anitpater's head with a single blow and returned to his place before the blood spurting from the neck could soil his white robe.

Two days later, Herod died at last. Then Hades opened its black gates and the Furies were let loose on Judea and Galilee.

CHAPTER NINE

As soon as Judas and Deborah reached Nazareth after the long journey from Hebron, Judas went straight to Joachim's house, which was near his own, to tell him that his daughter and grandson had escaped Herod's butchery in Bethlehem.

"My husband is still campaigning with bar Abbas in the south, somewhere near Jerusalem," said Anna, his wife. "We have all heard of the dreadful deeds that took place in Bethlehem but I am so grateful to you, Judas, for bringing the glad tidings of our family."

"I must inform your husband and bar Abbas as soon as possible. Do you know when Joachim will return?"

"His last message said about the middle of Shevat (late January)."

"Then as soon as things are in order in Joseph's house, I will go to him."

"Do you know where to find him?"

"He'll be at the winter camp."

"Then I shall write to him if you would take the letter with you."

"Of course I will, Anna. I will collect it in two days' time."

Joseph underestimated how much opposition Judas would face when he and Deborah returned to Nazareth. There had always been underlying resentment, especially from the steward Ephraim, at the speed with which the newcomer had been promoted to the position of business manager. Although totally incapable of handling that role himself, Ephraim nonetheless thought it should have been his by right, and had collected together a few sycophantic supporters from within Joseph's household to make life difficult for Judas. While Joseph was present, this confined itself to small things such as forgetting to prepare Judas' noon meal or replenishing his writing quills, none of which troubled him in the least, but when he returned from Hebron without the master of the house things changed.

Judas still lived in his own house in the lower town, which was his little sanctuary free from the poisonous atmosphere generated by Ephraim; however, two days after his return, matters came to a head when he arrived for work and found Ephraim in Joseph's office thumbing through some of his master's business scrolls.

"Ephraim! What are you doing here? Even I do not sit at Joseph's desk." The steward did not trouble to look up from the scroll he was reading. "I am checking the master's accounts are in proper order and, from what I have seen so far, they are not."

The slur on his professional integrity was too much and before Ephraim could react, Judas leaned over the desk and snatched the scroll from the steward's fleshy hand. Ephraim stood up, eyes dark with anger. "How dare you! I will have you expelled from this household."

"I think not. Did you not read the master's letter? I am appointed the manager of his business until he returns."

"But nothing was written about excluding his steward from decision making and overseeing. I am the master's substitute in his absence; therefore, you must report all business matters to me."

"That was not his intention as you well know."

"How can I know? I was not present when he made this decision."

"Indeed, you were not so let us ask someone who was and who has no reason to favour either of us. I will summon Deborah."

Now Judas saw uncertainty in the steward's face. "Well, I err... I don't think that will be necessary."

"Clearly it is. I will fetch her." Ephraim drew breath to object, but by then Judas had already left the room in search of Deborah.

A few minutes later, he returned accompanied by a flushed and panting Deborah. She did not like visiting the master's office at any time because it meant climbing stairs, still less did she want to witness two men squabbling. Ephraim, who had recovered his composure, was seated at Joseph's desk once more and spoke first. "Deborah, we have asked you here to verify a misunderstanding Judas has about the letter sent to me by the master."

Deborah could not hide her irritation, "I can neither read nor write so how do you expect me to help?"

"Were you present when the master handed this letter to Judas?"

"Yes."

"Good. Now Judas seems to think he is permitted to manage our master's business affairs without discussing them with me or involving me in the process of decision making. Obviously, Joseph would want me, his steward, to be aware of what Judas is doing just as I am involved in all other matters that affect the household. I need you to confirm that was his intention so that Judas can know his true place here. Think carefully before you answer. Unlike Judas you live here; this is your home and I am sure you do not want to put that at risk." That last sentence was a bad miscalculation on Ephraim's part. The implied threat had the opposite reaction he was hoping for. Deborah's already flushed face now reddened even more but this time not from stair climbing. "Ephraim, you may be steward here but you have no right to threaten me. Only the master may dismiss someone as senior as me, so I shall ignore what you said and speak only the truth as always." Judas relaxed. On the long sojourn to Bethlehem and back, he had learned that Deborah was not to be trifled with, so now he quietly anticipated Ephraim's imminent discomfiture.

"When we were in Hebron," began Deborah. "The master realised he would have to go to Egypt with his family to avoid Herod's murderous soldiers so, in front of us all, he appointed Judas in sole charge of his construction business. He said he had absolute faith in him and gave him the authority to act as if he were Joseph himself. There was no quibbling about referring to you or anyone else for that matter, and if you try to obstruct Judas from carrying out his work it will be the worse for you when our master returns."

Even Judas did not remember it quite as favourably as that, but Ephraim had heard enough. He ponderously got to his feet and announced, "Well, if that was what the master said then so be it." Then, with as much dignity as he could muster, he stalked out of the office and went downstairs.

"Deborah, I hope I have not got you into trouble," said Judas.

Deborah shut the office door so they could not be overheard. "Ephraim is just a pompous old fool, but there's no real harm in him; he hasn't the backbone for it. He'll be his old self tomorrow, full of hot air as usual just as if nothing has happened."

"Why does Joseph employ him?"

"He was married to Joseph's sister."

"Was?"

"Yes, a lovely lady but she died in childbirth. It would have been her first one."

"So Ephraim is without wife and children?"

"Sadly, yes. This is why this household is so important to him. He has nothing else."

"I understand better now. Thank you, Deborah for being so supportive to me in these difficult circumstances. I feel less of an outsider now."

On the journey back from Hebron, the robust matron had become fond of Judas in a motherly sort of way. She could sense the sadness in him which was not of his own making. "Judas, I believe Joseph is fortunate to have you in his service but even so, you may have to become accustomed to being an outsider."

"I feel you're right, though I don't really understand why."

"You will soon enough."

Judas was uncomfortable with too much familiarity and drew the discussion to a close. "Be that as it may, there is work to be done and I need help. Would you send Ehud to me please?"

"I will, but he is in Sepphoris today and will not be back until this evening."

"Very well, I shall stay here until his return."

"And I will send something up for you to eat while you

wait."

When Deborah had gone, Judas picked up the scroll Ephraim had been reading. It was the contract for the work on Herod's weapons store. He could not imagine what interest it might have for the steward so he rolled it up and locked it away.

The man who arrived at Joseph's study that evening was short and stocky, but his sinewy arms and weather-beaten face implied that hard outdoor work had given him fitness and strength before he left the tools of the trade to become a junior manager. Judas knew Ehud was twenty-six- years-old, but he looked nearer forty.

"Ehud, welcome," he said pointing to a chair. "Please sit down."

"Thank you, sir."

Recalling how Joseph had put him at his ease, Judas said, "Ehud, we are going to be working together for long hours to make sure this business is in good health when our master returns, so please call me Judas."

"I prefer 'sir', if you don't mind, sir."

So much for that then thought Judas. "As you wish. I have worked here for some while, yet this is the first time we have met."

"Yes sir."

Talking to this man was not easy but Judas persevered. "How is it we have not seen each other before?"

"I spend most of my time at the contract sites in Sepphoris, but my home is in Nazareth in the lower town where my mother and father still live."

"Well that explains it then. You are also Ruth's betrothed I understand; a fine woman."

"Maybe so sir but she needs discipline."

"And you are the man to give her that?"

"I am, sir. It will be my duty as her husband."

Judas kept his thoughts to himself, but Ehud and Ruth sounded like an unstable blend. He dispensed with preliminary chatter and spoke of the business. "As you know, we have two contracts going at present, one as a main contractor building the weapons store, the other as a subcontractor working on the gymnasium. The weapons store is almost finished I believe?"

"Yes sir. We have about three weeks' work left fitting out the guards' barracks, then we are finished."

"And the gymnasium?"

"Not long started sir. I estimate we have at least six months' work there but we are dependent on other subcontractors finishing the preliminary works first."

"Good, so we need to find work soon to replace the weapons store contract or we will have men on the payroll with nothing to do."

"That often happens in construction work."

"Of course, but we must do our bit to limit it. Now, I believe there is a new government contract coming out for the public baths. Our lawyer in Sepphoris has sent me the specifications so I would like you to prepare the costings." Judas took out a scroll from his desk and opened it up for Ehud to examine. The undermanager scrutinised the document for a while then sighed, "This is a large job, too large for us perhaps. We would be the main contractor I suppose?"

"Yes."

"It is always easier to be a subcontractor, less complex and without the headache of negotiating, direct with Herod's people."

This irritated Judas because negotiating and agreeing contracts was not Ehud's job. He found himself on the verge of telling Ehud where the limits of his responsibility lay, but checked himself in order to foster the new relationship he was trying to forge. He patiently began to explain. "The disadvantage of being a subcontractor is that you are the last in line when the cash starts to flow. The client pays the main contractor who invariably finds reasons not to pay his subcontractors on time. But the subcontractor must still pay his workers and suppliers or he will find himself without men and materials to carry out the contract. So to pay them, he must borrow and ends up paying interest on money that he is himself owed. Many a profitable subcontract business has gone bankrupt because of late payments."

"But that's not fair."

"It's business and I'm afraid there's no law against it. Now who will be our main competitors for the public baths contract?"

Ehud scratched his head. "Well, there'll be the bar Micah brothers here in Nazareth; they have a similar size of business to us, and there's the Amos business in Sepphoris itself. The rest are too small or unreliable for a contract like this."

"All right then. Tomorrow I shall be leaving on a business trip to Jerusalem, but I shall be back within seven days. While I'm away I would like you to do two things. First, prepare the costings for this contract; it's quite complex so how long will it take you?"

"Three or four days I should think."

"Good, that leaves enough time for your second task. Visit the sites that Amos and the bar Micah businesses are working on, and estimate how close they are to completion. Do not reveal what you are doing, just look in from the outside."

"Why?"

"So we can assess how hard they will try to win the public baths contract, or whether they will even bid at all. If they already have plenty of work to keep them going for another six months or more, we may be the only serious bidder."

"How does that help?"

"It means we can bid at a higher price and make more profit."

Ehud scratched his head again. "When the master was here, we never used to bother with all this."

This time, Judas could not help letting his annoyance show. "Well you should have, which is exactly why Joseph employed me."

"But you don't know the business like I do. I have been working here for ten years, first as a brick maker, then a carpenter and now as an undermanager. Nobody does what you are doing. We always work out our costs and then add a margin to get to the bid price."

"Ehud, will you follow my instructions or not?"

"I will, sir," answered the undermanager stiffly.

"Very well, I will send for you on my return."

***

II

Judas came back from his meeting with bar Abbas elated. The Zealots already knew about the slaughter of the children in Bethlehem and feared the worst for the Messiah's fate, so Judas' news was greeted with joy and relief. All agreed the

Messiah should remain in Egypt at least until Herod was dead, and a celebration followed where wine flowed freely, the after effects of which delayed Judas' homeward journey by a day. Meanwhile, Ehud had carried out his instructions and seemed to have got over his surliness as he gave his report to Judas in Joseph's office.

"Well, the bar Micah brothers look to be at full stretch. They are working on three smallish contracts but none are near completion. Amos is engaged on a contract in Sepphoris, but I could not tell how far advanced it is without asking someone. The roof is not in place yet and all the fitting out is still to be done."

"That is most helpful Ehud, thank you. What margin does Joseph usually put on his bid price?"

"One twentieth of the total cost."

"How successful is he?"

"He nearly always wins."

Judas nodded, "I thought so. In view of the information you have gathered, I think we can safely double the margin to one tenth." Ehud did not respond. His face remained impassive; he was always a difficult man to read. "Well Ehud, we are in this together. What do you think?"

"It's a bold move, sir; I would not risk it."

"I understand, but we'll give it a try this time. I will seal our bid now and you may take it to Herod's agent tomorrow morning. The bid closing date is the day after. When you're with him, find out when the bidders will be advised of the result."

"I will, sir."

Judas rolled up the scroll, tied it with a ribbon and sealed the knot with hot wax. While the wax was still viscous, he rolled the ceramic cylinder of Joseph bar Jacob across it leaving the impression in the cooling wax. The bid was ready. The two men shook hands, then Ehud departed with the precious document, the first commercial bid Judas had made. If his carefully calculated price was successful, he knew he would gain the respect of his sceptical undermanager and the praise of Joseph when he returned home.

Exactly a week later, just before Judas was about to start his midday meal in Joseph's office, a messenger arrived from Sepphoris and delivered a scroll. As soon as the messenger left, Judas sat at his desk and pushed his food to one side. The new seal on the scroll was Herod's; this must be the bid result. His stomach heaved with nervous tension. After all his confident talk to Ehud, he was now to be tested. Slowly, deliberately but with shaking hands, he slit through the seal and opened the scroll. Right at the bottom, just below the bid price, was one word — 'Rejected'. He dropped the scroll, grabbed a pot of flowers, emptied them out and was violently sick into the pot. Afterwards, the nausea did not leave him; he thought he was going to faint. He kept telling himself not to be a fool over one failed bid; it was not the end of the world and true businessmen accept failure as well as success in their stride. But this bid had meant so much to him; it was to be the means of proving his skill not only to Ehud but to himself as well.

Judas tried to pull himself together but it was no use. He felt too ill to finish his day's work; he could not even tidy his desk the way he always did at the end of the day. Still feeling very sick, he walked unsteadily downstairs and left Joseph's house. Someone asked him if he was unwell but he could not answer and tottered like a drunken man back to his house where he went straight to bed and slept though the afternoon and most of the night.

The long sleep healed him and next morning he was ready to face the consequences of his failure. When he reached the office, he saw that someone had tidied his desk and the flowers had been returned to their pot which had been washed and filled with clean water. This had all the hall marks of Deborah. He sent for Ehud who happened to be at home in Nazareth; in his black depression, Judas had forgotten it was the Sabbath. Even so, Ehud arrived within the hour.

"Ehud, I owe you an apology. I should not have called you here, but I forgot today is the Sabbath."

"That's all right sir, we can still talk without breaking the law."

Judas handed him the scroll, "You were right and I was wrong. I pushed the bid price too high. I am sorry."

Ehud glanced at the failed bid and handed it back. There was no gloating in his voice, "Sir, you were doing your best for our master. No-one will blame you for that. Do you know who won the contract?"

"No, but I shall find out tomorrow when I go to Sepphoris. I will also investigate what other contracts are coming up but this time we'll do it your way with a margin of one twentieth of the cost, no more."

"I'm sure we'll have better luck next time sir."

When Judas returned from Sepphoris he felt much better. He had lost the public baths contract to the local Amos business so maybe there had been an element of support for the home town bidder in the decision process. Amos must have been closer to completing the Sepphoris contract than Ehud thought. Better still, Judas was bringing home the bid instructions for the building of a large private dwelling on the southern outskirts of Sepphoris; this was a bid free from governmental contamination. He had three weeks to prepare a well thought out, professional offer; this time, he felt sure he would win. Work on the weapons store would finish in ten days, so he would only have to pay the men for doing nothing for a short time.

It took Ehud nearly a week to complete the costings. He laid out his calculations on Judas' desk and both men went through the final checks together. When they had finished Judas said, "Well Ehud, I think we have covered everything. I shall now add Joseph's margin, one twentieth of the cost. Are we agreed?"

"Indeed, we are, sir." Once again, Judas sealed the bid with Joseph's cylinder seal and instructed Ehud to take it to Sepphoris.

This time the wait was longer, almost a month, but at last, on a bright but cold early spring morning, the client's messenger arrived with the returned bid. As Judas broke the seal sitting at his desk in Joseph's office, he calmly recalled how nervous he had felt last time he had been in this position. Now that he knew he had Ehud's support, he felt no fear. His hands were perfectly steady as he opened the bid and looked at the result. 'Rejected'. But how could this be? He had done everything as Joseph would have done, yet he had failed once more. He was dumbfounded, his confidence was shattered again, but at least this time there was no vomiting into the flower pot. He sent for Ehud.

Once more, Ehud trod the road back to Nazareth guessing from the urgent nature of the message that it was likely to be bad news. It was late afternoon by the time he presented himself to Judas.

"Is it the bid sir?"

"Rejected!" Judas tossed the scroll across the desk. "We did everything Joseph would have done yet we lost again. I wonder who won?"

"I can guess sir because there were celebrations taking place at the premises of the bar Micah brothers as I passed by a few minutes ago."

"But they're fully extended on other projects! You saw that for yourself when you observed the status of their workload."

"Perhaps they have decided to hire more workers."

"Perhaps," agreed Joseph. "But make sure they are not ours. When you leave here tell our men they will receive full pay until our next contract. We must continue to show loyalty to our workforce even when times get tough, whatever the cost."

"I will sir, and may I be so bold as to say I commend your decision. The men will appreciate your generosity."

"Thank you, Ehud"." said Judas then, recalling the time he found Ephraim looking through Joseph's papers, he added, "'It's almost as if our competitors know our bid price before they submit their own."

"Unlikely, sir. All sealed bids are opened at the same time in front of witnesses; that's the rule."

"Well it's supposed to be."

"Don't worry, sir. I'll find another contract to bid for and we'll win the next one, I'm sure we will."

"I hope so, Ehud, I really hope so."

***

III

That same evening, Judas slowly walked back in the twilight to his house pondering on the day's events. Could Ephraim really be a traitor? He had certainly been upset by Judas' promotion, but did he have the guts to risk everything by betraying his own master? He did not really seem the type and maybe, thought Judas, you yourself are just trying to find excuses for your own failings.

"Good evening, Judas," said a familiar voice as he reached his house.

"Eli, is it really you?"

"And me," said Joachim. "It's chilly out here. Aren't you going to invite us in for a drink? We bring welcome news."

Joachim wiped red beads of wine from his grey beard. "Ah, that's better. We've been walking since daybreak with hardly a stop." The three of them were sitting in Judas' reception room. Judas had lit the fire to drive out the cold of the evening and was eager to hear the news his friends had brought, but they would say nothing until they had wine and warmth.

Judas asked, "Have you not been home yet, Joachim? Your house is but fifty paces from here."

"Time enough for that," answered the old campaigner. "I will let Eli speak; he is more eloquent than me."

Both looked at the young Zealot leader who was smiling broadly. "Judas, our time has come. Herod is dead at last. He executed his eldest son and heir, Antipater, just before he died and proclaimed another son, Archelaus, as his successor. Now we must arm ourselves properly before the new king has settled on his throne, for the battle that is about to come."

"You mean the weapons store in Sepphoris?"

"Exactly. I realise you already have the key to the armoury, but we will have to fight our way to get there."

Joachim added, "Our spies tell us there are about two hundred and fifty Galatians guarding the place, so we will need at least a thousand of our own, some to hold off the Galatians while the rest empty the armoury."

"And you will have to capture the outer wall first," said Judas.

"That will not be difficult," replied bar Abbas. "It will be a night attack and we will use the Shadows to carry it out."

"Who?"

"The Shadows are a group of special warriors that have been trained for missions such as this. They usually fight at night, they are invisible to the untrained eye and their weapons are stealth and the sicarius."

"No-one is invisible, untrained eye or not."

Bar Abbas laughed, "Isaac, you may reveal yourself now." There was a movement in a dark corner of the room. What Judas had thought was a shadow now glided towards them; the black hood was thrown back and standing before them in the flickering firelight was Isaac, commander of the Shadows.

"How on earth did you get in here?" gasped a wide-eyed Judas. "How long have you been watching us?"

"Please excuse the theatricals," answered Isaac in a quiet, almost whisper of a voice, "but our leader thought you are ready to see our skills for yourself." He was a small, ordinary looking man, but there was an unmistakable aura of menace about him. "I slipped in here when you briefly turned your back to close the door after Eli and Joachim entered."

"Well, you are well named," said Judas who was hugely impressed. "Come and join us by the fire and have some wine."

"I have brought Isaac and some of his comrades with me because tomorrow I am going to visit Herod's cousin Achiab near Capernaum on the north shore of Galilee," explained bar Abbas. "As you know, he is the commander of Herod's army which is based close by. It's about eight thousand strong and I hope to persuade him to join us when we move on Jerusalem to attack the Romans and Galatians."

"But might this not be risky Eli? Why does it have to be you who goes?"

"Because it would be disrespectful if I sent anyone else to a person of such high rank. He could either agree or arrest me. If he chooses the latter then, hopefully, the Shadows will be able to rescue me."

Joachim disapproved. "I agree with Judas. It's far too risky in my opinion. Eli you should let me go instead."

"We cannot foretell Achiab's response but, as leader of the Jewish army, he will expect to talk to the Zealot leader; nothing else will do."

"Then I should accompany you."

"And if Achiab decides to arrest us both or simply kill us then our army will have lost both its leaders at one stroke. Anyway, I need you to gather a thousand good men for the Sepphoris raid. The men respect you Joachim. Others may struggle to get a thousand to turn up at this time of the year."

"I don't think you'll need a thousand," said Judas starkly. "In fact, you won't need a quarter of that number." The three Zealots looked at him in astonishment. Judas got up and fetched a piece of parchment which he stretched across the

225

table in front of them. Then with a stick of charcoal, he drew a large circle. "From a bird's eye view this is the wall that surrounds the weapons store. The gates are on the west side of the wall here on the left." Next, he drew two parallel, north-south trending rectangles in the middle of the circle and to the right of them a small square which touched the east side of the circle. Judas pointed to the square. "This is the armoury itself, which is designed to accommodate four guards, an officer and of course the weapons we seek. The two rectangles in the middle of the circle are the barracks. They are built on the Roman model and can therefore accommodate no more than eighty men each, so you will be dealing with one hundred and sixty Galatians at most."

Bar Abbas replied, "This is encouraging, but the Galatians have the defensive position and will be fully armoured. I still think we should bring a thousand men to make certain of success."

"I haven't finished yet, Eli. All depends on Isaac and his Shadows quietly disposing of the sentries and opening the gates so we can get inside the walls undetected. Eli, you said this will be a night attack?"

"It will."

"And you may count on us, Judas, to open the gates before the garrison awakes," said Isaac.

"Good, then we will need about a hundred men to contain the garrison, while another hundred or so can empty the armoury; any more than that and they'll just get in each other's way." Judas noted the sceptical looks on the Zealot faces but continued. "This is how we will do it. Thanks to Joseph we already have the key to unlock the heavy iron door that protects the armoury, but we have also retained a set of keys to the barracks. I said they are constructed on the Roman model but they have been built to be little fortresses in their own right rather than simple accommodation blocks. So instead of wooden walls and reed roofs, they are made of mudbrick walls and tiled roofs. They have thick iron doors at either end which can be locked from the inside and..." Judas paused for effect "...from the outside too."

Bar Abbas immediately grasped the point, "You mean we could lock the Galatians inside their barracks so their little fortresses become prisons!"

"Precisely."

"But that's brilliant!"

"But what about the windows?" asked Joachim.

"That's why we will need about fifty men for each building to keep the Galatians inside. Once the doors are locked, we will hammer spikes into the key holes so they can't simply unlock them again from inside. The hammering will be sure to waken them. The windows have shutters which can only be bolted from the inside, but they are small so only one man at a time can squeeze through them. There are four windows on each side of the barrack blocks so we'll need to station at least four guards at each one to stop the garrison escaping that way. Once they realise they can't break out through the windows, they will try to force a way out through the roofs. We will need to station men on the roofs to discourage attempts to escape that way. We should be able to keep the garrison penned in long enough for you to get what you want from the armoury, but eventually they will break out by which time we'll need to be long gone."

The three Zealots remained silent for a while apart from Isaac lamenting the mudbrick walls. "What a shame the

227

barracks don't have wooden walls. We could have set fire to them after the doors are locked and got rid of a hundred and sixty Galatians at the same time."

Eventually, Joachim spoke. "Judas, this is a truly remarkable plan born from a fertile mind. The men already think you are a good luck talisman; I am beginning to think they're right."

Bar Abbas patted him on the shoulder, "Well done, Judas Sicariot. We will carry out your plan as soon as I return from Achiab's camp. Wait here until we come for you which should be in about two or three weeks."

***

IV

While he was waiting for bar Abbas' return, Judas set about the comparatively mundane task of winning a contract. Compared to his life with the Zealots, amongst whom he was highly regarded, managing Joseph's business with all the local jealousy and prejudice he was obliged to endure, now seemed less pressing. Even so, he remained determined to present a healthy and viable business to Joseph on his return; it was a matter of personal self-respect.

This time, he decided to be less ambitious and targeted two subcontracts which would yield marginal profits at best, but would at least keep the workers busy. As usual, Ehud calculated the costs but Judas reduced the margins to one fortieth of the contract cost which, in truth, was barely break-even.

As they were working on the contracts, news arrived that

the new king, Archelaus, was about to leave Jerusalem to travel to Rome to have his appointment as Herod's successor confirmed by Augustus Caesar. Although it was his duty as a subject king to do this, it was a bad time to abandon his kingdom, which was still seething with unrest after the slaughter of the children in Bethlehem. It only needed one more spark to ignite the dried tinder of rebellion; that spark was not long in coming.

It was the afternoon of the spring equinox. Judas was awaiting the results of his latest bids when Joachim arrived at his office.

"Judas, we are ready for you."

"Very well, I will leave a note for my undermanager saying I shall be away for a day or two. How many men have you brought?"

"Three hundred, and the Shadows of course."

"More than enough," said Judas. He went to Joseph's strong box, unlocked it and withdrew five keys, one large and four small. "The large one is for the armoury and the others are for the doors to the barracks. The four small keys are identical but we will need to lock and spike the four barrack block doors at the same time because of the noise. We don't want the Galatians swarming out of one block like angry hornets while we are locking the other." Then he placed four wooden mallets and four sharp iron spikes into a linen bag which he slung over his shoulder. "I am ready," he said.

Bar Abbas' camp was in the western hills about a mile outside Sepphoris. Judas was overwhelmed by his welcome. The Zealots crowded round him with 'here comes our good luck' 'blessings be upon you' 'may God grant you many fine sons' and so on. Evidently, word of his part in this campaign had already spread among the ranks. Along with Joachim, he was ushered like a hero to bar Abbas' tent.

"Welcome, Judas Sicariot," said the Zealot leader. "Come and sit with us." Already in the tent were two Zealot commanders whom bar Abbas introduced. "This is Ariel bar Eleazar." The older of the two men, a greybeard, nodded. "Ariel is in charge of transport which consists of eight wagons drawn by mules. He will ensure we escape with our prize before the Galatians can find us. And this is Jonathan bar Jacob."

The younger man smiled, "It is an honour Judas Sicariot." "Jonathan commands the hundred who will keep the Galatians locked up in their barracks. The remaining two hundred will empty the armoury and load the wagons; they will be under the direct command of Joachim."

"Is Isaac here?" asked Judas.

"As we speak, the Shadows are in place observing the weapons store. They already have their orders. We will leave at midnight but the wagons can only go part of the way because of the noise. The rumbling sound of the wheels will carry at night and we don't want to alert the sentries. The wagons will arrive once the Galatians are safely locked up. Two of the Shadows are here; they will escort you to their comrades for it will be the Shadows who lock the barracks while you supervise them. The rest of us will be behind you."

Judas' stomach heaved as the realisation of what he was about to do struck home. Until now, everything was just a plan drawn on a piece of parchment, but within a few hours he would be putting his life at risk again. But that was not what he really feared. What if his plan failed? More than three hundred men were about to face mortal danger because of their faith in him. All, including the leaders, had a child-like certainty everything would go well because their talisman, Judas Sicariot, was the mind behind the daring scheme. But what if he had overlooked something or an unforeseeable event threw his carefully worked out programme off course? These simple but immensely brave warriors would have died because of him and him alone. Their families would hold him responsible. That thought was more terrifying than death. He recalled how he had been ill because of losing his first building contract. What he was about to undertake put things in perspective; losing a contract would never trouble him like that again.

All this flashed through his mind in a few seconds. He was determined to maintain an outward appearance of confidence by moving the subject on. He asked almost as an apparent afterthought, "How went your meeting with Achiab?"

Bar Abbas shrugged, "Well, it could have been worse. At least I wasn't arrested. Achiab has agreed not to assist the Romans or the Galatians, but nor has he agreed to help us. This is not because he has failed to think through his policy; he's overcautious and wants to wait on events before committing himself."

"So his policy is to back the winner."

"It is as you say, Judas; though, he did commit to allow volunteers from his army to join us, but I do not expect much to come of that."

"So we fight alone again."

"Perhaps, but I believe many ordinary people will join us when we march on Jerusalem."

Joachim muttered, "They'll be of little value Eli, undisciplined, ill-armed enthusiasts who'll need to be fed but will either get in the way or disappear at the first sign of hard fighting."

"You are probably right" replied the Zealot commander. "Yet we may still find use for some of them, but now my friends we must prepare ourselves for tonight's work. Eat well and make your peace with God. We will assemble in one hour."

It was one of those nights that was almost entirely black because clouds obscured the stars but the moon had not yet risen. To begin with, one Zealot in ten carried a shuttered lamp which cast sufficient light to enable bar Abbas' men to see enough to walk without stumbling too often, but when they left the hills and entered the plain before Sepphoris, orders came to extinguish all lights, except for a select few, and to park the wagons until the weapons store had been captured. Fortunately, Sepphoris was easy enough to see because its street lights created a glow that reflected from the clouds, but that was little help in avoiding the irregular lumps and bumps in the poorly maintained road that awaited the unwary traveller. The Zealot column ground to a halt. Soon orders were relayed from the head of the column; 'Judas to the front quickly!' Stumbling through the dark, but with the help of many supportive comrades, Judas reached the front of the column where bar Abbas was waiting with two black figures in attendance. One of the black figures was Isaac, who was carrying a covered lamp that shed only just enough light for Judas to recognise his commander.

Bar Abbas shook Judas by the hand. "God be with you, my friend. The Shadows will guide you to the gates. When they are opened you will be in command. My only orders to you are 'no heroics' and 'keep to the plan'."

The weapons store lay at the eastern edge of the city of

Sepphoris. The Shadows moved quietly but swiftly across the last half mile speaking only in whispers to guide Judas to a concealed position just outside the walls where the other thirty or so Shadows were waiting. Isaac crept down the line tapping selected men on the shoulder and, without a word being spoken, they moved forward in small groups — some carrying ropes, others scaling ladders, like malevolent demons of the night. The rest, including Judas, crept stealthily to within a few paces of the city gates.

The waiting was nerve wracking; it seemed to be going on too long. Judas feared something had gone wrong but he dared not speak because everyone else remained silent. At last, the two gates swung open noiselessly on well lubricated hinges. Immediately, the Shadows around Judas entered the city and met their companions just inside the walls.

"Have you disposed of all the sentries?" whispered Isaac.

"All dead, sir," came the equally quiet response from somewhere in the night. "Judas, your orders please," said Isaac.

Humbled by being in command, albeit temporarily, of such superb warriors, Judas needed a moment to gather his thoughts. He unshouldered his sling and took out the keys, spikes and mallets. "Who is to deal with the armoury?"

"I am," came a voice out of the darkness.

Judas held out his hand, "Here is the key." The lightest touch on the palm of his hand and the key was gone.

Isaac whispered, "Give me the keys to the barracks and I will pass them on to the appointed men." It took just a few moments for the keys, spikes and mallets to be allocated. Then all waited for Judas' orders. Trying to whisper when your mouth is dry through nervous tension is not easy, but Judas managed to keep his voice steady. Just as he began speaking an owl hooted; the noise seemed deafening.

"When I say 'now' all of you move to your positions. At the same time, count slowly to thirty. When you reach that number lock the barrack doors and hammer in the spikes. Those at the weapons store must dispose of the guards and unlock the door to the armoury. Then each group send a man back here when your work is done. When all of you have reported back Isaac will send a runner to Ariel and Jonathan to bring forward the wagons and the rest of our men, but in the meantime, you will have to make sure the Galatians remain penned in their barracks."

The soft patter of shoeless feet in the dust was all that Judas could hear as the Shadows dispersed to their positions. Half a minute later, and almost simultaneously, four loud, metallic bangs reverberated into the night sky proclaiming that the barrack door locks had been disabled. At the same time a scream, followed by a throaty gurgle, confirmed that the guards in the weapons store were being dispatched. Isaac sent the runner back to Ariel and Jonathan without waiting for all the reports to come in. It was obvious everything was going to plan.

Amid the beginnings of a confused uproar emanating from the barracks, Judas said, "Isaac, I will go to the armoury and see what we have uncovered."

"Very well," acknowledged the leader of the Shadows, no longer bothering to whisper any more. "I will wait by the gates for the wagons to arrive."

Judas could not help but smile to himself as he heard the howls of frustration and banging on the doors coming from the barracks. He tried to imagine the pandemonium inside those buildings but was quickly brought back to more immediate matters when he tripped over the body of a dead Galatian sentinel and went sprawling to the ground. Satisfied that his lost dignity had gone unobserved, he dusted himself down and entered the weapons store.

Silhouetted against the lamps in the antechamber, which was also an office, stood six motionless, black robed figures holding unsheathed, bloodied sicarii. Their faces were covered leaving only small slits from which cold, killer eyes stared out. Around them lay five Galatians in the undignified poses of death where they had just fallen. One was just giving out the death rattle as Judas entered.

The nearest Shadow loosened his face mask. "Welcome Judas and forgive how you find us; you might have been another Galatian."

"I am glad I'm not! They are all confined like chickens in a hen coup. We are safe for the moment at least."

"Then you shall have the honour of opening the door to the armoury. We were placing the key in the lock when you arrived."

The fit was perfect and the key turned easily, but it still needed two men to push open the heavy, iron door. "Bring a lamp," said Judas and immediately a brazier was removed from its wall bracket and brought to him. Nervously, he stepped into the dark chamber and raised the flickering flame.

"Judas, what do you see?" asked one of the Shadows.

"Wonderful things. Shining armour, helmets and shields, hundreds of them!" He moved the lamp so that it illuminated another part of the chamber. "And there are swords, spears, bows, arrows and things I don't even recognise. There is all we need and more." He stepped back out of the chamber and handed the lamp to one of the Shadows. "Who commands here?"

"I do," said the Shadow who had first welcomed him. "I am Joab from Beth Shan."

"Joab, we must start moving the weapons outside so we are ready when the wagons arrive, but one of you must report to Isaac to let him know all is well here." Joab signalled to one of his men to go; the rest began the heavy work of emptying the chamber.

Ariel's wagons duly arrived and Jonathan's men released the Shadows from the duty of keeping the Galatians locked up inside their barracks. Loading the wagons was tiring work so Joachim, who was now in command, arranged for the rest of the men to work in shifts to maintain the work rate. They were about half done when a call came from inside the armoury. Judas and Joachim both went to see what caused it.

Behind a curtain, which screened off a corner of the chamber, was a neatly stacked set of wooden planks and spars placed on a wooden trolley with large wheels. Levers, ropes and strong, leather bags lay on the stone floor beside the trolley.

"What is this, sir?" asked the man who found it. "Should we take it with us? It will fill up one whole wagon if we do." Judas had no idea what the significance of the wood and ropes was but Joachim, who eyed the find with an appraising look, said, "If I am not mistaken, these are parts of a ballista, a Roman siege engine that hurls huge rocks to break down defensive walls and towers. I saw one being used in training when I was in Caesarea Maritima not long ago."

"Might we have a use for a thing like that?" asked Judas.

"It's possible. We may soon be attacking Romans and

Galatians in Jerusalem; a ballista could prove useful. It will certainly come as a surprise to our foe. We'll take it."

While the ballista was being loaded, bar Abbas arrived at the armoury. "We must go. The Galatians will soon break out of the barrack blocks; we can't hold them much longer. The carts must leave now so they can be far away before the pursuit starts."

"But one of the carts is still empty," objected Judas.

"That can't be helped. You have all done well, but you must leave now with whatever we've got. Joachim, appoint some men to escort the carts; the rest of you come with me."

Outside, the clouds had broken up; a half moon cast a silvery light on a fierce battle taking place around the barracks. Despite the best efforts of the Zealots, the Galatians had managed to smash their way through the mudbrick wall at the narrow end of one of the blocks where the frame of the iron door was attached to the brick work. The gap was, as yet, still narrow and the Zealots were holding them back, but Judas could see another section of wall moving where it was being pummelled from the inside. It could not be long before the Galatians broke free, but at least the carts had all got away.

The Zealots fought like demons; they gave bar Abbas another quarter of an hour before he was forced to begin the withdrawal. "Shadows to me!" he shouted. Seemingly out of nowhere, thirty black figures gathered around him. Then he called to Joachim. "Leave now. We only have a few minutes to get clear. Take your men and run to the meeting place. I will be just behind you. Judas, stay beside me." He spoke quietly to Isaac. Moments later the Shadows relieved Jonathan's men and took up their positions around the barracks, just fifteen of them to each block. They were armed with long swords and shields taken from the armoury.

Bar Abbas and Judas were young and fit and soon caught up with Joachim's men. As they slowed to the pace of the others, Judas asked, "What will happen to the Shadows when the Galatians finally break out?"

"Have no fear for them," answered Joachim. "They are the ultimate night warriors. They will hold back the Galatians as long as they can then, just before it's too late, they'll fade into the night. The Galatians are armoured so the pursuit will be slow, but the Shadows have already selected hiding places in olive groves, reed beds and even Sepphoris itself, so they do not have to follow on behind us. Then tomorrow, dressed in the normal day time clothes they always carry with them, they will be unrecognisable for what they are and can simply walk home like normal travellers."

"So the Shadows are invisible in day time, too, in a way."

"Just so. Unless you know any of them personally, you would never know their identity; even most of the Zealots have no idea who they are, yet they work among us as storemen, messengers, drivers and other unexciting non-combatant roles."

"Do the Shadows not fight as daylight warriors too?"

"Generally not," replied Joachim. "They are too valuable for that. It takes years to train a Shadow so I wouldn't want to lose one to a stray arrow or in a pointless skirmish."

"They are most admirable men. Could I be trained in their ways?"

Bar Abbas interrupted, "Absolutely not. Judas, you already have your mission. I do not doubt you would make an excellent Shadow, but you cannot be risked. You already know that. Quite apart from guiding the young Messiah, you have an excellent mind. Look at tonight's raid. Without you, it could have been a costly failure. As it is, I think we may have accomplished our task without a single fatality which is truly amazing. The men will tell this story to their families and the name of Judas Sicariot will be remembered for ever more."

At least bar Abbas was right about Judas being remembered but sadly, it would be for a different reason.

CHAPTER TEN

The accession of Archelaus passed almost unnoticed. When Herod died, an unnatural hush seemed to descend on Jerusalem; the bustle was gone, there were no crowds in the streets, even the vendors in the market spoke in whispers. This was not the quiet of peace but the calm before the storm. Everyone seemed to be waiting. We Romans knew something was about to happen; we were not sure what it would be except it would not be good. Clearly the new king did not sense the tension in the air. He mistook the silence as acceptance by the people of his inheritance and decided now would be a good time to visit Rome to have his accession confirmed by the emperor. Although it was his duty to do this, the timing could not have been worse.

Meanwhile problems were beginning to appear in the Roman camp. It was early April and Archelaus had only been gone three days when we centurions were called to a meeting in our tribune's office.

A grim faced Piso announced, "Last night, another two of our men were murdered. Their stripped and tortured bodies were dumped outside the camp for us to find this morning." A growl of anger greeted this. Piso continued, "That makes four men lost in this way since Herod died."

"Returning from brothels?" enquired Severus Pollio,

centurion of the first century.

"Yes. We shall have to suspend all visits to the city ladies of leisure until further notice."

"But sir, you cannot expect four hundred healthy young men to live like Vestal Virgins."

"I do not expect that, Severus. Today, I shall write to the governor requesting that some of the legion's own felicifera are transferred here from Antioch. I have no idea what his response will be." 'Felicifera', bringers of happiness, was the title of a legion's ladies of leisure; we knew them informally as the 'cats,' which was a term the refined Piso disdained to use.

"If he approves, how long do you think it will be before they get here?" asked Severus.

"At least one month, possibly two."

"That's a long time."

"I know, so I suggest you put the men to work building a suitable accommodation block for the felicifera; at least the men will feel they are helping to prepare for the great day, if it comes."

"Sir, while we're waiting, might we temporarily employ some local girls and base them in the camp?" asked Gnaeus Servilius, centurion of the fourth century and an old friend of mine.

"Possibly," answered Piso. "But the Zealots are everywhere and they aren't necessarily all male. There's a good chance the murderers of our men were tipped off from within one of the brothels. Let us wait for Varus' response and then discuss this again." That seemed reasonable to us all, so the meeting closed and we departed to delegate the working parties for the new accommodation.

Five days later, the spark that was to ignite the flames of rebellion reached Jerusalem. It took the form of a certain Sabinus, the financial prefect sent by Varus to manage Herod's estate during Archelaus' dutiful visit to Rome. He arrived at the head of a column, three hundred strong, as we centurions were finishing our noon meal. He rode in the comfort of a covered wagon drawn by four mules which stopped at the gates of our camp. One of the drivers stepped down from the riding platform and bellowed, "In the name of Caius Petronius Sabinus, Prefect of Jerusalem, open these gates!"

Severus looked at me. "By Vulcan's sacred balls! Who in Hades is that?" I volunteered to go to the gate and find out, but when I arrived the prefect himself had emerged from the wagon. I do not recall what I expected, perhaps a fusty, old insect of a man or an emaciated accountant, but what I beheld was very different. Standing beside the wagon driver was a squat, rotund figure no taller than an ape. His hair was cropped short to the round, bony skull which reminded me of one of those rare northern fruits called a gooseberry. His body was immensely broad and his legs, concealed by a toga, must have been extraordinarily short; in fact he must have been almost as tall lying down as standing up. But the distorted frame gave the impression of great physical strength; he looked more like a wrestler than an accountant. I drew breath to speak but he anticipated me.

"What apology for a man are you?"

Resisting the urge to plant a fist on his broad nose, I answered, "I am Lucius Veranius, centurion of the sixth century of the fifth cohort of the Third Legion Gallica. Who are you?"

"None of your business, Centurion. I will speak only to

the cohort tribune. Bring him here at once."

"You do not give orders here."

"Do I not? Then read this," said the ape-like man thrusting a scroll into my hand. "You can read I presume?" The seal was undoubtedly Varus'. I broke it and read the neat script, no doubt written by Brasidas. It was clear that the Governor of Syria had given Sabinus full executive authority to manage Herod's financial affairs until Archelaus' return. Whether or not he had authority over Piso was unclear so I paused for a moment and looked at Sabinus' followers. They were certainly not soldiers. They looked more like ruffians and blackguards, their scruffy attire and slouching stance suggested origins from the mob in Rome. I handed back the scroll but Sabinus attempted to brush past me as if I were nothing. I braced my left arm and pushed him back, but only just. Had he tried, he could have swept me aside like an irritating fly but he checked himself.

"Wait here," I said. "I will bring the tribune."

"And be quick about it, Centurion of the fifth cohort, or whatever you are, or you shall answer to me!"

I returned with Piso and, to add extra weight, Severus Pollio. Unlike me, Piso was not in the least overawed by Sabinus. He introduced himself with the confidence only the breeding of the senatorial class creates. "I am Licinius Piso, Tribune of the fifth cohort of the Third Legion Gallica. What is it you want?"

"Your co-operation so that I can carry out the governor's orders."

"Which are?"

"To acquire King Herod's assets and manage them until King Archelaus returns from Rome."

"Really? Do you realise that means entering the Jewish temple?"

"So what?"

"You understand nothing about the sensitivities of the Jews."

"I don't give a monkey's fart about the sensitivities of the Jews. They are a conquered people. I obey orders even if you don't."

"Then there is no place for you here. Go back to the governor and ask for new orders preferably sending you a thousand miles from here."

Outclassed in debate, Sabinus reverted to threats. "I do not take orders from you Tribune. My authority comes direct from the Governor of Syria."

Piso seemed unimpressed. "I know Varus well enough to understand that he has no wish to create a rebellion even if his creature does. Leave now with your band of guttersnipes before I order my legionaries to teach them a lesson in true soldiering."

Sabinus turned to his driver, "Come, we'll deal with these fools later. Putting children in charge of men never worked and never will."

As I watched the stocky, grotesque figure climb back into his wagon, I said to Piso, "That man is dangerous, sir. Should we not arrest him now?"

"I admit I am tempted to, but arresting the governor's personal prefect would be going too far."

Severus spat into the dusty ground, "Sir, I think Lucius is right. We should detain Sabinus and send his ruffians back to whatever hole they crawled out of."

Piso frowned, "Let me think about it." It was easy for Severus and me to encourage our tribune to get rid of Sabinus, but the decision and responsibility were his; at best it would be insubordination but a humiliated governor might consider it treason. Anyway, by the next day the decision was taken out of our hands.

It started in the early afternoon. Work had just begun clearing the ground for the foundations of the cats' accommodation, when we heard shouts coming from within the city. This was not especially unusual and often started in the market place over a minor matter. But now it was different. It came from the east end of Jerusalem and instead of dying down it became louder. Gradually, our building work stopped and we all looked towards the city where a dust cloud was beginning to emerge from below the temple mount. Piso, who was watching from the parade ground, called Severus over. After a few words, Severus turned, stood to attention, and bellowed, "Fifth cohort stand to!" We all ran to our barracks to armour up and returned to the parade ground in our allocated positions within ten minutes.

Piso addressed us. "Men, there is trouble in the city. We must find out what it is. I shall take a century with me while the rest of you take up defensive positions around the perimeter of the camp. You must assume that we might come under attack at any moment. In my absence Severus Pollio is in command. Sixth century stand fast! You shall come with me."

The sixth century was mine. At the morning roll call, we numbered seventy men fit for duty plus me; that would surely be enough for what we must face. We marched into the city by the west gate with the citadel on our left. There was no sign of the Galatians who remained firmly ensconced behind the lofty walls of the citadel. We marched in a single column, three abreast, with Piso and me leading at the front. Trouble was not long in coming. As we neared the temple mount, we reached an intersection between two main thoroughfares where there was an open area in which people often gathered to meet friends, listen to one of the many weird ascetics preach his particular brand of the Jewish religion, or simply pass the time with strangers. This time we came across a few hundred young men who began jeering as soon as they saw us. The insults did not matter because they were all in Aramaic, which was unintelligible to most of us, but the attitude became more threatening as we got closer to them. Then, seemingly out of nowhere, a large stone struck my helmet. I was momentarily brought to my knees by the shock of the blow, but that initial success encouraged others to follow the example and soon my entire century was under missile fire.

Piso kept his head and shouted, "Sixth century, close up! Testudo!" We shortened the column so that the outside ranks could link their shields and create an unbroken defensive wall to face the mob, while the men of the inside ranks raised their shields over their heads to provide shelter from missiles coming in from above. This manoeuvre was carried out without halting and must have discouraged our assailants, or so we thought, because they quickly melted away into the side streets when they saw they were having no effect on our progress.

Now Piso shouted, "Resume marching order! Draw swords!" Then he turned to me. "Lucius, are you all right?"

"I think so, I am thick skulled, but I'll have a headache later."

"Well, we'd better hurry to the temple; things are looking

246

ugly." He ordered us to advance at the trot, but as we entered the open precinct just below the temple mount, we stumbled into more than a thousand angry Jews. Our appearance only made things worse. The Jews were mostly unarmed but a few carried clubs or sticks and, of course, there were the inevitable stone throwers.

As we trotted towards the steps below the Hulda Gates they closed in on us, which at least ended the stone throwing for fear of hitting Jews instead of Romans, but though they approached to within a few paces, the sight of our drawn swords discouraged a direct attack. When we began ascending the steps the gates swung open and we entered the outer courtyard which was deserted except for a few of Sabinus' ruffians. It was with a great sense of relief that we heard the gates slam shut behind us.

Piso grabbed one of Sabinus' men. "Where's your master!"

Pointing to the main temple buildings, he answered insolently, "Up there somewhere."

Piso said under his breath, "Jupiter! What's he done!" Then he pressed the point of his sword into the corpulent ruffian's belly. "Take us to him now." The sword had the desired effect and we were led through another court and then into a building which the Jews regard as the most sacred place in the world, their Holy of Holies. Piso and I went in leaving our men just outside and found Sabinus sitting between two of his cronies on a stone altar with a chicken leg in one hand and a goblet of wine in the other.

"Well you took your time," he said through a mouthful of masticated chicken, some of which found its way on to Piso's clean, red cloak. "What kept you? Aren't you supposed to be protecting Roman citizens?"

Piso noticed some large wooden boxes on the marble floor behind the altar. "What's in those boxes?"

"None of your business, Tribune."

"Centurion, remove the lids." I was delighted to follow Piso's orders. One of Sabinus' men tried to stop me. I pushed him aside and he went sprawling onto the stone floor, then I kicked off the lid of the nearest box. Inside was a jumbled-up assortment of coins and ingots, all gold or silver, goblets, rings, brooches, necklaces and other precious items studded with red, green and blue jewels. There were beautifully carved statuettes in green malachite and jade, while the blue figures, I guessed, were carved in the highly prized lapis lazuli from the distant east. I kicked off the lids of the other three boxes which were similarly filled. There was more treasure here than in a large kingdom.

Piso turned angrily on Sabinus. "So not only have you defiled the Jewish temple, you have looted its treasury!"

For the first time, Varus' prefect found himself at a disadvantage; he had been caught in the act. He began to wheedle, "Oh come on, Piso, we're both men of the world. There's plenty more where this came from. You and your centurion with the dented helmet will get your share."

"You idiot! Can't you see what you've done! Most of the Jews accepted us as their masters because they could never agree amongst themselves what to do about us. Desecrating the Holy of Holies and looting their treasury will unite them. You have managed to create a full-blown rebellion in what was before a generally peaceful province. Is all you have stolen in these boxes?"

"No, the first consignment left for Antioch this morning."

"Then there's no going back, we must send word to Varus immediately."

Sabinus, recovering his arrogance, sneered, "So what's your problem, Tribune? You have your cohort and the Galatians. If you are the men you pretend to be, you will make short work of that rabble outside."

"You have not seen the Jews fight. The Zealots will already be on their way here. As for you, you're under arrest."

"Tribune, before you do something you'll regret, you had better see the governor's personal instructions to me." Then turning to the man who had tried to stop me reaching the boxes, he ordered, "Fetch Varus' slave and tell him to bring my operating brief with him."

A minute later, none other than little Brasidas appeared carrying a small scroll. He did not seem surprised to see us. Sabinus held out his hand, "Give it to me." Then addressing us again he said, "This is Varus' spy sent to watch me. He will report back to the governor if he thinks I have done wrong provided," he added menacingly, "he survives these troubles we are encountering. I will read the relevant passage to you. After outlining my duties, it says here, *'and the prefect has my authority to deduct from King Herod's estate all his expenses incurred while carrying out his duties'.*"

"Let me see that," snapped Piso. Reluctantly, Sabinus handed over the scroll and while Piso was reading, Brasidas covertly slipped a small piece of parchment into my hand. I waited a moment then took a surreptitious look. On it were written just five words; *Get me out of here.*

Piso handed back the scroll. "You left out an important word. It says *'all his **reasonable** expenses'.*"

"Does it?" shrugged Sabinus. "Well that's a matter of

judgement and I judge that what I have removed is barely adequate."

Before Piso could respond, I intervened. "Sir, could we have a private word?" We withdrew from the violated Holy of Holies and I showed him Brasidas' note.

"I wouldn't give two sesterces for poor Brasidas' life," said Piso shaking his head sadly. "Sabinus will do away with him before he can report to Varus."

"Then we must help him."

"Of course we must. I will think of something. Come, let us return."

During the short walk back to Sabinus, Piso's agile mind came up with a plan. He took on a more conciliatory tone. "Sabinus, I may have been a little hasty earlier. We cannot afford to be divided now that our enemy is united."

"I agree," responded the prefect, warming to the change of heart.

"I will leave now and meet the Galatians to work out a strategy to put an end to the rioting. You stay here within the safety of the temple walls; have you enough men? I could spare a few if you wish."

"Thirty left this morning with the consignment I spoke of but I still have two hundred and fifty. That should be plenty." It was a predictable reply from someone who wanted to get rid of us as soon as possible.

"Very well. Come, Centurion, form up the men." Just as I was beginning to worry, Piso said as an apparent afterthought, "Sabinus, the slave you call Varus' spy is known to us. He could be useful in the next few days because he speaks Aramaic. I may need an interpreter I can trust should I want to speak to the Jewish leaders. May I borrow him for a while?"

"Keep him as long as you like. All I need is for you to sign a temporary transfer of property. Varus likes his books to be kept in order."

"Very well, I'll do that now."

And with that, Brasidas was saved.

***

II

When we left the temple, it was dark and the rioters, who as yet were not hardened rebels, had gone home for their suppers so we were able to march at ease. As before, Piso and I were in front but this time we had Brasidas between us.

He said, "I saw you at the Hulda Gates and knew at once you were my only hope of escape. For a terrible moment, I thought you were going to leave without me but now I understand what you were doing."

"If Sabinus had realised I was trying to save you, he would never have let you go," replied Piso. "Instead, he is glad to be rid of you."

"He does not like criticism, especially from a slave. Once I'd expressed an opinion about looting the temple treasury, it was only a matter of time before I'd have had some sort of fatal accident."

I asked, "How is it that the Governor of Syria could employ such a man?"

Brasidas answered, "Two reasons. Firstly, Sabinus is undoubtedly good with figures and finances, he even excels me and there are not many who can do that, but more importantly, he made a good marriage in Rome and as a result, is distantly related to Varus."

"If the senatorial class allows such as Sabinus into its ranks then there is little hope for Rome as we know it," grumbled Piso.

"The emperor already draws more heavily on the equestrian class and even lower, than happened in the days of the republic," agreed Brasidas, "but there is also plenty of talent there."

"Perhaps," muttered an unconvinced Piso; he was of course from the senatorial class.

When we reached the citadel, it took a few moments for us to persuade the nervous Galatians to open the gates, but eventually Attalus himself came out to see what was happening and immediately let us in. As always, he was pleased to see us, especially Piso, and provided my century with plenty to eat and drink while Piso, Brasidas and I followed him to his quarters. Here, we were joined by Eumenes, his second in command and a man of Greek descent like Brasidas, though there the similarity ended for Eumenes was tall and handsome in an aquiline sort of way.

Food and wine were ordered and, over a meal of cheese, dried fish and bread we held a council of war. Attalus was already well aware of what Sabinus was up to in the temple.

"Just before Sabinus arrived, we heard there was trouble in Galilee," he said. "The Zealots carried out a daring night raid on Herod's weapons store in Sepphoris and escaped with a large quantity of arms and armour. I am ashamed to say my men were guarding it. We are in the middle of an investigation into how such a thing could have happened."

"What were your losses?" asked Piso.

"Very light in casualties, but devastating in terms of pride."

"So the Zealots are now properly armed and equipped?"

"Well, some of them. I have not received an inventory yet, but we estimate enough equipment for six or seven hundred men was stolen. The Zealots fled once my men were able to get to grips with them and left a great deal behind, so the weapons store still needs to be guarded. After the raid, my men were withdrawn and have now been replaced by some of Achiab's Jewish soldiers."

Eumenes, a much younger man than his commander and about our age said, "I'm not sure we'll ever get to the bottom of this. It seems the Zealots were equipped with keys to our barracks and the armoury. Certainly, the armoury door was opened without damage and our men were locked in their own barracks long enough for the Zealots to achieve a stunning success."

Attalus added, "The latest news we have is that rebels are assembling in large numbers about a day's march north of Jerusalem, but over the last day or so all our sources of information outside the city have been cut off. Now we're in the dark."

Piso took a drink of wine from his goblet and placed it firmly on the table. "Well you certainly know more than we do. I think the time has come to get word to Varus. I will ask for two legions to be sent to Jerusalem immediately."

"But what if this is only a city riot after all," I said. "Varus won't be pleased to be dragged down here on a fool's errand."

"That's true, Lucius, but I would rather see a disgruntled governor than a lost province. Look at what we know; the raid on the Sepphoris weapons store, the desecration of the temple which has united the Jews despite themselves, rumours of an army assembling in the north and finally, our communications out of Jerusalem cut off. It all points to a full-scale rebellion."

Attalus agreed. "Yes, but who will you send to Varus? Whoever it is must cross enemy territory before he can reach Antioch."

"It will indeed be dangerous," acknowledged Piso. "But he will not have to go as far as Antioch. There is a cohort of Numidian mounted spearmen based at Caesarea Maritima, only two days' ride from here. They are fierce, frightening but above all fast. I am sure they will come to our aid but they are light cavalry and more suited to scouting and pursuit rather than head-on charges."

"I will go," I volunteered.

"Thank you, Lucius, but I need you here with your century and me."

Brasidas suggested, "One or two men disguised as Jews might get through."

Piso answered, "None of us has a beard and there is no time to grow one, but any one of us could pass as a Greek I suppose."

Eumenes shook his head. "It will make no difference. There is going to be a bloodbath here. Once the Jews get the bit between their teeth, they will show no mercy. Greek, Roman or Syrian, we are all gentiles and that will be enough to put us to the sword. They have vowed to cleanse their land of all non-Jews; men, women and children will be slaughtered."

"In that case, I propose that I go with Caius Pantera," said Brasidas. "We can leave tonight on fast horses and outrun the Zealots. We can wrap ourselves in Jewish clothing and cover our heads in Arabian headgear. I speak Aramaic, Caius speaks Hebrew, so we can at least try to talk our way through any roadblocks we come across. Caius is well acquainted with the area already; he was born and bred in Caesarea and his father still lives there."

There was no arguing with such logic so we quickly finished our wine and rose to leave. As we gave our two Galatian comrades the customary hand on forearm handshake of departing friends, Attalus said, "Licinius, do you not think you should abandon your camp and join us in the citadel?"

"It may come to that," replied Piso. "But I do not want to hand an easy victory to the mob; that would only encourage them. We will fortify our camp and be ready for whatever the Jews throw at us."

"I hope you have enough time."

"After fighting, the legionary's greatest skill is digging. The ground here is hard but we should be ready within seven days."

"Well, if you run into trouble sound three horn calls followed by three more. If we hear that we will sally out to help you."

"Thank you Attalus," smiled our tribune. "We will do the same for you."

***

III

By midnight, Brasidas and Caius were ready to leave. From a distance, they looked like two Nabatean, desert tribesmen, but close up Caius' bright blue eyes ruined the disguise. He was mounted on a sturdy, brown cob, which easily carried his considerable weight, while Brasidas rode a grey pony as light and agile as he was.

"Good luck," whispered Piso as the camp gates quietly swung open on well-oiled hinges. "Here is my letter to Varus; he can't get here too soon." Caius placed the letter in a small satchel, saluted and rode off into the night with Brasidas close behind.

They skirted round the south of the city with the walls on their right. There was enough light left in the waning moon to allow them to pick their way through the mounds and ditches of the heavily cultivated land, and soon they reached the main road to the coast. Here they headed westwards but within a few hundred paces they came across a group of men clustered round a small camp fire at the side of the road warming themselves against the chill of the night. Two of them got up and stood in the middle of the road blocking the way. One held up his arm and spoke in Aramaic, "Halt! Who are you and where are you going?"

"And who is asking and blocking our way?" demanded Brasidas.

"We are the night watch appointed by the Sanhedrin and you are ordered to stop." Caius whispered, "Ride on and stay close to me." He dug his heels into the cob's flank.Brasidas did likewise and the horses broke into a fast canter. It was enough to scatter the night watch. Shouts and insults followed them but there was no pursuit because the night watch had no horses. Even so, Caius and Brasidas galloped on for another mile before Caius drew rein and they slowed to a walk again.

"Shouldn't we keep going?" asked an anxious Brasidas.

"The coast road is well maintained but there are still cracks and pot holes in the surface which could cause our horses to stumble at night. The last thing we need is for one of our mounts to go lame. As soon as it's light enough we'll break into a steady canter but for now we'll keep to a walk."

They kept going for about three hours but by then the moon had set and it was difficult enough just to see the road, never mind any pot holes in it. Brasidas was dozing when his mount suddenly lurched forwards almost unseating him.

Caius called a halt. "We must have put a good twelve miles between us and Jerusalem. It's too dangerous for the horses to keep going and dawn cannot be far away so we'll rest until then. You get some sleep while I watch."

"I must admit I could do with a nap," said Brasidas as he slid to the ground. "But wake me before daybreak so I can take over the watch from you." They left the road, leading the horses carefully into a clump of trees which were mainly cedar by the smell of them, then Brasidas handed his reins to Caius and was asleep as soon as he touched the ground.

It seemed just moments later when Caius woke him. As he drew breath to speak, Caius put a large hand over his mouth and whispered, "Quiet, something's wrong." It was no longer pitch black because Brasidas could clearly see the outline of the large Roman against a slightly greying sky as he leaned over him. "The horses are uneasy. We'd better leave now rather than wait for dawn. Be as quiet as a mouse and be ready to mount if I give the word."

They left the shelter of the cedar trees, leading their horses and nervously peering into the darkness around them. When they reached the road, Brasidas noticed a patch of black, darker than the surrounding night, which he took to be a boulder or a tree stump. But it moved.

Caius, just behind him, saw it too.

"Mount! Now! Ride as fast as you can and don't look back!" Brasidas needed no second bidding as a group of shadows appeared seemingly out of the ground and came rapidly towards them. He leapt onto his mount and dug his heels into its flanks. The horses were already nervous and sensed the fear in their riders; the pony lurched straight into a gallop. Brasidas felt something brush against his leg. He kicked out viciously, but a hand gripped his foot. He kicked out again; there was a dull moan and the hand released him. He heard a cry of pain behind him; he hoped it was not Caius. Later, he was ashamed he did not even think of going back to help, but it mattered not because within a few seconds he heard the sturdy cob pounding up beside him.

A friendly voice called out, "Brasidas, are you all right?"
"Yes, what about you?"

"A couple of nicks, that's all. Just keep galloping." "What about the pot holes?"

"Bugger the pot holes! We'll take the risk. Just behind us lurks certain death. These night hunters may have horses too."

The cob and the pony kept going until there was daylight enough to see a good distance behind them as well as the road surface. Caius called a halt.

"How far have we come?" asked Brasidas as he gratefully dismounted and rubbed his sore buttocks.

Caius looked back down the road and shielded his eyes against the red rim of the sun which was just appearing above the Judean hills. "Seven or eight miles, I should think. No sign of a pursuit, though."

"So those night hunters must have followed us from Jerusalem on foot."

"Yes, a twelve-mile night march; they must be fit. I think we may have come across them before."

"When?"

"Last year, the night before the battle with the Zealots at Mount Carmel. One of our sentries was discovered in the morning with his throat cut. He was on duty only a few paces from Varus."

"I remember; he was only young," replied Brasidas who noticed blood on Caius' hand. "You've been wounded."

"It'll mend." He wiped the blood on his tunic and cleaned the wound with water. "I see your pony's been hurt. I'd better have a look." He cleaned and washed a deep gash on the left rear leg of Brasidas' mount; the blood still flowed but slowly. "I think they were trying to hamstring your pony, but they missed the target in the dark; he'll be fine, but we'll need to slow down for a while, at least until the bleeding stops."

"So when will we reach Caesarea?"

"Tomorrow night. We should be with Varus five days later. If he moves quickly, the legions could reach Jerusalem ten or eleven days after that."

"Then let's hope Piso can hold on that long."

"Amen to that, but if anyone can he can."

***

IV

"Wake up! Wake up! We're under attack; the enemy's in the camp!" As I struggled to wake up, my door flew open and a soldier of the fourth century gasped breathlessly, "Centurion hurry! There's been a surprise assault on the unfinished side of the camp." I leapt out of my bunk and began putting my armour on. "Where is your century now?"

"Holding an improvised line between three barrack blocks, but the Jews are in overwhelming force; we can't hold for long."

"Zealots?"

"Not sure, sir. They're armed with swords, shields and cuirasses."

"Sounds like regular Jewish soldiers; we'll soon see. Get back to your century and tell Gnaeus we're coming."

My barracks were on the easternmost side of the camp and furthest from the fight, so we were the last to be roused. I quickly gathered the men outside and addressed my oldest and ugliest section leader. "Galerius, your section must stay here and guard the ramparts; there may be more Jews outside. The rest of you, follow me."

We trotted through the camp casting long shadows; the sun was rising behind us. I remember the golden rays warming my back and feeling I was not ready for death just yet. The scene that met us on the western rampart was a full-scale battle. The armoured Jews had broken through the perimeter and were pushing up against a ragged crescent of legionaries holding a thin line which stretched from the junction of the southern and western ramparts, through gaps between barrack blocks all the way to the northern rampart. The Jews were at least double our number and more were streaming into the camp to support their comrades. Our line was about to break. The din and clash of battle made thinking difficult. I looked for Piso and saw him with Severus Pollio and Gnaeus Servilius just behind the centre of our line so I led my century towards them.

When I reached them, Piso spoke as calmly as if he was attending a senatorial garden party. "Welcome, Lucius; we're in a tight spot. We must restore the western rampart in the next few minutes or be overwhelmed. At the same time, we must protect the causeway link to the city's south gate; that's our only way out of here. Severus, your century will guard the causeway and the south gate; keep them clear of the enemy at all costs."

"I will, sir," answered our grim-faced, senior centurion.

"Gnaeus, your century is the only reserve we have. I will join you in a counter attack in a minute." Gnaeus, centurion of the fourth century nodded and touched the hilt of his sword. Then Piso addressed me. "Lucius, I want you to take your century to the southern extremity of our line. When you see Gnaeus and me charge, you must lead your men in a narrow column and force yourselves between the enemy and the western rampart. When they feel their escape route being cut off, they may be less eager to go forwards; well, that's the theory anyway."

Severus asked, "What if they attack from the east? We have nobody there."

"Well, at least we'll have warning," I answered. "I left a file there to keep watch."

"Good thinking, Lucius," said the old campaigner. "We'll make something out of you yet!"

Piso drew his sword. I noticed it was his favourite, long-bladed cavalry spatha. "Centurions, to your posts!"

A few moments later, we were in position. My men were eager to do their bit. I had the large, comforting presence of Rufio beside me. "Pity Caius isn't here," he muttered. "He'll be sorry he missed the fun."

"True, but I suspect there'll be plenty of 'fun' waiting for him on his mission. Are you ready?"

"Ready as I'll ever be, but I don't think our enemy are regulars even though they are clad like regulars."

"What makes you say that?"

"With the numbers they have, they should have broken our line by now, so while you were with Piso I watched them closely. They're not using their swords properly. Instead of thrusting with the point, as all professional infantrymen should do, they're wielding them like clubs and using the edge instead of the point. It looks spectacular but it's ineffective against properly trained soldiers."

I scrutinised the fighting more closely. "Apollo's balls! Rufio, you're right! They're clubmen dressed as regular Jewish soldiers. Must have been part of the haul they made from the Sepphoris weapons store. Pass the word to the men."

It was full daylight when Piso led his counter attack with Gnaeus' century. He made little headway because the Zealots saw him coming and prepared themselves. By contrast, our attack came as something of a surprise and initially we made good progress capturing the southern half of the lost rampart. Just as Piso predicted, some of the victorious Jews on our right began to look behind them concerned at seeing their route back to base being cut off, but then our advance slowed due to the efforts of a single man. He was a fine-looking fellow standing on top of the western rampart calmly giving orders to his officers. It was he who rallied his wavering men and inspired them to halt and turn on us. He was about thirty paces from me.

Rufio was still beside me taking a quick rest. "Rufio, cover me while I try and knock over their leader." The big

Pannonian stood in front of me while I bent down to pick up a fallen pilum which must have been lost at the start of the fight. The Roman throwing javelin is an effective weapon at ranges up to thirty paces, so this was going to challenge the limit of my powers. I took careful aim and hurled it at the Zealot leader. He was young and fit and easily saw it coming. With a minimum of effort, he deftly parried it to one side with his shield as if it was made of straw. He was already carrying a shoulder wound, but it did not seem to impair him. There was another pilum near me. I stooped to pick it up but, just as I was taking aim, he saw me and deliberately lowered his shield challenging me to try again. I knew the result would be the same so, rather than give him the satisfaction of another little victory, I simply let the pilum drop to the ground. The young leader threw his head back and laughed and, despite myself, I could not help responding in kind. There is no harm in respecting your enemy.

Now the fighting became particularly hard. The reformed Zealots fought back spurred on by their brave leader and, no doubt, the fear of being cut off from their retreat. For a while, it was touch and go, but gradually the better sword play of the legionaries began to tell. Whenever a Zealot raised his arm to strike with his sword edge, he was forced to move his shield a little, sideways or downwards, in order to give his sword arm enough clearance to deliver the blow. If he left his shield in place, he would inevitably strike the rim with his own sword, so when he lowered his shield, the Zealot's body was open to a counter thrust from the Roman gladius. I encountered this myself when a heavily built Zealot tried to decapitate me with a powerful stroke at my neck. I parried his sword with my shield and easily dispatched him with a sword thrust to his undefended groin. He sank back onto his haunches with a quiet groan. I pushed him over with my shield and moved forwards.

A quick look round gave me hope. For every fallen Roman, there were at least seven dead or badly wounded Zealots; they began to give ground again. Their comrades facing Piso and Gnaeus became discouraged and they too edged backwards. Fear is contagious, especially amongst inexperienced troops, and soon they were in headlong flight despite the best efforts of their leader to rally them. Piso and I met on the western rampart. Every soldier knows that the greatest damage to a defeated enemy is caused during the pursuit rather than in the battle itself, but our men were so tired they just collapsed onto the ground where they stood. We had no need to restrain them so we watched, as exhausted as they were, while the Jews ran back to their starting point somewhere out of sight from us. The last to disappear was their leader.

By noon, we had assessed our losses. Although we had almost been beaten, our casualties were less severe than we expected thanks to the poor skill-at-arms of our enemy. Certainly, there were plenty of superficial bruises and flesh wounds caused by sword cuts, but these would soon heal. Our butcher's bill was only twelve dead and fifteen wounded of whom just three were unlikely to recover. Against this we counted forty-one Zealot corpses which increased to sixty-six after we had finished off the wounded. Knowing the value the Jews place on a proper burial, Piso ordered us to dump the enemy dead, less their armour, outside the camp for the Jews to collect under a flag of truce, which they did later in the day. Anyway, we did not have enough combustible material to burn the bodies ourselves and we certainly did not want rotting corpses contaminating our camp.

Next morning, Piso summoned his centurions again to review our situation. "Gentlemen, I am delighted to see you all got through yesterday unscathed, well more or less," he added as he noticed a bandage wrapped round Gnaeus' arm. "I have called you here to ask your views about what we should do now. We are down to just over three hundred men fit for duty but face an enemy that gets stronger by the day."

Severus replied, "So much depends on when Varus gets here, sir."

"Well, he should have received our message by now so if he acts promptly, which I believe he will, he should get here with the legions in twelve or thirteen days."

"I checked this morning, sir. We have water for a month at least, so there's no problem there. If we go to half rations now, we can make the food last that long too."

"That's good to know. Thank you, Severus."

The centurion of the second century, a tough, one-eyed veteran from Hispania called Titus Cotta, said, "Should we consider abandoning the camp and joining the Galatians in the citadel, sir? Our combined forces would be a tough nut to crack and the citadel walls are a far more formidable obstacle than our earth ramparts here."

"You make a fair point, Titus," acknowledged Piso. "The Galatians would welcome our support, but we will only be able to bring what we can carry because we'll have to fight our way through to the citadel and leave our food, stores and equipment behind for the Zealots to plunder. Another three hundred mouths to feed might put a strain on our friendship with the Galatians. Much depends on when the Zealots try again. Any thoughts on that?"

There was no immediate response so I answered, "Not for at least ten days, sir."

"How do you work that out, Lucius?"

"Yesterday, the Zealots matched us for courage and this time they were properly armed; they nearly won. They lost because they did not know how to use their new weapons properly. It was obvious and their commanders will have seen it as clearly as we did. They will need time to find weapons trainers and more time to learn and practise sword play and the aggressive use of the shield. It takes months to train a legionary but the Zealots know they haven't got that long. My estimate of ten days assumes trainers can be found in Jerusalem."

Severus agreed, "Lucius is right sir, though none of us can know if there are enough retired professional soldiers in Jerusalem to train so many men so quickly."

"There will be plenty in Capernaum," replied Piso thoughtfully. "That is where the Jewish army is based. If the Zealots decide today to contact General Achiab for trainers, they could be here in four days. Then, using Lucius' estimate of ten days to train them all, we have a respite of fourteen days. Varus could be here by then."

"Unless Achiab decides to throw in his lot with the Zealots and join them with the Jewish army." said Gnaeus sombrely.

"True," agreed Piso. "But there is nothing we can do to influence that. On the balance of what I have heard, we will remain here in the camp and do what we can to improve the defences around it and reinforce the link to the city's south gate." There was a murmur of assent from us then, lowering his voice a little, Piso added, "I have one more thing to say. I have got to know you all well so I should tell you that I bitterly regret allowing us to be caught out yesterday. I am responsible for the deaths of twelve of our brave men. It will not happen again."

Severus responded on behalf of us all. "No-one could have foreseen that attack, sir. Your centurions have already discussed that. I know you will forgive me for saying that you are still young for the rank of a tribune, but yesterday you led from the front and, when the crisis came, you conceived a plan to recover the camp's perimeter and gave your orders as clearly and calmly as any true veteran. We would have been lost without you; the men know it as well as the centurions. Now they will follow you to Hades and back if you ask them to."

"And so would we," said Titus Cotta.

Humility is a quality not greatly valued amongst the senatorial class, the class which included Piso's family, but it is highly regarded in the army. Piso had it in abundance. He blushed and was lost for words. Eventually, he managed to stutter, "I, err… I thank you for your support gentlemen. We did it together." Then, recomposing himself, he asked, "When will the west rampart be completed?"

"The day after tomorrow," answered Severus.

"And the barricades round the city gate?"

"By tonight."

"Good, then I think—" Piso was interrupted by what sounded like a huge thunderbolt landing just outside his office. The ground shook under our feet.

"Ye gods!" exclaimed Gnaeus. "What in the name of all the Furies was that!" We rushed outside. The gable end of the barracks next to us, which belonged to the third century, had been demolished.

Piso looked skywards. "Well it can't have been a thunderbolt, there are no clouds in the sky. Start searching the debris." Fortunately, no-one was hurt because the third century was outside on digging duty. We carefully started to sift through the splintered wood and, after an hour or so, I came across a large rock half buried in the ground beneath the shattered barrack block. I was about to speak when someone shouted, "Watch out above!"

We all looked up and out of the blue sky a large flying object approached us at great speed. It landed with a thud in the middle of the parade ground. Severus grimaced, "Arms and armour were not the only things the Zealots looted from Sepphoris. The bastards have got a ballista!"

CHAPTER ELEVEN

Ten days passed since the raid on Sepphoris. The tender results for the two subcontract bids had been rejections and now the financial impact of paying men with no work was beginning to show in the accounts. Judas was disconsolately checking the financial statement for the month of Nissan (March) when Joachim arrived at his office.

"Welcome, Joachim. I was about to have my midday meal. Would you care to join me?"

"Thank you, yes. I bring great news. While the new king is absent in Rome, the Governor of Syria has sent his financial prefect to manage Herod's estate. This prefect has not only set up his headquarters in a part of the temple forbidden to gentiles, he has looted the temple treasury!"

"And this is good news?"

"The best, for he has done what we have been unable to do; to unite our people. The wealthy commercial class accepted Roman occupation, as you well know, because of the stability the Romans brought. Trade flourished and we were ruled with a light touch; we were even allowed to keep our religion so there was no incentive for the Judeans who govern us to risk change. To them we are primitive, uncouth Galilean country folk who cause trouble. Now, all that has changed. The rich use the temple to store their wealth just like a bank, but now their money has been stolen they are baying for blood.

The smug priests have seen their sanctuary violated; they are furious. Already there are riots in Jerusalem. Even Achiab is considering joining us but though he has not committed yet, his men may force him to. Judas, we are a single people again just like in the days of David and Solomon. Bar Abbas has summoned all his men. We will be gathering at the spring camp."

"How many?"

"About four thousand. We will march on Jerusalem in a few days' time."

"Should we not wait for Achiab and his army?"

"We dare not wait. We must strike while the people's anger is still red hot. If we wait, the faint-hearts' resolve will weaken, but if we win, success will nourish it to greater heights. We must get as many as possible to commit to our cause while we can."

"Very well. After we've eaten, I'll pack a bag and join you."

"Tomorrow will be soon enough," smiled Joachim. "This afternoon I have something to show you. It's a surprise."

Joachim's surprise was an hour's march into the hills west of Nazareth. As they walked along a winding shepherd's path Judas asked, "Did we really manage to raid the Sepphoris weapons store without losing anyone?"

"Not quite," answered Joachim. "One of the Shadows lingered a little too long not realising the Galatians had already broken out of the barrack blocks. He was cut off from his comrades, but there was still enough moonlight for Isaac to see him slit his own throat before the Galatians could reach him."

"Very brave."

"Yes, but standard Shadow procedure. The nature of their

work means they know most of our secrets so they cannot be taken alive. Expert torture will break even the strongest man; suicide is a much easier choice."

Judas pondered on this for a while. The unquestioning faith the Zealots possessed of a glorious afterlife unsettled him. That was why they were so formidable. He wished he could feel so sure. Perhaps he lacked faith? But now was not the time for too much introspection. He brought the conversation down to a lower plane. "Was any of our plunder recaptured?"

"No, it has all been dispersed to safe places. In fact, we had only just hidden the last of it when the call to action came. Speaking of plunder, my surprise is in that olive grove just ahead."

Waiting at the entrance to the olive grove was Jonathan, the young commander who had led the men that kept the garrison penned in during the Sepphoris raid. He beamed a radiant smile, "Hello Judas, have you come to see Joachim's new toy?"

"I think so."

Jonathan called to a group of eight Zealots standing beside something hidden under a large, grey shroud. "Uncover it!" Two of them pulled the shroud away to reveal the fully assembled Roman ballista.

Joachim chuckled, "Well, Judas, what do you think?" "It's beautiful; was it difficult to assemble?"

"No, a child could have done it. The Romans are nothing if not thorough. Detailed assembly instructions were in a drawer in the trolley that supports the ballista."

"Can I see it work?"

"That is why I brought you here." Then Joachim

addressed Jonathan's men, "Prepare to shoot!" While four of the Zealots began winding the mechanism that created the tension in the rope sinews strapped to the ballista's wooden spars, the other four dragged a large boulder towards the leather hood of the ballista and, with huge effort, carefully lifted it into the hood. When all was ready Joachim said, "Judas, do you see that deserted shepherd's hut near the cedar tree about three hundred paces yonder?"

"Yes."

"Well it will disappear in a few seconds. Watch." He signalled to the ballista crew. "Shoot!"

The tension lock was released, the spars sprang forwards and the great boulder shot skywards in a beautiful arc against the blue Galilean sky. Moments later, the cedar tree was flattened but the hut remained untouched as the sound of splintering wood reverberated towards them.

Joachim cleared his throat. "Yes, well we still have one or two matters to sort out regarding accuracy, but you get the general idea."

"I certainly do," smiled Judas. "I suspect you will be more than accurate enough to cause havoc with the Roman garrison in Jerusalem."

"I hope so. Now watch this." Joachim gave new orders to the ballista crew. "Prepare to use shot!" This time the ballista was loaded with many large stones about the size of a man's fist. When the crew had finished there must have been at least fifty in the hood. Now Joachim said, "Do you see that line of olive trees to the left of the shepherd's hut?" Judas nodded. "Well imagine it is a line of Roman soldiers." Joachim shouted to the crew "Shoot!" The shot soared skywards like a flock of angry birds but this time the target was hit and almost all of the olive trees were shredded.

"Now what do you think about that!" boasted Joachim triumphantly.

"Good shooting, but what will the farmer say?"

"Nothing, he is one of us. If we had possessed this weapon when we fought the Galatians at Mukhmas we would have broken their ranks well before the Roman horsemen arrived to save them. The ballista is not just a siege weapon, it can be used in open battle too."

"Obviously," agreed Judas. "Then the sooner we use it the better."

***

II

Judas left the frustrating problem of winning building contracts to Ehud while he joined Joachim and his levies who were itching to meet bar Abbas and the Zealot army for the march on Jerusalem. His failure to win more work for Joseph was a stark contrast to his successes with bar Abbas. He could not understand where he had gone wrong, he had always thought he had a good business brain, but he resolved to put his disappointment behind him as best he could until he returned to Nazareth.

While Joachim's column of irregulars was heading south, disturbing news came from Sepphoris. Judas the Galilean had reappeared with the unwelcome consequence of presenting a second messiah to the united Jewish people. He had also attacked the weapons store with more than a thousand men and slaughtered the garrison taking all the weapons that bar Abbas' men had left behind. Unfortunately, the Galatians had been withdrawn after the first raid and been replaced by some of Achiab's men.

"So," growled Joachim when the news reached him. "The Jewish people have been united for less than a month and already they are killing each other."

Judas, who was walking beside him as the day's march was drawing to a close, said, "Judas the Galilean is always going to be trouble. We should deal with him once and for all as soon as we have captured Jerusalem."

"That will mean Jews killing Jews again."

"I have met him. It is impossible to reason with him."

"Maybe a great victory in Jerusalem will persuade his followers to abandon him and join us."

"Maybe," agreed Judas. "But they will need help because they live in terror of him. Now I have seen what the Shadows can do, it may be best to use them to remove just one man and avoid harming the rest. With the Galilean dead, I am sure his men would flock to us."

"That makes sense, but we will have to strike while he is far from his home base in the north; not even the Shadows could get to him up there."

Jerusalem was still a day's march away. Bar Abbas had already entered the city under cover of darkness with his personal bodyguard when a messenger arrived in Joachim's camp. He was a handsome, enthusiastic youngster recently recruited from the angry city population and had run so hard he was too breathless to speak clearly.

"Take your time," said Joachim paternally. "Speak when you are ready."

"My Lord—"

"I am not a lord, just a warrior of God like you." The young messenger glowed with pride at the compliment from such a senior officer. "Sir, I bring a message from bar Abbas. He says the Romans are expecting trouble and are fortifying their camp, but the work is not yet complete. He wishes you to halt your men and join him in Jerusalem with all the armoured soldiers you have as soon as possible."

Joachim was surprised by the order. "Messenger, what is your name?"

"Joshua bar Amos."

"Well Joshua, are you absolutely sure bar Abbas wants my column to halt?"

"Yes, except for the armoured soldiers. He was most clear on that point."

"Very well, I will arrange some refreshment for you then I'll carry out the orders immediately. Have you enough energy to run back to the city after you've eaten?"

"I will go now, sir."

"I am sure you would, but you will get there sooner if you eat first. Tell bar Abbas that we will be with him in three hours. Where is he?"

"In the safe house."

"Thank you, Joshua bar Amos, you have done well."

A tired red sun was setting when Joachim and Judas reached the safe house. With them were sixty-seven clubmen who had been re-armed with the loot from Sepphoris and looked for all the world like true Jewish regulars. Judas smiled to himself; the safe house may have been safe until now, but with nearly seventy men crowding round it, the Zealots would have to capture Jerusalem or find another one.

"Welcome to army headquarters," said bar Abbas as Joachim and Judas climbed the well-trodden stairs. "How many men have you brought with you?"

Joachim shrugged, "Difficult to say. Men keep joining us as we march. They do not ask for payment but just the chance to rid our land of foreign occupation. They are ill-armed and untrained, but they will be good for at least one charge. As we speak, I estimate there are between four and five thousand but that will increase by the time we reach the city."

"And armoured men?"

"Sixty-seven."

"Good, that makes about eight hundred fully-armoured men in all." Bar Abbas dismissed the various messengers and assistants who were in attendance so that the three of them were alone. "We have an opportunity for a quick victory but it's risky, so I'd appreciate your advice. The Romans are well aware of the progress of your column and are preparing their camp against an attack."

"We've brought the ballista"," said Judas helpfully.

"We may not need it. I wish to avoid any kind of siege if possible because our numbers will wither the longer it takes. The Roman camp is roughly square in shape. Although it is outside the city walls, the north wall of the camp is only fifty paces from Jerusalem's south gate. The Romans have built a fortified causeway linking the two."

"So they control who comes and goes by that gate," remarked Joachim.

"Yes, which gives them a tenuous link with the Galatians in the citadel and with the temple but, more importantly, their fortification work is not yet complete. They think they have at least another day, possibly two, to prepare for an attack. So far, they have dug a deep ditch round three sides of their camp and thrown up the spoil to create a rampart ten paces high with an earthen wall on top. They have stuck sharpened wooden stakes in the rampart which point towards any potential attackers and have also placed large boulders on top of the earth wall ready to roll down on them."

"Very thorough as usual," muttered Joachim.

"But," continued bar Abbas. "They have only completed three sides of the camp. The fourth, the western one, is but half built. They are working on the ditch and the rampart, but above the rampart the wall is still low and as yet there are no stakes or boulders. I propose we attack at dawn tomorrow with only our armoured warriors initially. We can bring forward the rest of our men once we have broken into the camp, but it is crucial they stay out of sight for now because the assault must come as a complete surprise. The Romans usually finish work at dusk but, if they suspect an attack is imminent, they will work throughout the night and be well prepared by dawn. Well, what do you think?"

There was silence for a while as Joachim and Judas digested what they had heard. It was Judas who spoke first. "How many Romans are there?"

"We know the cohort has not been reinforced since it got here so, allowing for casualties at the Mount Carmel battle and the usual wear and tear of campaign, I estimate a little over four hundred."

"Where are our men?" asked Joachim.

"Scattered in small groups outside the city. The Romans have no idea they are here. I can concentrate them for an assault in less than two hours. When we have beaten the Romans, the Galatians will surrender the citadel if we offer

277

them terms. They are only mercenaries and I doubt they've been paid since Herod died."

Joachim said, "Then let's do it."

Bar Abbas turned to Judas, "Your view, please."

Flattered by being consulted by his hero, Judas replied, "A most excellent plan Eli and well worth the risk."

"I'm glad you both approve. I shall lead the assault in person."

"No!" responded Judas and Joachim together.

Bar Abbas smiled, "My friends, I understand and appreciate your concern but this time I must lead. This is likely to be the most important battle we ever have fought. Victory will keep our people united and give us time to prepare for the inevitable Roman response. Achiab will stop dithering and maybe the Parthians will come at last. If ever a leader needs to lead from the front it is now. Joachim, as soon as the attack begins, send a messenger to bring up the rest of your men in case they are needed. You and Judas will stay here and direct them into the battle when they arrive."

Joachim shook his head. "Eli, you are too valuable to risk but, if you order it, I will obey."

"I would never give you an order. I ask you as my friend and guardian."

"Well, if you put it that way, I will do as you ask."

"And you Judas will stay with Joachim. Now that is an order!"

Judas looked at his feet and said quietly, "I understand."

As bar Abbas was finishing speaking, the young messenger, Joshua, ran up the stairs and announced, "Sir, you have two visitors, both are priests from the temple."

"Well that didn't take long," replied Joachim. "They have

spies everywhere. Send them up."

Two white robed figures entered. The tall elegant one Judas immediately recognised; Caiaphas. The older one, clearly full of self-importance, looked slowly round the little room as if the walls were made of something untouchable. His grey streaked beard was long and his eyes bloodshot with too much good living. "Who commands here?" he asked in a rich, well rounded voice which was pleasing to the ear.

"I do," answered bar Abbas.

"Then you must be the brigand Elijah bar Abbas."

"Just bar Abbas."

"Well, you know who I am of course."

"No," lied bar Abbas. Well done, Eli, thought Judas.

The priest raised his bushy eyebrows in mock disbelief. "I am Ananas bar Seth, chief secretary to the high priest and with me is my assistant, Caiaphas, who is betrothed to my daughter." That will speed up his promotion mused Judas ruefully; nothing will stand in the way of his ambition.

"What do you want with us, Ananas bar Seth?" asked bar Abbas in a neutral tone.

"I demand you free our temple from Roman occupation immediately."

"You do not give orders here."

"The temple is defiled, the treasury is being looted. It is your duty."

"Are you an expert in military tactics?"

"I am the chief secretary."

"Then listen well, chief secretary. When I presume to walk into your temple and lecture you on the laws of Moses, then you may tell me my duty as a military commander."

Ananas could no longer restrain himself. "Zealot fool!

279

You dare speak of the laws of Moses while you allow God's temple to be desecrated and plundered!"

In contrast to the chief secretary, the young Zealot leader retained perfect self-control. "As you say, the temple is already defiled so waiting a day or two longer will make no difference. As for the treasury, we Zealots are poor people. What little wealth we have is in our small farms and livestock; the treasury means nothing to us. And as for the laws of Moses, who do you think the great prophet would recognise as closer to the Israelites of old, the well-fed priests and lackeys of a gentile empire occupying the Promised Land, or the simple tillers of the soil?"

"You will regret this, I promise you that."

"You have said your piece, chief secretary. Now you may leave."

Just before they left the room, Caiaphas at last noticed Judas. "I see you have one of those well-fed lackeys you speak of with you bar Abbas. Judas' father is a rich merchant who lives in Jericho. Doubtless his wealth will now be in Roman hands."

"The son of the father is made of different mettle," replied bar Abbas. "Now leave, my patience is wearing thin."

***

III

The night was cold. Judas' bones felt chilled as he joined Joachim at the top of a small knoll about four hundred paces from the western rampart of the Roman camp. In the low ground around them, eight hundred armoured Zealots were kneeling in serried ranks waiting for the command to advance. There was to be no horn sounded, no shouting; surprise was everything so the order was passed down the ranks by word of mouth from man to man. Consequently, the centre, where bar Abbas had stationed himself, advanced first with those to the right and left a little behind. The result was that the assault went forwards in the shape of a spearhead rather than a line, with bar Abbas at the point. The night sky was beginning to lighten in the east; sunrise was just minutes away.

"The Romans haven't seen our men yet," whispered Judas. "And they must already be more than half way to the rampart."

"It's going well so far," agreed Joachim. "The light is behind the Romans so we are coming at them out of the dark. Even so, they should have seen us by now; they must be very confident."

The spear point of the attack had almost reached the ditch at the base of the rampart when the alarm was sounded. Soon Joachim and Judas could just make out a flurry of activity along the top of the wall, but there still only seemed to be a few defenders in place when the Zealot tide reached them. Shouts of anger and screams of pain began to echo back to the watchers on the knoll as the fighting began in earnest, but it was still too dark to make out what was happening. As far as they could tell, the attack had stalled at the wall but so far only the leading Zealots were engaged.

Quite suddenly, the rim of the sun appeared on the eastern horizon casting a golden light over the battlefield as if a warrior angel had just lit a huge celestial lamp. It was just in time for Judas and Joachim to see the main body of the Zealots surge up the rampart and over the wall like a wave of sparkling silver steel.

"They're in!" exclaimed Joachim. "By Holy Jehovah, they're in!"

"Have we won then?"

"Not yet, Judas, but we've made a good start. The rest of our men will be on the march by now. They should be here in half an hour or less."

"It looks like they won't be needed."

Judas' words were premature. Ten minutes passed, the battle raged and, if anything, grew more intense. Joachim began to worry. "The fighting seems to be confined to the area near the wall; we should have pushed forward into the main body of the camp by now." As if to confirm his misgivings, one or two Zealots scrambled down the outer face of the rampart and took cover in the ditch below. Soon, a few more followed — some of whom began to retrace their steps to the starting point of the attack; not all were wounded. It was not long before the entire Zealot force was in full retreat; something had gone badly wrong.

Joachim's reinforcements were still a few minutes away and too late to affect the result of the battle. He said, "Judas, let us go and find out what has happened."

"And pray to God Eli is unhurt."

"Amen to that."

Fortunately, there was no pursuit; the Romans were too exhausted but by the time Joachim's men arrived, the camp was safely back in Roman hands. Without even waiting to have his shoulder wound bandaged, bar Abbas called an immediate meeting of his war council while Joachim's fresh men took up positions to hold off any possible Roman counter-attack.

The meeting took place in a tent behind Joachim's and

Judas' observation knoll. Ariel bar Eleazar, Jonathan bar Jacob and Isaac, the leader of the Shadows were present as well as bar Abbas, Joachim and Judas.

"We should have won today," lamented bar Abbas. "We almost did. If an adult messiah had been present, we would certainly have won."

"We will have to wait twenty years for that," said Joachim sadly.

Isaac asked, "Eli, what went wrong?"

"Training, or rather the lack of it. I should have seen this coming. For the first time, we were properly armed and armoured but when the fighting started it soon became obvious that underneath that armour, we are still just clubmen. We wielded our swords like clubs while the Romans simply took the blows on their large shields and cut us to pieces. It would have been better if we had kept our clubs; at least we know how to use them."

"Then what now?" asked Jonathan.

"I will not send our brave men into battle again without proper training."

"But we have no trainers, Eli," said Ariel.

"I know, but Achiab has. We will ask him to send as many as are needed to train all our armoured men in the correct use of the sword. If he acts quickly, we shall still have enough time to beat these Romans and capture Jerusalem before Varus can send help. We have news that Achiab has moved his army south from Capernaum to Beth Shan. I suppose he thinks he's doing something, but at least that puts him only two days' hard march from Jerusalem. Judas, I want you to go to him immediately and persuade or threaten him — I no longer care which — to send us trainers. He can surely do that and still sit on the fence like the coward he is." "I will leave immediately, Eli," replied Judas.

"And take twenty armoured soldiers with you as your bodyguard."

"Thank you. I would like to take Joshua too."

"Joshua the messenger?"

"Yes."

"But why?"

"I may need to get a message back to you quickly, more quickly than the speed of an armoured bodyguard."

Bar Abbas paused and looked at him strangely in a way that made Judas feel uncomfortable. "Very well, Judas, if you think it necessary, but hopefully you will be back here with trainers within five days." Then the Zealot leader turned to Joachim. "And now, old friend, while we are waiting and training, let us see what your ballista can do."

***

IV

It was now Iyar (May) and the days were becoming hot. The most direct route from Jerusalem to Beth Shan is along the Jordan valley, which is low lying and much hotter than the capital, but for the sake of speed, Judas chose to go that way. This meant travelling through Jericho. As he passed the walled city, he resolved to visit his father on the return journey. The last meeting had ended badly and, at the back of his mind, he knew his father was not a well man who would not wish to die without a reconciliation with his only son.

Judas and his bodyguard reached Achiab's camp, which

was just south of Beth Shan, at around noon on the third day of the journey. Unsure of his reception, he decided to try diplomacy first rather than demanding the help the Zealots required; he could always resort to threats if persuasion failed. Surprisingly, Achiab granted him an immediate audience and allowed Joshua and the armed bodyguard to accompany him. They were first taken to a large tent where they could wash after the arduous journey. Then bread, cheese and dates were brought together with a little wine and cold spring water. By the time they were ushered into Achiab's campaign tent they were thoroughly refreshed.

Achiab was not at all what Judas expected. From bar Abbas' account, he thought he would meet a weak, cringing apology of a man; far from it. Despite being his cousin, he bore no resemblance to Herod. In his mid-forties, Achiab was tall and imposing. His hair and beard were iron grey and his large, dark eyes seemed warm and perceptive. When he addressed Judas, it was as an equal not a commoner.

"Welcome to my campaign headquarters, Judas bar Menahem. I see from your credentials you are from Jericho."

"Yes sir."

"So am I. I am sure our families must be acquainted though I confess I do not recall Menahem."

"Sir, we are of humble stock and you are the cousin of our late king. It is unlikely our families know each other."

"Maybe so, but think nothing of it. Allow me to introduce you to my senior officers."

While Achiab reeled off the names of the ten officers with him, only one of which Judas could later recall, he observed his surroundings. He was surprised at how simply furnished the campaign tent was; no rich tapestries or gilded trinkets, just a simple wooden table with a jar of water in the middle, ten plain goblets and a few bronze lamps for light in the evening. The chairs were unpadded but comfortable and the floor was bare earth. There was no concession to luxury anywhere.

"And now, Judas," said the general. "We are aware of the situation in Jerusalem as of a few days ago. Perhaps you would update us and tell us why you are here?"

Judas briefly described the battle for the Roman camp and the shortcomings of the Zealot swordsmen. He concluded, "So although we now have the weapons, we urgently need training in sword handling so that we can attack again before the Governor of Syria can send help. Once we have destroyed the Roman garrison, we will fortify the city and take on Varus' reinforcements from a position of strength."

"What about the Galatians?" asked Achiab.

"We will offer them terms and let them leave."

"What if they do not accept your terms?"

"They must; they are only mercenaries." Even as Judas uttered these last few words, they sounded hollow — more like wishful thinking than reality.

Achiab raised an eyebrow but did not press the point. "You will be pleased to know that I have not been entirely idle. I have sent two thousand light infantry and five hundred horsemen to Sepphoris to hunt down Judas the Galilean. You may already know he murdered my men guarding the city under a flag of truce?"

"I did not know about the flag of truce."

"Also, dealing with your namesake may persuade the Romans we were on their side if things go badly in Jerusalem."

"We will win," said Judas defiantly.

"You will pardon my scepticism, but you are taking on the

most powerful empire the world has ever seen."

"God is with us and we have the Messiah."

"Who is but a baby so I hear."

"So you do not wish to help us then?"

Achiab smiled, "I did not say that, but I have to think of the consequences if we lose. The Romans are not bad masters as long as they receive their taxes, but they treat rebellion harshly."

"It is taxes that are driving our people to starvation."

"True," agreed Achiab. "But not just Roman taxes. Most of the taxes we pay have funded Herod's extravagant lifestyle and his self-glorifying building projects, not to mention the voracious demands of the temple priesthood."

"At least we can agree about the priests," said Judas.

"Then consider this, my young firebrand. The Romans give us special treatment; we do not have to worship any god but our own and they leave us alone to govern ourselves. These are privileges not granted anywhere else in the empire. Until the end of Herod's reign, we seldom saw a Roman soldier in Jerusalem and, with the emperor as a distant overlord, Herod managed to expand his kingdom to a size rivalling that of David and Solomon. He was strong but he was also a monster and hated by his people. He was never really accepted by the Jews because of his fondness for Greek-style living, extravagance and cruelty. Under a more moderate king, who respects our traditional values, we could live well even if it means accepting we must be an outlying part of the Roman Empire."

"Will Archelaus be a good king?" asked Judas.

"Alas, I think not, but he has a half-brother called Philip who could be."

"But Herod has left Judea and Jerusalem to Archelaus."

"Yes, but a decision yet to be confirmed by the emperor who is an astute judge of character." Judas was beginning to feel a sort of empathy with this well-informed, avuncular cousin of Herod, but he was wary of being drawn into an easy way out of the struggle that must come. He needed to question Achiab further but to do this he must be respectful.

"Sir, you speak of empires, but we Jews had an empire once, so why could this not happen again?"

"You ask a good question Judas. It is possible that it could happen, but there are two reasons that mitigate against a new empire of the Jews as you propose. The first is numbers."

"I don't understand."

Achiab leaned forward in his chair, determined to make a fundamental point. "It is a matter of race versus citizenship. When the Romans conquer a people, they usually install a governor to rule over them but, after a generation or two has passed, they begin to confer Roman citizenship upon the local governing class provided there has been no rebellion against Roman rule. In effect, the native rulers are confirmed in their positions and are made into Romans with all the rights and privileges that brings with it. It has even started here. I am a Roman citizen as was my cousin. By these means, Rome has access to huge resources of manpower. There are very few true born Romans in their legions; their army is an imperial army drawn from all the peoples of their empire. Even the senate now has provincials within its ranks; I have no doubt there will soon be an emperor who will have been born outside Rome, even outside Italia. Now compare that to us. While the Romans include any subject peoples as citizens, we exclude all. We call them gentiles. I know it is possible to become a Jew by marriage or even by religious conversion but generally, if you are not descended from Abraham you cannot be a Jew. So while we must rely on natural reproduction for the manpower we need to become an imperial power, the Romans simply draw on the resources of the conquered. If we go to war against them, we may win victories in the beginning, but they have an inexhaustible supply of men which will overwhelm us in the end.

"So we have no hope then?"

"Our only hope is to wear them down so they get bored and tired of the cost. That means years of war with no guarantee of success at the end of it all."

"Yet David and Solomon created an empire despite all the disadvantages of manpower you have just described."

"That is true," acknowledged Achiab. "But there were circumstances surrounding their success which are unlikely to be repeated."

"Which were?"

"A power void. All the great empires of their time were in trouble. The Hittite empire was collapsing before the onslaught of the Sea Peoples, who also came close to overwhelming Egypt. The Assyrians were being swamped by hordes of nomadic desert tribesmen while in the east, Babylon was under attack from Elam. So there was no major power to prevent a small, well led people like the Jews from expanding their borders. And it is worth remembering that it did not take long for the quarrelsome nature of our people to re-assert itself when Solomon died, which led to the break-up of our empire without the help of an outside power."

Judas did not know enough about Jewish history to debate Achiab's opinions so he did not try to. "Will you send us weapons trainers or not?"

"Of course, but I will do better than that. I may be a Roman citizen, but I am a Jew first. My brother Asher will lead a thousand volunteers, including weapons trainers, to help you." One of the officers sitting near Achiab stood up and acknowledged Judas. He was of much the same appearance as his brother, but a few years younger. "But," cautioned Achiab, "Asher and his men clearly understand the terms upon which they will join you. If you win, they will be heroes, but if you lose, they will be deserters and hopefully the Romans will be persuaded that my army did not take the field against theirs. Be in no doubt, I believe you will lose and I have a responsibility to my men not to commit them to a war they cannot win."

Judas was delighted. This was far more than bar Abbas could have hoped for. "Thank you, sir, and if we do win, will not the Parthians join us in the struggle against Rome?"

"That may not be as straight forward as you think. The Parthians have a new king. His name is Phraates and I have met him more than once. He is young and ambitious, rather like you. If you take Jerusalem he will probably come, but he will expect a reward for his efforts. You could end up swapping one master for another but Parthia's capital, Cteisiphon on the Tigris, is much nearer to Jerusalem than Rome. You may find yourself with a less tolerant, more meddlesome overlord than you have now. However, my guess is that Rome will beat Parthia, as it usually does, and destroy us too."

"Then why are you helping us?"

"As I said, I am a Jew. Bar Abbas has set forces in motion which are outside his control, but when it comes to Jews against gentiles, I must do what I can to help the Jews. At the same time, I will prepare for the worst. What else can I do?"

Judas had no answer but, unlike bar Abbas, he respected this man. His own faith in absolute victory had been shaken by Achiab's simple logic. He needed time to think. "Sir, we are most grateful for your support. How soon will your men be ready to march?"

"Daybreak tomorrow."

"And what will you do?"

"I am not exactly sure yet but, for the moment, I will stay in Beth Shan and wait on events. And now you and your men will accept our hospitality until you leave tomorrow."

***

V

Next morning Judas, now accompanied by Asher and a thousand regular Jewish soldiers, began the journey back to Jerusalem. It was already getting warm, but Asher left his horse with a groom and chose to walk with Judas and his bodyguard at the head of the column. Judas looked back at the neat files of marching armoured men and said, "They don't look much like deserters, do they?"

Asher, less serious than his elder brother, smiled "Then let's hope for victory so they become heroes instead."

"Your brother thinks there is little enough chance of that."

"And he is right but holding back sits uncomfortably with him; you heard his reasoning."

"I could not fault it. Maybe now is the time when reason must give way to inspiration. Remember, we have the Messiah."

"Judas, is it really true that he escaped the slaughter in Bethlehem?"

"Yes, by a hair's breadth. I was there. We were saved by two Romans."

"Romans! But why?"

"I do not know. All Joseph, the Messiah's father, would say was that it was a debt of honour. He refused to say more when I pressed him."

"I do not understand."

"Neither do I, but at least we know the Messiah is safe in Egypt."

"How sure are you about his heritage? I thought all family records dating back to King David's time were lost when the Babylonians destroyed Solomon's temple five hundred years ago."

"Most were destroyed but not all. However, records tracing the Messiah's ancestry were saved. The true King of Israel now resides in Alexandria."

Asher was silent for a while. When he spoke, there was an air of resignation in his voice. "It seems we have acted twenty years too early. We cannot be led by a babe in arms."

"I am beginning to think you're right," agreed Judas. "But Herod's death and the desecration of the temple have forced the issue into the present day. The Zealots feel they are riding a wave of resentment strong enough to throw off the Roman yoke now."

Asher shrugged, "Then I suppose God will decide."

They reached Jericho two days later. It was evening and Judas suggested they camp near the city so that they would be fresh for the march on Jerusalem next day. While that made sound sense and was agreed by Asher, Judas had another motive. He was about to go into battle, he might not survive, so it was important he made peace with his father. The last meeting had been fraught, so there should be a reconciliation if possible, and Judas felt it was his duty to make it happen. So while Asher and the regulars made camp outside the city's lofty walls, Judas and Joshua entered Jericho by the north gate and headed towards the family home.

It was almost two years since Judas had last stood at the doors of his father's house. So much had happened since then. Then he had been but a callow youth. Now he felt he was a fully-fledged man with experience of the world, a senior Zealot commander with battle experience. Yet he was still his father's son.

Once again, anxiety assailed him as he knocked on the doors but this time he was not alone; he had Joshua the messenger with him. The door creaked open. For a moment, he did not recognise the small, shrivelled figure that faced him. "Arethus, is it you?" He could hardly believe the deterioration in the old slave since last they met.

"Master Judas, thank God! You have arrived just in time."

"Arethus what do you mean? In time for what?"

"Your father is dying. He had a seizure a week ago and has been unable to speak since. Your arrival may give him the strength he needs. Come quickly."

They went through to the reception room which Arethus had refurnished as a temporary sick bay. At the far end near the entrance to the courtyard Menahem lay in bed seemingly asleep.

"Shall I wake him?" asked Judas.

"You can try but he has been like this since the seizure. I

think he is unconscious rather than asleep."

Judas knelt down beside his father whose breathing was fitful and irregular. He held a wizened hand, which felt cold and limp, and rubbed it as if he could infuse some warmth into the cold, pallid body. There was no response.

"Father," he whispered. "It is Judas your son. Squeeze my fingers if you can hear me." But there was nothing.

"The physician says there is nothing more to be done," said Arethus without troubling to lower his voice, as if Menahem was already dead. "Your father's time has come."

"Not much of a physician then."

Joshua spoke, "Forgive me for intruding into a private matter, but I always carry salt of hart's horn. If there is perfume in this house, I can mix the two and it will make a strong, pungent smell which will revive anyone who can be revived."

"We are not short of perfume here," replied Arethus. "In fact, we have a bazaar full of it! I will fetch the lady of the house at once."

The old slave returned accompanied by Rachel, who was carrying a small, sleeping bundle in a sling strapped over her shoulder. She was as beautiful as Judas remembered and just as menacing. "So you are a doctor now?" she enquired sarcastically.

"I would like to wish my father farewell, that is all," answered Judas stiffly.

"And for this you need perfume?"

"Yes, to make a reviving solution by blending it with a powder that my comrade Joshua has with him."

Rachel handed Joshua a small phial. "It is not one of my best."

"For this process it does not need to be," answered Joshua

warily. "I only need a few drops."

While Joshua was preparing his potion, Rachel uncovered her sleeping bundle. "Judas, this is your brother. His name is Jacob; he is nearly a year old."

Judas looked at the tiny, perfectly formed features. He could not help smiling. "He is beautiful," he said.

"Yes, he is. Your father is proud of him. He began to walk a month ago which is very advanced."

"Is he a good boy?"

"Perfect. He already sleeps throughout the night."

When Joshua had completed his potion, he held up a small, cedar wood box. "I am ready. When I remove the lid, be prepared for an unpleasant odour." He put the box under Menahem's nose and took away the lid. A sickening smell of stale urine assailed them. Judas gagged. Suddenly, Menahem's limp hand gripped Judas'. He stirred and moaned. Now there were involuntary movements beneath the eyelids. Slowly, seemingly with huge effort, the eyes flickered open. They were bloodshot and vacant.

Judas whispered, "Father, can you hear me?" The old man's parched lips began to move, trying to formulate words, but no sound came. "Arethus, water quickly," urged Judas. The old slave held a goblet to Menahem's mouth and allowed a few drops to dampen his swollen tongue. Then, at last, Menahem managed to gasp through a hoarse whisper, "Judas, is that you?"

"Yes, Father." The grip on his hand tightened still more.

"My boy!" The eyes slowly turned towards him but were still unfocused. "Can you hear me?"

"Yes, Father."

At last, the eyes seemed to show recognition, but only

momentarily as they saw something behind Judas. Suddenly, blind terror flashed from them. Then the eyelids shut tight for the last time. The mouth struggled to speak again. Judas put his ear close to his father's lips; he could just make out the final words. "She knows."

Judas turned round. Rachel was standing close behind him. "What did he say?"

"It was too soft to hear," lied Judas. "I am not sure if there were words at all, just breathing." He put his head to his father's chest. "His heart still beats, he may speak again. I shall sit with him tonight. Joshua, thank you for your help. Now go back to Asher and tell him I will re-join the column at dawn."

Attempting a show of concern, Rachel ordered Arethus to prepare food and make up a bed for Judas next to his father's then, when they were alone apart from little Jacob and the dying Menahem, she said, "Judas, you seem to have matured since last we met."

"I have joined the Zealot sect. I am now a senior commander in bar Abbas' army."

"How senior?"

"I have a thousand warriors under my command."

Rachel clearly did not believe him. "Really? A thousand? Are you sure your numbers are correct?"

"They are camped outside the city walls. Count them if you like."

"I shall do that." For the first time, the mocking tone in Rachel's voice was absent. "Your father would have been proud to know of your success. What a pity he cannot appreciate it now."

"He is not dead yet. I have also learned that there are many shades of grey between black and white."

"Are you talking about me?"

"Not really, more about life in general."

"Well that is true enough. What will you do now?"

"Tomorrow I leave for Jerusalem to join bar Abbas in the fight to win back our freedom."

"Men! Is that all you can think about? Fighting!"

"The cause is just and the Romans have desecrated the temple."

Suddenly, Rachel became interested. "Have they, indeed? What have they taken?"

"Most of the treasury and we have heard they are burning the record library to keep themselves warm at night; years of family history is going up in smoke."

"What else has been destroyed?"

"The scrolls charting the history of our people, wills, contracts and so on. We will have to start afresh."

"Will you be in danger when you get to Jerusalem?"

"No more or less than any other man."

Rachel's voice softened, "Then go carefully, Judas bar Menahem. Dead heroes are plentiful and no use to the living." She returned to her quarters leaving the scent of rich perfume hanging heavy in the air. While he waited for Arethus to return with the blankets for his temporary bed, Judas pondered. That was the first proper conversation he had had with Rachel. She seemed almost human.

He sat up until the early hours, but there was no sign of consciousness in his father. Eventually, tiredness overcame him and he fell asleep on the bed beside the old man.

"Judas! Judas!" For a moment, he thought he was dreaming but, as he opened his eyes, he realised the voice calling him was Rachel's. "Judas, wake up, we must speak."

He sat up and wearily rubbed his eyes. "But it's the middle of the night."

"I know, I know but you will be leaving early in the morning. We must speak before then." She had brought an oil lamp which was on the table beside her; it cast enough light for Judas to see she had made up her eyes and lips as if she were going to a wedding feast. She wore a white, linen night shift. An embroidered shawl was draped over her shoulders.

"Judas, I know we have not been friends, which is mainly my fault, but now the time has come for us to be practical. Your father is dying and you are now a man. I shall soon be alone and will need a protector for little Jacob and me."

Judas was now wide awake and concerned by the direction the conversation was taking. "How can I help?" he asked nervously.

"When your father is buried, marry me. We are the same age and I could give you many children."

His misgivings were now fully justified. "But you must know that would be breaking the laws of Moses. No rabbi would marry us. The law does not allow a man to marry his father's wife, who is still legally his mother, or rather his step mother. If that happened, I would be both brother and father to little Jacob. It cannot be."

"But we could leave Jericho and set up home in a gentile town like Caesarea. The gentiles are far less fussy over who marries whom."

"But Rachel, we are Jews. We live by the laws God gave to Moses. They make us what we are."

Rachel was not deterred. "Judas, you are now a strong and handsome man. Despite our past differences, I could love you if you would only let me. See, I am beautiful; I could make you a wife you would be proud of." She moved so that she was standing between him and the lamp. Then she let her shawl fall to the floor. With the light behind her, he could clearly see the outline of her shapely body through the thin, white shift. "Judas, look at me. Am I not beautiful? Any man would want me, but I am offering myself to you."

When he had first met her, Judas felt an unwelcome stirring in his body, but now that was gone. For better or worse he spoke the brutal, unvarnished truth. "Rachel, I have no feelings for you and I am not just any man. My father, your husband, is not yet dead but you are already offering yourself to me. You should be ashamed." The rejection was complete.

The silence in the room was tangible. Slowly, Rachel bent down and drew her shawl round her shoulders once more. The warmth that had briefly filled her eyes was gone and the voracious, spider like beads returned. She wiped the red paint from her lips as the dawning of understanding, an understanding that even Judas did not yet appreciate, infused her mind.

Her voice was dull and threatening. "That boy Joshua, what is he to you?"

"He is my messenger."

"I know that but what does he mean to you?"

"I do not understand what you are suggesting."

"Yes, you do. I understand now. I always thought there was something strange about you. You are one of those abominations that prefer men to women!"

"I prefer men's company, that is true," protested Judas defensively.

"No, no! You prefer their bodies too!"

"I do not."

"I see it all now. You dare to quote the law to me yet you love men instead of women which is a sin far worse than I was proposing. You hypocrite! Why did I not see this before! As you said yourself, you are not any man. You are no man at all! Return to your sweetheart and indulge your sinful ways, but never contaminate the threshold of my house with your disgusting presence again!"

Rachel swept out of the room leaving the lamp behind. Judas looked at his hands; they were cold, sweaty and shaking. To be the object of such unbridled hatred unnerved him deeply. He did not sleep again that night.

As dawn broke, Judas prepared to leave. His father had not regained consciousness and from the sound of his light, sporadic breathing, he was on the verge of death. Arethus was already awake and walked with Judas to the city gates, which were just being opened for the day.

"You are quiet this morning, Judas." Judas had resolved to say nothing about his encounter with Rachel the previous night, but the invitation to talk changed his mind. Talking might help. He needed comfort from someone and Arethus was just the right person, so he told him everything.

"Well," said the old slave. "'She'll be in a foul mood this morning. I shall keep well out of her way."

"But what do you make of it all Arethus?"

"Is what she said about you true?"

"Of course not."

Arethus stopped walking and looked hard at him. "Are you sure?"

Judas had searched his soul most of the night. This was going to be difficult. "The truth is I don't think so but I'm not certain. I have never lain with a woman and felt no desire to do so, but nor have I felt desire for a man in that way. I have always been too busy to give much thought to it until now."

"The Zealot men of your age; are many of them married or betrothed?"

"Almost all I think."

"And Joshua the Messenger?"

"No, but he is still in his teens."

"Well it seems your comrades have found time for marriage or betrothal, but remember they will have been helped by their families. You have had no help in that way although I am sure your father would have liked to have found a girl of good family for you. Perhaps the opportunity has not arisen yet." Judas felt greatly relieved by this logical analysis but before he could respond Arethus added, "And if Rachel does prove to be right, there is no sin or breaking of God's law for what you may think; no-one can control that. It is your actions by which you will be judged."

This was an unwelcome sting in the tail even though unintentional. Arethus obviously thought Rachel might be right, but the comfort he was trying to give was not the succour Judas was seeking.

***

VI

The column set off an hour after dawn with Judas and Asher at the front again. Achiab's young brother glanced back at the well-watered oasis that was the reason for Jericho's existence and then at the parched desert ahead of them. "Judas, you know this area better than me. When do you think we'll reach

Jerusalem?"

"About the middle of this afternoon,"

"Should we send a message ahead to warn bar Abbas? We might be walking straight into a battle."

"Of course, I should have thought of that. I'll send Joshua."

As he watched the fleet-footed Joshua trotting off ahead of the column, Judas realised he had been so concerned about his own sexuality, he had even forgotten to tell Arethus about his father's last words, 'she knows', and the fear with which they were spoken. What was it that Rachel had found out? As soon as the fighting was over, Judas decided he would return to Jericho and investigate for himself.

The arrival in Jerusalem was greeted rapturously by the citizens. Bar Abbas welcomed the column just outside the north gate of the city amidst unfettered joy at Achiab's unexpected help. "Not only trainers but a thousand professional soldiers too," he beamed as he embraced Judas and Asher. "I must send Achiab a letter of thanks."

"He would rather you not do that," replied Asher. "If we lose, my brother will want there to be no evidence that he approved of this. Until we win, we are deserters."

"But how can he doubt we will win now?"

"He is cautious."

"Very well, I will write him a letter in a few days' time from Herod's own palace. Tonight, we will feast and you shall see how far we Zealots have come in the art of siege warfare!"

The next morning, there were a few sore heads when the Zealot war council gathered at the safe house to discuss tactics for the coming days. Bar Abbas opened the debate by asking Joachim to explain to Asher how effective the ballista had been.

"To begin with our accuracy was wayward," began the old campaigner. "The safest place to be was wherever we were aiming for, but gradually we improved and now all of the Roman barrack buildings have been damaged or destroyed. We have perfected our range, which has enabled us to continue using the ballista during the night, so although we can't see where the boulders are falling, we can assume the Romans are getting no sleep knowing the next one might land on any one of them. Lack of sleep becomes debilitating before long so, even if we have not caused a large number of casualties, the garrison will be dead tired by now."

"That will soften them up for the assault," said Asher approvingly.

Bar Abbas asked, "We have seven hundred and thirty armoured soldiers who need training in swordsmanship before we can attack again. How long will that take?"

Asher answered, "I have twenty officers with me who can train your men. Assuming one officer can train, say, thirty-five men at a time and, allowing time for them to practise what they learn, we will need about ten days."

Bar Abbas frowned, "That's too long. Varus could be here with his legions by then. Can't you do this more quickly?"

"Only at the expense of inferior training."

"Well, do what you can in seven days or eight at the absolute most. We will attack as soon as the training is finished. Meanwhile, keep the ballista busy Joachim."

Asher's men were deployed outside the citadel to support the Zealots who were keeping the Galatians penned up inside, but only a few days later disturbing news came from the north. Bar

Abbas immediately recalled the war council to the safe house after the evening meal had been taken. "The Romans have moved more quickly than we expected. Five days ago, two legions were observed marching down the coast road towards our border with Phoenicia. They will have passed Caesarea by now."

"Then they'll be here in three days," said Joachim.

"And they were accompanied by three auxiliary cavalry cohorts who could even be here by the day after tomorrow."

Asher replied, "We can deal with the cavalry."

"Maybe so," agreed bar Abbas. "But we must capture Jerusalem before the legions arrive. Two legions plus three cohorts amount to about eleven thousand men. Also, to that number we must add the two thousand Galatians in the citadel and the soldiers in the camp here. That makes over thirteen thousand in all. We have six thousand we can rely on plus Asher's thousand and goodness knows how many irregulars, who are adequate for guard duty and carrying supplies, but who will melt away when the serious fighting begins. Asher, how goes the training?"

"Half of the armoured men are ready, but the rest need at least another three days."

"We cannot wait that long. We must attack tomorrow night. Withdraw your men from the citadel and replace them with the half-trained men. Your own men can take part in the assault on the camp; they will make all the difference. We cut all communications between the camp and the outside world when we surrounded it, so the Romans probably don't even know you're here. We'll save that for a surprise when the time comes. "

Isaac, the Shadow commander, asked, "Do you want my men to try and infiltrate the camp just before the attack? We could perhaps eliminate some of the sentinels."

Bar Abbas thought for a moment. "No, I think they will have greater value putting some backbone inside our irregulars."

Suddenly, there was a commotion at the door, then a breathless Joshua ran up the stairs. "I am sorry to interrupt, but the officer of the watch sent me. He says the Romans seem to be preparing to abandon their camp. Horses and provisions are being moved towards the city's south gate."

The room fell silent. Everyone turned towards bar Abbas. The Zealot leader, fully aware of the significance of this news, looked at each of his officers making them understand without the use of words that now was the moment of truth. It was at times like this that he was at his best.

First, he spoke to Joshua. "Return to the officer of the watch, commend him from me on his sharp eyes, and tell him to stand by for further orders in the next few minutes." Joshua ran back down the stairs, half tripping over the last one in his excitement. Then bar Abbas addressed his officers. "We must bring forward the attack to dawn tomorrow and abandon the cover of darkness."

"My men prefer to fight in daylight anyway," remarked Asher.

"And so they shall. Ariel, I remember how well you carried out your task at Sepphoris. You will take command at the citadel. The Galatians may try to break out and help the Romans; you must stop them."

"What about the irregulars, sir?"

"Make sure they don't get in the way."

Now bar Abbas spoke to Jonathan. "You also distinguished yourself at Sepphoris. I want you to stay by my side when we attack the camp and take battlefield command if

I fall."

Joachim interrupted, "Your shoulder wound has not yet healed."

"It does not hurt and won't stop me knocking off a few Roman helmets. If I fall, you will be in overall command of the Zealot army, so you will have to stand back and be prepared to take over the direction of the battle."

Bar Abbas quickly turned to Asher before Joachim could object. "I will lead the attack on the camp with our fully trained swordsmen and five hundred clubmen. The aim will be to draw as many Romans into the fight as possible. Keep your men well-hidden but, when you judge the time is right, you will attack and capture the causeway that links the camp to the city gate. That is the only line of retreat the Romans have, so you must cut it."

Asher answered grimly, "I will sir, whatever the cost."

"Good. All of you need to remember this will be a fight to the death. The Romans must die so take no prisoners."

"Not even the Roman commander?" queried Asher.

"No prisoners. Now, if I fall you must all have your orders. Asher, you will return to Achiab and tell him of our victory. Ask, no, demand that he marches with all his forces on Jerusalem to help us confront Varus. He must also get word to the Parthians. Ariel, when the Roman camp has been destroyed, offer terms to the Galatians. They won't know how close the legions are, so you should be able to persuade them to leave the citadel; we will need it to fend off Varus. The terms can be as generous as you like; just get the Galatians out."

"I understand, sir."

"Jonathan, if you take command of the field army, you will need to prepare for the Roman counter-attack. Make sure you liaise with Ariel."

"I hope you will be there to make that order unnecessary."

"So do I. Isaac, my only order to you is continue to do what the Shadows do best and report directly to Joachim."

Then bar Abbas addressed his oldest friend and mentor. "Joachim, if I fall you will become the leader of the Zealot sect. Its future will be in your hands. I trust no-one more than you to lead us to victory. When Varus has been beaten, the time will come for you to oversee the cleansing of the temple. At the same time, the temple priesthood must be reformed so that they serve the people instead of themselves. Appoint a new high priest who shares our views before Archelaus gets back from Rome."

"Simon?"

"He will be perfect if he accepts. If he does not, then choose from a Levite family not tainted by corruption; there are not many of them left." Now bar Abbas lowered his voice and spoke almost apologetically, "Friends, things may not work out as we expect so we must also plan for the unthinkable. If God in his wisdom decides to grant our enemy the victory, you must know what to do because almost certainly I will have fallen. We will have lost the best chance of throwing off the Roman yoke in a generation, but we cannot give up the fight. However, great patience will be needed. If we have not secured Jerusalem before Varus gets here, we cannot engage him with the enemy at our backs. Therefore, we must melt away to our homes so that the Romans find nothing when they arrive. Go back to your families. Have many sons and bring them up ready to fight for our cause; that is exactly what I shall do if I survive. Resume normal lives until the Messiah comes of age to lead us in person. We can use this time to build more support amongst the people, especially the young, so when the Messiah is ready, he will have an army at his back of tens of thousands."

Ariel asked, "How long must we wait?"

"I am not sure; perhaps twenty years."

"It seems a long time," sighed Ariel. "I shall probably be dead. How can we be sure the Zealot cause doesn't simply fade away?"

"Because the dynamics will be the same; the Romans will still be here, the priesthood may still be corrupt and most of God's own people will be starving in their efforts to subsidise the degenerate lifestyle of their masters. But to be doubly sure, we six will meet once a year on Yom Kippur at the camp by the lone pine. Asher, you are also invited if your duties in the army permit it. There we will discuss and debate our hopes and fears but, most importantly, we will learn of the progress of the Messiah." Bar Abbas now spoke directly to Judas. "You have been most patient but I have not forgotten you. Before battle commences tomorrow, I will send Joshua the messenger to Alexandria with orders to recall Joseph and his family. Win or lose, the Messiah must now come home to be given your teaching and guidance. You will report on his progress when we meet at the lone pine and give us warning of when he will be ready to lead his people. Therefore, on no account must you join the battle tomorrow. Your mission lies in Nazareth. Is that clear, Judas?"

"Abundantly."

"Good. Then all of you go now, prepare your men for tomorrow's dawn and make your peace with God. You leave with my blessing."

CHAPTER TWELVE

The south gates in the city wall in Jerusalem are an imposing structure. The gates themselves are made of mature oak imported from the cold lands in the north with each timber weighing the equivalent of twenty large men. They are set upon huge iron hinges and secured from the inside by six massive bolts which require two men to slot them into place. On either side of the gates are rectangular bastions which overtop the city walls by thirty feet. Inside these bastions, the defenders can shoot arrows through slots cut into the walls at anyone who tries to attack the gates. On top of the bastions are crenulated battlements within which at least thirty men can drop rocks or hot oil over an attacking force. In short, the walls are proof against all but the most determined assailant.

It was eleven days after the ballista bombardment on our camp began. Although less than an hour after dawn, it was already becoming hot as the sun burned away the early morning mist. On top of the western bastion of the south gate, a group of men had gathered. To a perceptive observer the transverse crests on the helmets of six of them would have identified them as centurions. The bare headed seventh was Piso, the cohort tribune. They stood beneath the pennant of the fifth cohort of the Third Legion Gallica fluttering in the light breeze.

"Well gentlemen," said Piso. "Look about you. Our

barracks are mostly smashed by the ballista, the Zealots are now properly armoured and equipped and a mob of thousands stands between us and the citadel. Our barricades on the city side of the south gate look firm enough but they have yet to be subjected to a determined attack. Will they hold?"

Titus Cotta, centurion of the second century guarding the barricades said, "We could hold for perhaps a quarter of an hour sir, but not much more." Titus had lost his left eye fighting the fierce Danubian tribes with Tiberius, the emperor's stepson, but his injury in no way affected his fighting qualities.

"Well that will have to be enough then," replied Piso. "For tonight, we will abandon our camp."

"But our stores and equipment will be lost sir," objected Gnaeus Servilius, centurion of the fourth.

"I know Gnaeus. We will take all we can carry but the men cannot take much more of this punishment. The ballista is not only destroying our camp but our morale too. Our barracks are in splinters and no-one can sleep at night for fear of where the next ballista boulder will land; some of the men look like walking dead. We will not be able to withstand another attack like the one we repelled eleven days ago, and next time the Jews will come in greater strength. We need rest and stone walls to protect us."

"What do you suggest, sir?" asked Severus Pollio, centurion of the first.

"We do not have the numbers to make a sortie to destroy the ballista so, much to my regret, we must retreat to a stronger position. You can see the citadel containing our Galatian friends about six hundred paces to the west of us, but that way is blocked by the enemy. Yet less than two hundred paces to the northeast is the temple mount. The Zealots are well led. They expect us to try and link up with the Galatians but, as you can see for yourselves, there are far fewer of the enemy between us and the temple."

"But the temple walls are too long for us to defend," said Titus, "there simply aren't enough of us."

"True," agreed Piso. "But Sabinus' ruffians will boost our numbers and, more importantly, there is the Antonia fortress."

We all looked northwards across the city. Abutting the northwest corner of the temple was Herod's palace fortress which he had built to overlook the temple precinct to get early warning of trouble at festival times. It had four towers at each corner and thick masonry walls. It was a far tougher obstacle than our camp for the Jews to crack and easier for us to defend with our reduced numbers.

Piso asked, "Have any of you seen inside the Antonia fortress?" We shook our heads. "Nor have I, but it is said to contain luxurious rooms and even baths. It also has a staircase connecting it to the temple."

"Surely the enemy will have occupied it, sir?" I said.

"Probably, but not in strength for they will not be anticipating an attack from the direction of the temple. As soon as we reach the temple, we'll go straight for the connecting stairs, break down the doors and surprise the garrison. Lucius, how many are left in your century?"

"Fifty-three fit for duty, sir."

"Then detail some of them to carry one of the structural beams from our shattered barracks to use as a battering ram."

"What about the ballista?" asked Gnaeus. "Will not the Zealots bring that up and batter the fortress?"

"Unlikely, because of the danger of hitting their precious

temple. Even if they do, the fortress walls will give us far more protection than we have now." We all approved of the plan so Piso continued, "Now, the withdrawal from our camp must be carefully managed; we don't want to encourage an attack while we're doing it, so tonight we'll move all that we can carry to the barricades on the city side of the gates where Titus' men will be waiting. Make sure everyone carries two full water containers. Then at daybreak we will all join Titus at the barricades, gather our supplies and break out to the temple. Severus, your first century shall have the place of honour and guard the causeway until the other centuries have crossed. Then you will follow and shut the gates and bolt them in place which should hold off the Zealots at least until we have abandoned the barricades."

"And if the Zealots do attack while we're withdrawing?"

"Then we must fend them off. Severus, whatever happens, you and the first must hold the causeway!"

"You may count on it, sir."

"I know. Now, all of you brief your men. Today, everything must look normal to the Jews; give them no reason to suspect we're going to abandon the camp."

My men were delighted when I told them about Piso's plan, especially when they heard about the palace luxuries in the Antonia fortress.

Rufio said, "I would die for a hot bath. Why must we wait till dawn? Why don't we withdraw under the cover of darkness?"

"Two reasons," I answered. "First, there will be no moon tonight, so we would have to light torches to be able to see; that would give the game away. Second, when we reach the temple, Sabinus' men will need to see us before they open the gates. If they remain locked, we're finished."

The hot day seemed to drag interminably but at last, after another day of battering by the ballista which killed one of my men, the sun began to set and we prepared to move our equipment, including the improvised battering ram, to the barricades. By the time we finished, it was dark. We were exhausted but despite the lottery of death delivered by the ballista, most of us slept well for the remainder of that night.

A slight greying in the eastern night sky warned of the approaching dawn. I was woken by one of Piso's junior officers with orders to assemble my century at the mouth of the causeway. When we got there, we found the third, fourth and fifth centuries already assembling. The first was guarding the causeway and the second manning the barricades. All orders were given in a whisper as my sixth century joined the right of the line facing Piso and his staff. Our tribune raised his voice just enough so all could hear.

"Is everything ready? Answer by numbers." The centurion of the third century, Marcus Sempronius, answered, "Ready sir." He was followed by Gnaeus of the fourth, but before the centurion of the fifth could respond, a cry came from one of the sentinels on the western rampart. "Here they come!"

Suddenly, Piso's carefully laid plans were in ruins, but the experiences of war had provided him with the ability to give those around him the confidence that he was prepared for the unexpected. He had no need to whisper now. "Fourth century stand fast and guard the entry to the causeway! Third, fifth and sixth, follow me." There was just enough light for us to see our tribune trotting towards the western rampart, the exact same place where we had been attacked before, but this time we were ready. There were about a hundred and fifty of us in all, but we were able to form a line of interlocking shields at the top of the rampart before the first of the Zealots struggled up the slope towards us. Once again, the points of the sharpened stakes hammered into the earth slope broke up the solidity of their charge, and consequently they closed on us in scattered groups rather than a single wave. Each legionary carried two pila, the devastating throwing spears used to break up an enemy assault, and when the Zealots were within twenty paces of us, we hurled our first pilum at them. The effect was deadly and the leading Jews fell like wheat stalks to the scythe. But there were hundreds following, pushing forwards in an unstoppable mass. The second pila discharge brought down many more in screaming, tangled confusion; briefly the assault faltered, but the pressure from behind was inexorable and soon the Zealots closed with us along the earth wall at the top of the rampart. Our shield wall bore the full brunt of their fear and anger.

The fighting was even harder than before. Immediately, it was obvious to us that the armoured Jews had been trained in the use of their weapons since the last attack. I was taken by surprise as a burly Zealot smashed the upper rim of his shield upwards into mine nearly lifting me clear off the ground. I tried to recover my balance, but his sword point knocked me backwards as it struck my helmet, grazing my cheek at the same time. I was still reeling when he rammed his shield into mine again; his face and mine were now so close his beard was almost touching me. His foul breath swept over me as he panted with exertion. There was no time for fear, just desperation. All I could do was kick out. He dropped on one knee and briefly his helmeted head was level with my chest. I could not wield my sword properly, we were both too tightly packed for that, so I brought my pommel down as hard as I could on the back of his neck. I do not know if I killed him or just knocked him unconscious, but either way he fell as the tide of battle swept me away before I could deliver the final blow.

I was not the only one caught out by the skill of the armoured Jews; they gained a foothold on our side of the earth wall rather too easily for my liking. For a while, things looked bad as our line buckled, but fortunately for us these armoured Jews did not outnumber us by much, if at all, and as our line straightened again they were joined by the more familiar clubmen who were far less formidable; if anything, they got in the way of their comrades and eventually we were able to regain the earth wall and force them part way down the rampart slope.

There followed one of those brief, unplanned lulls in the fighting as the Zealots fell back a little way to regroup. Piso came up beside me. "How goes it with the sixth, Caius?" I drew breath but before I could utter a word, a cry of alarm came from the causeway. We both looked round. My heart sank as I saw our struggle had been for naught. Seemingly out of nowhere, hundreds of well-armed, regular Jewish soldiers had emerged from behind a cluster of hovels near the city wall and were advancing at a steady trot towards the causeway, our only means of escape. They approached in almost perfect silence, professional and determined; we were staring defeat and death in the face.

As always, Piso remained calm. The Zealots to our front had withdrawn about fifty paces from the rampart, which gave us a little breathing space. Once again, our tribune rose to the occasion. "Third, fifth and sixth centuries, follow me now!" We abandoned our position and followed him to the causeway where Gnaeus' fourth was guarding our side of the access. The causeway was only wide enough to take four men abreast, so we were forced to stop while the third century crossed followed by the fifth. By the time it was our turn to cross, the Jewish regulars had hurled themselves at Severus' first, who lined the causeway, while those we had been fighting swarmed over the rampart and assailed the fourth. The din of battle seemed to come from all sides at once; my memory of this part of the fight is fragmentary. I crossed the causeway behind the last of my men. I recall passing Severus, who had lost his helmet and was bleeding heavily from a head wound, as he fought off three Jewish soldiers trying to break through his line. Our thin defences were about to snap. Piso was just behind me calling Gnaeus' men to follow. We stumbled over bodies scattered at irregular intervals; all order was being lost, the retreat was becoming a rout.

At last we reached the city gates, which were being held open for us by men of the second century. We staggered inside but as soon as Piso entered, he ran up the stairs of the nearest bastion to get a better view of what was happening. I should have gone with him but was too exhausted. The men of Gnaeus' fourth were following us but were hard pressed by a determined pursuit. Some of them had not yet reached the gates when a sudden surge from the Jewish regulars at last broke through Severus' first century and cut off their retreat. The Jews flooded through the gap, swords and spears spreading death all round them. Some headed for the still open gates, determined to prevent us from shutting them. We hesitated.

Our friends and comrades in the first were still out there manfully fighting against huge odds; it ran contrary to all our instincts to abandon them. Then we heard out tribune's voice bellow down at us from the bastion.

"Close the gates! Now!" Still we hesitated, reluctant to leave Severus and his brave men to their fate. Piso called again, "The first is gone! Close the gates or we are all lost!"

This time, we reacted and began to push the great gates shut, but bodies lay in the way and the Jews were pressing forward from the other side. Suddenly, the toothless Galerius appeared with Rufio beside him. "Come on, sir, we can beat this lot. Remember Carmel!" That gave me the spur I needed. I sheathed my sword, threw down my shield and together with men of Titus' second, we pushed hard on the gates until they slammed shut. Titus' men slid the bolts into place and, for a few precious seconds, we could rest.

***

II

Our respite was brief. Within a few moments, Piso came down from the bastion. We were all crammed into the small space between the city wall and Titus' barricades, so there was no need to shout. Still our tribune, exhausted though he was, remained ice cool in the crisis.

"Listen men. We have just suffered a defeat but we are not yet beaten. There is still more work to be done before we reach safety and we owe it to our brave comrades of the first century to avenge their sacrifice." This was greeted with a murmur of assent. "The Jews are busy plundering our camp so we may rest here for a few minutes. Then we must break out of the barricades and head for the temple. Titus, your century will form the rear-guard and hold back the mob. As far as I could see, there are no real soldiers amongst them yet The rest of you, carry what you can. I do not expect you to fight again today."

During the short time available, we centurions reorganised our men so we were ready when Piso gave the order. "Cohort advance!" It was full daylight now and we could easily see the temple walls directly ahead of us. We scrambled over the barricades leaving Titus and the second to guard our rear, but the mob spotted us immediately and surged towards us. The second deployed into line on our left flank and gave us the protection we needed. We soon reached the wide steps beneath the Hulda Gates and gathered below them, but they remained shut. The noise of the mob was getting closer despite the best efforts of the second to hold them off.

Piso said to no-one in particular, "Sabinus' men must have seen us. Why are they waiting?" Someone answered, "Maybe they're asleep."

"Well then, I'll wake them up," and filling his lungs he bellowed, "I am Licinius Piso, tribune of the fifth cohort of the Third Legion Gallica. Open the gates!"

A head appeared over the wall above us. "Password?"
"Just open the fucking gates!"

"That'll do!" The head disappeared and just as the second was being driven in upon us, the gates opened at last. Galerius exclaimed, "Ye Gods! Piso's swearing like us! Now we know we're in trouble!" Despite the danger, this received a muted laugh and gratefully we staggered into the shelter of the temple's outer courtyard. I fell exhausted, onto the cool, paved floor without seeing the spirited rear-guard action of Titus' men, who covered us until the gates were slammed shut. For the moment, we were safe.

I must have fallen asleep as soon as I lay down, but it seemed only seconds later that Piso woke me. "Lucius, I'm sorry to waken you but we are not yet finished. I know we're all tired, but I must ask you for one last effort. The Antonia fortress remains in enemy hands, we must take it now before the Jews have time to prepare themselves. Use your battering ram and eliminate the garrison. Leave any of our seriously wounded men in the fortress and then return to me here."

"Yes sir."

"I want to make the Zealots think we are going to defend the temple, so they will have to prepare for an assault. That should give us a few more precious hours. Gnaeus' century will occupy the fortress after you have taken it; the fourth is well below half strength. Is all that clear?"

"Yes sir." I forced myself to my feet and wobbled on weary legs; close quarter combat is the most arduous activity known to man. As I moved off to find my men, Piso called after me,

"And get that cheek wound seen to as soon as you can." I gathered my exhausted men together in the middle of the temple courtyard; forty-four fit for duty, more or less, but there were three seriously wounded and unlikely to survive. I tried to sound confident. "Men, we have one more task to complete before we can take a well-earned rest. We must capture the Antonia fortress!" I could hear the groans. "Come on! Remember it's a palace as well as a fortress; you're only minutes away from a bath and linen sheets!" That was stretching it a bit, but it was enough. We trotted across the courtyard to the northwest corner where the stairs to the fortress were located. The door blocking the stairs from the courtyard was not designed for a serious assault. The lock broke at the first blow from the battering ram. We ran up the stairs unopposed. When we reached the upper floor, we found the palatial apartments defended by less than twenty poorly armed Zealots who we dispatched with ease. The water in the baths was cold, so I had no difficulty rallying the men.

"Galerius, remain here with your file and take care of the wounded until the fourth gets here. Send two men up to the fortress battlements to give early warning of a counter attack. Rufio, try and get the fires relighted to warm the baths and do what you can to make the doors we just broke open defensible again; we may need to defend them against the Jews soon. The rest of you, follow me back to the courtyard."

When we arrived, Piso had already placed the second, third and fifth in a thin line on top of the temple walls to make them look as numerous as possible. "Lucius, hurry," he said as we approached. "Spread your men along the west wall next to Titus. The Jews seem to be holding back."

"Perhaps they're tired too," I ventured.

"Very likely."

"Then will you rest now, sir?"

"Soon, but first I need to deal with Sabinus. I would arrest him if I could spare the men."

I have noted in my own humble way that command devolves reserves of strength that you never imagined you had. When men look to you alone as the final decision maker, the responsibility seems to lend you power to keep going, but as soon as a more senior commander takes over, your strength quickly ebbs away. Piso must have been drawing from these unseen reserves; at that time, I had never seen anything like it. Somehow, he just kept going while I was on my knees.

By mid-morning, the fighting ceased. Both sides licked their wounds and rested in preparation for the next bout. Piso found Sabinus huddled in the inner temple surrounded by his personal bodyguard. He soon persuaded him to release the rest of his ruffians to cohort control, which added another one hundred and fifty men of admittedly dubious quality to the two hundred or so legionaries defending the temple walls. Then we all fell asleep at our posts and even though it was broad daylight, the Jews had no idea that a determined rush might have overwhelmed us.

All remained quiet until early evening. About an hour before sunset, a group of Zealots approached the Hulda Gates waving a large, grubby white flag which was supposed to indicate a desire to talk. We had all had a few hours' sleep and were by now fully alert. I had a good view of events as they unfolded from my position only a few paces away from the Hulda Gates. The Zealots stopped about thirty paces from the wall and the spokesman, a short, thin fellow of mature years, called out to us in Greek, a tongue most in our cohort could understand.

"I am Ariel bar Eleazar. My commander has a message for the commander of the Roman forces."

"I am he," responded Piso, who was close by me and in direct command of the fifth century, whose centurion lay mortally wounded in the Antonia fortress.

"My commander makes you a generous offer," continued

the Zealot herald. "You are surrounded and have no hope of escape, yet instead of certain death you are offered a safe passage out of Jerusalem provided you hand over to us your weapons and the leader of those Romans who defiled our temple."

Piso answered, "If your commander wants our weapons, he is welcome to come and take them if he can. As for his offer of a safe passage out of Jerusalem, he may stick it up his own back passage."

"I do not understand."

"Shove it up his arse!" The men loved it and cheered wildly. This was the second time in one day that our refined tribune had sworn like a common soldier. An assortment of rocks, stones and other projectiles now rained down upon the Jewish negotiating party who quickly fled out of range. Just as they reached their own lines, their spokesman turned and angrily waved his fist at us. We greeted this with hoots of derision putting us all in fine spirits which was just as well in view of what was to follow.

Piso hurriedly called together his surviving centurions. We met behind the Hulda Gates; there were only four of us left. Severus had been lost with the first century and Marius Cerealis of the fifth was dying in the Antonia fortress from a sword thrust in the groin.

"My friends," said Piso, "We will soon be under attack again. Titus, you and the second will hold the Hulda Gates and the walls either side of them. You are now second in command and must take over if anything happens to me. Gnaeus, you will add the third to your century and hold the north wall; we need not worry about the east because the Kidron valley makes the ascent too steep for an assault force. The west wall will be guarded by Lucius with the fifth and sixth centuries, which leaves you Marcus Sempronius."

I have hardly mentioned Marcus Sempronius, centurion of the third century, yet. In appearance, he looked rather like Piso, tall, elegant and well-manicured. Also, like Piso, he was a true born Roman from a family of equites status, which is just below the senatorial rank. But that is where the resemblance to Piso ended. Whereas Piso tended to see the good in people rather than the bad, Sempronius was one of those men who could find nothing good to say about anybody. This manifested itself in a dark sarcasm which was unleavened by wit. I put this down to the fact that his family had fallen on hard times due to ill-judged financial speculation by his father. This led to Marcus joining the army as a humble private soldier rather than as an officer which his equites status would normally require. Consequently, he always felt himself to be superior to the other centurions, especially me, because of my lowly birth of which I shall say more later. He also had a habit of addressing Piso with the familiarity of an equal, which annoyed us more than it did Piso himself, because he always stopped just short of insubordination; otherwise, our tribune would have quickly put him in his place. But he was the perfect man for the job Piso now had in mind.

Our tribune said, "Marcus, Sabinus' men are now under imperial jurisdiction. They consist of one hundred and fifty ruffians in dire need of military discipline. Their behaviour could make the difference between victory and defeat. Can you prepare them in four hours?"

"Certainly, sir," answered the arrogant Marcus.

"Good, then take your two best file leaders and turn that rabble into something resembling soldiers as soon as you can."

"I'll give them hell, sir."

"Just make them fight; that will be sufficient for the present." Piso disliked him too, but he still knew how to get the best out of the man who would cause me so much trouble in time to come.

At nightfall, we had the unwelcome sight of the ballista being dragged to a firing position opposite my post. Piso's assumption that the Zealots would not risk damaging the temple was proved wrong. In the gathering gloom we looked on as the Zealot ballista team aimed the infernal machine directly at me, or so it seemed, and loaded it with medium sized rocks which meant an anti-personnel rather than a wall smashing load. The Jews were now proficient ballista operators and quickly adjusted the range before unloosing their first charge. The rocks soared high into the night sky, comfortably missing us. We all turned to watch them land and see what damage they caused, but sadly they fell short of the Holy of Holies and landed harmlessly in the courtyard below us. Oddly, there was a series of dull thuds rather than the cracking sound of splintering rock that we were expecting. One of the men of the fifth century went down to take a closer look. He walked across the courtyard, stopped at the nearest ballista rock and knelt down to examine it. Suddenly, he let out a wail of such utter despair and misery, that the blood seemed to freeze in our veins. They were not rocks at all, but the severed heads of our brave comrades of the first century! Without orders, some of our men left their posts and went down to look for themselves. Another grisly ballista charge landed nearby, then another. By now, we centurions were struggling to keep order. Some of the legionaries ran to the Hulda Gates and began to unlock them in their desperation to get to grips with an enemy they now hated.

Piso's voice rang out, "Men, this is just what they want. Get back to your posts!" His face was flushed with anger; his ice cool self-control was almost breaking. "You will have your revenge, I promise you!" With difficulty, we managed to cajole, persuade but not order our men back to the walls. The gates were safely relocked. Piso arranged a burial detail to collect the heads as they arrived and place them out of sight until they could be given the traditional Roman last rites.

If the Zealots sought to frighten us, they only succeeded in firing us up to send as many of them to their Hell as possible. Now, for us, the final assault could not come soon enough. The ballista crew stopped as soon as all the heads had been sent on their way; they did not, in the end, risk damaging the temple and all was quiet by the time the last glimmers of daylight were gone. The night was pleasantly cool, but I did not sleep well; I doubt anyone did. The thought of the noble Severus' body being mutilated by laughing, triumphant Zealots haunted me. The only comfort I could give myself was that he would surely have taken a good number of them with him before he finally fell.

Through heavy eyes, I watched the stars fade as dawn began to drive the dark into the west. All was silent. Sunrise approached and feathery clouds were illuminated from below in a rich, crimson colour as the great, gold orb neared the eastern horizon. Still we waited. The rim of the sun appeared and golden light flooded into the temple precinct. The Jews were leaving the assault late. At last, Piso sent out a patrol to investigate. A short while later, the patrol returned. The ballista was deserted, the enemy camp empty.

"They've gone sir, every last one of them," reported the

patrol leader. "They've just abandoned their camp."

"Any sign of the rioters?" asked Piso.

"Nothing, sir. They must have gone home. The streets are empty."

We did not have to wait long for an explanation. A patrol of Galatians appeared from the citadel led by Eumenes. Instead of reporting to Piso like he should have done, the excited young officer shouted to anyone who cared to listen, "Varus is here! We've won! We've won!

***

III

Varus had exceeded our expectations. When Caius and Brasidas reached Antioch with their Numidian escort, Varus ordered the Third Gallica and the Sixth Ironclads, who were stationed further south, to prepare for an immediate campaign in Galilee and Judea. Once again, he led the army in person and, within twenty-four hours, two legions were marching south on the coast road at a forced march pace. On the way, messages were sent out to bring in the nearest auxiliary cohorts who added fifteen hundred horsemen to the army under his command. This was a brave response because it left just one legion, the Twelfth Lightning, to guard Syria if Parthia decided to take advantage of Rome's difficulties in Judea.

All the able-bodied in our cohort left the temple and went to Jerusalem's west wall to watch the arrival of the auxiliary cavalry cohorts, who were a day's march ahead of the legions.

They were a wonderful mixture of peoples, Numidian

lancers, Syrian horse archers and camel mounted nomads from Arabia. Leading from the front, was Varus himself at the head of the Roman legionary cavalry. He knew how to make the most of this important but cheap victory; all the hard fighting had been done, but he could reap the glory.

We cheered him heartily. Now he had led two campaigns into the land of the Jews and both were complete successes. Never was his reputation higher than at this moment, especially in the eyes of the army, but he was a hard man to like. A tendency not to listen to advice from those qualified to give it, became overweening arrogance as he got older, which I was to experience personally when I served under him again a few years later. So it was no surprise that when disaster eventually struck, there were few who shed a tear for him.

The governor went straight to the citadel where he was welcomed by the Galatians, and set up his headquarters in Herod's palace. Piso, and the surviving centurions of the fifth cohort were summoned immediately. We met Varus in the audience chamber which still contained statues and frescoes showing the dead King Herod in heroic poses, smiting his enemies, hunting, accepting tribute from the defeated and so on, but now, apart from Brasidas, whom I was glad to see, there were only Romans present.

As soon as Piso finished his report, which included Sabinus' inflammatory behaviour, Varus said, "I shall inspect the battlefield, after which we will give our dead the last rites according to the soldier's god, Mithras, before the legions arrive. If our men see the mutilated bodies of their comrades, there will be blood."

"Good," said Titus.

Varus admonished him. "We are here to stop a war not to

start another one. There may be blood, but at my order alone. There will be no revenge massacres unless, or until, I give the word. Piso, have Sabinus placed under arrest and brought to me. You will find me at what is left of your camp." Piso nodded to Titus who departed for the temple.

As we walked through the city towards the sad remains of our camp, we were joined by Caius, who had ridden with Varus' escort. Our reunion was more restrained than it might have been because of the presence of the governor, but Piso and I were delighted to see him. The recounting of his adventures and ours had to wait a while because we soon arrived at the shattered wreck of the camp. Varus walked slowly through it, silently looking at the smashed barracks, scattered personal belongings and the blood-stained detritus of battle.

"Where are the dead?" he asked.

Piso pointed in the direction of a small, abandoned stone quarry about four hundred paces south of the camp, which had once been used for road maintenance. "Our dead were beheaded and thrown into that, sir. It is now used as a dump for the human effluent of Jerusalem. The Jews took their own dead away with them."

Varus' face reddened, but he managed to control his rage and spoke quietly to one of his cavalry decurions. "I want you to go into the city and break down as many doors as you need to gather two hundred able bodied Jews. Bring them to the quarry and force them to recover and wash every Roman body. Then make them collect firewood, wooden furniture from their houses will do, with which to build a pyre large enough to consume our dead. Then kill them and throw their bodies into the quarry. Be quick and take as many men as you need. The legions will be here by this evening so all must be done by then."

"Including the cremation to Mithras?" queried the decurion. "Especially the cremation to Mithras."

Varus' plan of action pleased all who could hear him, but nothing less than the sacking and plundering of Jerusalem would satisfy the thirst for revenge of Piso's cohort.

A few minutes later, an embarrassed Titus Cotta rejoined us. "Governor, I regret to report that Sabinus and all his personal bodyguard have fled. Shall I arrange a pursuit?"

"In which direction, Centurion?"

"I, err... I'm not sure, sir."

"Neither am I, so let us not waste time until we can find out. What about the rest of his men?"

"Under guard in case they try to run off too."

"Well keep them that way for now. We will be needing recruits to make good your cohort's losses. A few of them may make the grade."

At the time, I was surprised that Varus did not make a greater effort to track down Sabinus, but after he was recalled to Rome to receive an even greater posting than Governor of Syria, Piso discovered from one of his high ranking contacts in the senate that Varus had been toying with us. He had made a secret agreement with Sabinus to share the loot of the temple treasury, one half for himself, one quarter for Sabinus and one quarter for Sabinus' bodyguard. This arrangement was put in place well before Sabinus came to Jerusalem, which made Varus complicit in the very act of starting the rebellion, for which he took the credit for crushing so easily. When Varus was recalled to Rome, it was said he came to a rich province as a poor man and left a poor province as a rich man. As I said, he was a hard man to like.

In the late afternoon, the Sixth Ironclads and our own Third Gallica arrived exhausted after days of forced marches. By then our dead comrades were on their way to Mithras and the two hundred Jews were in the city's effluent, which partially appeased the fifth cohort. The legions camped outside Jerusalem with strict orders to stay out of the city for the time being. The two legates were summoned to the citadel along with Piso to decide on various promotions arising out of the campaign. Piso himself was promoted to Senior Tribune in our legion but, much to our great pleasure, he retained direct command of the fifth cohort. Within the cohort, our centuries were renumbered because we only had enough men left to make up four undermanned centuries. Titus was confirmed as Senior Centurion commanding the first century, which was in fact the second renumbered. Sempronius' third was renumbered the second, Gnaeus' fourth became the third and so on. The remnants of the fifth and sixth were combined to make up the new fourth under my command. There was now no fifth or sixth, so we needed to find transfers and recruits to man them and two new centurions to command them. The new centurion of the fifth was transferred from another cohort but, to almost universal approval in our cohort, Sempronius being the only exception, Caius Pantera was made centurion of the sixth at the tender age of nineteen. This was a remarkable promotion for one so young, but it was a prime example of one of the great strengths within the legions; promotion on merit.

Next morning, Varus announced he would hold an inquiry to determine the fate of Jerusalem. For us, this meant more delay in the eagerly anticipated sacking of one of the richest cities in the empire. Among those summoned was Joazar, high priest of the temple and the entire Sanhedrin, which consisted of eighty highly respected Pharisees and Sadducees who, amongst other things, monitored the complicated Jewish law and dispensed justice amongst the people. Achiab, commander of the royal but not so loyal Jewish army was also summoned; we were particularly interested to see what would happen to him.

The interrogations were to be carried out by Varus himself in the presence of his senior commanders and, because of our role in defending the city, the centurions of the fifth cohort were invited. Astutely, Varus selected the Sanhedrin's own meeting chamber in the temple portico, the scene of our victory, in which to hold the inquiry, but we were obliged to wait a frustrating five days so that Achiab could be present and witness the proceedings from the beginning.

Varus took great care in arranging the procedural detail; he was in his element with this sort of thing because of his experience as a senator. The inquiry was to be confrontational not conciliatory, so he placed the Romans on seats at one end of the oblong chamber while the members of the Sanhedrin were provided with simple wooden benches facing us. He had a raised platform built in the centre of the Roman end where he sat behind a large table with Brasidas at his side to take notes. From here, he could look down magisterially on the Jews whose fate he was about to determine. After so many years, I cannot remember all that was said but what follows is as accurate a summary as memory permits.

It was the first day of June. We began in the middle of the morning and the day was hot. My first thought as I took my seat opposite the Sanhedrin was that I had never seen so many beards in a single chamber before. Varus opened the inquiry with some surprising news. He held up a scroll which bore the imperial seal.

"I have just received a message from our beloved emperor, Augustus Caesar. He has not approved King Herod's will." There was an audible gasp from the Jewish benches. "The kingdom is to be split into three parts. Samaria, Idumea and Judea, including Jerusalem, go to Archelaus, who shall reign with the title of Ethnarch."

I whispered to Gnaeus who was sitting beside me,

"What's an ethnarch?"

"A Greek term for a national leader with all the rights of a king except succession."

Varus silenced us with an angry glare. "Galilee and Perea will be governed by Archelaus' brother Antipas, while Trachontis and Gualantis go to their half-brother Philip. They shall rule as tetrarchs."

Without waiting for me to ask, and risking further disapproval, Gnaeus quickly whispered, "Tetrarch means a ruler of one quarter."

So Archelaus was to take over the core of Herod's kingdom while Antipas inherited turbulent Galilee. Philip, son of Herod but by a different mother, Cleopatra of Jerusalem, acquired the northern and most peaceful part of the kingdom. Here, the population was predominantly gentile and not regarded by most Jews as an integral part of the old Davidic kingdom of Israel.

"I should say," continued Varus. "That Ethnarch Archelaus is on his way back from Rome and is but three days away from Jerusalem. He is not a happy man so you will need to do your best to manage his disappointment." He handed the imperial document to Brasidas and glared at the assembled

Jews. "And now we come to the purpose of the inquiry. As you know, Rome is a benevolent master to its provinces, especially to the land of the Jews. We bring peace, stability and freedom from foreign invasion. All we ask for in return is prompt payment of taxes and political loyalty. Most provinces understand and appreciate these gifts, and while we will tolerate a certain amount of grumbling, rebellion is the one crime we will not abide. You Jews have rebelled and it is my intention to give Jerusalem, the heart of the rebellion, over to the two legions waiting outside your walls to sack and plunder as they see fit. Such are the rules of war. However, knowing you as I do, I am holding this inquiry to give you a last chance to persuade me to show mercy. I will need some convincing mind you, especially since I saw the lack of respect your people accorded to the bodies of our brave legionaries. First, I call upon your high priest Joazar to speak."

A man stood up, utterly self-confident despite the gravity of the threat facing his people, and sat down on the witness seat placed directly opposite Varus. The Governor of Syria spoke first. "For the record, who are you?"

"I am Ananas, son of Seth, chief secretary to Joazar, high priest of the temple."

"Why is the high priest not here in person?"

"He is indisposed with a stomach condition that does not permit him to go far from the latrine. I am authorised to speak for him."

"How very convenient for him; an attack of nerves brought on by a guilty conscience perhaps. I shall speak to him later." Turning to Brasidas, Varus pronounced, "Let the record show that Joazar failed to attend this inquiry." Surprisingly, Ananas made no effort to object to this unfair depiction of his leader. "Very well, we shall proceed without the high priest," continued Varus. "Ananas, you have heard my provisional judgement for the destruction of Jerusalem. Can you give me a good reason not to carry it out?"

"Certainly, Governor." Ananas had done his research well. He exuded confidence. "Less than a hundred years ago, there was a great slave revolt in Italia which almost brought Rome to her knees. The slaves, led by a certain Spartacus, broke free of their chains and spread terror as far as the gates of Rome itself. Eventually, as you know, the combined forces of Crassus and Pompey crushed the rebellion but it was a close-run thing."

"What has this to do with the Jewish rebellion?" interrupted Varus impatiently.

"Everything. The rebellion in Herod's kingdom was caused by a small but vicious group of criminal fanatics who call themselves Zealots. Just like the slaves who fought Crassus and Pompey, they have no stake in our society. Their rebellion was aimed first and foremost at the Jewish establishment; the temple priests, the nobility and other supporters of King Herod who have always been loyal to Rome. We are the very people who encourage the Roman presence in our land, and for you to treat us all in the same way is a gross injustice to those who have always supported you. We opposed the rebellion though there may be a few who gave nominal support to it out of fear for their lives. So how can it be just for us to be judged responsible for the rebellion? That would be no different to condemning the Roman senate for the revolt of Spartacus."

"You say that you fought against the Romans unwillingly?"

"No, I say that we did not fight against Rome at all."

Varus thought for a moment. "But we have indisputable evidence that regular soldiers of the royal Jewish army were among those who attacked the camp of the fifth cohort."

"I cannot answer for that," replied Ananas. "You must speak to General Achiab, but all I can say is that the people of Jerusalem never rebelled against Rome. The few that did were forced into it by the Zealots, who are your true enemy and ours."

"Very well," acknowledged Varus. "You may stand down. I now summon General Achiab." A tall, stately man of middle-age, replaced Ananas in the witness chair.

"Identify yourself," said Varus.

"I am Achiab bar Antipater, cousin of the late King Herod and commander in chief of the loyal Jewish army."

"The 'loyal' Jewish army? Then why did you not come to the aid of your Roman allies in Jerusalem? Instead, you sent your men to fight them."

Achiab remained calm as he faced the accusation of rebellion, a crime with only one punishment. "Governor, nine hundred and seventy-seven men, including officers, joined the Zealots in Jerusalem. I did not send them. They deserted their posts while I was dealing with another rebellion in the north; that of Judas the Galilean. He had an army many thousands strong and captured Sepphoris, and with it, Herod's weapons store where he massacred two hundred of my men while negotiating under a flag of truce. At the time, he seemed the greater danger because, left unchallenged, the whole of Galilee would have gone up in flames. Of course I knew of the trouble in Jerusalem, but knowing the Romans and Galatians were there to contain it, I dealt with what I believed to be the more imminent danger."

"And what happened to this Judas?"

"Regrettably, he escaped to his hideout somewhere in the foothills of Mount Hermon, but we killed or captured most of his men. Even as I speak, my hunters are still searching for him."

"And what about your deserters?" asked Varus coldly.

"The officers whom I hold responsible have disappeared, but most of the men have returned."

"What do you propose to do with them?"

"Bearing in mind they were only following the orders of their officers, I shall use the ancient Roman punishment of decimation. That way most will live and learn and re-join the ranks as better soldiers."

That seemed to satisfy Varus. "Decimation is a good solution. I assume you are searching for the rebellious officers?"

"Yes, Governor; they shall be killed when we find them."

"Good, now tell me about Sepphoris. Did the people resist Judas the Galilean?"

"I cannot say they did, otherwise my men would not have been put to the sword like sacrificial sheep."

Varus did not respond immediately. He frowned and whispered something to Brasidas who scratched a few notes in response. Then he called forward the legate of the Sixth Ironclads and said a few quiet words to him. The legate nodded and went back to his place. Raising his voice a little, so that those at the far end of the chamber could hear him clearly, he announced, "I have made my decision. Jerusalem shall be spared on condition that the ringleaders of the rebellion and their close associates are brought before me for judgement. I expect there to be no less than a thousand and it will be the responsibility of the Sanhedrin to present them to me in the Court of the Gentiles at noon three days from now when they shall feel Rome's anger. I warn you not to play me false by sending vagrants and criminals as substitutes, for some of them will be interrogated and I shall know if you have tried to deceive me. If you are honest with me, not only will Jerusalem be spared the fate it deserves, but you will all keep your rank and status as if the rebellion never happened."

The looks of relief on the bearded faces of the Sanhedrin made it manifestly clear that Varus had judged his victims wisely, but there was a sting in the tail. "However, rebellion cannot just be forgiven and a fit and proper punishment must be meted out. Therefore, the city of Sepphoris, which willingly sided with the rebels, will be sacked by the Sixth Ironclads on their return march to base. No mercy will be shown to any who remain in the city for they will have ample warning of what is to come." He waited for Brasidas to finish his note taking and addressed Achiab again. "Finally, General, I must decide your fate." He paused for maximum dramatic effect as if he was making a speech in the senate. Achiab got to his feet like a condemned man about to receive his sentence.

"General Achiab, I find that you acted with the coolness of judgement in a difficult situation that was worthy of your rank. I am also impressed by the chief secretary's comparison of the Jewish rebellion with that of the slave revolt in Italia; it helped me understand the complexity of the problems that faced you. You diligently dealt with the immediate threat of Judas the Galilean and took the correct actions to get rid of Zealot sympathisers within your own army. Therefore, I confirm you in your post as General of the Jewish army."

"Thank you, Governor," replied a relieved Achiab.

"But now you have another difficult task ahead of you, one which I suggest you deal with before Ethnarch Archelaus gets here. Just as Herod's kingdom is divided into three, so must his army be similarly divided so that each new territory can defend itself. How you do this is up to you, at least until Archelaus takes up his post, so be quick. You will also have to decide who you will serve."

"I shall see to it directly, Governor."

The inquiry ended there. For Herod's ruling establishment, it was a success. At the cost of Sepphoris, Herod's second city, and a thousand troublemakers, who were eventually crucified outside Jerusalem's walls, the great city of the Jews was saved and the Pharisees and Sadducees retained their status and power. In some ways, they actually benefited from the settlement because amongst the thousand selected to face Roman wrath, many were creditors of the ruling class or had old scores to settle which would now never see the light of day. No wonder Varus was regarded as a hero by the Sanhedrin.

None of us knew how much, if any, of Achiab's story was true, nor did we care because the sack of Sepphoris would almost be adequate compensation for Jerusalem. Varus directed that a cohort from our own legion should accompany the Ironclads to make sure half the plunder was reserved for the Gallica. Better still, he announced that the survivors of Piso's cohort, who had done all the hard fighting, should each receive a double share. This meant that a frugal legionary could invest a lump sum in the legion's bank at a fair rate of interest so when he retired after his twenty-year term, he could add this investment to the cash bonus equivalent of thirteen years' pay that every man received on completion of his service. I suppose I should add that less than half the men recruited into the legions ever survived to the end of their term, but we were in no mood for such gloomy thoughts.

And soon, even better news was to come.

***

IV

Varus left Jerusalem at the end of June, by which time the crucifixions had taken place and an angry Archelaus had taken up residence in Herod's palace in the citadel. But we in Piso's cohort knew that the jubilation of the ruling class masked seething discontent within the rest of the Jewish people, for they felt their sacrifice had been betrayed by their masters. Of Herod's three successors, Archelaus proved to be the worst, having all his father's vices but none of his virtues. Antipas was the one most like his father and rebuilt Sepphoris on an even grander scale than before at the expense of taxing his people unnecessarily harshly. But Philip, on the other hand, turned out to be an excellent ruler who genuinely cared for his people. His building works were of use to everybody, roads, bridges, aqueducts and so on, and he limited his personal expenditure ensuring his people were lightly taxed compared to those suffering under Antipas and Archelaus. What a pity the emperor did not give him Archelaus' province instead.

But I am running ahead of myself. A month after Varus left Jerusalem with the Sixth legion, the legionary ladies of the Third Gallica, better known to us as the cats arrived. This was cause for a great celebration, especially amongst the sex starved fifth cohort. As part of Varus' settlement, the Antonia fortress was permanently occupied by a Roman cohort, the rest of the legion making do with a greatly extended camp outside the city walls where ours had been. Marcus Tullius, our legate, directed that the apartments in the north east corner of the Antonia fortress should be reserved for the cats' use, but that still left ample space for the occupying cohort. Needless to say, the cohort in the fortress was a prime posting which had to be rotated amongst the Third legion's ten cohorts on a monthly basis to avoid a mutiny.

For me, I had the pleasure of entering into the first long term relationship in my life with the beautiful Zenub, a dark-skinned cat from Nubia, who taught me most of what I know about the art of physical love. Such relationships were not uncommon with these ladies, who were not slaves but astute business women. I shall have much more to say about them but, at this point, I will speak only of the children who inevitably arrived as a result of the cats' business activities.

To be a child of the legion meant that you would never know your father. A boy or girl would be brought up by their mother and her comrades in the cats' 'sisterhood'. The children received a good education learning to read and write. The boys formed a pool of ready recruits but were not obliged to become soldiers. There were plenty of non-combat roles in a legion such as clerks, administrators, medical assistants, equipment buyers, grooms, to name but a few. The girls usually found husbands amongst well-off retiring legionaries, who would typically be in their late thirties or early forties unless they signed on again for another term, but some followed their mothers into the cats' business if they were good looking enough. All in all, to be a child of the legion gave you a good start in life. I should know; I was one.

And so, we entered a period of peace, but not tranquillity; underlying tensions caused by the increasing gulf between the Jewish rich and poor remained, except in Philip's province.

Varus had done his job well, but it was only a matter of time before the simmering cauldron exploded again.

END OF PART ONE

CAST OF CHARACTERS
*= non fictional

Narrator Lucius Veranius centurion 6th century 5th cohort 3rd legion (Gallica)

The Jews:
Abbas — founder of the Zealot sect.

Achiab bar Antipater* - Herod's cousin and general of the Jewish army.

Ananas* — chief secretary to the high priests.

Antipas* — son of Herod and Tetrarch of Galilee and Perea.

Antipater* — son of Herod.

Archelaus* — son of Herod and Ethnarch of Judea, Idumea and Samaria.

Arethus — house slave of Menahem.

Ariel bar Eleazar — Zealot commander.

Asher* — brother of Achiab, and an officer in the the Jewish army.

Caiaphas* — priest and protégé of Ananas.

Caspar — a Babylonian Jew.

Daniel — Zealot bodyguard.

Deborah — servant in Joseph's household.

Ehud — contract manager for Joseph.

Elijah bar Abbas* — leader of the Zealot sect.

Ephraim — steward in Joseph's household.

Ezra- owner of the outhouse in which Jesus was born.

Herod* — King of the Jews.

Isaac — commander of the Shadows.

Jacob — half-brother to Judas.

Jesus* — Messiah and King of the Jews.

Joazar* — high priest

Joab — a shadow from Beth Shan.

Joachim* — father of Mary and grandfather of Jesus. Jonathan bar Jacob — Zealot commander.

Joseph bar Jacob* — husband of Mary.

Joshua bar Amos — Zealot messenger.

Judas bar Menahem* (also Sicariot) — teacher and mentor to Jesus.

Judas the Galilean* — a false messiah.

Mary* — mother of Jesus.

Menahem — father of Judas.

Philip* — son of Herod and Tetrarch of Gaulantis and Trachontis.

Rachel — Menahem's second wife and step mother of Judas.

Reuben — Zealot bodyguard.

Ruth — companion of Mary.

Simon* — high priest

The Gentiles:

Arminius* — adjutant German auxiliary cohort.

Attalus — commander of Herod's Galatian bodyguard.

Brasidas — slave and secretary to Varus.

Caius Pantera — father of Jesus and legionary 6th century, 5th cohort, 3rd legion (Gallica).

Eumenes — deputy commander Galatian bodyguard.

Friedrich von Vechten — commander of German auxiliary

cohort.

Galerius — file leader 6th century, 5th cohort, 3rd legion (Gallica).

Gnaeus Servilius — centurion 4th century, 5th cohort, 3rd legion (Gallica).

Licinius Piso — tribune 5th cohort, 3rd legion (Gallica).

Lucius Veranius — narrator, centurion 6th century, 5th cohort, 3rd legion (Gallica).

Marcus Sempronius — centurion 3rd century, 5th cohort, 3rd legion (Gallica).

Marcus Tullius — legate 3rd legion (Gallica).

Marius Cerialis — centurion 5th century, 5th cohort, 3rd legion (Gallica).

Ostorius Rufio — file leader 6th century, 5th cohort, 3rd legion (Gallica).

Publius Quinctilius Varus* — Governor of Syria.

Quintus Paterculus — decurion, 5th cohort, 3rd legion (Gallica).

Sabinus* — financial prefect for Varus.

Severus Pollio — senior centurion, 1st century, 5th cohort, 3rd legion (Gallica).

Titus Cotta — centurion 2nd century, 5th cohort, 3rd legion (Gallica).

_____